Touch of Iron

TIMANDRA WHITECASTLE

EDITED BY HARRY DEWULF

CONTENTS

THE LIVING BLADE: BOOK ONE

IRON

CHAPTER 1

NORA WAS OUT HERE BECAUSE the baker's wife couldn't keep her mouth shut. Here, under the windswept trees. Here, on this hillock poised so neatly above the vast Plains she was tempted to believe the gods had created it to show off the horizon. The possibilities. The unfinished world to come. Nora stood with her brother at the brink of the Plains, in the wet, cold, gathering dark. It would take two days' journey on foot to get back to the Ridge, and half a day to the nearest homestead. But after Mother Sara's death, the twins were four years away from anyone caring.

The sky was tall. A huge crest of waves headed inland, shading the last of the sunlight in hues of orange and gray and purple. On clear days when the wind swept away the clouds, herding them over the Plains, Nora could just make out the line of the Crest Mountains in the distance. The Plains were a vast, flat bowl. Sometimes, when the summer sun shone down, the silver streams of water sparkled like jewels strewn among the green. It was pure pasture ground. Now, though, no herds of sheep roamed on the Plains. There were no trees, no roads, no shelter but little flocks of trees leaning against the wind. The long Plains were spoiled with space. You could see nothing but grass for miles and miles. And the sky. The ever-changing sky.

Crossing the Plains would take nearly three weeks. Nora sniffed the air. The autumn had been mild so far, unusually so. But surely Owen had no plans of actually crossing. It would be madness in the gathering winter, without enough warmth or shelter or food. They should sneak back home and at least stock up on provisions and warmer clothing. Maybe the clouds would bring more than rain this night. Maybe frost in the morning.

Her twin brother stood silhouetted before the glorious sky, unmoving, the high collar of his long cloak pulled up to his cheekbones. He turned when she threw down her backpack on the hard ground. Here the brown grass was undergoing its winter death. There was moss under the trees at the edge of the forest. As fine a place as any. They would camp here. And tonight, she'd talk to Owen. If she let him do the deciding, their bones would still be perched on this damned hillock before he reached a conclusion.

"It's been two days. You want to go back already?" Owen said, watching the rolling sky before him.

Nora scowled.

"I'm getting a fire started," she said. "It'll be cold tonight."

"Yes, do that. And cook us something hot while you're at it."

"You could help set up camp, you know."

"I could." Owen remained where he was, staring into the sky.

Nora set her mouth, stepped into the twilight under the trees, and kicked a dead branch. Dirt scattered. The earth was dark brown under the needles of the firs, closed cones lying around the visible roots here and there. She spotted some blueberry bushes under the conifers. It would be a good spot in summer to collect the berries. But now there was nothing, and they wouldn't be here in summer anyway. They each had a little bread and jerky left. If they skirted the woods, maybe she could catch hare or fowl.

She heard the screech of a falcon and ducked. It had sounded so close, yet above her in the branches there was nothing to be seen. A falcon cry at dusk? Nora crouched beside a tender young tree, the rough bark flaking under her hand. She waited in the sudden silence and her breath escaped in thin wisps, one at a time, one at a time.

A branch cracked.

Men passed her by. She held her breath. One of them was so close she could smell beer on his breath. She counted seven men in the dim light, moving not silently, but as stealthily as the leaves and needles under their feet would let them. Nora's heart was thumping in her chest. Her hand rested over it. She peered down. Her fingers seemed unnaturally white amid the black of her clothes. Or what had once been black but was now washed out, more charcoal gray. Still fitting, though—for a charcoal burner. And dark enough to fade into the twilight under the trees. Which was good, seeing as the men had weapons. And although they moved among the shadows with ease, no group of hunters would convene this large. For what prey? No large game lived at the skirts of the woods, though occasionally deer ventured onto the Plains to feed with the utmost caution. Soldiers, perhaps, but they wore no uniform. Mercenaries?

She sensed others moving among the trees behind her and remained as still as she could. The seven men were bent low, creeping toward the last of the trees. They had spotted Owen for sure, although Nora couldn't see him from where she crouched. Slowly, she let out her breath and took a deep one. Her thighs tingled, making her want to rake her fingernails over her legs to massage the numbness out of her flesh. She ignored it, accustomed to wearing light garments in all weather. They made it easier to go from motionless tending a charcoal burn to frenetically working hard and fast should a burn go wrong. Now, it seemed, she'd have to move hard and fast to save her brother.

She had a long knife tucked into her belt at her back. Slowly she reached for it. Eyes fixed on the men before her. Wary of the men she heard behind. Careful not to let any motion give her away. Just as her fingertips touched the smooth hilt, a soundless edge of steel slid close to her throat.

"Don't move."

The man's whisper sounded as loud as the falcon's cry had, though none of the creeping men had heard him. Or none turned around to see. The cold steel bit into the skin just below her chin. A warm hand took her own knife. The dagger at her throat remained. It tipped twice against her jawline, the thin cut burning. She rose.

"Be still." His whisper was a deep growl.

Nora watched as the seven men in front of her moved out. One of them gestured to the others. They had seen Owen and were fanning out to encircle him. She forced herself to breathe calmly. In through the nose, out between parted lips.

The blade moved to a hair's breadth away from her skin. Pins and needles rose in her feet now, the cold numbing them. She felt the warmth of the man's body radiate against her back. He was close. Very close. But he was careful not to touch her. She licked her lips. Of the seven men in front, she could only see four now. The one farthest back, closest to her, nodded toward another man in front.

So, now.

She rammed her left elbow into her captor's face and ran.

"Owen!"

She screamed her brother's name as she hurtled past the surprised men hidden in the undergrowth, who half rose, clutching their weapons. She heard heavy footfalls behind her as her captor gave chase. The second graze at her throat burned where his blade had left its mark. A trickle ran down her skin.

A few steps left. Five, perhaps six.

Now she saw Owen's surprised face in the twilight beyond the trees.

Now his wonderment.

Now his alarm.

But four men were already on top of him, wrestling him to the ground.

Then something hit her in the back. Hard. She fell forward onto the roots. One chafed against her cheek, tearing the skin open as she tried to move her head, winded, struggling to breathe, although in the confusion it seemed as though her lungs had forgotten how. Being pressed down wasn't helping either. Her mouth was filled with dead pine needles and earth. Rough hands pulled her up, and her arm was twisted painfully behind her back. Still no air. Face raw.

As the man's hand buried itself in her hair, his fingernails scratched her scalp. The tug on her head and the grip on her arm shoved her forward, regardless of whether her feet would follow. She was half dragged toward her brother. Owen was on his knees, bent over, as his arms were bound tight with rope behind him. His hair fell into his face as he looked up and saw her.

"Let her go, you bastard!"

The group of men gathering laughed. They seemed to be the dregs from the bottom of the wine cup—tavern brawlers, thugs who'd happily kill for money, and not even a lot of money at that, Nora thought. One of them strode into the middle of the loose circle the men had formed. The night was coming on quick now. His face was half shadowed but had finer lines to it. The man spoke with a quiet voice, but within the velvet was steel.

"Such passion! Your lover, boy?"

"My twin sister."

There was a pause as the man looked over at her and studied her face, then her brother's. Owen's eyes were narrowed on the man before him.

"Let's say I believe you," the man said. "What are you doing here? Speak quickly."

"We live here. Or not here, exactly. But near here." Owen swallowed and scrunched up his face. "We burn charcoal for the forge and are nothing but your humblest subjects, sire." His eyes flew open. "I meant lord. My lord."

The man's face paled. He pressed his lips so tightly together they were a mere line. "What did you just say?"

Nora closed her eyes. They were going to die. The leader drew his sword and held its edge to Owen's throat.

"I'm sorry," Owen babbled incoherently. "I'm sorry. Your ring! Your ring gave you away!"

"We were traveling to the Shrine of Hin," Nora chimed in. The blade rose against her throat one more time. She stared at Owen. The best lies were always those that were almost the truth. "We're traveling to the Shrine of Hin. We couldn't pass by Dernberia for fear of the bandits on the coastal road. My brother wishes to become a pilgrim. He can read and write and is otherwise very knowledgeable in lore." She shot Owen a look, but he didn't register. "We were going to ask Master Darren to train him in the way."

"Is that true?" the man asked Owen.

"Yes?" Owen nodded as the sword came closer to his face. "Yes! I've always dreamed of being a pilgrim, but our foster father wouldn't allow it."

"So you ran away from home?"

"Yes!"

At least that was true. The leader looked over Nora's head to the man standing behind her and lifted one thin eyebrow. Nora felt her captor shift his weight. She waited. The blade was taken away from her throat.

"Master Darren is dead."

Her captor's voice was deep like a well. When he spoke, the rasp was more pronounced, like he was drowning on land. His hand released its grip on her arm a little, and she turned to look over her shoulder and finally see the man. And nearly dislocated her shoulder with a yelp, trying to free herself from the grasp of the wight.

He—it!—was tall and lithe. Taller than most of the men standing around them and a hand-width taller than the leader. The skin of his face was a dark bronze, though she could not see much of it beneath his hood. And those eyes. Those deep, dark eyes with no pupil to be seen, pure black, like the reflection of a still lake on the high moors that held the memory of ages long past: wight eyes. The Everlasting, the old wives' tales also called them. The Lords and Ladies. Messengers of the old gods.

Nora struggled to get away and yet couldn't stop staring.

The wight shifted his gaze from her to her brother.

"Master Darren is dead," he repeated.

"No." Owen shook his head. "No. He can't be. We saw Master Darren last not even a month ago. At Nora's handfasting."

"Where did you see him?" the leader asked quickly.

"At the handfasting," Owen repeated.

Nora groaned. "We're from Owen's Ridge."

It was easier to look into the leader's eyes than the wight's, simply because they were a man's eyes. She felt his gaze wander up and down her body and tried not to shudder. They stared at each other in the chill evening breeze. He seemed like a man used to command. Tall and strong, a warrior lord, with dark hair and gray eyes and a beard that had been neatly groomed weeks ago. He scratched at his jaw.

"We were at the Shrine of Hin two weeks ago," he said. "Master Darren looked pretty dead to me."

"How did he die? How did he look exactly? Were his lips blue?" Owen asked.

The leader shrugged.

"I don't know. I was a bit distracted by the dagger in his heart to notice his lips. So, twins. Consecrated to Tuil and Lara, inhale and exhale, life and death. One soul in two bodies. Don't people here in the north kill you after birth? Leave you out in the woods for the wights to grab?"

The men chuckled and leered at Nora, held in the wight's arms. Her face flushed with heat. Her clenched jaw ached.

"We must continue east. The Temple of the Wind is still safe and open to us," the wight said.

"And from there south?" the leader asked.

The wight was so near, Nora felt his tenseness at the question. There was a slight pause.

"If we must," the wight spoke at last.

A ripple of movement went through the silent men around them as their leader shifted toward Owen.

"And these two?" he asked, looking at the wight.

Nora held her breath. She watched the tip of his sword closely as it rose above Owen's neck.

"The boy is under my protection," the wight said. "If he wants to become a pilgrim, I'm oath-bound to guide him to the nearest temple or shrine for education."

Nora saw Owen breathe relief. The leader nodded.

"And the girl?"

Nora raised her chin as the blade of the knife skimmed the soft skin of her throat. The gray, pale eyes of the leader fixed on her again. They reminded her of the dead eyes of trout when they pulled them from the brook below the Ridge. Cold and flat. She shuddered. The Fish Lord was a hard man.

And these were his men. She was one girl. Being held by a wight. And all this because the baker's wife couldn't keep her mouth shut.

"She goes with us to the temple," the wight said.

"Good," the leader replied, but the way he said it made the rest of his men smirk in the dark. Nora's stomach spasmed and she swallowed bile.

Owen's bonds were cut wordlessly, and he rose, rubbing his wrists. But the wight turned Nora around and bound her hands before her with a piece of rope.

"My name is Master Telen Diaz." He spoke quietly, tying a last knot. "Show respect; do not speak unless asked to; save your energy for running. For run we must. Go, get your things."

Owen stared at his new master, wide-eyed. He was about to say something, but Nora shook her head at him and he closed it again.

"Go, get your things," the wight repeated.

Owen turned and went to gather his backpack and Nora's. The wight turned to Nora.

"Your names."

Nora blinked.

"Tell me your names." He pulled at the length of rope, and she stumbled closer to him. She ripped her hands back.

"His name is Owen." Nora's voice caught. She swallowed the fear and looked into those deep eyes so close to her face. "You don't scare me."

"That's very brave of you to say." The wight stood tall and solemn and waited for Owen to approach. Nora's cheeks burned like the raw skin of her wrists.

"Owen of Owen's Ridge, that is your real name?" he asked.

"Yes."

"You know with whom you travel?"

"I think I've guessed as much."

"We must gain a few more leagues under cover of the night. You will follow me. You will watch me closely until we get to the Temple of the Wind. This is your first lesson, Owen of Owen's Ridge. Many will follow. You will run and you will breathe. Or you will fall."

And so they ran. Again.

Two days ago, at home, Nora had run out of ideas. With her back to the wall, she had one option left: flight into the unknown. Owen and Nora had bolted out into the night, unprepared, no plan. And here she was, still running. Still shackled to an undesirable future edging closer on the horizon no matter the direction she chose.

This was how it felt to run the night. First the cold got her. Then she was warmer, and she saw every breath in front of her. Then the sweat made her cold. After a while she felt the beginnings of a cramp in her legs. She had to start concentrating on her footfall. Made it regular. The ground below her, though it seemed flat, stretched out in ripples and slight arches. Treacherous. Suddenly there was no ground beneath her. It broke away and all she had was pebbles and water and a deep step that woke her up with a jolt, heartbeat rising a little more.

And then she burned. Her heartbeat pounded in the veins of her face. Her body was generating so much heat that even the cold wasn't helping anymore. Her lungs were burning with every breath. It felt like someone was stabbing her in the side. She wanted to stop. But the master wight wouldn't allow it. He yanked the rope and the raw skin broke open a little deeper each time.

The weariness crept into her bones from her feet up. It climbed her body until her legs were shaking from the effort to keep going. She felt sick. Maybe she'd been sick already and the back of her hand was wet with perspiration and vomit. The combination stung in the blood-red welts underneath the hemp cord. Her hands were cold and shaking. Breathing was torture. Her vision narrowed.

And Nora knew.

She knew she would fall.

She felt it coming. Her body would give in. It couldn't go any farther. Willpower or no, there was nothing left to fuel motion. And when she fell, the cold and pitiless slave master wight would have to drag her lifeless body behind him because there was no way she could possibly get up again.

And at last, as the red sun started to show in a pale line beyond the horizon, she didn't run anymore; she walked. The tired men gulped air in singing breaths. The mists swirled as she walked through toward the morning, and behind her the world lay gray, shapeless, formless, oblivious to what she felt going through it, what she shed to get here, how tired she was. Someone said, "We rest here." So she lay down on the wet grass like she'd never lain as sweetly or more comfortably.

And as always, when things seemed good, life turned bad.

Chapter 2

A warmth spread through Nora's right breast and a gentle squeeze made the nipple stand erect. Nora shifted in her waking slumber and rolled onto her side. She was stiff and her whole body hurt. Her nipple tingled again, sending a warm shiver deep down. Her hand moved to cover her breast but couldn't reach it. A hand slipped between her legs and touched her most intimate part. It was not her hand.

Nora woke in cold realization. Her body hurt because of running all night. She couldn't move her hands because they were still bound. The cold of the night had made her stiff. And one of those men was touching her.

If she screamed, would any of the others do anything? Could Owen do something? She listened hard, trying to ignore the hands. Trying to lie very still as they groped her body. Her eyes remained closed. Maybe if she pretended to sleep—maybe the man would give up and just go away?

His morning breath was hot on her face. His hand grabbed her shoulder to turn her onto her back.

If you fight, it'll only be worse.

A knee pushed itself between her legs.

Oh gods, no.

He gripped the rope around her hands and lifted her arms. Pretending to sleep was not an option anymore. Nora opened her eyes and saw the silhouette of a large man, shouldering a round shield and a battle-ax. When he grinned at her, his teeth were surprisingly white. He held a finger to his mouth and squeezed her thigh in a friendly way. She pulled her lips back mechanically to make a pass at a smile. He winked.

Nora inhaled. He smelled of unwashed man: sweat and grime and piss. She closed her eyes as he shifted his weight, fumbling with her trousers.

This would hurt. One way or another.

Her back muscles screeched in pain as she bunched her legs up. His eyes widened in surprise and his mouth was ajar in a perfect O. He didn't even see her boot coming. The cracking sound and the grind under her heel as his nose broke filled her with grim satisfaction. Blood gushed all over that pretty face. He cried out. Heart pounding in her ears, she reached toward his hips and unsheathed his hunting knife before he keeled over. She slashed the blade across his unprotected stomach, and he howled in pain.

Look for Owen. Cut the rope.

Don't stare at him! Look for Owen!

Men were waking only a few meters away. There was Owen! No one was guarding him. But they were all moving, sitting up, as one of their own cursed her with all kinds of names. This was it. Time to go.

"Owen!"

She shoved Owen with her foot. He woke, bleary-eyed, looking up at her.

"I see no smoke," he said and turned over.

"Owen, come on! We're not tending charcoal here!" She shoved him once more, frantically sawing at her bonds with the blade. Her fingers were still stiff and unhelpful, and she cut into the flesh of her thumb. "We've got to go."

Her eyes darted from one waking man to the next. Where was the master wight? One cord was loose. She could free one hand far enough to hold the knife and cut the other piece of rope. Too many men were moving, waking. They had camped on a little knoll, half submerged in fog. Behind her, when she raised her head, the open plain washed gray under a pale midday sun. On the horizon to the west stood a dark line of trees. To the east the Plains stretched far, far until the foot of the Crest Mountains.

No hiding place.

"You fucking wench!" the bleeding man shouted, reaching for his knife and finding it gone. He staggered a few steps toward her, wiping his sleeve across the red torrent gushing over his mouth, one hand clutching his belly. Nora stepped away.

"Come on, Owen," she said one more time, moving away from the man, who was reaching behind him to get a battle-ax.

"The wench is trying to escape!"

More men stirred. More were groaning and sitting up. Nora's gaze crossed the gray eyes of the Fish Lord as he wiped his face sleepily. She saw his eyes dart to her left. She turned and swung the knife.

Master Diaz was there. He dodged the blade gracefully.

Nora danced a few steps farther up the knoll. Run away and leave Owen behind? Yes? No?

"Stay away!" she cried.

The master did no such thing. He held out the palms of his hands to show he carried no weapon. But he was closing in on her. She backed off farther.

"Owen!" she shouted now.

Her twin brother sat up. His dark hair stood up on his head, and there was a red mark on his face where he had lain on his hand.

"What are you doing?" he asked, shaking his head.

The master was too close. Nora swung the knife once more. He dodged. She attacked, jumping toward him. But he was always a step out of her reach. Down, back down into the next vale he led her as she thrust the knife despite her protesting body. She looked to keep a free path behind her. Calculate her next blow. Heart beating, knees trembling. But her hands were steady.

She lunged, a desperate attack on the right. He arched away. She swung back to the left and he turned. But this time, she grazed his upper arm. Got him! A shout of raw triumph burst from her lips. The low panic she'd felt since waking up churned in her belly and made her faster but giddy at the same time. Her eyes ticked from face to face. The wight watched her with eyes partially closed, head tilted to the side. Half of the men behind him were sitting, half standing. The Fish Lord rose and grinned at her. The bleeding man had retreated and was being tended to.

Nora met the black eyes of the wight before her and took a deep breath. He moved more carefully now. His cloak was thrown back over his left shoulder, showing the hilt of his sword. She made a decision and withdrew. The Plains lay behind her; in two or three days she could be back at the Ridge. Get help and come back for Owen later. If she could break free now.

One last lunge.

CHAPTER 3

MASTER DIAZ HIT HER CHEST fiercely with the iron pommel of his blade. Owen winced as he watched his sister collapse. Laughter circled among the waking men. Owen stood up and wished he hadn't. His back screamed in pain and his legs faltered under him. He waited until the ache faded to a tingle, then half crawled toward his master. Master Diaz took Nora's pulse at her throat. Then he gently laid her left arm over her waist. He looked at Owen.

Owen lifted a strand of dark hair from his sister's face. A line of tiny blood drops dotted her throat where Master Diaz's blade had grazed her skin yesterday. No. Only a few hours ago. Owen rubbed his tired eyes and looked at the midday sun, then back down. Nora's wrists looked much worse. Red welts and blood, raw skin chafed from the hemp cords. Her left hand looked frail as it lay on her stomach, pale fingers and bleeding wrist. She was normally so robust, hardened like steel. Strange to see her knocked down. When was the last time he'd seen her hurt? Owen shook his head, trying to remember. Two years ago? The charcoal clamp had leaked, and as they were frantically shoveling mud onto it to control the heat, Nora had cried out and clutched her forearm. A burning ember. Still armed with his shovel, Owen had watched his sister stagger a few steps away from the clamp. She didn't hear his questions but closed her eyes and collapsed with a sigh. She'd gone still then, too. So still. Scared, Owen had continued shoveling mud onto the charcoal clamp and onto his sister's forearm, the white hand bone-pale under the black earth. Cool the burn. Cool the burn. And here he was again. All alone. Panic reached his throat, but he swallowed it down. This time there were others with him. He looked up into Master Diaz's black eyes.

"What happened?" Owen asked.

"Do you need me to spell it out for you? You seemed smart," the wight said.

Owen looked at the other men. Most were clustered around the bleeding would-be rapist, who shot him a dark look. The man spat a gob of blood to the ground. He seemed the type who'd kill you if he thought you'd looked at him funny. Nora wasn't safe here. But she wouldn't go home alone. Owen pushed another strand of hair away from his sister's forehead, giving his hands something to do while his brain worked on a way to get her to leave him.

The leader stretched and moved over to the injured man. The others made room for him. He slapped the man on the back before crouching next to him.

"Where, oh where has your charm gone? I quite think she didn't like you as much as the tavern girls seem to." The leader grinned amiably. "How many men do you lead?"

"Fifty, my lord."

"They're stationed with the rest of my troops?"

"Yes, my lord."

"Good."

The leader slashed a long, curved blade across the man's throat. He stepped away from the gush of blood and wiped his blade clean on the fallen man's cloak. Owen stared at him.

"No one who runs with me gets beaten by his chosen vessel of pleasure." There was silence among the men. "Weakness is punishable by death."

The leader nodded at Master Diaz and returned to his resting place to break his fast. Master Diaz reached into his own backpack and broke a small hard loaf in two.

"Prince Bashan," Owen began, picking at the bread. "He's not what I expected."

Diaz opened his mouth to say something, but Owen quickly added, "Nor are you."

Master Diaz raised both eyebrows at that. "And what would you know about me?"

Owen shrugged.

"About you? Nothing. Besides the obvious. You're a half-wight, aren't you? You look like the wight warriors that sometimes come down the Wightingerode to trade at Dernberia. But they don't have hair. So one of your parents is human, right? And you carry the rune of the pilgrim order on the back of your right hand. It's hard to make out because of the scar you have there—a burn, isn't it? I know burns. Got a few of them myself. Nora too. Our foster father is a smith, and he'd send us out to make charcoal even when we were still too small to be out alone."

"Explains your black clothes," Diaz said. "And a few other things."

Owen nodded.

"Most pilgrim masters I know are like Master Darren—old, sage, very wise in the ancient texts, and always first at the food tables at ceremonial gatherings like marriages and burials."

"And handfastings," Diaz said. "When was your sister to be married? Solstice, probably."

Nora stirred. They looked down, but she remained unconscious.

"You're not like them, are you?" Owen said. "And I don't mean your eyes or the color of your skin. I mean, you're a warrior. You're here on a quest. You must be, because you run with the exiled prince. I heard Moorfleet's library was torched to the ground a few weeks ago. It was the oldest, richest library left here in the north. A beacon of civilization. Gone. Just like that. Fire spreads. People could have died in the flames. Funny coincidence you and the prince were there at the same time."

They both silently chewed on a bite of bread. Owen swallowed first.

"'A pilgrim must honor the code and preserve wisdom in any form.' And 'If it lies in the power of your hand to do good, then you must do good.' Bands of plunderers and looters are raiding the villages between here and the ruins of Moorfleet. What are you going to do about them?"

"You quote the *125 Ordinances of Master Sulla* at me? That's impressive, and not only because you've just implied I broke them."

"I didn't mean to..."

"But you did." Diaz shrugged. "How did you guess it was the prince?"

Owen ran a hand through his hair.

"I didn't guess. I saw. I observed. The answers are right there if you choose to observe your surroundings. You could say the prince told me who he was himself: fully fitted with garb that's good quality but old. Means he had money to buy it at one point but doesn't have that money now. The warrior rings on his hand threw me off at first. They're not authentic. Warrior rings are shaped from the spear tips of the men you killed. His aren't. They're skillfully made to resemble warrior rings. So why have them? To show he is counted among the warriors? Although, assuming his right hand is his sword hand, warrior rings are cumbersome to actually use in a fight unless you want to bash someone's teeth in with your fist. So, he was clearly someone who doesn't often fight but has military education.

"And then the ring with the one-horned stag on his left hand. Kind of gave him away. Carrying the symbol of the heir of the empire? He's out to fulfill the prophecy, isn't he? That he'll find the Living Blade. The last master to hold the Blade died in the north. Bashan needs information. If there is any, it's probably here in a large, old library. Moorfleet." Owen shook his head. "Too easy, really."

After a long pause, Master Diaz nodded. "You observed all that while I held a knife to your sister's throat? If you truly do wish to become a pilgrim—"

"I do," Owen interrupted. "I really do."

"Then you could become one of our best assets. Bring new life to the old order."

Owen stared at the tip of his boots, ears red. "Yeah. That's not what most people say."

Master Diaz shrugged. "I am not most people."

Owen smiled.

"Your sister," the master began. "Her name is?"

"Noraya. Or Nora for short," Owen answered.

Master Diaz blinked. It was a sign, Owen thought. A visible change in the line of thinking.

"Owen as in Owen, the founder of the lost city of Vella?"

"And of Owen's Ridge."

"And Noraya, like the last northern high queen? Are you sure you're not of royal descent?" The hint of a smile was on the master's lips.

"I sometimes wish. But no. Our foster parents found us around this time of year when we were about a year old. No sign of a father. No sigil, no gold, no cloth of purple. Just a dead woman and two bawling children. Twins. But they took us in despite us being totally unnatural and raised us as their own the last sixteen years."

"Then why run away?"

"Are you kidding? Except for our foster parents, everyone distrusted us. I'm too much of a scholar to have any rapport among the tradesmen of the Ridge. Which is a laugh considering I'm probably the only one fluent enough in Kandarin to read the merchants' shipping information from here to Dernberia, but that doesn't matter because I can't swing a hammer in the forge. And Nora...well, let's just say she *can* swing a hammer in the forge. I mean, has anyone ever made the sign of evil against you when you walked past them?"

"Yes."

"Oh." Owen shot a glance at the black wight eyes. They looked like those of a lizard. Impenetrable and alien. He cleared his throat. "I see. Well then. I guess you know how it is."

Master Diaz stared down at Nora's face, his black eyes unblinking.

The prince ordered the group to move on after they had eaten. Nora was still unconscious, so Owen helped put her limp arms around Master Diaz's neck so he could carry her over his shoulder like a hunter would a deer. They ran at a more leisurely pace than they had during the night. Owen ran close to Master Diaz. The first few steps were agonizing; his feet were like stones, flint-edged, hard, and unwilling to roll. But as his body warmed, the going was smoother. He watched Nora's head bounce on Diaz's shoulder. She didn't wake up. The master carried her effortlessly, jogging without losing his breath. Now and then he would grunt and shift her weight but would not miss a step. Nora's arm dangled down the master's back.

Her hand jerked up suddenly. Nora tried to move and Master Diaz was thrown off-balance. She gasped in fright. Her arm clutched the wight's side to steady herself. He slowed to a halt. Up ahead, the prince looked back over his shoulder. He turned and ran a few steps backward as Diaz set Nora down on her feet and signaled the prince to keep going. The prince nodded and grinned at Owen in mock salute before turning around and running forward again.

Nora's arm swung wide as she shoved the master back.

"Don't you touch me!"

She retreated and held a hand over her chest in pain. Her eyes darted to and fro and then rested on Owen. She closed her eyes and sighed, clutching her cloak.

Master Diaz held up both hands. "Are you hurt?"

Owen thought Nora was going to faint again. Her face was drained of color.

"No," she said and knelt down.

"Give her some water."

Owen quickly unslung the waterskin and held it to Nora's lips. She took large, greedy gulps, storing the water in her cheeks before swallowing. Water spilled from her lips and dribbled into her cloak.

"I shall wait over there." The master nodded in the direction the men had run. He walked out of earshot and clasped his hands behind his back.

Nora was shaking. Her hands trembled as she gave the empty skin back to Owen. He searched among his things and took out a morsel of bread and a strip of dried meat. He crouched down with her and watched the clouds while she ate, so he didn't have to see the tears running down her cheeks. Dark gray clouds blew across the sky as though the whips of the wind masters were behind them. Owen had a theory that the shape of the clouds could reveal what the weather would be. But with this blanketed sky, they saw the sheets of rain hanging like brushstrokes across the sky from miles away. A cold northeast wind set in and chilled them.

"We're on the run with the Hunted Company," Owen said after a while. "Did you know that?"

"The Fish Lord is Prince Bashan? Holy shit, Owen!" Nora shook her head, sniffed, and wiped the tears away with the back of her hand. "You think he's found the Living Blade?"

"No." Owen frowned. "I'd say he was looking for information in Moorfleet and Prophetess Hin's shrine. Found none, though. He's been looking for it for eight years. Must be desperate now that his father's died and his half-sister is empress. I figure his best bet is to blow the search off, make alliances with some of the southern noblemen, and intrigue against Empress Vashti to get his throne back."

"You think he'll do that?"

"I certainly hope not." Owen looked down his long nose at her. "The Blade, Nora! Imagine being the first humans to find it after over two thousand years!"

"I imagine it as being a major disappointment. 'Oh, look! The legendary Living Blade is just a legend after all.'"

"What if it's not? What if the Blade is real? The prince seems to think it is."

"Well, then he's in for a big surprise, isn't he?" Nora shook her head.

They sat and watched the sky. Slowly the weak sun called it a day and gave her reign over to the creeping darkness. Owen looked back to where Master Diaz stood, as unmoving as a stone marker. He was far off. Owen lowered his voice anyway.

"But if you stay near the master, I don't think he'll let them touch you again."

Nora snorted.

"Or you could go back." He said it as casually as he dared.

"With you?"

He shook his head. "I think I will become a pilgrim. And who knows? Maybe I'll even be there when Prince Bashan and Master Diaz find the Blade."

"Just like in the stories." Nora sighed. "Remember when the coalers' families let us tend our burn with them? We'd listen to stories and sing under the stars all night."

"And read by the campfire."

"That was good. I wish it could be like that again." She ran a hand through her hair. "If I stay, I might be raped by this lot. If I go, I'll have to marry Wolfe at Solstice. Fucked either way."

"Noraya Smith! Swearing is a sign of stupidity, as though you lack the vocabulary for expressing yourself in an accurate manner."

"I'd say that was as accurate as can be. And shut up, Owen!"

"Wolfe seemed nice," Owen said quickly. "Or, well, I'm sure he *is* a nice guy."

"That's a bit vague for you, master of observation."

Owen shrugged. He opened his mouth as if to say more but then stopped himself. Was there a safe platitude you could say in moments like these? Nora raised one eyebrow at her brother's restraint.

"His hands were sweaty." She grimaced at the memory.

"So he's a nervous nice guy. Anyone'd be nervous who has to marry you."

"I know. He is a nervous nice guy." Nora gave him a smile, then took a raggedy breath. "But if I go back to the Ridge, I have to marry Wolfe to stop being the evil temptress from hell."

Owen flushed. There had been talk about Nora, and he'd never been entirely sure which rumors were false. This was tricky ground.

"Do you even want to marry him?"

Nora threw her hands up.

"It's not that easy, Owen!"

"Make it easy. Yes or no. A binary choice."

"I don't even know what binary means."

Master Diaz cleared his throat audibly. It sounded painful, a noise one couldn't ignore. He stood silently behind them, and both twins stared up at him.

"Can we move along now?"

They both stood up. Nora held out her hands, wrists first, forcing him to see the welts. The half-wight looked down at them. He reached behind him and gave her back her own knife.

"Here. This is yours, Noraya of Owen's Ridge."

She looked at Owen. She had made the hilt herself out of smooth antler this summer. Owen had watched her do it across the charcoal clamp they were tending. Their foster father had forged the blades for Nora's dowry, but she had carved and scraped the hilts. A good set of knives, three in all, rolled into a leather pouch. In the half-light, the rods the smith had beaten into one smooth blade curled and twisted against the warmth of Master Diaz's fingers like smoky wisps. Owen knew he'd never be able to craft such blades, even if the smith's work had interested him, which it hadn't. Nora probably could. She was good with her hands and had often helped out at the forge, hammering away at horseshoes and plowshares while Owen kept the books. She was right. Life had been good for a while. Very good. At least until Mother Sara had died. There was nothing for Nora here. Nothing keeping her but him.

She took her knife from the wight and left it unsheathed, tucked between her belt and her shirt. She didn't thank Master Diaz. Just stared into those dark eyes, black like the big sky above them.

"Use it well," Diaz said and went off.

A drizzle set in as they followed.

CHAPTER 4

NORA FOUGHT TO KEEP HER eyes open. She sat on the squelching earth, having no other choice after the rain, arms crossed over her knees with Owen's back against hers. She felt her brother relax as he fell asleep like a stone falls into water. His head lolled against her shoulder. She wished she could surrender to sleep like that, too. But as soon as her head nodded toward her chest, she woke with a start, heart pounding. She shifted into a more upright position, stared at the sleeping men around her, and tried to think of ways to escape the predicament they were in. Every time her eyes ripped open again from her moment of sleep, there he was—the master wight. Always on the watch. Never asleep. How did he do it? Was it some kind of wight magic? Nora tried to remember the old legends she'd heard about the Lords and Ladies, but her mind started to drift and she woke up a few moments later, a little angrier at herself.

When someone crouched down next to her, her hand was on her knife before her eyes focused on the master wight. He watched her lower the knife, but she didn't put it away.

"You can sleep tonight. I will watch over you." His voice sounded like he needed to cough even when he whispered.

"Yeah, right." She rubbed her stinging eyes, pulling her cloak tighter around her shoulders. Owen lifted his head from her shoulder, shook it slowly and curled up on the ground next to her. "Just like yesterday?"

"I assumed the men would be too exhausted from running to try—"

"Well, you assumed wrong!" Nora wiped her face, numbed by tiredness. She should get up and walk around. That always helped. She gave the wight next to her a glance. Would he let her?

"You are free to leave, you know," he said as though he could read her mind. "But I wonder, where would you go?"

And there was the crux. Where could she go? This was crazy. They never should have left the Ridge unprepared in the first place. They should have had a plan. Now she was stuck here in the middle of nowhere with nothing but a knife, and Owen seemed to be entertaining the thought of some grand quest with these last dregs of humanity swept from the gutters of the world into the open arms of a banished prince. She blinked the sleep away from her eyes, set her mouth, and stared right back at the wight.

"What do you want me to say? What do you want?"

"You were lucky it was I who grabbed you by the tree. Any of the other men and your death would have been slow and painful because you would have fought them. A little trust would be a good start, don't you think?"

Nora snorted.

"Yeah, sure. I trust any random stranger I meet in the woods who holds a knife to my throat, lets me get nearly raped by one of his mates, then beats me unconscious for trying to escape."

He sucked in air audibly through his clenched teeth, then held it in for a moment.

"He was not 'one of my mates.' Don't ever count me among them. I am a pilgrim master, and I swore to guide Prince Bashan through the northern realms to find the Living Blade. Yet foremost, I am oath-bound to protect the innocent."

"Well, if you're oath-bound to Prince Bashan, too, then your oath to protect the innocent is worth nothing, Master Diaz."

His eyebrows disappeared into the shadow of his deep hood and a short flicker of anger played around his jawline. Instead of standing up and walking away, he took a deep breath. Why was he trying so hard? Nora followed the wight's gaze downward to where Owen slept in the damp grass.

"Your brother trusts me."

"He does."

Those black eyes flicked back to her face. Nora sighed.

"Come on. You don't really believe all that mumbo jumbo about twins having a double soul? We may look alike. But we're not the same person."

"Did you run away from home because someone there realized you were not just brother and sister, but twins?"

"No. They knew and hated us for it."

"Because you didn't like the man you were supposed to marry?"

"No."

The truth was, she had liked Wolfe just fine. It wasn't his fault her life had become such a mess. That had been the baker's busybody wife. "What do you care?"

"Who taught you how to fight?"

Nora bit her lip and looked away.

"I'm not fighting. I'm defending myself." She shook her head. "And no one taught me. I learned through practice: kick hard when you have the chance. Aim for parts that hurt. Hope you get lucky and his surprise shocks him into being stupid. Then knock him out with the shovel if you've got one handy. If not, go find the shovel."

"And you've had much practice defending yourself? I can't imagine why."

Nora flushed. She scowled but kept her mouth shut. It wasn't easy. She rested her hot head on her forearms and hoped he'd go away before she fell asleep. After a moment, she heard the rustle of clothes and peeped over her arm to see the master wight settle down next to her, cross-legged, his pupil-less eyes staring off into the space inside his mind. She gritted her teeth. She'd wait and watch. He had to sleep sometime. And when he did, she'd run and take Owen with her—kicking and screaming, if need be. Both of them would be safe from this mad quest.

✧ ✧ ✧

IN THE RED MORNING, THERE was smoke on the horizon. It rose into the lighting sky in a dark plume. Nora rubbed her tired face and nudged Owen awake.

"I don't see any smoke," he muttered.

"Then open your eyes. It's all across the sky like a message from the gods."

"What?" Owen rose and stared at the black cloud looming in the west. He took a deep breath.

"The Ridge is burning," Nora said.

"No." Owen wiped a hand across his face. "Black smoke means un-burned charcoal dust lifting from a leak. In this cold, you could see a leak from this far away. You couldn't see a house burn."

Nora gave her brother a look.

"Charcoal dust?"

"Charcoal dust," Owen said.

"You emotionless lump of ore, Owen! That's cold. Really cold."

"What?"

"People tend the charcoal, Owen. People like you and me. Families. With kids. People we know and shared meals with. What do you think happened to them? Why aren't they watching for leaks?"

Owen paled, then shrugged. "Maybe they just, um...maybe they..."

"Days of work would go up in the smoke! Days! When would you leave a burn untended, Owen?"

"We never left a burn."

"When you have to run for your life, that's when. And if the coalers ran, it means the Ridge is burning."

Owen snorted. "Burning! How?"

"Bandits."

"It would take a large number of men to overthrow the Ridge, Nora."

"Yeah? You calculated how many?" Nora looked around at the Hunted Company, counting twenty armed men. Twenty armed men who would do nothing to help her village.

"Is something wrong?" Prince Bashan asked pleasantly.

Nora shot him a dark look and opened her mouth to speak her mind. But Owen touched her elbow in warning. The other men were breaking camp. And there was Master Diaz, staring at her with his beetle-black eyes. She clenched her teeth and fists. Her jaw ached with all the words she wanted to say.

"No, we're ready to go." Owen moved into Nora's line of sight, shoving himself between her and the prince. "Just wondering about the smoke."

The prince gave Nora a long look over Owen's shoulder.

"Enjoy the view as long as you can. We're moving out."

Nora grabbed her cloak and bag and touched her blade. Touch of iron. Touch of home.

✧ ✧ ✧

ALL DAY SHE MARCHED BEHIND Owen in silence, bare fingers tucked under her armpits. At dusk the company camped under the empty boughs of a small wood, the trees growing among a cluster of ruins. You could find the remains of stone houses, broken wells, and occasionally, partly overgrown cobbled streets all across the Plains. The stories told of the destruction of the ancient city of Vella. Master Scyld had smitten the god of air, Tuil himself, with the Living Blade. Crashing to the earth, Tuil had buried Vella beneath his massive body. Nora watched Owen's eyes gleam when he noticed the broken stone walls. Of course. He loved the stories. He touched the stones carefully, with awe, as though they were something more than the remains of a homestead long given up and left to crumble under the assault of the elements. When she said as much, he just smiled.

"Same story, different version. And all of them true."

She rolled her eyes and drank deeply from her waterskin before falling asleep. A few hours later, she woke with an urgent need, just as planned. Wight or no wight, there was no way she'd sleep through the whole night around these men. Nora rose. A small fire flickered in the middle of the circle of sleeping men. The huge man with a blind white eye hunched before it, leaning against his spear. He glanced over at her when she moved toward the darkness under the trees. She nodded at him and then made a show of stumbling over a root, as though she were still drunk with sleep. He grunted and turned back to the warming fire. Ha! It would be so easy to just leave now. Although, the wight was probably around somewhere nearby. During the day's march, every time she fell back to relieve herself, he'd slow down and wait for her to catch up again. Her own personal bodyguard. Annoying.

Nora ducked under a low branch and peered into the moonlit-crossed boughs of the trees to the west. She had seen a brook with high banks somewhere here earlier and didn't want to fall and break her leg. A fallen tree lay stretched over the creek, its upturned roots a marker. The flowing water had dug deep into the earth; for twenty or so feet it meandered through sandy banks, then constricted once more at the next elbow in its path. The spring floods carved it deeper every year, no doubt. She let herself down onto the smooth wet sand and looked in all directions, just to be sure she was alone. Above her, the bank formed a lip that sheltered her from view. Below it was a carpet of small pebbles and larger rocks. Perfect. And if one of the men was downstream now, drinking from the water, so much the better. She pulled down her trousers with a grin and a sigh of relief. Then she heard the voices.

It was the prince whining, and the low rumble betrayed the master wight. They were talking in Kandarin, but she could discern some of what they said, having a basic grasp of the empire's language through dealings with merchants. Diaz and Bashan weren't talking shop, though, and neither wanted to buy or sell iron. Still, she could guess some of the unfamiliar words by their similarity to her own language.

"...don't understand why you have to go away to meditate, Telen."

"I need quiet. Solitude."

"It's quiet now. Stay here and meditate tonight. We can go on tomorrow and reach the temple before winter comes on strong."

"I'm not asking for your permission, Bashan. I'm telling you I'm leaving for a day or two."

Nora pulled up her trousers and pressed herself against the bank. Her heart skipped a beat. If the wight was leaving, she would leave in the opposite direction. This was a window of opportunity. Diaz said something, but she couldn't make out the words. The men were moving upstream, so she followed under the bank.

"You swore an oath to me." The prince again.

"And I will stand by it."

"You wanted to help me find the Blade."

"I will."

"Then why leave? You've never left to meditate. You need peace and quiet? Fine. It's quiet here. Meditate now! It'll be quiet at the temple. Meditate all winter if you like. But I need you focused while we're on the journey."

Nora heard one of the men start to pace. Someone kicked a small rock over the lip of the bank and it splashed into the brook before her. She held her breath and pressed herself harder against the earth, into the shadow, in case one of them looked over.

"It's enough that we're dragging those kids along with us. They're slowing us down."

"I will hold you personally responsible if something should happen to either of them while I'm gone."

"I *will* be personally responsible if she keeps on staring at me like that, insolent wench. Peasants should look down when talking to their superiors."

"They are your future subjects. Treat them with respect. I believe Owen will be of great use to you, and he has an eager mind. You should pair him up with Shade. They'd both have the company of someone their own age. And they'd profit from each other."

"Oh, here you go again. 'You need to choose wisely, Bashan.'" The prince didn't get the timbre right, of course—no one spoke as deep as the wight—but Nora thought the tone was spot-on.

"You do," Diaz said calmly. "Your following is your reputation. These aren't men who befit your stature."

"They're loyal."

"For now."

"When everyone left me, they chose to come when I called for aid."

"They're desperate men. And that shows you are too. And they're a liability."

"Lara wept! Not Moorfleet again?"

There was a pause. Nora pricked her ears. Her heart was racing. What about Moorfleet? Diaz let out a deep sigh.

"The nature of a man cannot be determined by his actions alone, I guess.

Still. So much chaos. So much destruction."

"It wasn't my fault. Things got out of hand."

"Take the city, you said. Take the city. Do you know what that means to these men? You sowed death, Bashan. Moorfleet was loyal to you, loyal to the true heir of the empire, until you torched it to cinders."

"Then they should've given me what I wanted."

"You think you're closer to information on the whereabouts of the Blade now, after you burned the oldest, richest library in the north?"

Bashan snorted.

"Old, maybe. Rich? The realm of Moran has been dying for hundreds of years. It's cold and wet and poor, and everyone hates everyone else here. There have always been bands of brigands in this part of the country. Look at those twins and tell me with a straight face they're loyal subjects, if you can."

"No. I have never seen as many brigands on the roads or in the wilds as we have encountered so far. And it will become worse now that Moorfleet has fallen. Something is amiss here in the north. Empress Vashti has called back the last legions of the imperial troops in order to protect the rest of the empire from the unrest in the north. No one can help the towns and villages when they are overrun by bands of marauders and wild men. Yet if you'd return to Moorfleet and make reparations, take control of the city, you could become a beacon in the north and make the counts and barons in Arrun wish they'd allied themselves to your cause sooner."

"Diaz, I don't want to rule this shithole. No one does. That's why it's in trouble."

Nora held her breath. She could picture Diaz shaking his head in the brief silence.

"Prayers for the wicked must never be forsaken."

A sharp intake of breath.

"Careful!"

"It's what my father used to say." Diaz paused. "I have lost my way and must meditate to regain my focus. I must do penance for my failure to protect the innocent. And I must pray for those who are on the silent road by my hand. I must do this alone."

Bashan let out a long breath.

"Fine. Go do penance, then. But if you're not back in two days, I can't guarantee you'll see that insolent wench alive again."

"There are hundreds of ways I could lead you to your death, oath or no."

"I was just kidding."

"As was I. We will both remember it until I return."

From the rustle of the undergrowth, Nora judged that one of them left. It sounded as though someone was making his way farther upstream, back to the open Plains. After a short quiet, a stream of hot piss poured over the lip of the bank and splashed on the bed of pebbles below. She heard Bashan sigh and she crept away downstream as quickly as she could, one hand trailing the earthen wall beside her until she could hoist herself back up. Giddy, she walked back to the camp, but she remembered to walk slower as though she was tired when she came close to the huge man on guard duty. He leered at her, but it was more of a generic leer because she was a girl and not because he was thinking of making a move.

Lying back-to-back with Owen against the cold stone walls of the crumbling ruins, she wrapped her cloak around her and listened to the wind howl over the empty Plains. Diaz had left. Bashan was a prick. He had burned Moorfleet, the jerk. She could be back home in a few days, pick up some supplies, warmer clothing, and head toward Dernberia's port to take the first ship out of the north, out of trouble. She had a plan now.

CHAPTER 5

THROUGHOUT THE DAY, AGAIN AND again, Nora tried to get a glimpse of the lonesome black silhouette traveling northward until she couldn't see Diaz anymore. The prince hadn't been very amused in the morning. He had threatened the twins a bit but hadn't ordered her bound again. Maybe it had helped to keep her eyes on his boots while he ranted. It helped her stop grinning, at least.

Dusk found the group at the ford of a river. The river's fountains lay under the snow of the Crest Mountains, and the shepherds who walked the Plains in summer called it the Line. It was the natural boundary of the ancient realm of Moran, and beyond it was the Suthron Pass to the empire. Don't cross the Line, the shepherds always joked. It wasn't very funny, but then, they were shepherds. Sheep were an easy audience, Nora figured.

The river resembled the brook, only on a larger scale. The water had dug a deep path through the flatlands. Lots of rounded pebbles washed up on the embankments, with the occasional boulder strewn here and there, the water pooling around them, eating away at the bed beneath, though the water was shallow enough to cross at some sandy banks. Beyond lay another wood scene, a handful of trees grouped together against the wind. Nora nudged Owen's side.

"Hmm?"

"Fall back," Nora said.

"What?"

"So." Prince Bashan slapped his hands together in the cold. "Who wants to go first?"

The men grumbled.

"Yeah, me neither." The prince laughed. "Still, after we cross, I think we can risk a big fire or two tonight. Get warm again."

No one moved forward.

"Fine. Follow me," the prince said. He waded into the water, grimacing, but stopped after a moment to let the others catch up.

Nora let the other men go before her. She tugged at Owen's sleeve to keep him by her side and gingerly stepped into the water as though she wanted to cross. The river was icy cold and swirled white around her leather boots. Footing was tricky as the pebbles and stones all moved. She took a deep breath, readying herself. They were nearly the last ones in the water. The huge man was bringing up the rear. He rubbed over his good eye, the blind one bulging from the cavity due to a large scar that ran down his face. He seemed tired, putting his weight on his spear that he was using as a walking staff among the slippery stones. That was good. That would make this easier. She splashed closer to him, dragging Owen with her.

"What are you doing?" her brother hissed.

The water was clear and ran smoothly. She could feel the stream pull at her feet as she waded in a bit deeper to get behind the man. He was breathing heavily. Old man. He was the only one close enough to come after them immediately. She'd have to take him out. Then at least she'd get a few minutes. Her heart missed a beat as her foot sank deep into a patch of sand. She swallowed hard. They were nearly in the middle of the river now. The water seeped through her trouser legs and into her tunic and cloak.

Now.

Nora gathered speed. She kicked away the spear butt and slammed into the man as hard as she could, making him keel over into the water. As he did, she grabbed the pommel of his sword and unsheathed it. The man went under, so she turned and grabbed Owen's hand.

"Run!"

Her legs splashed the water up high as she ran, pulling Owen behind and raking the riverbed with the tip of the huge man's sword, which was too heavy to lift above her head for long. The noise attracted attention. She heard the shouts of the men behind her and the man she had shoved came up again, sputtering and coughing and angry. Owen tore himself free.

"What are you doing?"

"Getting a head start. Come on!"

"Nora!" Owen ran alongside her. "What's your plan?"

"Run and hope they don't come after."

"Well, it's not working."

Nora risked a look over her shoulder. Her heart fell. Some of the men were already plowing through the water. The huge man was getting up and aiming with his spear. She turned, zigzagging across the green.

"This is crazy. Where are you going?"

"Away from these guys."

The spear slammed into the ground next to her left foot with a sickening thud. She jumped to the right and bumped into Owen. He stumbled and grabbed her arm, unbalancing her. They both fell.

Her teeth clicked together hard and then she was kneeling, hands splayed on the ground. The sword was gone. There were shouts behind her, louder now, anger in the voices. But the sound was muffled by her pounding heart. Her hands tingled, and sweat dripped from her face. Nothing felt broken. Owen was at her side, groaning but stirring.

"Come on, Owen! We can still make it."

"Gods damn you, Nora! I think you broke my nose."

"Let me look."

She pulled him to his feet and pried his hands away from his face. He was glaring at her, eyebrows knotted in a frown.

"There's no blood. It's all right."

"No, it's not." A blade dug into her back with menace. "Kneel."

It was the young man Bashan had set to watch over them this morning. His voice still broke. A tall gangly youth, he was about their age, pale with close-cropped blond hair, and he obviously didn't need to shave yet. But he was fast. Faster than Nora had thought. He had waded into the river just after the prince. Dammit. If she could reach her knife—she felt another blade push under her ribs.

"I should kill you right now." The prince spoke with a flat, cold voice that made her knees buckle. "Give me a reason not to."

She closed her eyes against his spit.

"I'm leaving. You don't want me here anyway."

"That is so true. But, unfortunately, I can't just let you wander around telling people where I'm heading either. There's this awkward thing called banishment on my head, and some people believe that's the same thing as a bounty."

"And who could I tell? Who'd believe me?"

The prince twisted his sword against her ribs.

"Take me as a hostage," Owen said.

"What?"

Nora looked up, as did Bashan. Owen shrugged at them both.

"Isn't that how you say it? You could take me as a hostage, my lord. As a guarantee. I swear on my life, she will not tell anyone where you're headed then."

"Owen!"

"On your life, eh?"

"Owen, no!"

Owen shook his head. "You don't understand. I don't want to leave, Nora."

Nora stared at her brother and focused on just breathing for a moment. Anger churned her stomach and burned in her throat.

Owen shook his head once more, then looked at her beseechingly. "Where do you want to go anyway?"

"Owen, please!"

"You were the one who wanted to run away, remember?"

"Not like this! Not with these people! We'll find another way, our own way. Maybe go south, wherever you want to go."

"I want to go to the Temple of the Wind. I want to become a pilgrim." Owen looked up at Prince Bashan. "And I want to help you find the Blade."

Bashan nodded. "I'm listening. Keep going."

Owen licked his lips.

"There's a library at the Temple of the Wind. But it's not an ordinary library of books and scrolls. In the ancient world it was a collection of memories. If Kandar ever wrote down where he was headed with the Blade, that knowledge would be stored there. I could help you. I'm a scholar at heart, a scrivener by schooling. And I'm wasted in Owen's Ridge. Let me come with you. And let my sister go home if she wants to. Unharmed."

The tips of the swords were gone.

"Fine. You have a deal." Bashan sheathed his sword. "She goes, you stay. Say your goodbyes quickly before I change my mind. Shade, look after our new recruit."

"Yes, lord."

Nora scanned Owen's face. What she saw in his eyes made her heart break.

"You can't do this," she said.

He shrugged, then scratched the back of his head.

"I'm sorry. But I was trying to tell you all this time. You just weren't listening. I don't want to leave."

"Owen, these are not good people."

"The prince has a just cause. He should have been emperor. If it weren't for the prophecy of the Blade, he would be."

Nora hit the ground with her fists.

"The prince is a fucking jerk and isn't fit to rule. Look at the scumbags he's with. Murderers, thieves, mercenaries. They'd slit their own mother's throat if they thought it'd bring them coin."

"Careful, aye?" The young man called Shade still stood behind her, but Nora didn't care. She just talked louder.

"What? It's true! Owen, these guys torched Moorfleet without so much as a second thought because of a whiny, petulant princeling who acts as though he's still four years old and the world belongs to him. Well, hello, reality. It doesn't work that way. Stories are stories. Legends are legends. And there's no such thing as a magical blade that imbues you with the right to rule."

"Shh, Nora!"

"Don't *shh* me! You're better than this. You know better, Owen. You yourself carved the runes on those daggers and swords we made for those pompous pricks from Dernberia. What did you write? 'My wielder thinks I'm magical'?"

Owen clenched his teeth. "This is different."

"No, it's not," Nora yelled, and her voice broke. She wiped her nose on her sleeve. "Don't you see? Open your eyes."

He crossed his arms and studied her face as she cuffed away the tears.

"My eyes are open. It's you with the illusion that you can just carry on with your life as though nothing happened. Maybe this is your last chance. Come with me. Do yourself a favor and don't go back to the Ridge."

His voice was hard and tense. She stared at her brother's face. His eyes became her focal point, the fixed star. If she blinked now, she'd spin into the darkness.

"Oh gods. You believe it too, don't you?"

"I don't have to believe. I saw often enough."

She rose slowly, seeking to steady herself by his gaze.

"What did you see? You saw nothing. There was nothing to see."

Owen turned his head and looked across the river where the men were gathering. The world fell silent, and Nora took a breath as though it were her last.

"Yeah, well. If you're going to be all self-righteous, maybe you shouldn't have fucked our father," Owen said.

Cold gripped her heart and squeezed. Nora struggled for air as though she were underwater. Mechanically she gripped the straps of her backpack and twisted the rough hemp as though it were a lifesaving rope. She opened her mouth. He didn't believe that. He couldn't! It was too…too… Her head reeled.

You never called him Father, only Rannoch. I did, though. And that's all he ever was. She wanted to say that. But nothing came except the salty taste that heralded vomit. She shut her mouth again. She wanted to hit him. Wanted to shake him until his teeth rattled. But nothing she could do would make him take back the monstrosity of what he'd just said.

So she left. One foot in front of the other. First the right, then the left. Looking ahead, she saw nothing but dead grass and forlorn windswept trees dotting the Plains. There was nowhere to go and nowhere to hide. She would be one tiny speck in the vastness around her. She didn't look behind her until night had fallen and she was sure she wouldn't see anyone. Owen never called out after her, anyway.

CHAPTER 6

MASTER TELEN DIAZ SAT ON top of the collapsed stone aqueduct, legs crossed and palms open to whatever the heavens had to offer. Night had fallen around him, but it didn't make much difference to his wight eyes as he gazed over the emptiness of the Plains.

The world melted away beneath him and he saw himself from far above, outlined in a pale blue light. His condensed soul light pulsed steadily. The wights believed that all souls were of the essence of the stars and that everyone could tap into their innermost being and draw strength from the eternal stillness within if they so wished. But decades of watching humans had led Diaz to the conclusion that if they did know how to go far without and deep within, most chose not to know. They were content to be distracted, unfocused, carried about hither and thither wherever the winds would blow them, like the autumn leaves that swept past his lone figure. Few were like the stars above, striding in their set path untouched by any wind, a law unto and in themselves, unshackled by actions and words. How long had he let himself be bound, not giving heed to what his body did or said? When had he last gone far without and deep within? He had become too human, too much of a leaf.

He hovered over his body for a long time, lingering in the light and undisturbed quiet of the stars, and contemplated the web of interconnected cords surrounding him, some strands thicker than others. All the oaths he had chosen to take. The thickest was the cord that bound him to the pilgrim order, of course. It led from his body below him to the north in a faint blue line. To the north where the Shrine of Hin stood. With Master Darren dead—obviously not of old age—Diaz was the next eldest master in the northern realms, and thus he should be at the shrine. Should be. The pilgrim code was clear in this matter. Punish the wicked. Protect the innocent. Guide the lost. The daily grind of upholding law and order, passing out judgment, giving women over in marriage, and giving over the dead to the silent road in burials. Important, yes. Especially now that the north was without leadership. Moorfleet gone, the empire withdrawn, and the order's representative killed. However, perhaps there'd be someone more suited to take up that role of oversight. All these years, Master Darren had been doing Diaz a favor. Unknowingly, but still. Diaz should at least hunt for his murderer. A thin strand divided itself from that thick one. One more obligation. Yet it was one of need.

The next strongest cord was the oath he had sworn to Bashan. The two men's methods were different, as were their motives, yet perhaps their goals were still the same. Bashan was on a quest to regain all he had lost, however the young man defined that: mostly it was his right to rule the empire, yet some days it seemed to be only the loss of his riches and a comfortable life. And Diaz? When they had first met five years ago, Bashan's cause had given Diaz the possibility of regaining his honor and finding a new sense of purpose. Purpose he had lost after... An echo of a woman's laughter disturbed his thoughts. *Don't think that! Don't go back! Focus on what's before you. The Blade.* Find the Blade, find purpose. It was never that simple, though, was it? Moorfleet had shown that. Every day the young prince sank lower and lower to new depths of debauchery and, bound to him, Diaz was pulled down alongside, not knowing how to cut the cord. An oath was an oath, and once you broke your word, even in the least of things, then all words had failed and every oath meant nothing.

He frowned, remembering the same words spoken by the girl, Noraya. Two thin strands bound together. Maybe it was the twins who'd caused his doubts, made him feel the need for introspection. The boy, Owen, in particular. The way he looked at Diaz, as though being a pilgrim master meant being flawless, all duty and honor and sacrifice for the code. Hadn't he seen it that way once? Didn't he still? And the girl—Bashan was right. She was insolent, impulsive, and reckless, albeit with noble intent. She had said no one taught her how to fight—and why should they? She was a girl, and a charcoal burner. But also strong and capable. The order would profit from more female masters of that spirit. From more masters of that kind in general.

So twins really did have their own magic about them. He smiled. They'd be able to spend two or three months together at the Temple of the Wind before Bashan continued his search for the Blade come spring. And maybe Diaz could teach the twins a thing or two in the meantime. He'd never had students before. Maybe it was time.

✧ ✧ ✧

DAWN WAS CREEPING INTO THE world, coloring the last of the night charcoal gray. Some of the early risers among the men were waking as Diaz noiselessly walked into the encampment on the far side of the River Line. His wet clothes steamed as he stood next to the fire to dry. He nodded a greeting at the weary watcher on guard duty and then looked for Bashan's figure among the sleepers. There. The boy Shade slept close to the prince, as always. And next to the pale, blond boy lay the dark-haired head of Owen. Good. It was as he had told Bashan. Maybe Diaz's word did still have some influence on the man. Bashan was still malleable.

Then he doubled back. There was only one dark-haired head. The girl was gone.

Diaz blinked and checked he hadn't missed her among the men. No, she wasn't there. His gaze wandered over the grass around the encampment, looking for footprints leading away. There weren't any. She wasn't anywhere. He took a deep breath and tried to find the calmness within he had felt only a few hours ago. Instead, he stormed over to Bashan and grabbed him by his collar. The prince woke face-to-face with an angry wight.

"What the…?"

"Where is she?" Diaz demanded, shaking Bashan awake.

Bashan wiped a hand across his face and focused on Diaz.

"Where's who?"

"The girl. The girl, Noraya. The girl I told you I'd hold you responsible for."

"She left. It wasn't my fault!" Bashan held up his hands over his head as though warding off a blow. "She and her brother—they had a fight. She wanted to leave, so I let her go home. Why are you so—I don't know…what's the matter with you? I thought you wanted to go pray or something."

Diaz let Bashan go. He turned around to face west and stared back across the Plains in the direction from which he had just come. She had wanted to go home? It was a few days' travel to Owen's Ridge. If there was still an Owen's Ridge to go to.

"Talk about tranquility! You said nothing was to happen to her. Nothing has happened. I swear no one touched her." Bashan was still talking. It didn't matter. Diaz tuned him out.

She had left. He had been gone but one day, and she had just left.

Diaz looked down at the sleeping boy at his feet. He had only known the twins for a couple of days. In the aftermath of his meditation, it seemed as if he could still see the faint blue cord binding him to Owen now. Diaz, by his oath, was under obligation to guide Owen to the nearest temple or shrine for education as a pilgrim. He was the master and Owen an initiate. Protect the innocent. Guide the lost. The boy was his responsibility and under his protection.

Fuck!

CHAPTER 7

IT TOOK NORA FIVE DAYS to get back to the woodlands she knew. She told herself she would just be passing through Owen's Ridge. Pick up some extra supplies and winter clothes to get to Dernberia and leave the north. Where to? She didn't know yet. But her feet knew her heart and led her back home. In the chestnut grove below the Ridge, she could smell burned wood lingering on the wind. The charcoal clamps in the woods were cold and abandoned. Only prickly, empty chestnut shells were strewn here and there, peeking out among the dense fallen leaves. The ground before her was red and brown and wet from the constant rain that had set in on her way back across the Plains.

Owen's Ridge stretched along one main road that led up to the coastal road on one end and into the woods on the other. The village sat on a natural shelf of land, a sheer cliff that rose suddenly as though the earth had bowed before it in a time long past. The only way to climb up was a steep stone path that ran up in long curves, twisting this way and that way until it finally reached the top. At the foot of the cliff ran a small brook that pooled in the woodlands around the Ridge, attracting wild ducks and geese to rest before their flight south. Those birds were lucky ones, fed by the excited girls and boys who begged their mothers for breadcrumbs. And so some of the animals lingered longer than they should, becoming fat and lazy, and the unlucky ones who tarried landed in the cooking pots and ovens as autumn roasts. Those ducks were a lesson in life: that greed was bad and luck a thing of perfect timing. Farther up the brook was a huge stone slab laid across smaller stones, serving as a bridge to the winding path, but it was covered in lichens and thus treacherous to cross.

Nora hunkered down under a chestnut tree at one of the pools, among the empty shells covering the forest floor, and threw them into the water. She had no food left. She had run the last day on nothing but water and was feeling weak and hungry for it.

The ducks had all gone.

There were no children skipping down the stone path, being scolded by their anxious mothers.

And above, she could hear no sounds of the village. No dogs barking, no geese cackling. No human voices. She'd been right. The coalers had fled in fear. But it didn't make her feel any better.

There was another way to the village, one that led far around it, following the brook. She could walk around and come up on the far side. Not many families lived here at the neck of the woods, mainly woodcutters, hunters, the herdsmen who settled down for the winter with their smaller flocks of sheep, and the ewes that hadn't been slaughtered for the winter. Only a handful of houses were built of stone—and the bakery, the smithy, and the inn, of course.

In front of the inn, the dirt lane had been cobbled with stones, a proper road. A small space in front of the smithy served as the unofficial town square. On most days, the villagers gathered there to exchange news and gossip, or sheep and goats. She'd helped Rannoch shoe the Vale's horses. Young girls made themselves up and waited in the square for the young men to tell them how pretty they were, spending the summer nights dancing to music and stealing off into the woods for quite a different kind of dancing. There the spring tide fire roared. There the autumn fires warmed cold hands. There Nora had shared a sip from the same cup as Wolfe at her handfasting.

She fell asleep leaning against the tree trunk and woke at dusk. Shouldering her empty backpack, Nora climbed the steep stone way. As she reached the top, she crouched low, spying over the last cuff of rock to see what was up there.

The square was empty.

The flat cobblestones still shone with a wet gleam. The waxing moon snatched a peek from behind the clouds before veiling his face once again. Most of the houses were burned, leaving behind charred beams like raised fingers. The door to the smithy was gone, a gaping dark mouth. The torches at the inn were flickering in the wind, and behind the colored glass windows shone the only light to be seen in the whole village, right down to where the bakery once stood, the large bread oven now a tombstone looming in a forlorn heap of rubble, sagging like the shoulders of a widow.

Two men stood in front of the inn. Men wearing swords at their sides.

Nora hoisted herself up the rock and crouched down behind a bench. She slid her knife out and clutched it tightly. In the shadows, she ran to the smithy and pressed herself against the stone wall. After a moment she looked around the corner to the inn. The men were talking to each other in low voices. One had his back turned to her and was scratching his head. She passed along the wall to the far side of the smithy. To the front, facing the square, was where Rannoch had set up his shop with the forge. The old men liked to come and stand at the door or at the windows, chatting with Rannoch as he beat something into shape. Nora made her way to a window and climbed through, crouching low. It was strangely silent in the forge. The chatter, the men laughing and grunting, the hammering, the hissing, Rannoch cursing and shouting at the men not to tell lewd jokes in front of Nora—it was all gone. The only thing left was ashes and moonlight. And that smell. The smell of meat gone bad. It was the smell that made her feet step forward.

And in the dark, she saw something. A familiar shape. Beside the anvil lay a man's body, a body without forearms. The corpse was bloated and stank, and white maggots were wriggling and falling out of the dark rim of the severed neck. She doubled over, retching, holding the anvil tight. Face pressed against the cool iron, she wiped her mouth with her sleeve. The head was gone. It didn't matter. She didn't need his face to recognize him. There was the smith's apron. And the white cotton shirt with the new patch at the elbow. Nora had sewn it just before the handfasting. She swallowed down the dry heaves and hid her head in her hands. What had she been expecting? There would be no coming back home. No reconciliation. Owen was right. She had been chasing an illusion. Her world lay broken, chopped into ruins, rotten, full of maggots.

Don't look at him. Oh gods, don't look!

Nora flattened herself on the floor next to the body when she heard a commotion in the street. She crawled deeper into the shadows, away from the wriggling white mass. Through the other shop window she could see the inn door open and bright light spill onto the cobblestones. A young girl fell on the ground between the two guards. It took Nora a moment to recognize Becca, the innkeeper's daughter. Becca's normally artfully-styled blonde hair was a mess, and instead of her pristine, fashionable clothing, she wore nothing but her torn undergarments and bruises on her face.

"You beast!" Becca screamed and scrabbled to get up.

The two guards paid her no notice. One bent inside the inn's common room and called something. There was laughter from within. Nora pressed herself closer to the wall. She watched the girl scurry around the square, throwing all the loose cobblestones she could gather at the guards and the inn. Then she turned and ran toward the smithy. Nora quickly moved through the second doorway into her old kitchen, wondering whether Becca would enter the building. For a long time, it had seemed that Owen and Becca might...but Becca's mother had found a more promising future husband among the merchants of Dernberia. And so Becca's visits had stopped abruptly. Nora heard Becca run past the smithy.

Nora hesitated. She risked a glance over to the inn. Three men were standing in the light now. One was fastening up his trousers, slapping one of the guards on the back. They seemed to be in no hurry and like they were having a good time. She loosened her grip on her knife and then tightened her hand around the hilt once more. It was still there. In the shifting reality around her, she had one constant. The knife was still there. She moved through the kitchen, through the doorway, and into the garden.

Her garden was trampled. Sheets and clothes were strewn among the beds and rows of vegetables in disarray. Nora saw her own trunk split on the side, its contents scattered among the winter cabbage. Her brother's few books, spines snapped and pages torn. And they had been so expensive.

The garden was fenced in by trees, old trees that grew on the edge of the Ridge. Here stood oak and beech and sycamore. Nora ducked under the leafless branches and listened for noise. Before her, the white of Becca's garment shone clearly in the dark night. The other girl was standing at the edge of the Ridge, one arm around the trunk of the oak tree to steady herself, barefooted among the dead leaves, eyes as wild as her sobs. One false step and she'd topple over the cliff. But maybe that was what she was planning to do anyway. It was a bad plan, though. You could fall and break your neck, true. But you could also fall and only break your legs. With the men at the inn, lying helpless with a broken leg or two was not an option. Nora sneaked up as quietly as she could and held a hand over the girl's mouth. She bucked and struggled, and Nora fought to keep her away from the edge and close enough to whisper into her ear.

"Becca! Becca, it's me. It's Nora."

Becca threw herself into Nora's arms wide-eyed. For a moment the two girls embraced, both trembling.

"I thought you died," Becca wept. "I thought you all died."

"What happened?"

"I don't know," Becca sobbed. "There was fire in the night. Someone shouted that the bakery was burning. And it was, but then there were these men. All these men. And they...they killed everyone, my father, your father. And then, and then...the heads, they piled the heads before the butcher's. And the women and children were..." Becca couldn't speak on. Her formerly pretty face was a mask of grief and bitterness. Nora held her tight until she quieted.

Becca looked up with red eyes, wiping the tears from her cheeks with her fingers. Her eyes went wide as she took Nora's hands. The red marks around Nora's wrists were still visible. Though the pain had gone, the stiffness was still there.

"What happened to you?" Becca asked.

"Nothing like what happened to you," Nora said, squeezing Becca's fingers before letting them go.

"Where's Owen?"

"He's..." A choke stopped her. "Everything's going to be all right now."

"No, no, Nora. You don't know." Becca's blue eyes were wide in terror and she grabbed Nora's cloak, speaking in a hoarse whisper. "You don't know what they're like. And now you're here, and they'll get you too and we'll all die."

Their heads snapped around as they heard someone stumble over a chair in the garden and curse drunkenly. Becca flattened herself against the oak tree. Nora squeezed her arm and melted into the shadows. Her palms were sweaty. She signaled Becca to crouch down low. Becca mouthed, *"Stay with me."* Nora shook her head and held up her knife. Becca snapped into a rigid pose. Her eyelids closed and her lips quivered as though saying a prayer. But the gods were dead. Long gone. The wights, who the people thought were gods until they saw they could bleed, were dwindling. All cut down by the Living Blade. If it existed, the Living Blade brought nothing but death.

"Hey up, duck." The man was standing in the garden now, peering at the trees with a beer stein in his hand.

Nora could just make him out in the pale light. He edged closer, his feet going high over the random obstacles that lay in his way. He was tall and strongly built. His dark blond hair had been groomed carefully, and he wore no beard. He walked with confidence, though his run-in with the chair had made him limp a little. He looked not much older than Nora herself, nor as drunk as she would have liked him to be. He wore a shirt and trousers, but no armor, and he carried no weapon as far as Nora could see, only a leash in his other hand. She took a deep breath and closed her eyes.

Her first instinct was to run. Run far away. Her second thought was more coherent. Run to the Vale. Raise the alarm. Get help. Get Wolfe and his father to come back here on horseback and ride this rabble down. Her hand tightened its grasp on the knife's hilt. But Becca would have to suffer through one more night. There was no other help. They were alone. It would be like slaughtering animals, wouldn't it? How many animals had she cleaned in her cooking life? Sneak up close. No leather jerkin, no coat, stab under ribs from behind. Stab hard.

Rannoch's voice echoed through her mind. *Stab hard*, he had said when they were slaughtering the pigs just a few days ago. Or was it a week or two? Seemed to be another life entirely. He'd said, *Skin's tougher than you think. And every life fights*. Was that why they had cut off his hands? Because her father fought back? Her jaw hurt from gritting her teeth. When she unclenched them, her jaw clicked audibly.

The man was closer now. He stood under the branches of the first tree. His lips were full and soft.

"There you are, duck."

Becca whimpered.

"Don't you want to play no more?" He swung the leash playfully round.

"Go away," Becca said, dangling one foot over the rim of rock. "Please just go away."

"Come away from that edge. You'll hurt yourself if you fall. We don't want to get hurt now, do we?"

Nora edged around the tree trunk. Focus on the knife's edge. Work fast. Clean up when you're done.

"Please just go away." Becca started to weep once more.

Nora stepped softly on the wet leaves, crouched low. Her feet made no noise. Her fingers were cold, so cold. And her head was so hot, blood pounding in her ears and cheeks.

"You know I can't do that, duck. I can't let you hurt yourself now, can I?"

The man let the leash drop before Becca's feet.

"See?" he said, raising his empty hands. "Nothing to be afraid of. Now step away from the edge."

"No." Becca shook her head. Her ash-blonde hair shone silver in the moonlight.

"I said step away!" The man's voice changed now. It was harder, with a steel edge that reminded Nora of Prince Bashan, the jerk. *Gods, Owen! Let him be safe!* At least he wasn't here.

"No!" Becca screamed in defiance.

For a moment, only Becca's sobs could be heard over the wind. The man lifted his shoulders and squared them. He sighed. Just a few more steps before she could reach him. Nora halted and held her breath behind him. Stab hard.

"No is not an option!" he yelled and grabbed a strand of Becca's hair with his fist, forcing her to the ground.

Becca screamed.

Nora stabbed down hard.

The man gasped and twisted around to see her. She'd missed the heart. Nora's hand nearly slipped off the hilt in fright. She yanked the knife out, staring at the man's face. He looked at her in surprise, mouth open wide. His eyes were a dark blue, and the stubble on his chin was light as straw. He dropped to one knee before Nora, a gargling sound coming out of his mouth. With a deft stroke, Nora sliced down with her knife and slit half of his throat open. He fell and died at her feet, twitching. She stared down at the wet leaves, black with his blood.

He stopped twitching after a while.

Blood covered her right hand. It grew cold. She wiped the back of her hand against her trousers.

"Noraya?" Becca sat on the ground, arms around her knees, head on her arms.

"I'm fine," Nora said. *I'm fine?*

"Is he dead?"

"Think so."

Becca started to rock back and forth. "What about the others?"

What about the others? The question rang throughout Nora's whole body. Her legs gave way under her, and Nora shuddered and sat down. She was gulping air like a fish on land. Her head was reeling. This was not good.

"Don't know," she said.

Nora waited for the elated feeling of surviving, or a feeling of guilt over the life taken. She waited for the earth to open under her and Lara herself to drag her down to the silent road. Or maybe Tuil would strike her down with lightning or blow courage into her nostrils. A battle rage to take her into a killing spree. But nothing came.

She sat on the ground with her friend and a dead man. After a moment, Nora pushed the body toward the edge of the ridge. He was heavy. She placed her feet on both of his shoulders and shoved her weight against his. Slowly he budged, until the weight of his dangling legs pulled him over the rock shelf. There was a thud and a rustle of leaves below them. Nora sat sweating at the effort and then reached for Becca's hand.

She was just one girl with one knife. If they caught her—one more rape, one more death—would it really matter to them? But as much as her legs were ready to run into the dark and off to the Vale, her heart wouldn't let her. Because if she ran, what then? She'd be safe, yes. Becca would be safe with her. And maybe the trained men of the Vale would applaud the brave girls who fought back. But she knew if she left with Becca now, there would be no turning back. The Ridge was not her home anymore. Her home was dead, just like the body in the forge, and those men had taken it from her. Now all that was left was the possibility of a new home with Wolfe, looming over her head like the black clouds of the autumn skies. But that was what she had been running away from to start with.

She sighed. Marry Wolfe, and maybe the talk would stop. Stay, and she might die. But at least she'd have tried to do what was right. And if you didn't do what your heart told you was right, what was the point? You didn't let others suffer to save yourself. She couldn't live with that and the knowledge that she'd probably never see Owen again. Her empty stomach heaved with the thought.

Either way, it all seemed to boil down to never seeing Owen again. She should have stayed with him. Stayed with Prince Bashan, the jerk, and his company of scumbags. At least she'd have Owen close by. Even if he thought...Nora clenched her teeth as rage flooded her thinking. The anger swept an idea along with it, one Owen would have berated as stupid. But Owen wasn't here. She grinned in the dark and clutched her knife. The knife was always there. Touch of iron. Touch of home.

CHAPTER 8

"CAN YOU WALK?" NORA STOOD up and held out her hand.

"I think so." Becca nodded and grasped Nora's hand hard. She bent double, one arm pressed around her stomach, but gave her a faint smile. Becca's eyes were blue slits. She seemed as close to her former self as she could get tonight.

"At the inn, are there still horses in the stable?" Nora asked.

"I, I think so. Why?"

"How many men did you count?"

"What?"

"How many men were there, Becca?"

"I don't know."

"Think, please."

Becca took a deep breath and closed her eyes.

"Him and four in the common room."

"He's dead, though. Two guards at the door makes six."

"And their chief's in the suite upstairs. There's a guard there too, I think."

"Eight. Doesn't seem enough to overthrow the Ridge."

Becca shook her head. "No, there were more at first. A lot more."

"What happened?"

"I don't know. Some left the same day, took a few women with them. Most left after that. Only those few stayed. That's all I know."

So. One girl. One knife. Eight men. It was stupid.

"One of them has a bow," Becca continued. "I saw…when Widow Harris tried to escape, she was shot in the thigh. They pulled her back into the inn by her ankle. There was a blood mark on the floor where they dragged her in. She was still alive then. She's not anymore."

Nora squeezed both of Becca's hands.

"Who is this chief of theirs?"

"He calls himself Ubba Bearkiller. I believe it. He's huge. With bits of bone in his hair. Poor Ethelwyn. She was taken up to him earlier."

"Who of the women are still with you?"

"We were about twenty after they were finished butchering the men. Not many are left here, though. Ethelwyn. Sallima, the baker's wife." Nora groaned. "Malla the chambermaid, and two of the Forester's daughters. They kept us in my father's root cellar under the kitchen. Took us up one by one whenever they…needed someone."

Nora shuddered. Becca managed a faint smile. It didn't reach her eyes, and her lips were pressed thin. She squeezed Nora's hands back and swallowed. Gods, poor Becca! Her lower lip trembled a little, but she held back the tears. Nora felt ashamed. She hadn't thought Becca so strong before, the spoiled, rich only child of a well-connected family. They could have been sisters. And now that girl was gone. Before Nora stood a young woman, pale and gaunt. Her eyes were red and swollen, her hands shaking. But she was strong.

"What are you going to do now?"

Nora didn't immediately reply. The answer was madness. It was cruel death served on a platter. If there was an afterlife and the gods watched from there, surely they favored those who took risks.

"We need to get to the stable. Are there guards there?"

"I don't know."

"Come on." Nora took Becca by the hand and led her through the trees around the smithy.

They went parallel to the main street, crouching among the shadows until they reached a burned cottage they edged by. Nora peered around the burned-down wall. They were now three houses down from the inn. The two guards were still there, though one was now leaning against the stone wall of the inn, cupping a match in his hands, lighting a pipe. They had to cross the road to get behind the inn to the stable.

Nora looked up at the sky. The moon was submerged by clouds, but it was still light enough that Becca's white shift would stand out. The hilt of Nora's knife was moist with sweat. She switched it into her left hand and wiped her right dry on her trousers. Blood dried in flakes on the back of her hand. Maybe not just sweat.

The men talked. One of the guards moved, stretching. He said something to the one with the pipe and strolled behind the inn. Nora tugged at Becca's hand and they ran across the street, hiding in the shadows of another derelict cottage. Nora waited. She put her finger to her lips and snuck a look. The lone man's face was dimly lit by a red glow. He was smoking his pipe, leaning against the wall, leisurely blowing circles into the night sky. Nora motioned to Becca to come along.

The stable was warm, though dark, and smelled of horse. Nora lifted the bar on the door and they were in. She closed the door behind her and waited for her eyes to adjust to the dark, knife still in her hand. The horses could smell them, and they recognized Becca's scent. In the semi-darkness, Nora saw the white shift step over to the boxes, and she sensed the animals' delight as Becca stroked one of the two horses, muttering comforting sounds under her breath.

"Kitchen door seems unguarded. You stay here. I'll risk a quick look through there."

"The kitchen door is bolted from the inside," Becca said, nuzzling one of the steeds. "A couple of days ago, some boys in hiding came back to get us out. Tried to break in through the kitchen door. We heard the commotion from underneath. Since then, the door's been locked, and they stand guard when we're hauled up to cook them their meals."

Nora hid her face in her hands for a moment. As if in prayer, she held her hands against her lips. Five young women in the inn, the two of them out here, made seven. Seven couldn't ride off on two horses. But a fast rider could be at the Vale in hours, raise the alarm, get help. If the Vale wasn't similarly troubled. But they had strong palisades and trained riders.

"Which one's faster?"

"What?"

"Which horse is faster?"

"Neena."

"Can you saddle her in the dark?"

"I, I think so. Why?"

Nora didn't answer. This was it, then. The decision was made. She pulled the long silver chain from under her tunic and laid it into the cup of Becca's hand. Even without holding it, Nora felt the heavy weight of the silver wolf's head dangling from the chain. The guilt for taking it off was a needle prick. So easy to ignore.

"Nora?"

"You'll ride to Green Vale."

"We both will." Becca's lower lip started to wobble, but her jaw was set. Nora shook her head.

"Show the chain to Wolfe and Elderman Eol, and they will send horses and men."

"You show it to them yourself." Becca shoved the necklace back at Nora.

"No."

"Nora, if they find you! You don't know the horrible things—"

"No. These men don't even know I'm here. I can hide and be safe until the riders of the Vale come tomorrow. And you'll be faster riding there on your own."

"It's a half-day's ride to the Green Vale. Even if Elderman Eol were to come immediately, they wouldn't be here until tomorrow evening."

"I know."

Becca gasped for air and threw herself at Nora, weeping.

"I can't leave you. I don't want to."

Nora held her friend tight. She had never had many friends and even fewer the last couple of years. But now and here, the straw under her feet, the gentle sound of the horses, the lavender-scented strands of pale gold between her fingers, and the salty tears on Becca's face—this was good. Only it couldn't last. She was on her own. She held Becca at arm's length.

"You're the better rider."

"But they'll kill you if they find you."

"They won't find me."

"Promise?" Becca sniffed. Her sobbing had stopped. Nora stroked her thumb over her friend's grimy, soft face.

"I promise." It was easy to lie in the dark.

Their foreheads touched. She pulled away and swallowed hard. Becca busied herself saddling the horse. Nora sat down in the hay. Her bones ached, her stomach was churning; she tasted bile on her tongue, and all she wanted to do was lie down. Lie down and never have to get up again. She grabbed a handful of oats from a sack by the door and chewed them carefully. It wasn't much of a meal. Bits of straw and tiny pebbles among the oats ground like sand between her teeth.

She woke up with a start as Becca gently shook her shoulder.

"I'm ready," she said.

Nora's hand left the hilt of her knife. She nodded and rose.

"Good. Do you know how to ride to the Green Vale?"

"In the dark?" Becca asked. "Follow the road, I guess. You sure you're not coming?"

"I'm sure. Here, take my cloak."

"I already have your necklace."

"You're in your shift, Becca. It's a cold night. It'll be colder riding. Just take it."

"Thank you."

Nora gave her the thick cloak. Becca squeezed her hand before taking it. Opening the door, Nora listened into the dark outside for the guard who had left his post earlier. It was all clear, so she signaled Becca to come with the horse. It neighed softly as Becca sat up in the saddle, her naked legs poking out under Nora's short cloak. Well, there was nothing Nora could do about that. Her boots were the only thing of value left to her. Her boots and her knife. She'd need both. Becca tugged at the reins and the horse moved to the side. Nora looked up at her.

"Go slow until you reach the pine tree at the baker's," she whispered. "Then ride as hard as you can."

Becca nodded. "Stay safe."

"Just go, now. All right?"

Nora stood in the shadows under the stable's thatched roof, watching Becca vanish into the night. Her coal-black cloak helped mute the shine of white in the darkness. Her friend was a silver ghost light hovering along the path. Nora readied her blade. But the guard in front of the inn didn't come running. His partner didn't come running. No one shouted a warning. The well-trodden dirt in the back lane muffled the hoofbeats. And then the horse and its rider were gone.

CHAPTER 9

NORA WAITED ANOTHER FEW MINUTES. Then, not finding any conveniently placed barrels or ladders, she ran at the door of the stable, grabbed the top of the door frame, put one foot on the handle, and scrambled onto the thatched roof. All that shoveling and carting the charcoal had been good for a few things at least: building muscles, sleeping light, being out on moonlit nights. If she lived to see the morning, she'd be able to make a passable living as a thief. Nora chuckled to herself and scrambled up the wet thatch. She really needed food, though.

The two buildings, the stable and the inn, were adjoined. The inn's guestrooms on the first floor were higher than the stable, but now that she was on the roof, it would be simple getting into one of the rooms through a window. Nora crept to the ridge of the roof and lay down in the thatch for a breather. The moon was slowly setting into the pitch black of night. It was late. Or early. She crawled across the top to the inn wall. Here were two small windows, left and right. Becca said the chief had taken the suite to the right, the tax suite. The empire's tax collector, who made his rounds in the late autumn, always stayed a few days in the best room of the inn. Looked like he wasn't coming this year. Nora grinned despite herself and stepped closer. It was dark within. Quiet, too. She couldn't see anything.

Nora crept down the street side of the roof and crouched low, looking over the edge to the inn's main door. The smoker still leaned against the wall. His mate had not returned. She crept to the other side and peered into the backyard of the inn. There was no one to be seen. Maybe the other guard had gone inside? She bit her lip. But the odds were against her, however she calculated.

She crawled back to the window and slid the blade of her knife under the frame, lifting it a notch so that her fingers could reach under and push it open. She swung noiselessly over the windowsill and closed the window behind her.

Nora stepped into a dark corner and waited for her eyes to adjust to the gloom. It was warm inside, and she could make out a huge shape under the blankets. The chief was asleep. She stepped up to make sure his eyes were closed before she searched the room for Ethelwyn. He must be a big man, a fat man, filling the whole of the double bed. One arm lay beside his square, bearded face, and the size of his hand was such that she could easily imagine it grappling with a bear or grasping her entire head and crushing it. In the orange light that shone through the windows from the torches lit outside, she saw his armor leaning against the chair. The sword in its scabbard was nearly as long as her legs. Her knife seemed like a toy next to it. She crept even closer to the bed to check if Ethelwyn was smothered under the blankets next to the mountain of a man. No.

A gold gleam in the half-light caught her eye. Curiosity piqued, she slowly, slowly pulled out a dagger from under the snoring chief's pillow. The blade itself was about as long as her forearm and curved. The gilded hilt was heavy, making the dagger ill balanced. Pretty piece of crap. She half expected it to be blunt, but someone had sharpened the edge with care. The chief moved in his sleep, rolling his large body over to the side. She held her breath. But he slept on. His long black hair fell into his face, and his lips were fat and protruded out of his black beard like those of a sullen child. Here and there little trinkets had been tied into the hair: a pebble with a hole, warrior rings made out of the spear tips of his enemies, red prayer ribbons like those at the shrines all over the northern wastelands, pearls and glass beads, and a little bone that seemed tipped with gold. It all jingled as his barrel chest rose and fell.

Nora wiped the sweat from her brow with the sleeve of her tunic and held the two knives loose. She licked her lips and swallowed dry. The thirst made her head feel light, and the hunger made her giddy. She stepped away from the bed.

"Ethelwyn?" She breathed the name into the darkness. No response.

Nora searched the room, careful not to make any noise, watching the mountain sleep with one eye.

"Ethelwyn? It's me. Nora."

Nothing. Maybe Ethelwyn had been sent back downstairs again. Maybe they were all still alive. There were a few hours left until daybreak. If her luck held and all the men were asleep, she could unbolt the kitchen door from within and the women could sneak out into the dark, safe if not sound. There was a cave hidden in the woods close to the spot Owen and Nora had often used to burn charcoal. They could hide there until help came tomorrow. If her luck held.

The chief stirred and opened his eyes, only to close them again and snore. Nora froze before the pale light of the window. Had he seen her silhouette?

"Ubba?" she spoke in a low voice, testing whether he was still asleep. For a moment, she was unsure whether she had remembered the right name. The man's ragged breathing was all she heard. What had Becca said his name was?

"Ubba," Nora said once more, a little louder, gripping the daggers tight.

His eyes opened and darted around the dark room. His large hand slid under the pillow and, finding his dagger gone, his body jolted awake. He half rose and then he saw her. Nora nearly stepped back. She was tired to the bone but stood as tall as she could.

"Who are you? Are you—my queen, is it you?" His voice was soft and carried the lilt of the northern coast. "My dagger is gone, Prophetess."

Nora hesitated. *Play along.* She held up the gold dagger in her right hand and kept her own blade hidden in her left. The gold gleamed in the torchlight from the window.

"I took your dagger from you, Ubba."

He rolled out of the bed and landed on his knees, bowing low before her feet, blubbering. "No, I am worthy, Prophetess. I am worthy. Give me, please, your favor. Please."

It took all of Nora's self-control not to run away or scream. She held her breath until the urge subsided.

"Ubba, tell me what you have done here."

He peered up at her, squinting. His eyes were small and piggish compared to his large mouth. The lower part of his face seemed consumed by hair. He wrung his large hands together in anguish.

"I made them dead, Prophetess. I'm a good deadmaker." His voice broke. "I did as you told me. I did. I went to your shrine. The pilgrim master there, he was suspicious. But I lost your girl. And I thought—I thought you'd be angry. Because your pretty one was lost. There was some trouble in the big city. Men were raiding the countryside. I joined them and so I came here. Don't be angry, my queen."

"Where is Ethelwyn?" Nora asked.

"Ethelwyn? Was that the true name of your pretty one? Is she not with you, my queen? I—"

Waking realization was slowly creeping into his large black head. Nora had been lucky so far. She gagged in panic, swallowed. Her knuckles whitened on the hilt of the dagger as she turned it in the ray of pale light.

"I see a soul standing at the far shore. It is lingering. I have a message for you from the girl, Ubba," she heard herself say from far away. Her voice was cool and emotionless. Ubba Bearkiller leaned closer on his knees, his hands clasped in front of his chest, his eyes lit up with delight.

"Yes, yes?"

Nora thrust his golden dagger into his large belly. She stabbed hard into the softness and the handle kept going in after the blade, the fat closing in over it. She pulled her hand away in horror and watched Ubba paw his flabby flesh, trying to grasp the hilt but failing to find it. She stepped back as blood and black fecal matter spattered to the floor. The stench of his spilling intestines filled the air. Ubba groaned and fell forward. His hand reached for her ankle. She kicked it aside.

"Hnnnuhhhh," he groaned, holding his belly.

His breath was labored now. She stepped to the right, nearing the door. His eyes followed her movement. His body held a lot of blood, oozing out of the folds of fat. It seemed to take him hours to die. He reached out a bloody hand to her, dragging it weakly over the wooden floor, unable to draw his body up.

He made the noise one more time, a pleading sound. Nora felt the cold creep up her spine. He still thought she was the prophetess. She approached him then with her own knife, crouched low, and passed her hand under his wiry beard to slit his throat. Blood gushed out of the cut and washed into the hair, soaking the prayer ribbons black in the dim light. He died under her hand, eyes open, staring at some vision he'd perhaps had all his life.

She wiped her blade on his nightshirt and stepped away, listening hard. The stillness in the room made her own rushing heartbeat sound stronger, louder. It was stifling. The stench of shit overpowered the thick, salty scent of blood. Her stomach heaved suddenly, and a patter of spilled fluid broke the silence. Nora wiped the bitter taste of bile from her lips. She moved away from the large felled man and her heels knocked against a wooden chest at the foot of the bed. Her head snapped up, listening for the sound of running feet coming her way. But there was nothing.

And suddenly she knew where Ethelwyn was. She shouldn't open the chest. She knew she shouldn't. But just as she had stared at the maggots wriggling out of the headless body in the forge, something moved her cold fingers over the lid and pulled it open.

It took a moment for her to make out anything in the jumble of hastily stashed cloaks in the trunk. Her heart leaped. They were only cloaks. Ethelwyn wasn't in here after all. She was still alive, then. Nora was about to close the lid when her mind translated what her eyes had been seeing all along. The high round shape under the cloak was a shoulder, the flat fold to the front the knee and shin of a bent leg. Nora followed the folds and saw the body underneath them. The fold of the cloak in the corner...her hand felt the roughness of the spun wool as she tugged it gently. Her heart sank.

There was no blood. No sign of violence Nora could see. On the contrary, Ethel looked as though she were merely sleeping on her side. A bit uncomfortable in the trunk, maybe. Knees bent high, nearly touching her chest. But still, she could have been sleeping. Her hands lay folded under her cheek, her fingers curled by those long brown eyelashes. One of the fingernails was chipped and broken. Dark shadows lay under Ethelwyn's eyes as though she hadn't slept in a long time. Her golden bangs shone in the light, combed neatly to form a parting on the wrong side of her face.

Nora stretched out her hand to correct the hair but then let the girl rest. She closed the lid with the knowledge she'd done the right thing killing Ubba. Even if she'd join Ethelwyn tonight, she had done the right thing. The lid clicked shut.

CHAPTER 10

NORA STEPPED UP TO THE door. It was locked on the inside by a wooden latch. She listened, one ear pressed to the wood, straining to hear a sound where there was none to be heard. The other men must be sleeping now, surely. The corridor behind the door led down into the common room of the inn. Perhaps she *could* get to the root cellar to see if the other girls were still there and alive. They *could* all be hidden in the woods before the men woke in the morning and found their chief dead in his room. She pushed the wooden latch to the side and heard a faint click as the lock opened. She pulled the door wide and froze.

Before the door a man sat on the threshold, asleep. A young man. His head had been resting against the door, and when she opened it, the jolt woke him. The youth at her feet blinked up at her. He had gray eyes. His hair was sleep-ruffled and there was a red patch on his forehead. He looked only a few months older than Owen and herself. Any second now, he'd realize a strange girl had stepped out of his chieftain's room and call for aid. With a thrill of terror, Nora plunged her dagger into his eye. The tip of her blade jarred her hand and scraped the inside of his skull. The young man gasped and shuddered, and she quickly put her hand over his mouth and nose, pulling her knife out of his head and plunging it into his throat instead. He spasmed and fell back, drowning in his own blood, unable to scream.

Against the opposite wall another guard slept, an older man with a similar jawline and straight nose, legs crossed, head leaning against the wood, mouth slack. Father and son. Crap. As the son died, Nora looked to the other man. He closed his open mouth in his sleep and swallowed, moving his head into a more comfortable position against the opposite door. Nora held a bloodied hand over his mouth and felt him stir as she slit his throat.

She knelt between the two dead men, wiping her blade and hands on the father's cloak. His head lolled now. Half a hand was painted in red on his light brown beard. Her hand. Her fingers were wet, and there was blood everywhere. It ran down the father's chest, seeping into his cloak. She pulled the son's russet cloak over his face and shuddered at his broken eye. Otherwise, they both still appeared to be sleeping. The man who came after Becca, the chief, the son, and the father. Four men. She had killed four men. The sleeve of her tunic was red and wet with blood that was not her own. Her hand was stained red, red under her fingernails, red on the antler hilt of her knife. The tip of her right boot was splashed dark red, too.

This never happened with the shovel. She'd only bang her coaler's shovel against any pushy guy's head and then run into the forest to hide. She couldn't stop staring at the spot on her boot until her eyes watered and hot tears fell.

She knelt in the corridor, covering her own mouth for fear of letting a sound escape, and shook. She felt no sense of victory, no sense of justice meted out and revenge taken. *For the Ridge*, half of her heart whispered. *For Rannoch!* But they were dead already. And there were no gods, so there could be no afterlife, so what did the dead know or care about what the living did?

Nora was racked by sobs and silent laughter in equal measure. She was a murderer. A murderess? If the baker's wife had kept her mouth shut, she would never have left the Ridge! And now, who she was trying to save? The baker's wife! Nora was alive. But she was going to die here. The muscles in her stomach contracted and hurt, but she couldn't stop laughing. She wanted to go home. But there was no home anymore. She wanted to throw her knife away and lie down between the dead forever. Lie down and sleep and not feel anything anymore.

After a while, the spasms ebbed. Nora took a deep breath. She needed food. She was exhausted now, so tired. At first, her legs wouldn't budge under her. They were numb and stiff and then started to prickle with heat. She had to move, regardless.

In the dark, she crawled down the corridor to the stairs and paused at the top, staring down into the common room. There were various tables and benches and chairs on a flagstone floor, all assembled around a huge stone fireplace. Above it in a place of honor were the sword and shield Becca's father had carried as a soldier in the imperial army before he settled down here to marry Becca's mother. The shield still showed the emblem of the emperor: three blue dragons, claws readied to strike. Once, the empire had been everywhere. Now it was looking out for itself.

Four of the benches had been moved closer around the fireplace, where the fire had burned down to glowing embers for the night. On them, four men slept. On one of the larger tables was a huge pile of everything that she guessed had seemed valuable in the men's eyes: cups of tin and silver, platters from the kitchen etched with intricate designs, piles of coins, and a few jewels and gems from the women's jewelry. It seemed a meager treasure hoard for the whole of the Ridge. Furs were heaped on another table. These, Nora knew, would bring in valuable coin when sold. The riches of the Ridge weren't the gold and silver the people possessed, which was little. It was the furs, the steel, and the wool.

For a moment, standing at the top of the stairs, Nora considered turning away, walking back down the corridor, past Ubba's body, and out through the window into the freedom of the night. She could take the second horse in the stable, be away, far, far away by dawn. She'd done her fair share. She could ride over the Plains toward the Temple of the Wind, maybe even catch up with Owen and the Hunted Company and just...and just...Her mind failed to imagine what would happen then. Maybe it was a sign. Or maybe she was just too tired.

Slowly she crept down the wooden stairs. When she reached the bottom, she was so close to one of the men on the benches that she had to step over his hand, which hung to the floor. She inched away to the kitchen door beyond the bar, not letting the sleeping men out of her sight. One of the men nearest to the inn's entrance moved, shuffling onto his side. He pulled his cloak over him. Nora stood and watched, heart beating painfully in her throat. He slept on.

The kitchen was nearly as large as the common room and took up the entire far side of the building. The fireplace could easily fit three roast pigs. A huge metal stove dominated the room. On the wall hung copper pots and pans. Cupboards lined the free walls, filled with crockery and dishes of all sizes and designs, some plain, some with elaborate hand-painted patterns. There were glasses and mugs and pitchers and wooden cutting boards and wooden plates and spoons and forks and ladles and sieves. But no food. Nora groaned. This was a kitchen. There had to be *something* she could eat. Sausages or cured meat or cheese. Raw broccoli. She'd eat it. She'd eat anything. Her stomach growled, needy.

A cut loaf lay on the stovetop. It was going stale, but she didn't care, ripping off large chunks of bread and gobbling them down like a duck. A piece wedged itself in her throat and she choked, bent over the cold stove, retching and hacking until she could breathe again. Death by suffocation. Just as stupid as what she was doing here. Tears ran down her hot cheeks and snot poured into her mouth. She put the bread back on the stovetop, breathing breadcrumbs and eyeballing the kitchen door, expecting the men to run in any minute with drawn swords and doom. But her luck held and nothing happened.

Nora was still spluttering but plodded over to unbolt the outside kitchen door. She took deep gulps of the cold autumn night that rolled in. Only then did she turn to her left where the larder was. And below the larder's floor, under a trapdoor, was the root cellar, a cool, dark place where the innkeeper also kept the beer and wine. Nora knelt down and felt for the iron ring. She heaved the trapdoor open and peered down the steps, carved crudely out of the stone foundation the inn—and all of the Ridge—was built on.

"Please be there." Her voice broke. She cleared her throat of the last crumbs. "It's me, Noraya."

She couldn't see anything in the pitch black. But she heard the faint rustle of clothing and whispers. A voice wafted up from below in a hoarse croak Nora couldn't identify.

"Nora?"

"Yes. Becca told me a few girls were still down here. Quick, the men are sleeping. We can leave together now. But you must hurry and be quiet."

A shadow moved closer to the steps. Sallima looked up out of the dark. It would be so easy to close the trapdoor again. She'd deserve it, too. She was only a few years older than Nora, but she belonged to the company of the young wives. She had looked down on Nora. Now Nora stared down at her. Normally, Sallima had her small child on her arm at any given time. But her arms were empty now, and her hand fidgeted with a torn piece of her shift. Her long face was drawn and gaunt. Her hair, normally held up in a tight bun, hung lank and loose around her face. There was a dry red gash on her forehead. Nora felt the sting of pity. It rattled her a little. Another girl pushed forward into the half-light.

"You met Becca?" It was the inn's chambermaid, Malla.

"Sent her off to the Vale to get help. We have to hide till tomorrow, late afternoon, maybe evening. I know a place in the woods."

In an instant, Malla was up the stairs. Nora reached down to hoist her up. Her shift was torn and too thin for the cold autumn night. Her face was tired, but her eyes shone with hope.

"May the gods bless you, Nora." She leaned in to kiss Nora on the cheek. Then she turned and waved her hand. "Come on."

Sallima came up, dirty and disheveled, one young girl hanging on to each hand. When she saw their faces, Nora remembered the two Forester girls. The older, Kanna, had just turned thirteen; the younger, Laena, was six. They had wound wreaths of heather for Nora's handfasting. She tried to smile reassuringly at them, but they kept their eyes on the floor. Laena hid her face against Sallima's waist. Her blonde hair had been plaited into pigtails that were slowly unraveling from the bottom.

Sallima clutched the girls to her. She wasn't much taller than Kanna. It took Nora by surprise. Had Sallima always been shorter than her? She'd acted taller. Of all the people who could have survived, it had to be the baker's wife! Nora didn't know what to say. She grasped her knife.

"Are you all right?" Nora asked.

"Let's not talk. Just leave," Sallima answered.

They moved back into the kitchen, Sallima and the girls first, then Malla. Nora closed the trapdoor and stared at the iron ring. The ongoing strain of the last few days had made her mind fast and light, able to react with speed. But now it seemed to do nothing but repeat Owen's last sentence over and over again. *You shouldn't have fucked our father. You shouldn't have fucked our father.* It was a nightmare. This was not the time. But she couldn't stop it. Of all people, even Owen had believed Sallima. Nora's head reeled, but she stood and staggered behind the other girls. She'd lost Owen because of the baker's wife. Nora stared at the back of Sallima's head and her hands started to shake.

"Kanna, go get the bread on the stove for your sister," Sallima whispered. "You can eat it on the way."

The girl let go of the woman's hand and reached out for the stale bread loaf. Suddenly the door slammed open and a man came striding in, carrying an oil lamp. He wore a leather jerkin and a cloak hung over his shoulder. He was one of the men who had slept on the benches in the common room. They all stood frozen for a moment. The man in the doorway, Kanna with her hand on the loaf, Sallima with Laena at her side, Malla and Nora behind them.

Then Kanna started to scream.

Chapter 11

SALLIMA SNATCHED KANNA AWAY AND put her hand over the girl's mouth. They started to move backward, but Nora impatiently shoved the young women forward between the stove and fireplace, toward the unbolted rear door.

Nora whipped out her knife as the man fumbled for his sword. She jumped forward and rammed her blade into his throat. He lifted his hand halfway to the wound and then stumbled toward Nora. She ducked out of his way, and he slammed into a cupboard of crockery before he fell to the floor. The endless shatter of pottery echoed throughout the room. The door banged closed and swung open once more. In the moment it swung fully open, Nora saw the heads of the other men in the common room turn toward the kitchen. Great. Just great.

She grabbed a meat cleaver in her left hand and turned to Sallima. The oil of the smashed lamp was already burning fiercely, and flames were licking at the dead man's cloak.

"Go. Go now."

Sallima didn't even nod. As the crockery cracked in shards around Nora's feet, the young woman swung Laena up onto her hip and all four of them ran out of the rear door into the night.

Nora had maybe seconds left. Seconds until the next man came into the kitchen. Seconds left in which to choose. She could run or she could die. She felt the weight of the meat cleaver in her left hand, the weight of her bloodied knife in her right. She could choose her fight: with her back to the rear door, waiting for the next man to come at her through the fire. Probable death. Or keep the men in the common room, giving Sallima and the other girls a few more minutes' head start into the night. Very probable death. She should run, then. Run into the woods she knew and hide there. But that would mean spending the rest of the night and most of the next day with Sallima. Nora couldn't bring herself to run after the woman who had taken her brother from her.

She stepped over the flames licking the dead man's body and kicked the door to the common room open, walking into it head and knives held high.

There were four men in the room. She had counted on three. One of them must be the pipe smoker from outside. The other guard still hadn't shown up. Nora dismissed him from her thoughts. The men had been woken by the dying man's crash into the cupboard and were blinking owlishly into the lit room, half rising from their sleeping benches.

"What's going on?" one of those men said, dragging a hand across his face.

"Who is that?" The other pointed at Nora.

"I am Noraya Smith of Owen's Ridge. I just killed Ubba Bearkiller and his guards. If you let the girls go, I will spare your lives."

There was a pause. Then the man with a hunting bow at his side started to laugh. The others joined in. Nora rolled her wrist, twirling the meat cleaver in her hand. Let them laugh. Laugh at the silly little girl. But her father had made the heavy cleaver. It had a sharp edge that could bite into bone. The thought was strangely comforting. The laughter died slowly as the men saw the blood that covered Nora's sleeve and hands. Her own knife was in her right hand.

"Talgorn," the man with the bow commanded. "Go upstairs, check on the chief."

One of the men on the bench struggled to get his legs free of his cloak and shot a look at Nora as he ran up the stairs, two steps at a time. Nora stood in the common room with the three men, waiting in silence. Every minute gained was a minute more for Sallima and the girls to get away.

A loud curse rang down from upstairs.

"What?" the man with the bow shouted, his eyes locked on Nora.

"Mik and Mads are dead," the man called down.

"The guy in the kitchen is too," Nora added. "And the one who ran out after the blonde girl, in case you were wondering what took him so long."

The men before her were rallying around the man with the bow. He was a stout man, good-looking in a rough way, light brown hair tied back into a ponytail held with a leather thong. His nose looked as though it had been broken once. Nora stared back at his brown eyes. She heard the door to the room upstairs open. There was more cursing. Then silence.

"You found Ubba?"

"He's dead, Ravn." The man came back down the corridor slowly, standing at the top of the stairs.

A flicker of uncertainty passed among the men as they shuffled closer to the man with the bow. He looked Nora up and down.

"What you want, girl? Huh? Revenge? Share of the gold? Fame?" He spoke quietly.

"Take the coins. If you want, take it all." Nora made a sweeping gesture at the tables with the treasure and the furs, careful to let the men see her wield her blade. "Just go away. Stay away from Owen's Ridge. That's all I want."

"You hear that, lads? It's all she wants." The man with the bow drew out his own dagger. It wasn't as fancy as Ubba's, but a cold piece of gleaming metal with two edges and a sharp point was impressive enough to the right mind.

"Tomorrow morning the Ridge will be filled with thirty or more men on horseback, heavily armed and out to do justice," Nora said. "Go now, take what you want, and live. But go."

The man strung his bow.

"What if I don't want to?" he whispered.

"Come on, Ravn," the man on his left said. "Ubba's dead. We can move out now and take what we want."

"You afraid of one girl, Etch?"

The man called Etch scowled.

"That smoke plume attracted those two riders the other day. Scouts, I told you so. But Ubba didn't want to leave then. I say, if Ubba's dead, we leave now, before they come back. Find a new place. Plenty of villages along the coastal road."

"Ubba's dead and now you're leader or what?"

The man called Etch took a pipe out of his pocket, emptying it out on the flagstones. He *was* the smoker from outside, then. He shrugged.

"Are you?"

"You two, kill her," the bowman ordered.

The man on the stairs looked down at Nora. He had no weapon and remained standing where he was. The man on the bench stood up. He raised a huge ax and grinned at Nora, lumbering forward. If they all attacked at the same time, they could easily overpower her, so why didn't they do just that? But then again, they were killers, and she was just a stupid girl making a brave last stand.

He swung the ax high. Nora watched its curve. It was a show swing, meant to inspire fear in the opponent. It worked. She licked her lips. The man was heavily built. His arms were thick and his mighty biceps were covered with black tattoos that ran up in curves to his bull's neck. He came a step closer and raised the ax high once more to hammer it down and cleave her skull. And body. And all the way through to the stone floor, probably.

As the ax reached the peak of its swing, Nora hacked the meat cleaver into his leg, stabbing her knife upward under his ribs. The ax fell out of his hands behind him to the floor with a loud clang. She saw the three others step back collectively. Then the axman toppled. He fell to the floor with a crash, howling and thrashing in pain.

Nora danced a few steps back toward the kitchen door. She risked a quick glance up at the man on the stairs. He had the higher ground, the better vantage point, but he was watching his mate bleed and looked pale. She looked at the bowman and the smoker over the mess and flicked the blood spatter from the meat cleaver, twirling it in her hand one more time. She grinned at him.

"You think you're clever, don't you?" The bowman laughed. "You think you're gonna somehow survive tonight, you stupid wench. You against us?" He pointed at the man on the stairs. "Get down here and cut her, Talgorn. I think I've got an itch the girl should scratch."

The man called Talgorn swallowed hard but took one step after another, attention now on Nora.

"You don't have to do what he says," Nora spoke quietly. "You could just grab your things and leave."

"Shut your mouth!" the bowman roared. "Shut up or I will make you suffer."

He hissed the last like a snake. First Ubba, now this guy. Both of them insane. What was it with these people? Where did all the crazy come from?

Talgorn hesitated at the foot of the stairs. He looked at the bowman. Then he looked at the smoker, Etch. He picked up his cloak. Under it were two curved blades. Nora swallowed bile.

Etch made his decision and sheathed his sword.

"Come on, Talgorn. Help me with Janner!" He pointed to the downed axman and nodded at the front door. "And then let's go."

"You're not going anywhere, Etch," the bowman said. "Neither are you two!"

"I'm not going to die over a few furs and a stupid wench. Look, the kitchen's burning. We get the hell out, sell the furs in Dernberia, get some easy money—"

Etch got a dagger in his stomach instead. He opened his mouth as the bowman twisted the blade and then pulled it upward before wrenching the knife free. He lay jerking his life out in spasms on the blood-soiled floor. The bowman laughed again.

"Now you." He stopped abruptly and pointed the bloodied blade at Talgorn. "And you." He pointed it at the axman. "Stop playing and bring her over here."

Talgorn grabbed his twin blades and turned to Nora, jaw set, look grim. He sidestepped toward her, slicing the blades through the air in graceful movements, yet out of the corner of his eye he checked to see what the bowman was doing.

Nora tightened her grasp on the meat cleaver, at a loss for ideas. When her luck had held, it had held tight. Now, though, it had run out the door screaming and wouldn't be coming back any time soon. The element of surprise was gone. She was outmatched. She was alone. She was tired and had reached her limit. Everyone was dead. Rannoch was dead. The Ridge was dead.

And Owen was far, far away. At least one thing to be thankful for.

Talgorn stepped over the body of the axman. He glanced down at his squirming mate, distracted for a second.

Nora's body moved. She vaulted onto the bar as though to take cover behind it, but then ran two steps along it only to fling herself off the end. Surprised, she found herself in the air now, cleaver and knife ready. And in her memories of the moment, she seemed to hang suspended in the air for a long time. The man with the twin blades turned his head incredibly slowly. He followed her movement, but his body was still facing the wrong direction. His blades pointed at the floor. She would land on his back if he didn't turn around now. But he was too slow. Everything was incredibly slow. Her feet impacted his back.

They both toppled to the floor. Nora scrambled on top and hacked the cleaver down into the man's nape, cutting a deep gash into the flesh with the dull snap of blade meeting bone. Blood flowed up and she couldn't get the cleaver out. Her hand slipped off it. Didn't matter. Use the moment. She pounced onto the nearest bench and hurled herself toward the still-flailing axman.

He was slow, too. Too slow. Ha ha. Funny. His sword was only half drawn when she slashed her dagger across his face. His hands went up and he started to scream again. She plunged the knife into his armpit, then turned to face the bowman.

But he wasn't where he'd been standing a second ago. He was fast. His bloodied dagger swished only a hair's breadth away from her throat. Nora's eyes widened. She skidded on her knees, arching backward under his thrust, then ran those few steps back to the kitchen door. It was time to go.

Nora grabbed the door handle and yanked it open. Then she felt the burn of the iron on her fingertips. Fingers in her mouth, she stared into the kitchen. Red and yellow flames greedily licked toward her, blocking her path. The heat hit her like a blow. The small flame of the oil lamp had found fuel enough in the man's clothes and hair, the wooden cupboards, and the bushels of herbs above to spread. It was a furnace in there. She recoiled, protecting her face from the heat with her arms. The way through the kitchen was barred. She should have made her last stand at the kitchen door. Too late now. She let the door fall shut again and turned around to face the bowman.

Something hit her in the shoulder. Her back slammed against the kitchen door as white heat exploded in her arm. Her fingers would no longer grasp the hilt of her knife, and it clanged uselessly on the floor. Warmth ran down her arm and dripped blood red from her fingers. She tried to look down. Something like black feathers was obstructing her view. Then she realized they *were* black feathers. The tip of an arrow had buried itself in her shoulder. The bowman stood poised a few steps away, calmly drawing the string of his hunting bow back with a new arrow aimed at her.

"I wanted to pin you to that door. Watch you burn," he said with a smile, stepping over the axman's still body. "But I like it this way too. Kneel."

Nora slid down the kitchen door. It was no use, now. Do as he says. Ignore the pain. Try not to focus on the screaming white-hot pulsing flesh. She groaned. Her breath came hard.

It was over now. She knelt on the cold flagstones, arms dropped at her side. She heard the crackle of the fire behind her, felt its heat coming through the door. White smoke crawled underneath it, snaking between her fingers. She looked up at the bowman, past the arrowhead aimed at her left eye. He wouldn't kill her easily. He was one who liked to watch the pain. It should scare her. But Nora couldn't feel anything but the mind-numbing pain in her shoulder. She concentrated to keep the man's face in focus, but darkness lurked in the corner of her view and it was reaching out fast. Only the pain kept it at bay for now.

"I'm going to kill you," the bowman told her. "Then I'm going to take all the stuff we got here and won't have to share it with anyone. Thanks to you. Shame about the girl, really. Whatsherface. Blonde girl. Ran out earlier. I liked the way she moaned. Moan for me, will you?"

He kicked at the arrow dug deep in her shoulder. Nora didn't moan. She screamed. She bent over double, left palm splayed on the floor, panting hard, sweat dripping into her eyes.

"Look at me!" he commanded.

The bowman stooped to grab a fistful of her hair and forced her to face him. But then he fell on the floor face-first instead. Behind him in the gathering darkness of Nora's vision was Sallima, the baker's wife, with wild hair and a coalman's shovel. Nora fell forward. The flagstones were cool under her cheek. Gray smoke crawled into her mouth and nose. And the darkness waited.

CHAPTER 12

NORA OPENED HER EYES. SHE lay in a furry brown cloud. It tickled her nose, but it was warm. Her shoulder throbbed and she had difficulty swallowing, her mouth was that dry. She raised her head. It was heavier than any mountain, and she let it drop back into the fur.

"Rest." A cool hand patted her left shoulder, then fingers touched her cheek. "You are still weak."

"Water," she croaked.

An earthenware cup was brought to her lips, and a hand slipped under her head to raise it up for her. The water was cool and she quenched her thirst in long gulps. It ran down into her belly like a soothing balm. With every swallow, the ache in her throat subsided. The hand with the cup moved away. She reached for it but it was gone. Out of reach. She lay back and could have cried, only she fell asleep once again.

Nora woke up a second time. Her shoulder still hurt. This time, she raised her head herself and peered at her surroundings through sleep-caked eyes. She lay on a bundle of costly furs. She stroked the fur under her fingers. Sheepskins, deer, the pelts of the antlered minks of the woodlands around the Ridge. Fox and wolf. In her dream, she had seen a pile of furs somewhere, but it kept slipping from her mind. On a table? That didn't make sense. On a table in the inn? But something was wrong. Something…She sighed and settled her gaze above her head, on the wooden beams. They were familiar at least. She knew her own kitchen. Why was she in the kitchen? What was she doing on the table? She was in her house on the Ridge. Soot and blackened burns showed on the ceiling above. As if from fire.

The fire, the inn, all those men! Her shoulder throbbed where the arrow had pierced her flesh. And she lay in the furs that had been in the treasure pile.

Panic caught in her throat and she kicked at the furs, rolling off the table. Escape! She had to escape. She was in her kitchen, on the floor. She searched frantically for her knife, but it was gone. A figure stood between her and the open space where the door to the garden had once been. It didn't matter. She could escape through the smithy, past the forge.

Only she couldn't, could she? The leather apron, the body without its head, the burned fingers in the cold ash. The patch. The patch she had sewn on his shirt. She couldn't flee past the forge. Couldn't go in there again.

Someone was talking to her, trying to guide her back to the table.

"It's all right. You're safe now. Noraya! You're safe now."

"No! No. Don't touch me! I can't stay here!"

She broke loose from the grip and knew it was a bad idea. The ground couldn't really shift under her feet, yet it certainly felt as if it were doing so. She stumbled and instinctively held out her arms to break the fall. The pain exploded in her right shoulder again, and she saw black and white stars in front of her eyes as she clutched her arm and howled like a wounded animal.

When she came to, she was on the table once more and the baker's wife was hunched over her. Her eyes were dark blue and her lips were pressed thin.

Nora stared at the other woman.

"You're safe now," Sallima repeated. "But you need more rest. I stitched your shoulder for you after pulling the arrow. It was barbed." She held her hand out and Nora automatically lifted her head to look. The dark gray arrowhead had a dull gleam to it. The ends were curved like a fisherman's hook. Nora shuddered and went back to staring at Sallima.

"I'm home." Nora's voice had a rasp. She tried clearing her throat and repeating what she had said, but the rasp stayed. She sounded like the master wight.

"Yes. The inn was burning, so I dragged you over to this place. Most of it is still intact." Sallima knocked on the wall. "You can thank me later."

"Thank you?"

"For saving your life."

Sallima checked Nora's forehead for fever. Her hand was smooth and dry on Nora's skin. It smelled of yeast and garlic. It was a motherly gesture that came natural to the baker's wife. She snatched her hand away before Nora slapped at it.

"For saving—" Nora propped herself up on an elbow. "I saved *your* life! *You* should be saying thank-you!"

Sallima shrugged her shoulders.

"Should I? Well, thank you. Happy now?"

There was a long pause as Nora tried to find words. Her mouth opened and shut a few times. Then Sallima turned and busied herself in the kitchen.

Nora watched as the short woman lit the stove and found the kettle. She went outside to fill it with water and came back in humming a lullaby. It seemed she was going to make tea. Sallima stood ramrod straight at the stove while the water boiled, staring out into the garden. She kept pulling a woolen shawl over her tiny shoulders.

"Why are you here?" Nora's tongue felt heavy. It was cumbersome to talk. "Why did you come back for me? You don't even like me."

The woman shrugged again.

"It was the right thing to do."

"The right thing," Nora repeated.

"Yes."

They looked at each other. Nora started to laugh. It sounded cold and hollow and foreign to her ears. Sallima wrinkled her nose as though she smelled something distasteful.

"What's so funny?" she wanted to know.

"You are!" Nora's injured arm rested over her stomach. As she laughed, she clutched her ribs, grimacing at the pain. Moving her hand hurt her shoulder. "You come here from Moorfleet, laced and ribboned and all. Start making accusations that ruin my reputation. And do you know what happens when a girl's reputation is ruined? It's a good excuse for any guy to try and find out whether you're really as easy as they say. The ominous 'they.'"

"I did not—"

"I was fourteen. You shouldn't have to ward off older men's attention at fourteen. You should color your cheeks and wear silly dresses and tie up your hair with ribbons and think you're a lady already. All I had was my smarts and a shovel, and it's all your fault! You do not get to say you did the right thing, damn you!"

"Oh, warding off is what you call it? Didn't look that way to me. I saw you and that coaler in the woods together."

Nora blanched as Sallima crossed her arms.

"You—"

"No, you! And him. He's a married man, you know. Or was. His wife, she'd come to the baker's every day to bake her bread. And every day I saw her sit in that tiny cottage at the end of the road with her meal going cold, all alone. But what do you care? They're both dead now."

"That's your reason? That's it? You saw us in the woods once four years ago? We grew up together. We should have been together. He was only two years older than I was."

"And his wife was a year younger than you. You were the other woman.

He was married to her!"

"Nothing ever happened! And besides, he didn't want to be married. His parents arranged it!"

"And your foster father never arranged your marriage."

"That doesn't mean I fucked him, you stupid cow!" Nora screamed.

"How dare you!" Sallima stepped away from Nora's burst of rage.

"No, how dare you?" Nora slammed her fist against the table. "How dare you sow that lie in the minds of the people here, in my home, not yours! People here have known me from infancy. You turned them against me. You turned everyone against me."

"You did that yourself," Sallima hissed. "You think I chose to come here? To live here in this poor excuse for a village as the third wife of an old, lecherous baker? I did not! But I accepted my duty. The duty of a daughter. I accepted my fate. Every woman's fate. You, though, Noraya Smith, you think you're special. You think just because you're a twin, that makes you free to do as you like. Lara's daughter, I call you. Bringer of death. You wonder why your foster mother died? You and your brother cursed every child to ever enter her womb until it drove her mad. Everyone knew it but her and your foster father. The poor besotted man. And now, they all are dead. You think the mess in your life is my fault? Think again."

Nora swallowed hard. The flood of rage choked her. Her vision blurred treacherously. There was no way she was going to cry now. Not in front of that woman! She clenched her teeth together and ripped her eyes wide open. They stung in the corners. The kettle whistled and Sallima turned around deftly, pouring the boiling water into two chipped cups from Nora's cupboard. Nora cuffed the tears away with her good hand. It was shaking. Sallima was wrong. Twins weren't cursed. The miscarriages weren't their fault, nor was Mother Sara's death. It wasn't Nora's fault.

"He was my father in all but blood. Have you seen the body in the forge?" she asked when she had her voice mostly under control again. There was a tremble of emotion, but she couldn't help it. Didn't want to.

Sallima kept her back turned to Nora, staring out the window as the steam rose from the two cups before her.

"I saw." The woman nodded. "I saw everything."

She turned her head to the side and Nora saw the tears spilling down her cheeks, but Sallima's voice was calm and steady. "Those men did bad things. Really bad things. They were very bad people."

After taking a few minutes to compose herself, Sallima came over with the tea, humming the lullaby once more. She probably wasn't even aware of it. Nora tried to imagine the pain of losing your child to Lara's cold embrace but couldn't. If it felt anything like losing your brother and parents, it fucking hurt. She gasped and grunted with the effort but managed to prop herself up against the wall on her own. She took the proffered cup, hand slightly trembling, and the two women drank together in silence.

"You have to change the bandage daily at first." Sallima cleared her throat. "I found some sheets to use. They are not as clean as I could wish for, but...they will do until your betrothed gets here."

Nora nodded. "What?" she said.

"Wolfe, your betrothed." Sallima narrowed her eyes at Nora. "I thought you said you sent Becca to the Vale to get help. You did, didn't you?"

"Oh, that. Yes. I did."

Sallima blew on her tea.

"Of course," she started again, "you'll probably find it more...tasteful to postpone your wedding until the spring equinox. After your loss, I mean. Bury the dead and mourn them."

"My wedding?"

Sallima tutted impatiently.

"You were supposed to be married on Solstice, weren't you? That's in a few weeks. Highly inappropriate considering what happened here. But at least now you can finally do the right thing and marry him."

"What?"

"Did you knock your head?" The baker's wife raised her eyebrows.

"I can't marry Wolfe," Nora blurted. "I mean, I live *here*." She rapped a knuckle against the stone wall. "This is my home. This was my home. No, *is*. I don't know. This is my kitchen. This is my cup. That's my shawl."

Sallima clutched it tighter around her shoulders.

"Yes, that's why I said you should consider postponing the wedding."

Without thinking, Nora swung her legs off the table and onto the floor. It was still a bad idea. She stumbled and steadied herself against the wall, cursing. Sallima stepped toward her to fuss, but Nora held up her hand. The room spun before her eyes, but she was walking—stumbling—toward the garden. She leaned against the doorpost and looked outside. The sky hung gray and overcast. A slight drizzle had set in. It was already past midday. Crap! Wolfe and the riders from the Vale could be here in two, maybe three hours. What was she going to do? She rested her head against the wall and closed her eyes. When she opened her eyes again, her gaze rested on the coaler's shovel leaning against the opposite wall. She pointed with her good hand.

"I thought that was just my imagination. Did you really hit that bowman over the head with a shovel?"

Sallima looked between Nora's face and the shovel. She nodded.

"I hit him over the head. He was out cold, but alive. Then I tied him up and left him there. Inn's burned down now." The woman's drawn face hinted at a smile. "I watched the fire. I didn't see him crawl out."

Nora shuddered at the odd gleam in Sallima's eyes. You could judge others by their actions, and rightly so, but you couldn't see into the darkness of their hearts. And in Nora's opinion, Sallima was just a step behind the bowman if she enjoyed watching others die. Would the baker's wife be able to carry on now? Live a normal life? Would Nora? How many men had she killed last night? Then she frowned.

"Where did you get the shovel?"

Sallima shook her head. "Strange thing, really. Like in the old tales."

"What? It magically walked out of the woods?"

"Kind of." She gave Nora a sharp look and took a deep breath. "We ran into the night, past the stable. I had to put Laena down. She was so heavy. Suddenly there was this guy, one of the men from inside. He grabbed Malla around the waist and dragged her toward the forest. The girls were screaming. Malla was screaming. And then this wight walks out from under the trees and kills the guy with one sword stroke."

Sallima mimed the stroke. The hairs on Nora's arm rose as the woman smiled at her.

"A wight?"

"Just like the old tales: a wight at night." Sallima smiled with that odd gleam in her eyes again. "Only then he gave me this coalman's shovel. He said it's yours."

"Black eyes? Bronze skin? Dark brown hair?"

Sallima cocked her head to the side. "You twins run with a strange crowd, Noraya. I wouldn't be surprised to see Lara herself show up at your door."

Nora groaned and slid down the doorframe to sit on the cold, wet floor. Sallima took the shovel and gazed at it as though she'd never seen one before.

"He gave me the shovel as a message for you."

"Yeah?"

"He said you'd know what it meant. Do you?"

"Yeah," Nora said with a lump in her throat. "It means I really hate that wight."

Sallima shrugged and put the shovel back. She busied herself getting clean water to wash the cups and scrub the bloodstain off the table. Nora's bloodstain.

For a long time Nora sat on the threshold, one side of her body inside the house, the other getting wet in the drizzle of rain. Burned ruins on the one hand, on the other...what? The unknown future. The ever-changing future. Possibility, Owen would say. Owen. She didn't even know where he was. They had been heading for the Temple of the Wind. Could she find it on her own? Would she find him?

Diaz had come here. Her annoying bodyguard. He had come after her when he should have been looking after Owen. Oh, he had saved Sallima and the other girls from the one guard who had never shown up again—and now she knew why—but only after she had killed to free them first. Why not before? Why not rescue Nora? And then taunting her with his message? And then leaving in the night so she couldn't take that damned shovel and answer him right to his face?

Well, it was either sit here and wait for Wolfe and his father to come pick her up and live that arranged life, or...or buckle up and find Owen. Flight or fight? Fight or flight?

She touched her aching right shoulder.

And stood up.

THE LIVING BLADE: BOOK TWO

AIN'T NO MOUNTAIN HIGH

CHAPTER 1

OWEN WATCHED HIS SISTER'S FACE freeze into a guarded expression. Nora turned and started to walk away, across the Plains, holding on to the straps of her backpack as though her life depended on it. His feet started to follow her, but he stopped himself. It was better this way. She'd be safe. She'd go home, get married, and live a good life. And hate him forever. But she'd be safe. And that was the main thing, the right thing. Duty first, emotions after—that was the way of the pilgrims, the way he aspired to. He swallowed, but his throat was choked up, too constricted to call out and stop her from leaving. He coughed, then hawked the bitter taste from his mouth.

A few days ago, she had tiptoed into his room back home in the middle of the night. He had been reading by the light of a candle and looked up to berate her as the draft blew out the flame.

"Do you mind? I thought you were at the slaughter feast with Wolfe." He groaned, reaching over for the tinderbox with one hand, trying to keep his finger between the pages.

He felt her move toward him in the dark. Her footsteps made no sound.

"Shhh!"

"What?"

She stood so close to him he smelled the scent of burned wood that always lingered in her hair, that charcoal scent, but also the honey-sweet fragrance of mead.

"Nora, are you drunk?"

"I'm still standing, aren't I?" she whispered angrily, taking the tinderbox and lighting the candle for him.

The stairs creaked under the weight of their foster father coming upstairs. Nora's head whipped toward the door and her hands shook slightly. Her eyes were wide and darted across the tiny bedroom. Bed, trunk, and desk. There was nothing else. She stepped behind Owen and bent over as though looking for something on the floor.

"Nora, what are you doing?" Her strange behavior was making his hair stand on end.

She pressed a finger against her lips and shook her head.

Owen heard Rannoch's heavy steps scrape across the wooden planks in the small corridor. His foster father was drunk. He heard it in the way Rannoch's left foot dragged over the floor. Either very tired—or very drunk. When he passed Owen's door, Nora squeezed her brother's forearm. Their eyes met as they heard their foster father pause before Nora's bedroom door next to Owen's. The other door opened. Owen strained to hear anything but the creak of wood. Nora's fingernails were buried deep in his forearm. The door closed again and the heavy footfall carried on one door farther to Rannoch's bedroom.

Nora's eyes were brimming with tears.

"I have to leave," she whispered. "I have to run away."

"When?"

"Now."

Owen nodded.

"All right."

✧ ✧ ✧

"SHE DIDN'T REALLY…FUCK YOUR FATHER, did she?" Owen turned to the voice outside of his memory, turned his eyes away from the distant silhouette of his twin and met the gray eyes of the pale boy next to him.

"No." He made no effort to conceal his frown.

The boy shrugged.

"Did you two ever…?"

"No!"

The blond boy shrugged again and scratched the back of his head.

"I've seen twins do it before. Only it was two red-haired girls. People paid a lot of money to watch them."

Owen flushed a dark red and gave the boy another look. He was tall and wiry, with a clean-cut face and a hint of broadness in his shoulders that might someday make him a decent fighter. If he lived that long. If they both lived that long.

"What's your name?" Owen asked.

"Shade Padarn."

"What kind of a name is that?"

"Mine." The boy's hand settled on his hilt.

Owen's eyes flicked back to Shade's.

"The name's Owen, destroyer of maiden hearts." He held out his hand.

Shade looked at the outstretched hand before he grasped it with a strength his lanky limbs belied.

"Yeah. I knew you'd be the evil twin."

✧ ✧ ✧

OWEN WOKE THE NEXT DAY with a bad taste in his mouth and a half-wight crouched next to him. He ran a hand through his unkempt hair and managed a smile.

"Master Diaz! You're back!"

"Indeed."

"That's good. I was worried when you left that—"

"Your sister. Where is she?"

Owen's smile died. He sat up, then squinted at Diaz's pupilless black eyes to figure out where this conversation was going. It didn't help much. Those wight eyes were unreadable. Owen cleared his throat.

"Ah. Nora. She's gone back home."

Another look at Diaz. The master didn't say anything.

"So...we had a bit of a fight. And, well, see, Nora wanted to leave the company, and I wanted to stay."

More nothing. Owen knew this tactic. Knew it and stepped right into it every time, trying to fill the silence, his words sounding more like excuses the more he spoke.

"Look, the best way of getting Nora to do what you want her to do is to make her angry enough to do it. If I tell her to do something, she'll just flat-out refuse. She's stubborn that way. If you tell her *not* to do something, challenge her, then she'll go the extra mile to prove you wrong. I figured she didn't want to stay, and let's face it." Owen lowered his voice and cast his gaze about the campfire, where Prince Bashan's men were waking. "With this lot? It's not really safe for her to stay, but she would never just leave me here on my own. So I had to make her leave. To keep her safe."

"And you decided this without consulting me, your master, first?"

"Um. Yeah. That was probably wrong."

"Owen, do you realize why we're running across the Plains near winter?"

"Um...because you don't want to be seen?"

Diaz sighed.

"Because all the roads are teeming with bandits and looters. The countryside is infested with roving bands of masterless men, some of them ambitious enough to prove themselves against the Hunted Company. Fighting them off would be tiresome and time-consuming, and the bodies we'd leave behind would show the direction the Hunted have taken. So we run the Plains."

The hair on Owen's forearms rose, but not because of the chilly morning breeze.

"You mean she's not safe?"

"I mean you sent your sister alone into the wild, and there's no safety of home left to go to, even if she arrives at Owen's Ridge unharmed."

"Oh. Oh crap!"

Owen felt sick. He stared into the flames and clasped his hands over his knees in an attempt to hide their shaking. Why hadn't he thought of that? His head turned to the direction Nora had taken. It'd take days to reach the Ridge. He'd never catch up with her. And even if he did, what could he possibly say? *You shouldn't have fucked our father.* There was no way to misunderstand that. No way he'd been joking. You couldn't just apologize after that sentence. Oops, sorry. Didn't mean it. He'd said it to get her to leave him, and it had worked. He groaned and hid his face in his palms.

"I need you to do something," Diaz said.

Owen looked up through his fingers.

"Keep close to the prince. And to Shade. They'll keep an eye out for you on the journey to the Temple of the Wind. But you must in turn keep an eye out for them. Understood?"

Owen nodded, although he wasn't too sure he understood.

He watched Master Diaz move among the waking men, watched him pull the hood of his cloak farther down over his face as he strode westward.

CHAPTER 2

THE LAND CRAWLED PAST THEM as they continued farther east day by day. The Plains were a vast bowl of grassland surrounded by the Crest Mountains, dotted here and there with scraggly trees shaped by the northeast wind, boughs reaching out toward the south like outstretched hands. The Hunted Company had slowed down their pace from a run to a solid marching rhythm. Some of the company came and went whenever they broke camp, bringing felled game back with them. Owen watched despondently as Shade shot hare on the Plains with a frequency and aim that outclassed Owen's mediocre attempts by far. The boy was younger than him, for the love of the gods, if only by a few months. They'd be talking about something, and then Shade would raise his hand, attention suddenly drawn away. He'd string his bow, aim, then follow the arrow's flight to his prize. Every single time. It felt like having Nora back around him—except that Nora never talked about brothels or tits—and so Owen stuck close to Shade.

Every day that passed uneventfully was another day his sister lived, Owen told himself. The first few days after Master Diaz left, Owen had slept badly, straining for any sound of the half-wight's return. That would surely mean Nora was dead. And it would be his fault. After the first week had gone by with no sign of Diaz, Owen pictured Nora having reached the Ridge in safety and Diaz checking in at the forge to see that she was all right. Then the master would return soon and tell Owen so, and he could sleep restfully again.

After the second week had gone by with no sign of Diaz's return, Owen started to worry again. There were too many factors. Too much he didn't know. Maybe Nora had thrown a fit at Diaz when he arrived at the Ridge. Maybe she hadn't, and the master had stayed to perform the marriage at Solstice himself. There was always the need for a pilgrim in the villages along the coastline. Sometimes the young pilgrims from the shrines in Dernberia came by on pilgrimages to the larger temples. Once a year at least, Master

Darren had made his rounds. But maybe Diaz had decided to do the rites himself. Who knew? Not Owen, and that was his problem. But he trusted the master and he knew his sister. And every day they weren't by his side was a day that Nora lived longer. Maybe.

By the third week, they left the Plains and entered dense woodlands. The lonely groves of trees had joined forces to become a thick forest. A rutted dirt trail passed as a road under the close canopy of trees, even though the last people to come through had certainly been dead and gone for decades, if not a century. Camping in the woods off the trail was a slight improvement, Owen felt, as the trees protected against the constant blasting wind of the Plains. At night, he huddled as close to the fire as he dared and read by its light.

Owen was never without books. Nora said he carried them like a disease. Even in their great haste to run away from home, as Nora was packing food, Owen had grabbed two books from his desk. She had scoffed, of course. But he always had books, even when tending the charcoal clamps. He read until his vision blurred and his mind couldn't focus on the words before him.

He awoke cold and sore. His book had tumbled out of his hands and lay dangerously close to the glowing embers of the fire. Weak moonlight filtered through the empty boughs above his head and flashed on metal near his feet as he reached for the book. He looked up and made out a dreamy, hazy silhouette standing over him.

"Nora?"

Nope, it wasn't Nora. It was a man. A man with a sword. A man with a sword who was about to kill him. Owen rolled against the trunk of a tree, heart pounding. He held the retrieved book high over his head like a shield—as though that would help—and scrabbled back as the blade slashed down where he had been a second earlier. His other hand was on his paring knife. It wouldn't be much good against a sword; neither would the book hinder the stroke. He readied himself for the pain that would come any second now. He was going to die. Now. Here. And the worst part was that he couldn't even see his killer, so he'd never find out why that man wanted to kill him. Metal flashed and he closed his eyes, calling out in terror.

The killer grunted as Shade hurtled into him from the side. Owen watched them scuffle. What could he do? What should he do? If he stabbed randomly into the dark with his paring knife, he might hurt Shade instead of the other guy. He took a deep breath and yelled instead.

"Attack! We're being attacked!"

On the other side of the fire, Prince Bashan, exiled heir to the throne of the Kandarin Empire, woke with a jolt as though he had been shot with an arrow. His eyes took in the situation and his hand was already drawing his sword out of its scabbard. All around the camp, torches lit up among the trees. The attackers started a wild howl that made Owen's skin crawl with primal fear.

"All to me!" the prince yelled, voice still hoarse from sleep. "Shield wall! All to me!"

With a deft swoop Owen grabbed the man punching Shade and pressed his face down into the glowing embers of the fire. The man screamed and twisted violently, flailing with his arms and legs, but not for long. Shade sat up and stabbed him in the back three times. His young face was a snarl. Owen rolled to his feet and ran.

He ducked between the trees as chaos erupted around him. Cries rang out. He heard the clang of weapons, and arrows whirred unseen through the night. Beyond his speeding world of half-glimpsed faces and whipping branches, Owen knew running away was not a good idea. In fact, it was probably a stupid idea. He now found himself alone, surrounded by archers and men with swords somewhere in the woods before him, and he wasn't sure in which direction he was running. Toward the dirt road? What if the main force of the enemy lay in wait there? Deeper into the forest? Then he'd be all alone without a weapon, and that was not a good situation to be in, either. His best chance of survival was going back to the prince and the Hunted Company. But his feet weren't listening to his reason. He willed himself to stop and turned back toward the sounds of fighting.

The men around him were occupied with their bloody work, but he was in the middle of a nightmare. Shadowed fighters choked and blood gurgled in slit throats. Torch flames waved to and fro hellishly, distorting the men's faces, their limbs, and their weapons. Fear gripped him hard and, in turn, he gripped the hilt of his paring knife. It was pathetic. Now that his feet had stopped, they just wouldn't move again. Blind rage gleamed in the eyes of the men around him, killing and hacking and grunting and falling. They'd kill him in their battle rage. Kill now, mourn friendly fatalities later. Ha! As if any of them would give a damn about him.

A loud crashing sound boomed to his right, and he ducked instinctively, then ran to his left. Now at least he was moving! He tripped over something—a root—and fell face-first into the wet dirt. He scrambled to get back up, spitting pine needles, his face raw and chafed, blood trickling from his forehead over his left cheek. He couldn't see and staggered forward, one hand outstretched before him, one hand pressing down on his brow. He swallowed and tasted blood and earth.

Dizzy and disorientated, he bumped into a tree and steadied himself, still clutching his face. The sword of a man with an unkempt beard whacked into the trunk beside him. It stuck. Owen glanced at the blade that had nearly chopped into his side then across it at the man, rank with fumes of mead on his hot breath. He grinned at Owen, revealing two incisor teeth filed to sharp points. Owen stepped back. Still grinning, the man tugged at his sword. Bark rained down, but the sword remained stuck. The man frowned at his hilt. Owen sprang at him with his paring knife, slashing it across the man's face before running back into the fray.

Where was Shade? Where was the prince? Owen tried to listen for their voices in the din. He zigzagged between the trees, slipping on the pine needles and wet, rotting leaves, stumbling over roots and stones. Footsteps thudded behind him, but he didn't turn around to see whether the Tooth-man had managed to pull his sword out of the trunk. Or perhaps he had decided to kill him with some other random weapon, like his bare hands around Owen's neck. Owen ran straight through a line of five archers. One of them shouted out. If they turned to shoot at him and missed or just didn't bother, he never knew. But archers? What was going on? He was going in the right direction at least. He could tell because the noise was becoming louder. Shrieks heralded death and pain and steel—and lots of it.

Before him, a huge man bellowed with rage and knocked back another man with his shield. As the other man hit the ground, the giant warrior impaled him on his spear. Owen stopped mid-step and nearly ran back in the other direction. But he knew where that would lead him: straight to his death. The man before him, he knew that guy at least. It was Garreth. His hair was gray stubble under his hood, and his face was broad and covered in pockmarks broken only by a huge scar that swept from his jaw across his left eye and beyond his hairline. The left eye was blind white and bulged out of its cavity. The scar slit this eyelid into two pieces, and the tissue had pulled apart as it healed, leaving the eye open even when the man blinked. It was fascinatingly revolting to look at, but right now Owen was so glad to see it he didn't care. Garreth was the closest thing to a captain of the prince's rabble of men. He shadowed Shade Padarn like a mother hen and always stayed close to the prince. If he didn't turn and kill Owen now, he was probably Owen's best bet for survival.

"Garreth!"

The huge man turned and sighted down his spear, aiming at Owen's heart. Owen's first impulse was to curl together, but he straightened and held up his hands, though his voice broke as he called out,

"It's me, Owen! I've lost Shade Padarn!"

Recognition flickered across the old face. It wasn't pretty to watch. Garreth was also the man Nora had dunked under the icy waters of a river just before she left. Obviously, Garreth remembered only too well. The warrior grunted.

"Where's your sword 'n' shield, boy?" His voice was like gravel.

"I've got this," Owen answered, holding up his small paring knife. Seeing Garreth's expression, he wished he hadn't.

Garreth picked up the sword of the man he had just felled and pressed it into Owen's hand. The hilt was covered in blood and sticky. Owen nearly let it fall. The sword was a heavy piece of crap, not well made. The metal was inferior, and the steel was nicked badly and so brittle it would probably break under one hard blow.

"Beggars can't be choosers," Garreth rumbled as he grabbed Owen and shoved him half behind his huge body. "Stay behind my shield. Kill anything that comes before it. Got it?"

Owen nodded and stumbled after the older man into the dying chaos. The tide of the fight was ebbing already. Only minutes had passed since Owen had woken. Garreth smacked his shield against anyone in his path toward the main campfire, cursed them to their faces and jabbed them with his spear. But in the small clearing that was their campsite, those left standing were those of the Hunted Company. Those who stood alone with bloodied sword and shield in hand took a breather or were looting the bodies of whoever had attacked them. It was ghoulish, Owen thought and shuddered, looking away. A corner of the fight still raged over by the main fire, where a short line of shields was pressed tightly together, the men behind them hacking and slashing at the attackers before the wall. The prince was making his stand there, brow furrowed in concentration, but his eyes were shining with ferocious joy. Next to Bashan fought Shade. Blood was spattered across his young face, a stark contrast with his blond hair and beaming eyes. Those eyes. Steel gray and merciless.

They're enjoying this, Owen thought and swallowed hard. Distracted by the sensation of horror crawling over his skin, he never noticed the hand that slid around his ankle and toppled him to the ground.

A rough hand was holding him down, clasped around his throat. Owen couldn't breathe. He opened his eyes and saw the Toothman bent over him, lips parted in a demonic grin, flashing those pointed teeth. He was muttering words in a tongue Owen didn't recognize. He struggled against the hand that held him down, pummeling the arm with his fists. Voices rang out behind them. Shouts. But all Owen heard was the crescendo of the man's incantation. His own heart beat louder than the mad screech the man howled as he raised a golden dagger high above his head, as though it were an offering to the moon. Owen's lungs burned, aching to inhale. He had to breathe now, and he kicked up high, hitting something hard. But it wasn't enough to free himself from the deadly clutch. The sounds were muted now, growing dim. All he saw was the arc of the golden dagger curving toward his chest. He was going to die. This was a moment when even grown men called for their mothers.

Owen curled up into a ball, one hand on the forearm of his attacker, the other raised as if it could ward off the blow that was certain to come. And if he'd had breath, he would have screamed his sister's name.

CHAPTER 3

NORA ADJUSTED THE STRAP OF her bag again. Her right arm was swaddled in a makeshift sling, the shoulder wound still oozing. Food for three weeks, extra clothing, it all had to be carried on her left shoulder. Didn't matter. It would get lighter fast. The dull ache in her shoulder turned into a sharp cutting pain, and she winced as she hoisted the bag up a little. In a long row of stupid ideas—leaving Owen, killing a number of marauders with a kitchen knife, grandstanding the vicious bastard who had injured her—this was probably the stupidest. There was no way she'd make it across the Plains during winter in this condition. No way she'd find Owen before her meager food supply ran out. She didn't even know where he was. There was nothing for it, though. If she tarried, her betrothed would come riding up on horseback to save the daring damsel in distress. And she couldn't hold with that. One step at a time. One step, then another. That was all she could do.

Her original plan had been to sneak down the path of the Ridge, go over the slab of stone that served as a bridge across the brook, and then walk into the woods until night fell. No one would find her there. Especially not a horse rider.

She scrapped that plan after walking just a few steps beyond her garden, sweat running down her face, every footstep shaky business. New plan. She and Owen had often burned charcoal near a small crag, a hiding place. It was close enough to home for them to wheelbarrow the fresh coal back. As children, they had often climbed into the split rock and weathered the winter storms under the crag's protection, huddled together safe and dry, yet still able to peer out and watch the charcoal clamps for telltale wisps of smoke.

Her goal was clear: find Owen. It was a deceptively simple goal but included a rattail of other smaller tasks to carry out first, like get dressed and get food, difficult because she had to raid for supplies while the busybody baker's wife wasn't looking. But it wasn't impossible. The baker's wife stood motionless in the village square before the inn. She had been doing so for a long time. Nora waited to see whether she would come back inside after a while, but she didn't. Nora had considered knocking out the poor woman who was so intent on getting Nora married. It would have been satisfying in a swift retribution kind of way. But grabbing hold of the coaler's shovel with her left hand had felt awkward and cumbersome. And now, she was into the woods, unsure of her way other than the next few steps ahead.

Nora slung the heavy bag into the split before scrambling in herself. Her right shoulder banged against the rock as she squirmed. Nora groaned, the pain blinding her for a moment. *Now just breathe, breathe the pain away, wipe the sweat from your brow and push a little harder, Nora*—and she was inside. Autumn winds had swept in a carpet of brown crackling leaves. She maneuvered herself so as to sit and stare out of the opening in the rock, arranging a wolf's fur around her shoulders to keep her warm. Wounded and shivering with exhaustion, she hadn't come all that far from the Ridge, from her home, but she was hidden well enough away that the riders wouldn't find her here. This was a place only coalers knew. It was safe and dry and though she meant to stay awake and keep watch, she fell asleep and dreamed of flames and blood, blades and the thunder of hooves.

She woke late the next morning, stiff and aching, a wight waiting for her.

Nora stared at Master Telen Diaz, who sat cross-legged before the entrance to the cave, blinking out of his meditation, his black pupilless eyes now fixed on her face.

"Good morning," he said.

She stared.

"You look like Death herself," he said. "How badly hurt are you?"

He watched her throw her bag out first, then wriggle out of the split rock, the pins and needles in her feet making for an inelegant landing. She collapsed in a heap on the leaf-covered woodland floor and slowly managed to stand up, leaning against the rock wall behind her. One-handed, she pulled the strap of the bag over her head and glared at him, trying to snatch one of the many responses that welled up in her throat. Her right elbow caught on the rock before she could decide which profanity to hurl at him, and she winced in pain, a short moan escaping her lips.

"So, you plan to travel across the Plains in near winter all on your own, unable to use both your hands." Diaz rose in one effortless movement, dusted himself off, and shouldered his backpack. She hated him already. "Reckless, yes. Stubborn, definitely. However, I did not take you to be stupid. I was obviously mistaken."

He turned and made to leave.

"That's it?" Her voice was hoarse. He paused and looked over his shoulder. "That's all you have to say? Where's Owen?"

"Perfectly safe."

"With Prince 'Let's Torch Moorfleet' Bashan?"

Diaz shrugged.

"Owen is safer than you. And if you truly do want to find him, you're going to need help."

"Your help?"

"Yes."

"Fuck you and your help, Diaz!"

Diaz sighed and looked up at the gray skies as though praying for strength.

"I would prefer you call me 'master.'"

"And I'd prefer you call me 'queen.' But you and I both know that's never going to happen."

Diaz held on to the strap of his backpack, one knuckle tapping his upper lip. Was he smiling? It was hard to tell with those large black eyes, so unlike a human's.

"Go home, Noraya Smith. Heal and be well."

He was gone in an instant, leaving her alone. For now. Because that was the thing with the wight, Nora thought. He had followed her all this way, had looked out for her in secret, and had waited for her to wake this morning—all to tell her to stay put? Who was he fooling? She shook her head and sat down, leaning against the rock. Breakfast first. He could wait and catch her again later.

✧ ✧ ✧

THREE DAYS LATER, NORA APPROACHED the hillock poised at the brink of the Plains, cold and aching. Winter was coming on stronger now. Huddled into the gray wolf's fur, she staggered the last few steps under the nearly bare trees, puffing white wisps before her. The cold numbed her feet, every step jarring her. The wind clawed at her relentlessly. She rested against the tree where they had first met, where Diaz had held a dagger to her throat only two weeks ago. Gods, it seemed a lot longer. But here she was, still just Nora. Beyond the trees, on the hillock, she half expected to see Owen's silhouette. Instead she saw the orange light of a fire and smiled. He remembered, too.

She pushed away from the tree, nodding at Diaz in tired greeting and sat down, warming her shaking hands over the fire. Her fingers were stiff as though frozen at the joints. The master wight sat at the fire, fingers intertwined in his lap. With his large black eyes, he watched her shiver and rub her hands together. Then he cocked his head.

"So you didn't go back home," he said.

Nora nodded, not trusting her chattering teeth to allow her to speak yet.

"Why?"

She shook her head.

"I'm not here to prove something, you know? I'm not walking the Plains wounded in winter because I want to. It's because...I didn't want to stay there. I couldn't. The...the men at the Ridge, the men I killed, they killed my father in the forge. Took his hands and his head. Right there." She paused, looking for words in the chaos of emotion that followed those last ones. *My father.* She had left home with Owen, run away after her handfasting. She'd left that night after...she'd never told him how much...That was a pretty shitty feeling. She took a deep breath, focusing once more.

"I told Owen hundreds of times. I said, 'Look! Our actual mother was probably going to set us out in the wild. The double soul. The unnatural. Leave the twins for the wi—'" She shot the wight opposite her a look and corrected herself. "Wild animals."

"Nicely saved."

She glared at him, cheeks hot.

"That's how it is, isn't it? Stupid tradition. We could be dead. *I* could be dead. But I'm not. We're not. We belong together, Owen and I. He's all I've got. So that's where I'm going. Wherever he is, that's where I have to be."

She looked across the fire and into the wight's eyes.

"I won't go back. And you can't make me."

Diaz leaned forward a little.

"You think I want to?"

Nora ran her good hand through her hair. It was getting greasy. When was the last time she had washed her hair? When was the last time something normal like that had been her concern? She had tried braiding it out of her face earlier, but her right shoulder screeched in pain when she tried to lift her hand above her head.

"I don't know what you want. Or what you think you're doing." She paused. "Master Darren and the other pilgrims at the Shrine of Hin—they're more like...well, like Owen."

"We pilgrims are rather individualistic." Diaz cleared his throat; the rasp in his voice stayed. "Some say our order collects those who do not fit elsewhere. And they are right. To be a pilgrim means to travel the world, to know no ties of kin or origin, to never fit in anywhere, to be the distant observer who can settle legal issues objectively, speak justice, give guidance on morals."

His dark eyes reflected the fire, and it made the iron of his sword's hilt shine.

And how's that going for you? Nora thought. Out loud she asked, "And which do you do?"

"All of it. Although now I'm more of a personal guide to the wayward, exiled Prince Bashan."

"To find the Living Blade?"

"To help him find the Living Blade, yes."

Nora shook her head again. It was getting heavy. She pulled up her legs and rested her chin on top of her knees.

"And you really believe it exists?"

She saw him nod once as her eyes closed.

"Who's stupid now?" she whispered.

Diaz was gone when Nora woke in the morning. She didn't see him again until a few days later.

CHAPTER 4

SOMEONE WAS PULLING HER PILLOW out from under her head. Nora grunted and shifted her arm underneath the bag to hold it tight. Again someone tugged, and a wave of warm air spilled over her shoulder, reeking of rotten meat. Nora wrinkled her nose and turned to look over with one eye, sure it was just a nightmare impressing itself on her mind. Her head twitched up—then she was flailing all four limbs at once in a mad scramble to get the hell away from the bear tugging at her bag. She shored herself up against the tree she had curled under and stayed there, trying not to scream, a low moan escaping her lips. The pain in her shoulder flared up again and she grabbed it.

The animal had one half of her bag between its teeth, and now the other half was dangling from the bear's huge jaws, the contents falling onto the ground between its paws. Apples and bags of nuts and dried berries. And, of course, the cured strips of meat she had ransacked from the pantry. She could see the bear's nostrils flaring; the exhalation hit her like a breeze, drying her wide eyes in a flash.

Larger than a normal bear. She stared into the black eyes in front of her, the scent of animal rising heady in the chilly dawn. Meat eater. It sniffed the air cautiously on all fours, but if it rose it would be twice her height at least. Maybe taking in the strange scent of human for the first time and wondering whether the meat—her meat—was tasty. A young male. A common brown bear's paw was already as wide as Nora's forearm. This bear's paw was larger. A lot larger. Because a mountain bear was larger. Nora guessed that if this mountain bear hit her with one paw, he would probably not only swipe off her head but also the top half of her torso at the same time. It wasn't very reassuring that she'd be instantly dead at that point and wouldn't feel the pain of being ripped in half. *Oh, gods.* Her knife was in her left hand, but it felt tiny. And wouldn't a slash with it just make the bear angry? And would she even be able to hit the bear with her left hand? Eating with the left was difficult enough—there was no way she'd be able to defend herself against the beast.

He let out a low growl and his head came closer, sniffing and slobbering. Dry sobs racked Nora's chest as she leaned into the tree. She was gasping for breath, and the meat eater's stench hit her hard. He seemed very interested in her bleeding shoulder. Maybe if she stuck the knife into his eye? Would the blade penetrate deep enough to kill the bear instantly? *Oh, gods,* she repeated to herself.

"Don't move."

Relief dripped off her like her rolling sweat. The whisper behind her had a deep rasp to it. She closed her eyes and prayed Diaz was stringing his bow and had an arrow at the ready. The mountain bear's head swayed from side to side, trying to identify this new scent.

He bellowed in her face and Nora screamed, hands raised above her head instinctively despite her shoulder bleeding and hurting—she didn't care. Didn't feel. The fear numbed everything else. Then the arrow impacted straight into the bear's eye. The shot was lethal. Only the bear hadn't realized that yet. He rose and bellowed once more, paws swiping in blind rage. Nora stared up at him through the rain of bark chips, then rolled to her feet and ran. Diaz's arrow, Diaz's problem.

She ran through the trees, trusting terror and distance to keep her safe. Then she saw an oak with low branches and jumped at one of them. As her hands grabbed the rough bark, her arms tensed, and before she realized what was happening she was lying on her back, winded, looking up at the branches of the trees, the dawn skies oblivious to her beating heart and the world of pain blooming in her right shoulder. She sobbed, voice cracking, curled on her side in the dry leaves. The bear bellowed once more. She tightened her throat and rolled to her feet, clutching her right arm at the elbow. The wound in her shoulder had ripped open and was bleeding profusely. She staggered a few steps toward the fight. This was it. Where her fate would be decided. If Diaz died, then she'd die, too. Eaten by a mountain bear, then shat back out to the ground whence she came. Symbol of the wheel of life right there.

Diaz had ditched his bow and was fighting with his sword and a long knife, dancing around the bear, dodging his mighty blows. He freed his sword from a deep thrust into the bear's side and slashed across his belly, crouching under a swipe from the towering beast. He was fighting in a way Nora had never seen before: both weapons held steady at a point above his waist, twisting the blades in his hands by movements of the wrists and elbows, swinging the tip of his swords with an economy of strength but at the same time with precision and speed. He stepped to the side and lashed the sword across the bear's broad back. The beast bellowed and lumbered around to get his attacker back in view, but his going was slow, bleeding from a dozen wounds, weakened by too many cuts, arrow shaft wedged deep into his skull.

Turning on two hind legs, the bear caught sight of Nora and roared in pain as Diaz sank his sword into his flank. The mountain bear fell to all fours and howled the pitiful sound of a wounded animal. He snapped his jaws at Diaz, who was inching around the huge frame, blood dripping from his sword, black eyes intent on the bear. The mountain bear was dying, but he wasn't beaten yet and growled as Diaz came closer. Then his head turned to Nora, staring at her with small black eyes as though he knew she was the cause of his death. She held her breath. Still dangerous and fast, he ran toward her on all fours, ignoring Diaz's shout for attention.

Nora stood still, clutching her arm and watching her own death approach. Those large teeth would break her bones in one bite. Those claws could rip her to pieces in one swift move. She'd die right now. She saw Diaz take up pursuit, but he'd never make it. She watched the two of them approach her, the black-eyed bear, muzzle snarling as he came upon her, followed by the black-eyed wight. Diaz hurled himself forward, plunging onto the huge mass of fur. His sword dug down deep into the bear's nape, and the snap of bone was audible under the trees. The bear's paws were buried underneath his huge body as he skidded forward, lifeless, carried by his own momentum, finally coming to a halt inches before Nora's feet.

Nora looked up into Diaz's face, not even an arm's length away from her own.

"Are you all right?" He wiped the bear's blood from his jaw with the back of his sleeve.

She nodded and then threw up.

CHAPTER 5

THE TASTE OF BILE IN her mouth could not be fully washed away with the sweet cold water from a small brook just beyond where the bear lay. Nora gargled one last time. Finally trusting her legs to carry her weight, she stood up and turned to Diaz, who was busying himself removing the bear's claws and teeth.

"What are you doing?" Her throat was sore. She coughed up phlegm and spat it out.

"I know a few people who pay good coin for mountain bear claws. Maybe they'll pay for the teeth. I'd skin him, too, if there was time." He looked up, squinting at her. "Better?"

She nodded. He went back to work. Nora cleared her throat.

"You fight good."

"And I guess that's as close to a thank-you as I'll get." He put the last tooth into a small pouch and rose, walking past her to the brook to wash.

"So what now? Will you leave me again?" Nora opened and closed her left hand, which was clamped around her right arm. "Shall I catch up with you in a few days' time at a different campfire? Is this how it's going to be?"

"No." Diaz splashed his face with water. "Not anymore. We journey together."

"What changed? You think I'll be attacked by another bear?"

He glanced at her over his shoulder.

"Maybe." He pointed at her. "Your shoulder's bleeding."

"Yeah."

"Let me see."

She bristled but then did as he said, kneeling down next to him at the water. He had saved her life. She could do what he wanted for once.

Slowly and painfully, she slipped her shoulder free of her woolen tunic sleeve. The baker's wife had stitched the wound together while Nora had been unconscious. Under the bandages it had sealed into a horrible red crust that was puckered and ragged and reached under her collarbone into the flesh of her shoulder joint. That crust had opened in three places. Diaz pressed a piece of cloth over the bleeding. It hurt. She sucked in air through her clenched teeth and looked away, tears stinging her eyes.

He hmm'd and tapped her shoulder.

"You left the stitches in too long. Then put pressure on them."

"Yeah, I was kind of running for my life."

Diaz cut through the threads with his hunting knife and grasped the knot end of the first stitch firmly between his finger and thumb. He looked at her.

"This will sting," he said.

That was all the forewarning Nora got. He pulled immediately. It did sting and worse. She swore loudly. Then he pulled the second thread, then the third. Nora's eyes watered. He did it quickly, most merciful man. When all five stitches were out, her forehead was pressed hard against his shoulder and she felt like throwing up again. He pressed a cold, wet rag against the wound. A dribble of water ran down her bosom, and she shuddered. For a moment, they sat close together. Then he shrugged his shoulder and she lifted her head from it.

"Here, dry it with this." He pressed a soft piece of cotton cloth into her hand and rose, looking at the huge carcass of the bear.

"You lost your provisions."

"Bear ate them." A nervous giggle crawled up her throat. She coughed, fighting it down. "I guess it came down from the Crest Mountains and caught the scent of the meat in my bag. It doesn't matter. There's enough meat on him to last the two of us until way past Solstice."

He gave her a look.

"You don't want to eat this bear."

"I'm going to have to if I want to get to the Temple of the Wind."

"Follow me."

"Follow you? What? Where? Hey!"

And Diaz was back to being annoying again. He'd just walked off under the trees, expecting her to follow. Nora pulled her collar back up, tightening it around her exposed throat, and followed.

Not far from the carcass, the reek of rotten flesh was pervasive and it grew ever stronger the farther they went. It hung on the air like a fog. No sound stirred the place; only the indignant caws of ravens broke the silence as they hopped away from Diaz's feet. He stopped just ahead and gestured her to come closer. Nora tugged her scarf over her face and breathed through her opened mouth.

Before her feet was a sudden drop in the ground, a hole dug deep and wide, but dug by human hands. Wooden stakes lined the pit, driven into the hard earth, spikes with pointed ends. And on top of those ends a number of dead people hung impaled—and they hadn't hung there for long. She turned away hastily, retching. But her stomach was empty already and she hadn't even had breakfast yet. Men lay at the bottom of this hole. Men killed by other men. Only humans were this cruel to their own kind.

She shook her head.

"Your bear smelled this, I reckon," Diaz said and pointed at the pit. "And he's eaten his fill. You can see the bones of the leg torn from this man and eaten over there."

Her legs shook. She would definitely not eat the bear. She'd rather starve.

"What is this place?"

"It's a death pit." Diaz stared into the hole. "In ancient times, men believed that the gods desired human sacrifices. Before or after battles, sacrifices were made to beseech the gods' blessing. A pit was dug, stakes were sharpened and prisoners were offered, but sometimes, when the need was desperate, a more valuable sacrifice was made. A nobleman, the chieftain's beautiful virgin daughter. You get the picture. This is the third time I've seen something like this. The first time was in the south."

"The gods are dead. They were destroyed by the Living Blade."

"The Blade you say does not exist?" Diaz turned to look. Nora opened and shut her mouth a few times. "There are some people who believe that the Blade did not destroy the gods, but merely robbed them of their incarnation. They still linger among us, ready to answer an earnest prayer if given the right incentive: blood."

They both stood for a moment, gazing at the brutality before them. Nora wanted to turn her head away from the wreckage but couldn't. Her gaze was fixed on all that death. *Remember that you are mortal,* she thought. But this? This was just sick. Who would do this kind of thing? And for what? She thought of the chieftain she had killed at the inn on the Ridge. He had been just as crazy, just as deluded as the people who had done this, believing in prophecies, summoning dead gods with human sacrifice—it didn't make sense to her. They should bury these poor people, shovel the pit full of earth and let those who were sacrificed to dead gods have whatever peace they could in the afterlife. She felt giddy and light-headed as though she were drunk, the stench of blood and guts was so overpowering.

"Well, there's nothing for it." Nora paused for dramatic effect, then gestured at the humans in the pit. "We'll just have to eat them on our way."

Diaz slowly turned his head to her, and she couldn't hold the laughter in anymore.

"Sorry. But…your face!" She clasped a hand over her mouth but couldn't stop the rib-hurting laughter until she was crying and bent over double with a red face. "So funny!"

"You have a very disturbing sense of humor."

He straightened his cloak and walked past her, back straight. She followed, giggles like hiccups disturbing the icy silence. It was nerves. She knew it but couldn't stop herself. It was either laugh or fall down and weep. And she couldn't allow herself to weep right now. Weep and her feet would falter and she'd never see her brother again.

Diaz did skin the bear after all, while Nora searched the ground around her sleeping place for unspoiled food she could take along, still giggling to herself occasionally. It wasn't much. A few apples, some small pouches of dried berries and nuts. She drank a sip of fresh water to fill her rumbling stomach and watched as Diaz rolled up the large pelt. She cleared her throat.

"You said this is the third time you've seen a death pit?"

"Yes." He didn't look at her but continued rolling. Yeah, he was still mad, she thought. She tried not to smile at the memory of his shocked face.

"Once in the south, you said. One today. And the other?"

He strapped the pelt onto his backpack and shouldered it before turning to face her.

"Are you sure you want to know?"

"Moorfleet?"

He shook his head.

"Just behind Owen's Ridge."

CHAPTER 6

THEY SPENT THE REST OF the day walking in silence. There was little to say. Any inclination to laugh had died the instant Diaz said those last words. Nora clutched her now uncomfortably light bag, willing her feet not to run back to Owen's Ridge. What was done was done. There was no going back. She bit the insides of her cheeks until they were raw and followed Diaz across the Plains.

Dusk was falling already when they finally reached the river ford. Somewhere beyond the rolling gray skies the sun was setting, though Nora could neither see it nor feel its warmth. Around the pebbles on the banks, among the reeds and brush, were little pools of ice that broke away easily enough if she tapped them gently with her foot. The water would be colder this time. Her every breath hung in a mist before her mouth. Well, there was nothing for it; she couldn't wait here for spring. She fumbled with her belt buckle and shot Diaz a sidelong glance. His head turned back to the river.

"The water will be cold," he said. "We can make a fire on the other side."

She grunted, stepping out of her boots, and pulled her trousers down as nonchalantly as she could. It wasn't as though she were naked underneath. Her underwear covered anything Diaz could possibly catch a glimpse of. Not that he gave the impression of wanting to. And that was totally understandable: she was grimy and smelly and wounded, and besides, he likely thought her just a tiny bit insane for even trying this whole stupid quest for her brother. But...well. He could see all he liked, but there was nothing to see. Except the goose bumps that puckered the white skin of her legs. Gods, it was cold. However, trousers would soak up the icy water and she'd be freezing for hours to come, fire or no.

Diaz walked onto the riverbank, cracking the ice under his boot.

"Be mindful of your footing. The river isn't deep, but its current is strong and the pebbles—"

"Pffft!"

Nora raised her chin up, shouldered her boots and trousers, and took the river in a storm, bare feet and all.

It was fucking cold! It was physical, and it punched with violence. Her feet were numb in an instant, and the cold coursed up her legs and sank its teeth into her hips. She automatically quickened her pace, her legs stepping high through the shallow water like a stork searching for frogs only finding none because it was splashing so godsdamn much! In the middle, the water reached her hips, and she snatched in deep breaths of air as though she were drowning. The cold seeped into her underwear as she raced to the other bank. Just get out. Of the water. Get warm soon.

With stiffly frozen fingers, getting dressed on the far side of the river was more than difficult. Her wet legs snagged on the woolen trousers, and she cursed them and her trousers and herself in breathless whispers. Her teeth chattered and wouldn't stop for a long time, even after she had slipped back into her warm, dry clothes and curled into her sleeping furs.

She watched as Diaz strode out of the river, water gushing off him. He seemed oblivious to any feeling of cold or discomfort. His trouser legs stuck to him as he busied himself with lighting a fire under the branches of a little gathering of trees too big to be called a copse, too small to be a wood. Once the fire was going, he rolled out the fresh bear pelt onto the ground and nodded for her to sit on it.

Nora sat in front of the fire, knees clasped to her body, lower jaw shivering.

"Not cold?" she managed to ask him.

"I am. But I'll get warm again. Tea?"

She nodded and Diaz heated some water over the fire. He was still dripping. She winced and massaged her aching legs, feeling awake and utterly spent at the same time. It was a strange state of being, but one she was accustomed to. It was what tending the charcoal burning had sometimes felt like. The only difference was, she had shared that state with her twin. Never anyone else.

Diaz sat down on the bear pelt next to her and offered a small metal mug full of hot liquid. Nora took it gladly. A fresh scent rose in the steam, of balm and fennel and peppermint. For a long time, they both stared into the fire, holding the mugs to warm their hands if not their hearts.

"I've never seen anyone fight like that. Who taught you?" Nora asked.

Diaz took a sip from his cup. Then he licked his lips.

"Mostly the other man I was fighting," he answered. "If you survive a few fights, you pick up a number of tricks to keep on surviving. But if you're talking about the basics, my father taught me those."

Nora held her face above the steam rising from her cup, inhaling the warmth and the scent.

"My mother was a human. Like you," Diaz said after another sip from his cup.

Nora's eyebrows went up high.

"My father...," Diaz started. Then he shook his head. "The wights say I'm human. The humans say I'm a wight. Now I am a pilgrim. It seemed to be the most obvious choice. I never went back. Even when my mother died, I never went back."

He took another sip.

"How did she die?"

"Of old age."

Nora's face must have shown her puzzlement. Diaz didn't look much older than his late twenties, maybe early thirties. Although, the wights were also called the Everlasting.

"I'm eighty-seven," he explained and half smiled at her expression. "Wights can live to be a thousand years old. Can you imagine how young I am to them?"

Nora's eyes widened. "And you? How long will you live?"

"All in all? Probably about three hundred, four hundred years. If I don't fall in battle before."

"Well. That goes without saying."

Nora was stunned. She pondered how long three hundred years were. Owen was good at the histories of the world. What might the world have been like three hundred years ago? Or even one hundred years ago? She had no idea. Probably not that different. Same people doing the same things, she guessed. Eating and drinking and making sure they had enough of both, working, marrying, and being given in marriage. Children. Blah, blah, blah. Nothing ever really changed, did it? Or maybe humans didn't live long enough to see the change.

"Are there more like you? Half-wights?"

He ran a hand through his dark hair. Owen did that too. Did full wights even have hair? Every picture Nora had seen of the wights showed them as lizard-like, hairless. She cocked her head and studied his face for the first time. If the eyes didn't put you off, he was handsome in his own way. Handsome not as in good-looking, but striking in his hard masculinity. *Yeah, definitely striking,* she thought. Those eyes, though.

"Not in the north, no. But far in the south, beyond the desert sands, there are large clans of half-wights in the mountains. They stay among themselves mostly."

He emptied his cup.

"Why do you ask?"

Nora shrugged.

"You're a master pilgrim. A master warrior. I was wondering..."

"Yes?"

"See, my father was a master smith. You can only be a master when you teach someone else your trade. You call yourself master. I assume you've had apprentices?"

"Ah." Diaz stared into the fire. It reflected in his black eyes. "No, I have not."

"No?" Nora's brow furrowed. "Why not? No one asked you before?"

His face was unreadable. Diaz took a deep breath and checked the depth of his cup for a last sip of tea. There was nothing left, though. He pursed his lips.

"Teaching another person is a weighty commitment. For now, I have given my oath to the prince to aid him on his quest to find the Living Blade."

He gave her a look as though daring her to ask him already. Nora gave him back her empty cup.

He took it; their fingertips brushed briefly. The back of his hand was scarred white like the snow. The scars were old, but looked as though he had held his hand against a burning ember. Or someone had held a burning ember against his hand, anyway. She snatched her fingers away and glanced at his black eyes.

"Thanks," she said.

"You're welcome."

"I'm warmer now. And I think I'm going to drop unconscious for a long while."

He nodded.

Nora lay back on the rank, untanned bear pelt and was only mildly surprised to still be alive while the mountain bear was now dead. When her back touched the fur, she moaned in relief. Lying down was so, so good. Being warm was so, so good, too. Her eyes closed, and she was asleep before Diaz had stowed away both cups.

CHAPTER 7

THEY WERE STILL IN THE midst of the Plains when the weather finally decided to play by its usual strength. The storm moon, the month was called. And storm it did. The winds howled around the two travelers on the grassy Plains with nothing to stand in the way, no shelter for the pair to hide under. They kept moving from one small woodland to the next along the Plains, heads bowed and hooded, leaning against the wind. The already sparse conversation died as the wind snatched every word from Nora's lips, tearing at her voice. It was pointless to try any talk. Besides, Diaz didn't even bother to turn around to answer her most of the time. He always walked a few paces in front, leading her forward. And by the end of the day, when she was utterly exhausted, he was so far in front of her that she would have to yell for him to hear. Not that she had the breath for it. Sometimes days would go by without an exchange. It was very silent traveling with Master Diaz.

Day took long to break in the brooding gray, and dusk fell early. And always the icy wind, sheets of sleeting rain. The last few days, Diaz had them march on for what felt like hours as night fell around them in the early afternoon. His half-wight eyes could see in the dark, Nora guessed, because under the clouded sky, with no heavenly light to guide her, she stumbled and groped while he kept going straight.

She tripped over something and fell, instinctively reaching out with both hands to break her fall. The jarring impact with the sodden ground sent a flare of blinding pain into her shoulder, which was still healing. She fought her way back up to a kneeling position and tried to peer into the gloom around her, massaging her hurt shoulder. She couldn't see anything but grass before her. She rose clumsily, first to one knee, then pushing herself up. But there was still no sign of the wight. Her heart rose into her throat.

"Diaz!"

She called his name softly, but the wind was stronger. So she called louder, her voice breaking with effort. There he was, more to her left than she had thought, and her heart skipped to see him coming toward her in the darkness. That felt...weird. But still, he had saved her life. She was depending on him getting her to the Temple of the Wind. And though she resented the thought of being dependent, she understood she'd never make it across the Plains on her own. So she took his hand as he reached out to her, muttering something in his own language she was happy to not understand—although the tone was such that she *could* understand.

Hand in hand into the dark, like in the old stories: a long time ago, not far from here, but far enough, a wight met a maiden fair and took her with him into the night. And she was never seen again. Only, in her own tale, it was a half-wight, and Nora didn't consider herself to be very fair, considering all the grime building up.

Diaz had meant for them to reach a small wood they had seen before the light had faded. But now they sat in a shallow bowl of grass, the winds whistling above their heads, no firewood, no light, no warmth, no talking—all because Nora had fallen. She was so drained she felt like crying. Because why not? But she was too tired to cry. After a few shuddering dry sobs, she half hid her face in the fur she had huddled into, breathed onto her cold fingers, and closed her eyes. She felt Diaz sit down next to her. He moved so close that their legs were touching. For a moment she just sat there, hands curled in her lap. Then she pulled out her leather waterskin and took a sip.

"You know Ridger's Muck?" she asked.

"No." He moved beside her, trying to get comfortable. "But I know Fisherman's Muck. They drink it on the coastline villages around Dernberia. Strong brew. Is it the same?"

"Yeah, pretty much. Although every village, every household has its own recipe, of course."

She frowned after taking another gulp of water. They were talking more than they had the last few days.

"I like mine with elderberry syrup. Sometimes I put fennel seeds in as well. I wish I had some. My throat really hurts. Good job we don't have much food. I couldn't swallow it properly anyway."

"You'll be out of the cold soon."

"How soon?"

"Depends on you." She stiffened and he amended his statement. "Probably another two weeks of traveling."

"What's it like? The temple?"

"It's a haven of peace." Diaz cleared his throat. The rasp stayed. "There aren't many pilgrims left there. A handful, maybe. We used to be many, hundreds. But now, few want to live by our code. Too ancient, too restrictive. Things may have changed. I was there last three years ago. But I have a good friend there. Perhaps my best," he added, frowning.

"Is he…human?" Nora prompted.

Diaz's lips twitched.

"He is a she. And yes, Master Cumi is very much human. She's a…a healer, a very talented one. One you haven't seen the likes of before. She's also a very capable leader."

"A woman as a leader, huh?" Nora half smiled. "I'm shocked at the thought."

"The temple is also safe and warm. And the food's good, too, as far as I remember. But the best thing? Deep down under the temple are caves with small pools of hot water sprung from the depths of the earth. Hot springs make for hot baths."

"Hot baths without hauling buckets? You tease." She closed her eyes. "I can't remember warmth."

"They'll be the first thing I show you, then."

"I'll bathe after I've seen Owen."

"You should bathe first."

She flushed and buried her face deeper into the fur. It was true. She smelled like…well, like a person who hadn't bathed in a while. Her fingernails were black, and she had managed to tie her hair into a tight braid to keep the grease out of her face. She washed her hands and face fastidiously whenever possible, but she'd been in the wild for nearly a month now and it showed. And smelled. As if he were better, though!

Diaz cleared his throat. Again. It never helped.

"I meant to say…" he started.

"It's all right." Her voice was muffled by her cloak. She was too tired to fight.

"Women usually smell better than men, anyway," he finished.

She laughed through her nose. There was a long pause after that. She leaned back, trying to relax the aching muscles in the small of her back. The two of them lay side by side, shoulder to shoulder.

Suddenly Diaz twitched beside her. He jumped up and lay flat against the other side of the bowl. It was hard to make out his shape, even though he was barely an arm's length away.

"Do you see it?"

He pointed into the dark. Nora leaned forward, eyes watering, staring into nothingness.

Diaz's hand cupped the back of her head and turned it slightly to the right. Something was there. Like a twinkling star, only on the ground.

"A firc?"

"A fire. Under the trees we wanted to reach earlier."

Her heart lifted.

"Maybe it's Owen. I mean, Prince Bashan's company."

"No." Diaz hoisted himself up to the bowl's rim. He bent back down to Nora. "Stay here. Stay quiet. Stay out of sight."

"How do you know?" Nora strained to see something in the dark. "Wait. I can't come?"

"No." His hoarse whisper was already fading.

Nora grumbled a little as she lay back in the grass, but she was secretly relieved that she didn't have to get up and run around in the dark with Diaz. Funny, though. The night was colder without him by her side.

When a hand touched her shoulder, Nora woke with a start and realized two things instantly. First, it was daytime already. The sun was a low white drop behind the clouds. And second, her knife wasn't in her hand. She was defenseless and alone and—*fuck!*—they were coming to get her! Strong hands held her flailing arms tight, and panic crawled up her throat. She screamed.

"It's me. Noraya." She saw the now-familiar wight eyes staring down at her. Diaz had returned.

"It's me," he repeated softly and let her go.

"You were sleeping," he then said disapprovingly.

"I was only resting my eyes!" Nora said. "Yeah, I was sleeping. You told me to stay here, so here I stayed. I'm tired and wounded, you know?"

"The sun rose two hours ago."

Diaz started pacing around the bowl. She wasn't moving fast enough for him, Nora knew, but couldn't will her body to hurry up. A thin coat of hoarfrost lined her sleeping fur and she was stiff.

"So, the fire?" she prompted, though she knew she wouldn't like the answer.

"There are more than fifty men camping in the woods between us and the Temple of the Wind."

"Fifty?" Nora stopped rolling her fur together, shocked at the sheer number, then hastened to stow it away. Goose bumps rose on her forearms that had nothing to do with the cold. Her mind was racing.

"What do you think...?"

"...they're doing crossing the Plains?" Diaz glanced around. "I'm not sure. They're not refugees, as there are no families. Not mercenaries—too few have weapons of worth. It matters not. I don't plan to ask them. We are two. They are many. We should be able to be quicker and overtake them by this afternoon."

He looked down at her with a grim expression.

"I shudder to think what would have been, had one of them found you sleeping."

Nora stuck a few strips of cured venison into her mouth, chewing mechanically, and nodded.

They struck out north and walked a wide circle around the forest where the fire had been. Nora picked up Diaz's speed and kept close, watching the horizon as they marched. The Plains were deceptively empty. They saw no one before darkness fell once more, and this time, Nora took Diaz's hand.

CHAPTER 8

NORA TWISTED AWAY FROM THE thrust of the dagger, and her nose squashed against Owen's shoulder blade. Ah. It was just a nightmare, then. Her right hand still felt flabby flesh close around it, felt the scrape of the young man's skull at the tip of her knife, jarring her hand, half waking her.

She buried her face deeper into the warmth and felt the steady rhythm of another person breathing next to her. It calmed her pounding heart a little. Her hand still held her dream knife so tightly her fingernails had imprinted little half-moons into her palm. She consciously opened her fist. It was just a dream.

Owen smelled different, though. What was that scent? Mostly bear. And reek—that was her. But there was a trace of something. She took a deep breath. Like a fresh woodland smell. Owen didn't smell like that. Leather, ink, paper, and charcoal, yes. Was it rosemary?

Her brow furrowed in her dream-hazed wakefulness. Owen wasn't even near her. He was far, far away. She tensed and was fully awake.

It wasn't Owen. It was Diaz. Her face was buried so deep in the folds of his cloak her eyelashes scraped against the wool when she blinked. Oh crap. Should she roll over? Pretend to still be asleep? He must have noticed her bump into him. She waited for some agonizingly long seconds, but he continued breathing regularly. Fine. Maybe he was sleeping too. She relaxed a little.

Strange how sleeping together was so intimate, she thought. Not *that* sleeping together, obviously. Rather, you let down all guard, trusting the other person not to abuse your vulnerability. You were close, moved together, always half conscious of the one next to you.

Diaz knew her much better than she knew him, Nora realized. Because he was mostly awake, keeping watch while she slept, watching her when she had nightmares or shifted when her shoulder ached, and probably, when she drooled all over her arm, too. This time he was asleep and she was awake, and now she'd watch over him. Pay the trust back.

Darkness still lingered. Dawn had not yet broken. She sighed and curled up closer to Diaz to relish his warmth a little bit longer and to breathe in more rosemary scent. It made her feel a little homesick—a yearning for simple kitchen work, chopping herbs, roasting vegetables from the garden. He had pulled the bear fur over the two of them while she slept. It was warm and dark and safe. Maybe she could still get some sleep.

"Bad dream?"

Nora threw the bear pelt off in a huff and jogged ten paces into the brisk cold, slapping her arms and stomping her feet to get warm.

"Don't you ever fucking sleep?"

"I do." Diaz shifted from his side onto his back. He squared his shoulders while his eyes remained closed. "Though not as much as you."

She ran her hands over her numb face.

"What time is it?"

"About three hours to dawn."

"You didn't even open your eyes."

"I don't have to."

"Because you're so perfect."

"Keep the noise down, will you? There might be people nearby who'd kill us as a sacrifice to the gods."

"I'll kill you as a sacrifice to the gods," she muttered.

He laughed at that. It was the laugh of a glacier at the sight of a single flaming torch. Her ears burned.

"Come on then." He beckoned her with one hand raised out of the fur.

"What?"

"Kill me."

Nora snorted.

"Said the guy with his eyes still closed." She stuck her fingers into her armpits for warmth and moved from one foot to another.

Diaz opened his eyes and stared into the nighttime skies, sighing deeply.

"Battle flashes. It is natural and most warriors know them. During a fight, the body is a vessel for the mind. It is focused on survival. Though it does take in all other details, it switches them out of your consciousness. Later, those details come back to haunt you. You see the deaths you have caused, see the fear in your opponents' eyes before they go down the silent road. You have dealt out death, Noraya, and you are still alive to know it. Be glad."

"'Glad' is not the word I'd use." Nora swallowed hard and stared at the dark sky above, treading the ground. "What about you, master warrior, do you ever...?"

"Have bad dreams? All the time. I remember every face of those I killed. And in my memory, they will live longer than they have walked this earth. Sometimes I feel regret. Sometimes, remorse. Most days, though, I feel alive. Killing is an art. And I am a master. Now ask me."

"Ask you what?"

"What you were going to ask me the other day." He sat up effortlessly and rested his elbows on his knees.

"I was going to ask you something?"

"Don't pretend."

Nora bent over, fascinated with the tips of her boots. She laughed quietly and shook her head. A minute ago she had been lying next to him, guiltily enjoying a little physical contact. And now this conversation was turning bizarre. Maybe she was still asleep and only her dream had shifted. But it was too cold to be a dream. The air smelled of snow and was as refreshing as a bucket of ice water.

"Yeah, well, will you teach me how to fight like you do?"

"I told you I cannot at this time take a student, as my commitment lies elsewhere."

"I didn't say 'apprentice' me, did I?"

"Indeed. But the answer is still no."

She shook her head once more and pressed her lips together.

"Why? Because I'm a girl?"

"No," he said slowly. "Because every art needs discipline. And that is something you need to learn first."

"Discipline."

"Yes."

They shared a look.

"You know..." Nora took a deep breath. "For a master warrior craftsman, you talk a lot of philosophical bullshit."

CHAPTER 9

THEY HAD BEEN SKIRTING THE Crest Mountains and now drew close to the woodlands that lay at their feet, marking the end of the Plains. In the evening, they ate their last meal of scraps of whatever they had left in their backpacks. She felt his eyes on her all the time now and it got under her skin, irritating like a splinter she couldn't quite pull out.

During the night, it started to snow. As they set out again by daylight, tiny white flecks danced before their eyes and speckled the grass. It was cold, but the snow wouldn't yet linger. The pale sun melted most of it as it fell, and by midday it would be gone, leaving muddy slush behind.

Moving through the woods was more straining than walking the Plains, with their rolling waves of grass. The undergrowth was thick, and even when Nora and Diaz stuck to the wild paths of deer and other woodland creatures, Diaz had his sword at the ready to chop through the brambles and bushes. Underneath the intertwined branches, there was no snow slush, but Nora cursed a few times under her breath when her long braid snagged on the grasping, low twigs, jerking her head back again and again. Nora noticed Diaz pulling up his hood and wordlessly followed suit shortly afterward. They plowed on through the rest of the day. At dusk, the wight raised his eyebrows at her hood with a hint of a smile playing in the corners of his eyes when he turned to check on her. She spoke before he could commend her for her observation skills.

"What is it?" Her legs wouldn't carry her another mile. "Are we stopping already?"

Diaz sheathed his sword.

"Here is as good a place as any. The sun is down already. The next hour would only find us stumbling over bushes and into thorns."

She nodded and collapsed onto a heap of old leaves caught in the roots of a birch tree.

"What if he doesn't want to see me?" Nora's eyes were closed.

"Who?"

"Owen."

"Why shouldn't he?"

"We didn't really leave each other on a positive note. And I've...done some really bad stuff." She swallowed hard and then winced in pain at her sore throat.

Diaz crouched next to her. His hand tapped his leg as he thought. After a while, he sighed deeply.

"He'll want to see you."

It was Nora's turn to sigh.

After surviving the attack on the Ridge three weeks ago, she'd been waiting for the divine hammer to come blazing from the sky to smite her down for the sacrilege of taking another human's life. Waiting for the earth to swallow her up, for the world to be changed at its core. Nothing had happened. The world was the same. And for the most part, Nora was the same. Just add some gruesome nightmares.

In the same situation, she'd kill the marauders and their chieftain over again. She knew as much. But did that make her right? How did you judge morals when the gods were dead and long gone and there was no celestial standard to go by, only your own conscience? She wanted to ask Diaz about that, about the pilgrim's code, the passing of judgment, and how he dealt out death as penalty, but she fell asleep before she found the right words.

The next days went by much as the last day had. More trudging through woodlands. More snow, even under the trees. Nora registered the white specks around her from a far-removed place within. Normally the first snow was always her favorite. The white formed a pure blanket, a clean slate, making everything fresh and new. She tried to feel excited. But she felt frozen to the bone. And oh, look! More trees.

Diaz and Nora came upon the temple suddenly as they stumbled onto the road leading to it from the underbrush in the late afternoon. One moment there was snow-brushed canopy, then the phallic structure of the temple piercing the sky.

From afar, the Temple of the Wind looked like the gods of old had taken the spiraled horn of a huge animal and planted it apart to stand alone, a white, beaming watchtower across the Plains. It was shaped like a high pinnacle, with jutting balconies, smaller towers, and platforms with hanging gardens; the temple could be seen far and wide. A wall encircled the foot of the temple mountain, and in the wall was a gate flanked by statues of a man and a woman carrying pilgrim's staffs.

Traffic clogged the road. A lot of traffic. And all of it moved steadily toward the temple in clusters and family circles. Diaz pulled his hood far over his face to hide his eyes in shadow. It didn't help. Whenever they passed a group of people, one look at his face made them blanch and turn away, making the sign of evil as Nora scowled at them. The odd pair walked by the other travelers with loaded backpacks or wagons full of homey things, bored children, and animals, too. Droves of cattle and sheep lined the broad road, and hens squabbled between the hooves.

Ahead was a bit of a jam—a long waiting line that sluggishly moved forward at the pace of a snail. They overtook a large family wagon, and Nora strode past a group of three young men about her own age when a grumpy goat decided it had had enough and knocked its head into a bystander. The big lad tumbled over, dragging one of his mates down with him. The last of the three boys bumped into Nora and turned around to berate her but then caught sight of Diaz looming next to her. The boy's mouth worked around the cursing and his eyes darted between Nora and Diaz. Poor boys. They looked like farmers. One of them had a sword, though it was old and nicked.

"Fuck!" the skinny boy in front of her said. "Is that a wight?"

"No," Nora answered. "He's a half-human pilgrim master on his way to the temple."

Diaz snorted and pulled the rim of his hood deeper over his face. He passed her by without another glance, moving toward the front of the gates. People were flowing around the disturbance, muttering and grumbling; the family next to them was wrestling with the kicking goat. Nora was keenly aware of the three young men ogling her like they'd never seen a girl before. Or maybe they'd never seen such a dirty girl before. She smiled, though it never reached her eyes.

"Are there usually so many people on the road to the Temple of the Wind?"

The skinny boy regarded her up and down.

"Dunno."

She had to refrain from rolling her eyes.

"I'm Noraya. I'm looking for my brother, Owen. Have you seen him?"

"Dunno," he said again, his voice breaking into a squeak. "What's he look like?"

"Like me."

More ogling.

"Can't say we have," the youth said. "You look like you come from Nessa. But you speak as though you're from up north."

Nora gazed at the boy in front of her. He was the youngest of the three and the skinniest, yet he also seemed to be the smartest. Even though his dirty blond hair looked like his mother had pulled the kitchen pot over his head and cut along the rim. She hesitated, but—whatever—she saw no harm in telling them a version of the truth.

"I'm from Owen's Ridge. Or what's left of it. My brother and I crossed the Plains to reach the temple. But I wasn't expecting so many on the same road. And I've lost him."

Well, it was mostly true.

"No one crosses the Plains in winter," the lad with the sword said, finally dislodging himself from his mate. They were both lucky not to have accidentally impaled themselves on their sad excuse for a weapon. "That's just dumb."

"Owen's Ridge? That's a long way." The skinny boy stared at her again. "We're from Woodston. Or, well, from a village close by Woodston. Elmswell. You wouldn't know it. When the raiders came, we ran through the woods up to Woodston's gates, but they wouldn't take us in. Too many refugees already. No more room, they said. So we figured we'd come down to the temple instead. Guess that goes for everyone else here."

"Your village was attacked?" Nora asked.

"Marauding bands. They're everywhere now." The young man shrugged.

"They are?" Nora frowned.

"Neeze wept! You always asking dumb questions? Where've you been the last few weeks?" the big lad with the sword said.

"I've been running for my life across the Plains." Nora gave the young man a sharp look. He turned away, blushing.

"Don't mind Brenn." The skinny lad hawked a load of green slime from his nose. "He don't mean harm. We look after each other, you know? We could look after you, too. Until you find your brother, I mean. Better than the…other company you were traveling with."

The skinny lad lowered his voice at the last sentence and glared at Diaz's back far up front. Nora bristled.

"You look after yourselves? And you have one sword for the three of you?" She pinched the bridge of her nose and then held up her hands at the sight of his puzzled look. "I'm sorry. Thanks for the offer, uh…?"

"Larris." The skinny boy pointed two thumbs at himself, then introduced the other two. "Brenn, and the silent guy is Bow."

Bow leered at her while holding up a hunting bow.

"Thanks, Larris. And if you do see someone our age who looks like me..."

"We'll tell him his sister's looking for him."

"Great."

Nora walked briskly forward until she reached Diaz's side once more.

"People just love seeing you, don't they?" she asked.

"I've become used to it."

"Really?"

He gave her a sidelong glance.

"So?" the half-wight said in his familiar deep rumble. "How far does the chaos reach?"

"Well, good old Larris over there says Woodston's gates are closed. He means the town Woodston on the Suthron Pass, doesn't he? How far is that from here?"

"On foot? About a week. Wagons are slower."

"Moorfleet's fallen."

Diaz remained silent.

"And Master Darren's dead. That means there's no one with authority to unite the north under one banner, no last vestige of peace and law and order. Something's going on. There are marauding bands everywhere from Moorfleet to Woodston. Death pits. Fugitives. End of the world." Nora shook her head. "What are we going to do?"

"We?" Diaz raised one eyebrow. "*We* are taking you to the temple and to your brother. That's what we are doing. And then Prince Bashan and I are going to find the Living Blade. And when we find it and the rightful emperor sits on the throne, the north will see peace again."

"You really believe that?"

"I believe it."

Nora raised an eyebrow. If they had been alone, she would have asked him for an explanation. But they weren't. All those weeks of solitude on the Plains and now—

She shrugged and decided not to poke deeper. They were already attracting unwanted attention. He was being unbelievably ignorant about Prince Bashan's character, about legends and mythical objects. But she was following him. So who was really being stupid? She pulled up her hood as he had and they walked the road in silence.

CHAPTER 10

BY DUSK, NORA AND DIAZ passed through the gates, entering the temple courtyards. The grounds of the temple were built like a stone island set in the wide and shallow bay of the Plains. The island's summit was the actual Temple of the Wind, an airy palace filled with light, with spires and balconies overlooking the green sea below. It was easy to imagine white linen curtains billowing in the breeze in the sweltering summer, yet inside it would always be cool, the air filled with the sound of wind chimes made of seashells and exquisite wood, humming eerie music whenever the wind blew through. Now, in winter, the temple glittered like an icicle, sparkling in pure white.

In concentric rings around the base, cobblestone streets branched off the broad but steep causeway, which led ever upward before spooling out into a wide square at the foot of the temple itself, closed in by a round wooden gateway painted red. In the streets stood lime-washed stone houses with slated tile roofs, with balconies and gardens and alleys that shaped the lower courtyards into a labyrinth of passageways. Fountains and springs with statues of pilgrim masters and springs bubbled forth fresh, clean water into carved marble troughs, where Nora and Diaz stooped to drink. The water was hot but not scalding in Nora's hand and it steamed in the cold like breath, a tribute to the god of air.

Nora had never seen so much stone. But the outer rings were in disrepair—crumbling, broken structures with saplings growing between the weeds and grass and cracks in the streets. One elder tree had taken over a forlorn square in one of the side streets. Now there was an elder grove breaking up the cobblestones, roots thick under the crumbling walls. Green lichen grew on the white stone, and the Temple of the Wind showed a twin face. The towering temple itself left Nora with the impression of a regal lady looking down resentfully on the dirty neighbor's children, clutching at her faded skirts.

On the one hand, the streets along the temple's outer walls housed the ghosts of former splendor, while newly arrived herds of sheep and cattle ruminated among overgrown pillars and statues. On the other, the rings closest to the temple were crowded with refugees as though the surrounding lands had been stripped bare of people. Every house there was cobbled together from the pillaged ruins of the outer rings, or by breaking through walls to join them together to sleep at least fifteen to twenty people. Makeshift stalls had been put up in the square. Women haggled, girls carried water, men hammered wooden boards across caved-in roofs, and washing lines hung full of clothes and sheets. The smell of garlic and freshly baked bread wafted down the causeway, making Nora's stomach rumble. Children ran and shrieked in their wild games, and above all, the sounds of industry rang loud and clear.

No one paid the two worn travelers any attention until they reached the round red gates. Beyond that threshold the temple began. Here, as though the temple had chosen its own personification, an elderly woman stood in white robes whipping in the wind, her gray hair tied into two long braids, chains of silver dangling from her earlobes. Her stern face broke into a smile and she opened her arms when Diaz approached.

"Telen," she said as he embraced her. "We have been waiting for your return. I kept a lookout on the road to spot you firsthand. It's been a long time, my friend."

"It's good to be back, Talitha. You grow more beautiful every time."

The woman blue eyes wrinkled in pleasure. Her laugh rang clear and high over the busy marketplace in the courtyard below.

"He is a courteous flatterer, this one." The woman bent over to Nora and winked mischievously.

Nora smiled. A courteous flatterer was not what she would have called Diaz.

"I am Master Talitha of Cumi, pilgrim master and guardian of the Temple of the Wind." The woman bowed, one hand to her heart. Nora bowed lower, just as was expected before age and wisdom. The master turned and gestured for them to follow her up the stairs. "You must be Noraya. I have heard much about you from your brother. He's holed himself up in our library and has set it upon himself to read through every scrap of paper he can find there. Or so it would seem."

"That sounds like Owen."

A huge weight lifted from Nora's heart and it skipped a few beats in an aching yearning as they walked up the stone staircase.

"Are the courtyards full?" Diaz asked Master Cumi with a frown.

"Most of the refugees from the surrounding countryside are in some of the courtyard houses. So much unrest all across the north since the emperor died! And I fear that after the fall of Moorfleet, more people will stream to this sanctuary."

They climbed the stairs, the two masters in front, Nora behind them. It was a steep, narrow staircase with no railing. Nora stayed in the middle and hoped no one would come down while they were going up.

"But I dare say there's room enough. Perhaps we could convene tomorrow, you and I, and Master Akela?" Master Cumi spoke to Diaz while climbing.

Master Cumi didn't need to catch a breath and here Nora was, sweating already. She really hated heights. Really hated depths, too. And they weren't even a quarter of the way up.

"Akela still hasn't left for Lara's embrace?" Diaz asked.

"He keeps on saying he'll live to be ninety. I believe it." Master Cumi smiled. "Prince Bashan told me you found Master Darren dead in the Shrine of Hin. This is bad news in itself, especially now, amid the chaos. Though it may also be good news. I do believe you are still the oldest master in the north."

Nora looked at Diaz, who winced.

"Darren was murdered," he said. "I will find the one behind his death and avenge him."

"Of course. Well then, Akela is the next oldest. Though I doubt he will accept the position of oversight of the entire northern lands. That is something to discuss. I took the liberty of filling some of the empty sleeping chambers of the temple with the prince's men. Though, if you do not approve, Master Diaz, I could still find some accommodation elsewhere."

"The temple is yours, Talitha. I was merely surprised." Diaz waved his hand, dismissing any objection.

He glanced back at Nora to see whether she was still following. They had reached a small platform overlooking the courtyard below. It was far down. Very far down. Nora wiped the sweat from her brow.

"How many flights of stairs are there?" she asked, glancing up.

"Seven," Master Talitha said with a smile. "Everyone hates the stairs. But they are the best protection in case the outer wall and gate should fall."

Nora looked back over her shoulder to the high wall and the heavy gates that were lifted by wheels and pulleys.

"Have they ever?"

"Many times," Diaz answered. "Though not in a long while."

"Let us hope it shall remain that way," Master Cumi said.

"We ran into some trouble. Nora is wounded in the shoulder," Diaz said as they climbed again. "Perhaps you could take a look later."

Master Cumi stopped and looked at Nora.

"Really? Is it a fresh wound? Right or left?"

"The right shoulder. I was hit by an arrow three weeks ago."

Three lifetimes ago, more like.

At the top of the everlong stairs was a smaller courtyard before the actual Temple of the Wind. It was a beautifully tended garden area even in winter, with bushes of sage and lavender with their silvery leaves next to laurel trees in darker shades of green. In the middle of the slender trees, a statue of a woman holding a long sword to the sky dominated the small space. Water surrounded the statue's feet and pooled there before running into a stone basin leading into the temple itself.

"Scyld." Master Talitha knelt down, reached over the water, and touched the statue's bared foot. The toes had been sanded down by generations of people touching them as they walked past. "The founder of our order, and our guardian."

Nora nodded at Scyld in greeting. "I guess that's supposed to be the Living Blade."

Talitha exchanged a glance with Diaz, who shrugged. She smiled at Nora, waving them onward into the temple. It was airy and light within due to the many windows arching around the walls. Nora groaned at the sight of more stairs. Leading up and down in winding spirals, this time.

"Our temple is on the very site she smote Tuil, Lord of the Wind, to the ground with the Blade. He fell and the ancient kingdom of Vella was buried underneath him. The earth swallowed them up, and the Crest Mountains were born. And out of a rib taken from Tuil's side, Scyld fashioned the Temple of the Wind. To remind us that we must never again cower."

"A rib, huh? That's nice," Nora said, tripping on a step. "I know who Tuil is. Patron saint of twins. Everyone always thought Owen was Tuil's twin."

Talitha's sharp eyes flashed.

"Indeed. That would make you…?"

"The other one's."

"I see." Master Cumi turned to Nora and Diaz in front of two large wooden doors. "Telen, I have arranged for your usual quarters to be cleaned and ready for you. I shall accompany Noraya to hers."

Nora opened her mouth, but Diaz was faster.

"Noraya will be wanting to see her brother before she retires. I can show her to the library and to her sleeping quarters after."

"Very well."

Talitha clapped her hands together, and her silver bracelets dangled on her wrists like bells ringing out her departure. She gave Diaz directions to Nora's room and then bowed.

"I shall see you in the evening. I must prepare dinner for over forty people, and I'm running short of ideas as it is. Ah, I know. It'll be roasted something, like all the other evenings so far."

She smiled one last time and vanished around a bend.

"I like her. Your friend. She's nice." Nora followed Diaz up the winding stairs. "So, let me guess—the library is on the top floor?"

"No, just the next level up." He looked over his shoulder.

"Oh, good."

"The sleeping quarters are on the top floor."

Diaz gave her a lopsided smile as she grimaced.

"A joke. They're far below us. Be of good cheer, Noraya. Down is always easier than up."

Nora wheezed. A joke? Maybe there was some magic to this place to have Diaz remove the stick up his ass. Shocking! First he said he wasn't all wight; now he wasn't all jerk. Next thing he'd tell her, he wasn't a proper master pilgrim. They took the next bend and the half-wight pointed at a wooden door carved with patterns resembling vines and flowers. Nora paused to catch her breath. She bent double, hands on her knees, strength nearly giving out. But not yet.

This was it. Journey's end. Behind this door was her twin brother, firmly wedged into the place he loved best. A library. Among all the other geniuses of the past, their tomes whispering their thoughts to him even centuries after they had gone. Her heart was beating loudly in her ears. There would be no more danger, no more sudden jolts of nauseous leaping into action. No more cold and deprivation. And tonight she would sleep in an actual bed. In an actual room. In an actual building. And alone. Her half-wight heating system wouldn't lie next to her. Diaz had his head cocked to the side, waiting. She stared across an ever-deepening abyss of awkward silence into those dark eyes, conjuring up the words within her. He had saved her life. And she'd never be able to repay him. And how did you put that into words exactly?

"I wanted to say…" she started. "That thing you did…"

He raised his eyebrows and waited, hand on the doorknob. She took a deep breath and pressed it all out in one go.

"I'm glad you came for me, Diaz. I wouldn't be alive or here if you hadn't."

She looked up into his face, which hadn't changed much in the last few seconds. Maybe the eyebrows had gone up a little higher.

"You're still very welcome," he said and pushed open the door.

Chapter 11

THE LIBRARY WAS A LARGE rounded room that curved with the temple's tower shape. No wall was a straight line, so all the bookshelves stood not up against the walls but in double rows like eager soldiers, leaving a small passageway between them that smelled of dust and parchment. Rays of light with specks of dust swirling in their unseen currents slanted down each of the rows, and the middle of the room was dominated by a long reading table. It was heaped with paper and scrolls and codices and lost half-empty mugs of some liquid, making it look just like Owen's desk back home on the Ridge, only on a larger scale.

Nora saw her brother and her heart leaped painfully to the back of her tongue. He holding an engaged discussion with none other than Prince Bashan, the once and future emperor as it were. They both stood, hands on the table, like generals poring over maps of war. Her smile wavered with emotion. She swallowed the lump down.

"I'm just saying it would be more logical to look for the Cauldron of Arrun than for the Blade itself. Every source I've read so far shows that every wielder of the Blade breaks down after a time. Kandar came to this temple spouting nonsense in an ancient tongue no one could identify and sometimes thought he was a woman. The Cauldron holds no such risks." Owen held up his hands.

"I don't want the fucking Cauldron of Arrun!" Bashan interrupted, throwing his hands up. "I want the City of Arrun. My city. The imperial city. And for that I need the Blade. So just find me the Blade and spare me your sidetracking."

Owen ran a hand through his hair. It stood up like raven's feathers. He looked tired, with dark rings under his eyes, his jaw clenched tight. Nora took it all in at once, drunk on the sight of that so-familiar face she hadn't seen for such a long time. One thing was new: a thin red scratch ran along Owen's left cheek, from his nose to his ear, like someone had carved him an extra smile. He kept picking at the scab while Bashan talked.

"Well, the Blade must be here," Owen said. "In the north. Our safest bet is if we strike north as Kandar did, past Moorfleet, and head through the Wightingerode."

"And ask the wights where the Blade is?" Bashan threw his head back and flared his nostrils.

"You have connections, don't you?"

"Oh, yes, when Telen shows up, we can just ask him whether he knows where exactly his great-grandfather killed my ancestor, the founder of the empire," Bashan scoffed.

"If it helps," Diaz spoke into the ensuing pause, "I could ask my father what he knows. Though I doubt it would be much. If the wights knew where the Blade was, they would have used it themselves to gain back their lost lands."

Bashan and Owen looked up and saw Diaz and Nora standing at the edge of the row of bookshelves. The prince sighed audibly in relief.

"Thank the gods, reason has finally returned."

"Nora!" Owen actually sounded surprised.

She took a step forward but then hesitated, suddenly unsure what to do. All this way—what if he didn't want to see her? What if it'd be awkward between them?

She needn't have worried. Owen leaped over the table, scattering paper all across the floor, and smothered her in an embrace before the paper stopped falling. He was warm and smelled of knowledge and soap.

"I am so, so sorry," he kept saying over and over.

"It's all right," she answered again and again.

They heard the soft talk of Diaz and Bashan in the background, but mostly the familiar sound of each other's heartbeat. Nora started to laugh. Or cry. She wasn't sure which. Owen's shoulder became damp, either way. Her brother took a deep, shuddering breath and rested his chin on top of her head. He sniffed.

"You reek," Owen said after a moment.

"I'm sorry." Nora dug her face deeper into his shoulder, laughing. Then she looked up. "What happened to your face?"

"It got cut. What happened with you?"

"I got shot. Long story."

Two heartbeats of silence.

"You didn't happen to bring my stone collection?" Owen asked.

Nora shook her head.

"Pity. I've found a translation of Kerrulan's essay on the nature of minerals here. It's quite fascinating. Especially his theory of similarity. He says if you smash a mineral into pieces, each piece will resemble the structure of the larger stone. If you were able to grind it down to its very last piece, that piece would still have the structure of the large stone. His conclusion: the essence of stone is embedded in every part. Although, he then finishes his essay with a catalog of stone categories instead of asking the real question."

"And what would that be?"

Nora pulled away from her brother to look him in the eye. His sharp mind flashed before her in a mischievous wink.

"Does the similarity exist merely in stones, or in all life? Look at you and me. We're similar enough on the outside, but crushed into our very essence, I wonder whether we'd still resemble each other."

"I missed you, Owen." Her voice broke, but her smile didn't.

He nodded sagely.

"I missed you too."

Chapter 12

Master Akela, Master Cumi, and Diaz had all convened in the kitchen. The great hall was too chilly for Akela, who had grumbled into his cowl and then promptly fallen asleep in his chair next to the fire. Akela was younger than Diaz, if only by two years. But then, those were a lot of years for a human. Diaz looked about the kitchen, thinking of a painting that hung in the great council chamber of the Temple of Arrun, depicting a Convening of Masters. In oil colors on canvas, twelve masters sat on identical chairs in a perfect circle, a symbol for the equality of all opinions, all viewpoints. The masters in the picture were discoursing with solemn expressions, as though they were discussing matters of great social and political import, the fate of the world, perhaps even "philosophical bullshit," as Noraya would say. Diaz smiled. In all his years as a master, he had never been to a meeting that had even come close to that picture.

Right now, though, this was ideal—much better than the painting. He was clean, rested, warm, and not hungry.

"Calla, pour the tea," Cumi told a young blonde girl who hovered behind her.

"Where's Kenneth?" Diaz asked.

"He asks you to excuse him. He has to be with his bees," Cumi said, watching the girl pour scalding-hot water into their cups. "I don't know why. It's winter, after all. You remember Calleva, Telen?"

He was about to say he didn't, then stopped himself.

"Master Rallis's initiate? You're training to become a midwife?"

Calla blushed and cast her eyes down.

"Yes, master."

"A very useful skill. And Calla is very good," Cumi said. "I'm thinking we could specialize in healing, too."

The girl blushed a deeper red. Then she looked up and considered Diaz with large eyes. There was no fear or repulsion in them. Just curiosity. That was...different. Diaz shifted on his chair, cupping his tea with both hands.

"Where is Master Rallis?"

"She died, Master Diaz," Calla said. "Last summer."

Diaz arched his eyebrows at Cumi across the table.

"Oh, that," Cumi said and waved a hand. "Must have been a heart attack. There was really nothing I could do. She was quite old, you know. One minute she was standing right there next to the sink, and the next she was on the floor. Calla has all but replaced her. She's not a master yet, but she'll get there. That was your cue to leave, Calla."

They had tea and almond biscuits. All was set. Cumi waited until the girl closed the kitchen door behind her.

"So, what do you think?"

He shrugged.

"She's copying your styling, and it doesn't suit her. You should tell her. However, I don't know her enough to decide whether she should be a master or not."

"Akela? What do you think?" Cumi beamed at Akela's answering snore. "Yes, I think we should wait, too. She's still very young."

"You're still very young," Diaz said.

"I don't feel it." Her bangles jingled as she picked up her cup and held it to her lips. "I'm old, you know. Very old. And tired."

"One is as old as one feels." Diaz took a sip of tea.

"And how would you know?" Cumi gave him a sharp look. He held the tea in his mouth, cup still half raised.

She took a deep breath and smiled an apology.

"I'm sorry. Shall we start over?"

Diaz swallowed and put down the cup.

"Very well."

Cumi neatly folded her hands before her on the table.

"There are a number of things we need to discuss. We'll need to talk about the refugees and the situation in the lower courtyards. And the untimely death of Master Darren, of course, and the vacancy he leaves. I think I can speak for Master Akela and say he turns down the position of Guardian of the North."

"It's the third row to your right, my boy," Akela said, eyes opening for a moment before he settled back into his slumber.

"So there's that to discuss," Cumi continued. "I've sent word to the Temple of Arrun, but as it's winter, who knows when we'll get an answer back? Though that is probably to our advantage. Have you met the boy they sent to the Shrine of Hin last year? Twenty-three-year-old arrogant little flunky. Every letter Darren sent me was one of complaint. So, naturally, the mother temple in Arrun will want to name the flunky Guardian of the North."

Cumi smoothed her hair with a hand, adjusting a silver chain caught behind her ear.

"Did you know Empress Vashti has issued a decree which undoes the taxation laws her father imposed on the order? She's trying to break the chain, poor girl. We'll see how long she lasts among the lions of Arrun. But who knows? Maybe it is true what they say and the world would be a better place if a woman ruled it."

"Don't you already?"

Cumi smiled.

"I wish. My main job right now is keeping the dignitaries of various small villages and hamlets from lording it over each other. Having second thoughts on joining Bashan on his quest?"

She lashed her question out like a whip. They gazed at each other over the table. A candle flickered its soft light across Cumi's face, blurring the creases that showed in daylight. Diaz remembered when her hair was black and not gray. Her piercing eyes were still the same, though. He leaned on his elbows, folding his hands before his face.

"No," he said.

"Liar." She smiled. "So, Telen Diaz, as the eldest pilgrim master among us, do you accept the authority and duty of Guardian of the North?"

"I have given my word to help find the Blade. When I return, though, I will," he added.

"You will?" Her eyes narrowed.

"Yes."

Her eyes narrowed even more.

"Such change." She tilted her head and gazed at him intently with a pinched mouth. "I wonder…is it the girl?"

He laughed at that.

"You have met Noraya, yes? She's hardly what would inspire a man to any action other than throwing one's hands up in despair."

"She did seem to have a wild manner about her." Cumi's eyebrows arched high.

He shook his head.

"She has no manners whatsoever," he said. "She is a mixture of pride and impertinent independence. But she is tough, enduring. Uncomplaining. In her home village, she took on a number of men alone with nothing more than a kitchen knife and a meat cleaver."

"So she is insane as well. Or did she know you were there?"

"No, she did not."

"You like her," Cumi observed, a smile playing around her lips.

He frowned. "I am…intrigued, perhaps. She—"

"What?"

He folded his hands on the table and stared at his intertwined fingers.

"I've never met anyone more fit to train as a swordsman. Swordswoman, in this case," he corrected.

"Then why don't you train her?"

"I can't," he said simply.

"I see you have both hands still remaining to you. They are capable of holding weapons, yes?"

"Yes."

"Aren't you still the best warrior in the order?"

"Again, yes."

"Then I don't see your problem, Telen. Train the girl if you want. If she has the talent you think she has, no one would suit her better as a master than you."

He sighed.

"A male master shouldn't take on a female student," he said.

A short silence followed that statement.

Cumi clicked her tongue in disapproval. "A woman can never be a warrior, never be a leader, never be better than a man—that is what you would hide behind."

"What is this girl to you?" He ran a hand through his hair, exasperated that the subject still hadn't changed.

"A test, Telen." She shrugged. "I had expected differently from you after what I heard about your time at the Temple of Fire."

"What you heard?" The sensation of a hand trailing over his burning chest played on his heart. His breath faltered.

Opposite him, Cumi watched his expression ardently.

"I was visited last summer by a few young pilgrims from the Temple of Fire," she explained slowly. "They came bearing a message from the prophetess there. A message of hope. A hope they desired to spread throughout the north. They left for Hin's shrine and Moorfleet shortly after, lamenting that they hadn't had the chance to meet Master Diaz in person—the great Master Diaz—but still glad to hear you were in Bashan's company, looking for the Living Blade. You never told me you had been to Shinar's temple."

His mouth was dry.

"I've been to every temple and shrine as part of my pilgrimage," he said, his voice raspier with the heaviness of emotion. "It was…before your time here."

"It was what inspired you to lead the simple life of groundskeeper, I suppose, because that was what you were when I first came here. Some things *do* change."

They shared a long look.

"These pilgrims who visited you—they were young girls," he said.

"Beautiful young girls."

"Each carrying a golden dagger, I guess."

"Gold ever was Shinar's most beloved metal, as it so perfectly reflects the face of his sun."

"What was the message?"

"That your quest will be successful. Bashan will find the Blade," Cumi said with a gleam in her blue eyes. "And that once more the world is about to change because of that mythical sword."

CHAPTER 13

NORA WOKE AND PUSHED HER legs over the edge of the bed. She had slept straight for three days, only dragging her heavy body from the bed to drink, eat, and avoid soiling herself. She felt a pang of guilt whenever she woke and saw sunlight peeking in through the small window, but her limbs just wouldn't move. Lying in a proper bed felt so good. It even relaxed the muscles in her back she hadn't known were tense and sore.

She looked around, her bare feet on the wolf's pelt that had traveled with her all the way from home. Her room was shaped like a slice of cake and had a bed and a trunk in the widest part and a small wash table by the door with a fresh bowl and jug of water every day. Food appeared by her bedside as if by magic while she slept—though if it were magic, it didn't last to keep the food warm until she woke. No matter. The bowls of stew with hunks of fresh bread to dunk in it tasted like heaven, even lukewarm or cold. But now there was no bowl. It must be between mealtimes, then. Listening to the noises of the temple around her didn't reveal much, either. A quiet lull lay beyond the thick wooden door. She checked the window, but the day was overcast so it could just as well be late morning or late afternoon. Nora stretched.

When was the last time she had woken and not had to immediately do something? Like walk for miles for the rest of the day, defend herself from bears, or ward off killers and rapists? But even before, there was always the charcoal that needed tending, the goat that needed feeding, the garden that needed care, the stomachs that needed to be filled. And now? What was she supposed to do here? Now there was nothing but bare feet tickled by the wolf's pelt.

On the bright side, she was finally clean. There were clean clothes in the trunk, clean sheets on the bed with a mattress of crackling, rustling hay. And as she sat on the edge of her bed, she saw someone had scrubbed and polished her boots to a shine, cobbled them new, and put them neatly under the wash table.

The boots did it. The sight of them choked her up. Here she was in this safe, clean place, with her brother and people who were so considerate they took care of her smelly old traveling boots while she slept. Her lower lip trembled slightly, and then suddenly the realization she was safe came crashing down, inundating her with tears. She had functioned for so long now being driven by survival, carrying on automatically. And here she was blubbering, wallowing in self-pity and relief with rib-hitching sobs. It was pretty pathetic. But she couldn't stop it and quickly gave up trying.

She was still breathing in shuddering gasps when a rapid staccato of footsteps announced someone approaching her door. She hastily threw the blanket around her shoulders and cuffed her wet eyes with it, taking one last deep breath before the door opened. Master Cumi poked her head into the room.

"Sleep well?" she asked, stepping inside, her long robes swishing as she closed the door. She stepped up and bent double to see into Nora's eyes. The elderly woman's eyes were a dark blue today and wrinkled at the edges from smiling.

"I came to check on you. But I can leave if you need to be alone for a while."

Nora shook her head as a treacherous tear rolled down her cheek.

"I'm fine, really I am," she sniffed. "I just can't stop crying. It's so stupid."

Master Cumi sat down next to her on the bed. She wrapped her arm around Nora's shoulders and just sat there, holding her, the thin silver bands around her wrists jingling with Nora's every sob.

"It's all right," she whispered into Nora's ear. "Salt water always heals. You just let it all out. Personally, I believe it has something to do with the glands balancing out, you know? Discharging all the pent-up stress."

"Stress crying?" Nora managed a watery laugh.

Master Cumi shrugged.

"Maybe because for the first time in a long time you *can* cry."

Nora's heart sank.

"Diaz told you everything?"

"*Master* Diaz? Yes. Of course."

"Oh." Nora wiped the wet corner of the blanket across her face again. She looked about the tiny room, then at the woman next to her, eyebrows raised high. "Oh. Well. Did he tell you how stubborn, reckless, and dumb I am? I think those were his exact words."

Master Cumi laughed.

"To you he said that, maybe. To me he said he's never seen anyone with such a natural talent going to waste. That you were fast, fearless to the point of being reckless, and very talented with a knife. Or two." She winked. "He also told me to work my best charms on you to make you become a pilgrim."

Nora blinked. "No, he didn't."

"No, but it's what he meant." Master Cumi stared at the closed wooden door, focusing inward for a moment. She turned her attention back to Nora. "I need you to strip."

"What?" Nora laughed nervously, leaning back.

"I've had a look at your shoulder while you were sleeping, but I'd rather heal you properly when you're awake."

Nora shook off her blanket and pulled the neckline of her loose cotton shirt down over her shoulder, wincing as she threaded her arm through the opening. The scar was still an angry red line on her pale skin, dotted red on either side where the stitches had held the flesh together. Master Cumi knelt before her on the wolf's pelt and pinched and poked and prodded with nimble fingers before leaning back. "Hmm," she said.

"What?" Nora wanted to know.

"You were lucky," Master Cumi said, poking Nora again, this time under her collarbone. "There's a vein just here that goes from the heart to the arm. If that had been pierced, you wouldn't be here anymore."

Nora pressed a hand to the spot.

"It still hurts when you move your arm?" Master Cumi asked next.

She had Nora lift up her right arm over her head—she couldn't—to her side, stretching and flexing her muscles. Finally Master Cumi tilted her own head to the side. Her eyes were slits, but her finger traced lines on Nora's shoulder.

"I could heal the muscles beneath the skin. You could move your arm properly again, without the pain."

"Do it." Nora's answer came like a shot.

Master Cumi looked up.

"It'll feel…strange, though."

"I've been walking the Plains with a half-wight the last few weeks. A mountain bear nearly chewed off my face. Occult death pits everywhere. Define strange."

"Strange as in not the way other healers would heal you."

"That sounds…intriguing."

"Then watch."

Master Cumi rose to her feet. She stretched out her hand to the small table next to the door. The water in the jug rose to meet the elegant flicks of her wrist. It flowed through the air in a tear-shaped drop and twisted itself around Cumi's forearm like a snake, writhing up and down, across her shoulders and back again.

Nora snapped to attention.

Don't lose it! This is a test, she thought. *It's just a test. And you asked for it.*

So instead of scrambling away in sheer panic at the *fucking blood witch* in her room, she stared at Master Cumi watching her, twirling the ball of water expectantly. And she remained as still as she could.

Talitha Cumi was a blood witch! A blood witch from across the Great Divide, that ocean of water between the ports of the northern coast and the Blessed Isle of Nessa. Nora had heard tales of the women of Nessa, tales she would never have believed if her eyes weren't seeing what they were now. *I don't believe in magic.* How stupid that sounded right now. Owen had told her stories of the goddess Neeze holding court in Nessa by the island's tidal pools, half woman, half fish. And the mortal children of the goddess sat on the throne, the blood witches of the ancient wars, mighty sorceresses with the power to influence their enemy's very body by calling to their blood. Neeze dwelt in all water. Water of life. The blood of all living things. Even in Nora's veins. *"She's a very talented healer,"* Diaz had said. *"A capable leader,"* he had said. *Yeah, well, he forgot to mention that his friend could turn people into living, breathing puppets shackled to her every whim, didn't he?* Nora thought.

Master Cumi made the water dance in the air between her hands. She tutted.

"I see your face," she said. "You need to learn to control it better."

"Funny. Control was the very word I was just thinking of." Nora licked her lips.

"Please, do tell." Master Cumi let the ball of water pass before Nora. "I'd love to hear what exactly you were thinking. Fear is the most common reaction, you know. Followed by disgust and then distrust."

"I know. And I'm not afraid," Nora lied.

"Very good, my dear. I nearly believed you. Shall I heal you now, or would you prefer another bandage with some ointment?"

Not a drop spilled on the floor. How did she do it? Magic, right. But *how* did she do the magic?

"You'll heal me with the water?"

"The human body is mostly water. We are of water, born from water, made of water. It runs through our veins, courses through our hearts, and touches our minds."

"That's a yes, then." Nora sniffed. "So can just anyone learn how to…heal the way you do? Or is it a special gift?"

Cumi smiled and beckoned the water back to her fingertips.

"I can't say for sure. I know how I do it, but maybe it would be different for you. Water is a part of all of us. So maybe everyone could learn the push and pull of water calling, though not everyone does. Why not?"

"Because it's magic?"

"Many things seem magical if you don't know how to do them. Even simple things. How does the farmer cultivate his vines to produce wine? I don't know. Magic. How does the cook makes a meal that, once you taste it, you never forget it for the rest of your life? Again, that must be magic. How does a charcoaler make charcoal? Pure alchemy, if you ask me, for I have absolutely no idea. The truth is, Noraya Smith, if no one believed these things were possible, no one would reach out to attain them but those who believe they are chosen to."

"We're still talking about water magic and not about a certain quest certain people are on to find a certain mythical object, right?"

The water encased Master Cumi's hand and became like ice, a white and blue gleam with a sharp edge.

"Don't worry." Master Cumi bent and took Nora's arm. Her eyes sparkled blue. "Afterward you'll feel a lot better, I promise."

After? Great. That was very reassuring. Nora gritted her teeth. It was a test, right?

"Do it."

Cumi ran her fingers over Nora's shoulder. They were so cold their touch felt like a burn.

"Relax, the cold numbs your skin," Cumi said. "Watch how to do this."

Nora looked down at her naked shoulder. The blue glow left Cumi's fingertips and danced over Nora's skin in a weaving motion. It tickled beneath the blue, but Nora dared not scratch nor touch the magic. She swallowed hard. Cumi's fingers were poised above the scar now. She looked up to make sure Nora was following her every move, her hungry eyes reflecting the eerie light from her hand. Her fingertips pushed slowly into Nora's shoulder. A strangled gasp escaped Nora's throat. Her eyes went wide as she saw the fingers pass through the flesh, feeling very much like the arrow penetrating the same spot, only slower. Much slower. A dull expanding throb stretched the tissue, which was unaccustomed to invasion. The white heat of the arrow piercing was missing, though. There was only cold.

Gradually the glow subsided and Master Cumi smiled. Her hands withdrew and dropped to her sides, where she wiped them clean with the hem of her robe. She pulled Nora's shirt over the shoulder and then patted her twice. It was over. The skin around her shoulder prickled like Nora's legs had after she'd stepped out of the river, waking up as the blood coursed hot underneath the chill.

"And?" Cumi rubbed her fingers against each other. "How did I do it?"

"I—I have no idea."

"Try lifting your arm over your head."

Nora did so and her shoulder moved smoothly. There was no pain, no daggerfall of hurt after a certain point. She moved it to and fro easily. Wide-eyed, she looked up at Master Cumi's mischievous smile.

"Just like magic." Cumi's eyes twinkled over her steepled fingers.

Nora nodded and touched her shoulder.

They heard a timid knock on the door.

"Come in!" Master Cumi called out.

A young woman opened the door, balancing a tray on her arm. She was dressed in the same billowing robes Master Cumi wore, girded with silver, though her sleeves were tied up, exposing her bare forearms. Her pale golden hair was similarly fashioned in two long braids. She cast her eyes down as she entered.

"Dinner?" The young woman's voice was barely above a whisper.

"Noraya, I want you to meet Calla. She's been keeping an eye on you, too. She's a capable midwife and a pilgrim here at the temple. And the cook I was talking about earlier." Cumi pointed at Calla behind her back.

"Pleased to meet you," Nora said as Calla set the tray with a steaming bowl of soup down next to the bed.

Calla smiled and rose. Or tried to. A silver chain dangling from her hair had caught in a silver chain dangling from her belt, making her bend over in an awkward position. She turned a violent shade of red.

"Um. Help?"

Nora sprang to action, fiddling with the chains.

"Here, let me just—there you go."

She unhooked a chain and her hand brushed against Calla's.

Nora's vision dimmed as though she had been hit over the head. Her hands filled with blood. The incessant wailing of an infant strained her ears. Images flashed before her eyes. Some she recognized as her own memories. The flabby flesh closing around her hand. Blue gleaming fingertips piercing her flesh. The scrape of her knife on the inside of the young man's skull. But then a silhouetted man, unknown, belt in hand raised high above his head.

Nora blinked. The room was back to normal. Except Calla knelt on the floor, arm raised before her face as though Nora was about to slap her. They stared at each other in shock.

"Oh yes. I forgot." Master Cumi's voice seemed to come from far away. "Calla is also an empath."

"A what?"

"I can…know you," Calla whispered, slowly lowering her arm. "Through touch. I'm sorry."

Nora shook her head.

"Is it just me?" she said slowly. "Or is no one else fucking normal around here?"

Chapter 14

Nora slept long the next morning. She woke and stretched and got dressed, making her way down the stairs to where she supposed the kitchen area was. The yeasty scent of freshly baked bread led her feet. As Nora opened the door, Calla looked over her shoulder, her blonde hair in a knot, arms elbow-deep in a huge kneading trough.

"Good morning," she said. "You missed breakfast. Grab a bite, if you want. It's still fresh."

Nora didn't need to be asked twice. Her stomach was rumbling. She stepped up to the tabletop Calla was working at and saw a large platter with a few slices of soft flat bread and ham. She dug in.

"Can I help?" Nora asked between mouthfuls. "You need something done?"

"Look in the pantry, will you? Tell me how many sides of mutton are still there."

Under Calla's direction, Nora walked over to a small larder and opened a heavy wooden door to see carcasses hanging from the ceiling. She counted and told Calla: "Forty-three." Calla smacked the flour from her hands and scratched under her eye, leaving a smudge of white on her pale face. She came over to Nora, cleaning her hands on her apron, and sighed.

"Well, we have a few racks of pork and beef left that we were saving for Solstice, but it won't last that long with all these men and their constant cry for meat, meat, meat."

"The prince's Hunted Company?" Nora asked. Calla nodded. "Well, they probably want copious amounts of beer and free sex, too. Doesn't mean you have to give it them."

Calla's eyes widened and she blushed deep red.

"Why don't they hunt game?" Nora quickly suggested. "The weather's still holding. There's only light snow. They could find deer or boar in the forest around the temple. Replenish the larder. Or do they have anything else to do here?"

"Er...no. Not really. But..."

"But?"

Calla wrung her apron. "Frankly, the prince's captain scares me. And the prince himself is even worse. I feel sick when I'm around him too long. I feel just a thin coating of control over a bubbling turmoil, even when we're only in the same room together. And the way he looks at me..." Calla shuddered.

"He needs food, just like everyone else. The worst he can do is say no."

"You'd just ask him? Prince Bashan?" Calla laughed nervously. "Are you sure you're normal?"

"Most of the time, I'd like to be." Nora shrugged. "Anything else I can do? You need help in here?"

"No." Calla took a look around the kitchen, as though taking a mental tally. "The dough can rise, and we'll have enough bread for lunch. Eggs are hard-boiled, ham's still there. Dinner's all set and slowly cooking." She pointed to a large cauldron. "Vegetable stew. I'll grill the fish later. But you can accompany me on my rounds, if you like."

"Sure."

Before the unrest, as Calla explained on their way, her rounds had usually meant doing chores and jobs around the nearly empty temple palace, along with making a regular circuit around the lonely homesteads and hamlets in the surrounding lands. Master Cumi and Calla went around, mostly healing and helping in the houses, changing bandages, distributing ointments, talking, and listening. Mostly listening. Master Cumi was also the local justice and priest in one person, marrying young people, burying dead people, and settling legal issues for those in between. The only difference after the unrest was that now they made their rounds below in the courtyards of the temple, much closer. But they also saw many more people. And a lot more pregnancies. Nora frowned at Calla.

"I'm a midwife," Calla explained.

"Animal or human midwifery?" Nora asked, eyeing a group of young girls carrying baskets of washing. She and Calla were going down the long stairs and were between platforms. They would have to walk uncomfortably close to the edge to let the girls pass by. Uncomfortable for Nora, at least.

"Both, but mainly human. I prefer animals, though."

"Why?"

"You did not hear this from me, but if all goes right, women don't really need a midwife. Babies are born, even if we don't make it in time. On the other hand, when things don't go well, or go very wrong, well...there's only so much you can do. The unspoken rule is, if you can save both, then save both. If you can't save both, save the mother. Dealing with cattle and sheep is easier in that situation."

"How is it with the…how do you cope with…you know. Do you wear gloves or something?"

"Mostly it helps when I can feel the women under my hands."

"Mostly?"

The young girls stopped, and Nora shuffled nervously even closer to the edge as they talked to Calla, swinging their baskets enthusiastically. They were on their way to the laundry in the depths of the temple. Hot water from the springs made the backbreaking, dull work slightly more endurable. One girl had a wobbly tooth and showed it off. The other had skinned her knee. The third told Calla that her mother hadn't yet returned from mushroom gathering. Calla promised to come by later. She looked up and took a step back, knocking into Nora. Nora rowed with her arms, cold sweat pouring off her face at the closeness of a long plunge to her death. She found her balance again, heart pounding in her throat.

"It's him," one of the girls screeched. Suddenly, all three were shrieking and jumping up and down around a handsome young man on his way up the stairs. Owen was following him.

"Oh dear," Calla breathed. She straightened and put on a smile. It stayed on while she talked, making her look slightly mad. "Noraya, you've met Shade Padarn?"

Nora looked Padarn up and down. She remembered his sword at her throat. He grinned at her over the girls' heads. Yeah, he remembered too.

"Briefly," Nora said.

"Well met, ladies." Shade bowed low.

"Shade! Look at my tooth! It bleeds when I do this!"

He obediently looked and then pulled a face.

"That," he said slowly, "is the most disgusting thing I have ever seen in my whole life."

The girls giggled.

"Are you going up or down?" Owen asked Calla.

"Um…" Calla blushed.

"Down, if you lot get out of the way," Nora said.

"Better do what she says," Shade told the girls in a stage whisper. "She's a twin, and so evil that even the wight master brought her back."

He winked. The girls ran up, jostling with their baskets, wary of Nora's scowl.

"Thank you very much, asshole."

"Shocking! There are children present. And I only spoke the truth, Briar."

He grinned. She wanted to punch him in the face.

"My name is Noraya."

"I know."

"You're not in the library?" Nora asked Owen, gritting her teeth.

"No, not today. Master Cumi is in the lower courtyards, laying down law." Owen clutched a thick notebook to his side. The spine had been broken and the book fixed to accommodate more sheets of paper in the back. Those last sheets stuck out more and were filled with Owen's careful handwriting. "I was volunteered as her scribe by Prince Bashan."

"What Prince Bashan says is what gets done," Shade said, stretching, both hands at the small of his back. There was an audible *crick* as something snapped into place and Shade exhaled. "Gods, I took a beating yesterday. Every single bone knocked out of place, I swear."

"Who cares?" Nora said, stepping around Calla to walk down the middle of the stairs again.

"Not Master Diaz, I can tell you that. I have to train with him again this afternoon."

Nora froze.

"I thought Garreth was a mean swords teacher," Shade continued. "Sent me flying every time we knocked shields together. And whenever I'd mess up, he'd send me out to get a beer. From the lower courtyards. Master Diaz, though. A battering ram is nothing compared to that half-wight. But what am I saying? You know that, eh, Briar?"

She straightened next to Owen and met Shade's gray eyes, muscles tensing.

"You're training with Diaz?"

"Yep."

"You?"

"Uh-huh."

"With him?"

Her jaw ached. For a moment, she imagined shoving Shade over the edge and listening to his scream on the long way down. But pushing Diaz over would feel so much better. She scraped a hand over her face to feel if she was grinning. *No discipline, my ass.*

"Nora?" Owen spoke to her, but she hardly heard him. "Are you all right?"

"Excuse me, lots of things," she managed.

Calla followed closely as Nora stormed down the long stairs, and she didn't have to be an empath to know how Nora felt.

Chapter 15

So Calla made her rounds, checking in on new mothers with their screaming, pink bundles; little old ladies with runny eyes; and snotty, lice-ridden children. Nora stood by her side, lending a helping hand where necessary, silent except for the most basic conversation. Her jaw was still clenched tight. There was a lot of medicine and bandaging, scolding and explaining, but also a lot of gossip and listening happening. Whenever Nora and Calla reached a house, the neighbors would come by, too, exchanging news and remedies.

Calla explained between visits that most of the refugees had settled in the tiers of the courtyards depending on where they came from. Neighbors fleeing from one village would naturally look for empty houses next to each other. So the courtyards had their own little order, depending on the origin of the people. There were a few open areas for everyone, like the square before the red gates at the bottom of the stairs. This was where most merchants had put up their stalls, and where farmers sold their last fresh produce. One street was dedicated to all sorts of crafts, carpenters, and smiths with their portable forges and anvil stumps. The men greeted them courteously, and occasionally one of them would strike up a short, monosyllabic conversation with Calla about the weather or something else, and it turned out to be a code for an ointment against joint ache or pain in the knees or an arranged political meeting with Master Cumi. Nora couldn't quite work out the code, though.

Sometimes, one of the old ladies would hand Calla a few balls of wool, freshly made biscuits, or a cured leg of ham. Nora would carry it a little farther to the next house they called at, where Calla would then pass it on to someone else. It seemed like a very elaborate game of what goes around comes back around.

"Is this payment?" Nora asked Calla as they walked down the main road.

Calla looked shocked.

"A pilgrim is never paid. That would be against the code. No abundance of personal possessions. No personal gain. You do what must be done. Nothing more. Nothing less." She hesitated. "Sometimes, out of gratitude, a person may want to contribute what they have, if they can. We then pass this on to another person in need."

"Who then owes you a favor."

"Yes. It all evens out in the end. Balance. A perfect cycle."

"Why were the temples so rich in the past, then?"

Calla looked hurt, so Nora quickly apologized and let the subject drop. Calla honestly seemed to believe in the code's inherent force for good and chose not to see the hypocrisy. She was, Nora mused, in that regard a bit like Owen, who often reasoned that all people were decent deep down, even beyond the point when he was proven wrong.

The last tier of the courtyards ran along the outer walls. This was where the domestic animals were kept when the gates were closed for the night, grazing between the ruins of some of the largest houses. Calla led Nora down the broad road where birch saplings grew and were eaten by the sheep. They stepped over chickens and pushed aside the goats. Once, a long time ago, these buildings had been warehouses full of wonders from the farthest corners of the earth, Calla said. Now, though, they were the most derelict ones in the courtyards and, besides the animals, no one lived here. Or nearly no one.

They stopped at one of the houses facing the outer walls. It was partially caved in; a ragged piece of colored cloth had been pulled over the huge hole in the ceiling. They had to duck to get through the broken doorway, which was curtained against the wind by a thick sheep's pelt. Inside, the smell of sheep and turpentine hit Nora's nose hard. She sniffed as her eyes adjusted to the semi-dark. Inside, the house was an explosion of colorful wool carpets. They were everywhere: on the floor, on the walls, across the ceiling. Three small looms stood along a far wall, and three old women sat at them, only turning briefly from their work to see who had arrived. One called out a name Nora didn't understand.

A short woman came in from the next room, belly round before her, her skin darkly tanned from the time she spent outside, a staff in her hand. A shepherdess. Nora's heart missed a beat. The shepherdess was about her age, seventeen, eighteen—maybe a few months lay between them. She was a sturdily built young woman, like Nora, a living reminder that Nora could have been married, could be a mother. A cold sense of foreboding seized Nora's heart. She felt the urge to leave but stayed as Calla bustled about, taking the woman's pulse, feeling the baby, checking the insides of the mother's lower eyelids for signs of anemia.

"I hope it'll be a boy." The shepherdess beamed at Nora. "A gorgeous boy like his daddy."

And where was his daddy exactly? Nora wondered. She remained silent, though.

"Two boys." Calla gave the mother a worried smile.

"Yes," the mother-to-be laughed. "My two gorgeous boys."

"No, I mean you're expecting twins," Calla said.

✧ ✧ ✧

NORA WAITED OUTSIDE THE BROKEN house until dusk fell. Her feet ached and her legs felt like tree trunks from walking around all day. Funny, she had done so much walking the last few weeks. One more day should be nothing. She could still hear the wailing inside through the carpet roof.

The outer walls were mostly in good repair. Farther down the road she saw a part of a crumbled house, spewing its bricks onto the streets. A few men were gathering them in wheelbarrows and carting them to some sort of construction taking place on top of the wall. Maybe they were the husbands of the women inside the house. They scaled rickety wooden poles of scaffolding, and Nora watched to see if someone would fall down and break their leg, because then at least she'd have something to do. Finally, Calla stepped carefully through the doorway. She looked tired.

"Let's get back. I still have to grill the fish. And I feel dirty now."

"Why? What did you do?"

"I mean, I need a bath to get rid of the smell of sheep, Nora. All I did was soothe the mother. She was in a lot of emotional pain." Calla gave Nora a sharp look. "And the other women were a nightmare. I'll have to keep checking on her every day now. They have...opinions on the nature of twins. They might persuade her to...do something...inexpertly."

"Have you ever delivered twins?"

"I haven't myself. But I've seen my former master do it. It's a bit fiddly. You have to take care of three people instead of just two. But I think I can manage."

"What will you do when they're born?"

Calla stopped. A cow ambled by between them. Nora stepped back to let it through. She folded her arms.

"Nora..."

"What did your former master do with twins?"

"You're taking this far too personally. What the mother decides to do is what she decides to do. It's not your call to make."

"So you'll just allow these stupid people their stupid traditions?"

"I can't just *not* help because people are stupid. That's not the way it works."

"I thought you pilgrims were all about moral guidance. Don't you know right from wrong? Let me explain it to you: killing babies is wrong."

"I'm not going to kill them."

"Good."

They walked on in silence until they reached the red gates.

"So what are you going to do?" Nora asked.

Calla groaned. "Can't you just let it go?"

Nora arched her eyebrows.

"If the pregnancy goes well and the birth runs smoothly," Calla said, staring in front of her as they walked up the steps, "I shall lay the babies in their mother's arms with instructions for her to follow."

"And then she'll walk out into the night and throw the babies to the wolves. Great."

"You do what must be done. Nothing more."

"Fine. If you want to be that way, I'm going to tell Owen you'll let babies die because they're twins."

Calla reached out and grabbed Nora's arm.

"No, don't," she started to say.

Nora's vision dimmed. A baby cried in her ears. Blood everywhere, on hands that were too thin to be hers. The unknown man with his belt in his hand. The looks the women of the Ridge cast her way whenever she walked into a group of them. Her father, making the sign of evil at her. No, not that! Nora gasped.

"Get off me!" She snatched her arm back. "And stop doing that! Who is the guy with the belt anyway?"

"I'm sorry," Calla called after Nora, who was storming up the stairs two steps at a time. "I wasn't thinking! Nora!"

CHAPTER 16

THE NEXT FEW DAYS, NORA worked in the kitchens with Calla but went on the rounds with Master Cumi. While Calla worked in a sea of women, Master Cumi dealt with the menfolk. There was considerably less small talk—and biscuits—and more getting down to business, which suited Nora just fine. They stood side by side in the broad road leading along the outer walls and listened to a pompous, red-faced man deliver reasons why he was ransacking the houses to build a windmill on top of the walls.

"I understand," Master Cumi was saying. "Many people feel like you do."

Nora had figured out that this sentence meant Master Cumi was getting annoyed. When she spoke it, the conversation was usually over soon.

Master Cumi smiled sweetly at the man. "However, the outer walls still belong to the temple. You're attempting to put up a business in my temple. And you have to ask my permission before you start building. It's not that I wouldn't want a mill here. In fact, I think it's a very good idea and a signal to all the other refugees that this place is indeed their new home instead of simply a waiting ground before moving back to wherever they came from. However, the outer walls belong to the temple, the temple belongs to my order, and I don't approve of you not asking me. That sends a very different signal to the rest of the refugees, you see. One I can't be holding with."

"I can't just stop building right in the middle, master."

"I'm sure you can," Master Cumi said.

"We've got the millstone here already. Do you know how difficult that was? It'd be a waste of time and money."

This was where the haggling started. Master Cumi had a refreshingly open mind toward the rules of the pilgrim order when it came down to business. It was one thing to go on the rounds and expect nothing for it, she told Nora on their way back. It was quite another to be the Guardian of the Temple. And as such, Master Cumi considered taxation a completely legitimate tool to use.

"If they want to live here, they accept the order as landlord. Or they move on."

The miller would get his business, the growing community would get a mill and a piece of normality, and the temple would profit as well. As they passed along the road, Nora glanced at the crumbled house with the piece of cloth as a roof. Master Cumi noticed.

"Have you spoken with Calla?" she asked.

"Loads of times," Nora said, frowning at the outer walls instead. "We work together, as you know."

"I meant about whatever you have fallen out over."

"She told you?"

"No. She radiated. You pick up these images whenever you're near her then." Master Cumi sighed. "Nora, do you want to become a pilgrim?"

"I…I don't know." She glanced at Master Cumi. "Why did you become a pilgrim?"

"You know what I am." Master Cumi shrugged. "I could tell you the story of a young woman, fed up with the life that was handed to her, looking for a fresh start. Running away from home. Sound familiar? Joining the pilgrims seemed like the safest bet against having to live the life that was forced on me."

"But?"

"Joining the order doesn't change who you are. You know that." Master Cumi gave her a long look and adjusted her cloak around her shoulders. It was fastened on the side with a raven's wing that hung over her shoulder. The black feathers shone with a luster no dead thing should have. "There are rules and obligations people expect you to live by. Just of a different kind. You are never free of other people's opinions just because you choose to run with a new crowd. You better make sure you like the crowd before you run with them."

"Why are you telling me this?"

"You know your brother wants to be a pilgrim. You know that he is proving himself to be very useful to Prince Bashan's undertaking."

"So?"

"So Owen will take the vows, leave with the Hunted Company come spring, and go on his pilgrimage to see the world. What are you going to do then?"

She arched her eyebrows high. But Nora had no answer.

They parted at the square, Master Cumi giving Nora one last errand. One of the smith's boys had burned himself working the portable forge. Nora dropped by the craftsmen street to pass on a jar of something that squelched as she walked, the liquid contents splashing against the inside. The smell of charcoal hung in the air. Hammer blows ran hard and clear. This was as close to home as she could get. She paused for a moment and closed her eyes. Everyone needed a smith.

Someone bumped into her from behind.

"You shouldn't be daydreaming, girl."

It was Bashan. His dead fish eyes assessed her coldly. He smirked.

"My lord," Nora said and moved to go around him.

It was a good thing to say. *My lord* could mean anything. *Good day*, for instance. Or, *I understand and follow your implied order. I know my place*. Or it could just mean *fuck you*.

"Are you looking to replace that knife of yours?" Bashan asked. "You should be. You should trade it for something more suitable. Like a pot or a pan."

"The knife's still pretty sharp. I think I'll keep it awhile. My lord."

He grabbed her arm and squeezed it painfully.

"Want to become a female sellsword?" The calm of Bashan's whisper belied the strength of his grasp. "Train with the best master? Well, I don't think I need to explain Diaz's skill to you. There is no one who can match him as a warrior. It's what makes him so valuable in my service. However, I'd hate for you to remain under the impression all warriors are like Master Diaz."

"Then it's a good thing I have met you, my lord."

He smiled and squeezed harder.

"Diaz likes you. Ridiculous, I know. But the great thing about Diaz is he'll never admit that, not even to himself. So if you act up, don't do as you're told, are impertinent, I can destroy you. And there is nothing Diaz can or will do about it. Are we clear on this?"

Nora struggled to free her arm from his grip.

"My lord," she swore.

"You know what happens to female sellswords when they are beaten? Hmm? I think you know."

He pushed her away and she stumbled over the cobblestones, cheeks hot. With a last creepy smile, Bashan was gone in the bustle of the crowd.

CHAPTER 17

ON THE WHOLE, NORA THOUGHT, it felt good to be busy again. Mind-numbingly good. It gave her hands work to do and made her tired enough to sleep. A few nights ago, Nora had woken from a nightmare, reliving every kill on the Ridge in her silent chamber in the temple. While her shaking hands had tried to light a candle to hold the darkness at bay, she'd wished herself back on the Plains. Safe. Not ever alone. His calm breathing next to her. *Dammit!* she'd sworn. Keeping busy distracted her enough to forget how much she hated Diaz training Shade every afternoon under the watch of that ancient woman warrior, Scyld.

Like now.

She had walked up the long stairs, feet dragging after a long day. And now this. Diaz had said he wouldn't train her because she lacked discipline. Discipline, ha! As though Shade had more discipline than she had! It was because she was a girl. She gritted her teeth and kept her eyes fixed on the statue of Scyld so as not to look over and see the half-wight's face.

A wooden sword skidded toward her feet. The old one-eyed warrior Garreth had knocked Shade's play sword out of the youth's hands. The two of them had been running at each other under Diaz's supervision with large shields strapped to their arms, clobbering the rims of the shields with practice swords and circling one another. Now Shade came jogging up, right hand waving away the pain of Garreth's hit. He grinned when he saw her. His face was flushed and sweaty despite the cold and the small snow piles that had been swept aside into the bushes.

"Hey, Briar! You mind bending over…and picking up my sword?"

Garreth chuckled and said something to Bashan, who was watching from the sidelines. The prince's cold eyes narrowed on Nora as though she had brought in something nasty. Nora's eyes flicked back to Shade's before they could wander any farther. She wedged the tip of her boot between the cobblestones under the wooden sword and kicked up, and the sword arched into the air so that it was nearly too easy to grab. She twirled it around, a tiny bit proud of herself, and held it out to Shade hilt first, grinning.

"Come and get it."

Shade, though young, obviously knew enough about women to be on his guard. He looked over his shoulder back at Garreth, Bashan, and Diaz to make sure he had an audience.

"Come on!" Garreth urged Shade. "I'm not gonna stand in the cold all damned day."

Shade moved to grab the sword. Without thinking, Nora flicked it across his fingers first, and Shade was bent down on one knee before the burning sensation on his knuckles and the dull throb in his knee would tell him he had been hit. Twice. By a girl. He grunted, then stood up.

"Come on, kid," the old warrior said. He worked out something from his throat and hawked it into a snow pile. "I'm still waiting."

Nora held the sword at her hip and backed off a few steps. Shade followed. He wiped his brow with his forearm.

"You know the sword is a symbol for a man's best part?" Shade grinned. "You're handling mine. So this is kinda like foreplay."

"What's your problem, Shade?"

"I'm seventeen years old and just wanna get laid."

"Learn a girl's name, then. It's Noraya."

"Oh, so that's what's holding you back?" An odd gleam entered the gray of the young man's eyes. "You want to hear me scream your name?"

His shield was up before she could hit him again. The wood banged loudly against the leather coating. Nora felt the reverberation echo in her arm, and her numb hand let the sword go. Shade took advantage and leaned in to grab her wrist, pulling her toward his laughing face. She accelerated the forward movement and jerked her head at Shade's face as if she meant to smash his puckered lips with a head butt. He flinched and brought the shield up.

That was his mistake. It left his groin unprotected from Nora's incoming knee. Shade doubled over, gasping for breath, face paling dramatically. Nora knocked his feet from under him and he was down, gargling and rolling onto his side.

Nora scratched her ear and turned away to gaze at Scyld and let Shade have a moment to gather whatever was left of his dignity. She had seen the veins in his throat bulging and thought about how easy it would be to strike a killing blow if she had a real sword. A cut through those veins, a quick stab into his exposed side. She shuddered, remembering what that felt like.

Garreth was wheezing behind her. Bashan clapped his hands twice before turning back to cleaning his fingernails with the tip of his paring knife. Diaz regarded her with one raised eyebrow, then let out a small sigh. The pent-up energy in Nora spiked as Diaz looked away. She clenched her jaw shut and willed her feet to stay where they were.

Shade was breathing hard. But at least he was breathing again. Nora turned back and crouched beside him.

"Still want to scream my name?"

"You're mean," Shade croaked.

"You're stronger than I am, heavier than I am. If I fought fair, I'd never have a chance. So that's not much of an incentive for me to fight fair, is it?"

She offered Shade a hand and after a moment's hesitation, he took it, hauling himself to his feet. They stood facing each other. He was about a head taller than her, dirty blond hair tied back into a foxtail. Nora bent down and picked up the wooden play sword. She balanced it on the flat of her hand, offering it to the young man in earnest this time. He took it, his face color improving by the minute.

"There," Nora said. "We tussled."

"I'll remember it on lonesome nights."

They both grinned, dusting themselves off.

It would be easy to just keep on walking, head past the statue and into the temple. It would be the sensible thing to do. Nora's feet just wouldn't move, though. The short confrontation with Shade made her skin tingle. Everything was sharper. The scent of lavender leaves around Scyld's feet, the empty boughs of the trees outlined against the gray skies, the shine of sweat on Shade's brow. She clenched her fists and turned on her heels to walk over to Diaz. He arched his eyebrows high as she approached like a storm cloud.

She took a shaky breath and planted herself before him. Nora looked Diaz in his pure black eyes and then slapped him in the face as hard as she could. His head jerked back.

"I challenge you to a duel."

CHAPTER 18

THE SATISFACTORY ECHO OF THE clap of flesh on flesh rang through the courtyard, bouncing off the statue of Scyld. Nora's hand prickled and stung. She shook her fingers, then curled them into a fist. She imagined Diaz's cheekbone felt similar. A small red welt was blossoming under his cinnamon skin. He stared at her with those dark eyes. She waited for his reaction, holding her breath.

"I decline your challenge," he said after a moment.

Wrong answer.

She struck out once more with her right hand, but he caught her by the wrist this time and pulled her close, twisting her arm at a painful angle. She winced.

"Try that again," he said, "and I will break your arm."

A mix of triumph and panic made her stomach crawl into her chest as a spasm of anger flickered across his usual poise. A heartbeat later, he pushed her away. She stood, rubbing her wrist.

"You saved my life," she blurted and grabbed his upper arm as he moved to turn away from her. "You watched me kill all those men. Then you saved my life. You half dragged me here across the Plains, protecting me along the way. And now, not one word? You haven't even spoken to me once since we arrived. You fucking…half-wight!"

He cocked his head to the side, eyes narrow.

"You're…angry?"

"Yeah, I'm angry! You know what they say about the life you save? It's your responsibility. There's a connection between us. How dare you save my life only to drop me into the nearest kitchen you could find! Is that what you saved me for?"

He brushed her hand off his arm and squared his shoulders.

"What do you want from me?"

Nora stood her ground and crossed her arms.

"I want you to train me. As a warrior."

If Diaz could roll his eyes, he would have. It was hard to tell without seeing pupils. Instead, he laid his head back to glance above as though issuing a silent prayer for patience.

"I told you: I've given my oath to find the Blade. After that, I might take someone as an apprentice. Maybe it will even be you."

Nora threw her head back, tossing her long hair over her shoulder.

"I never said 'apprentice me.' I said 'train me.'"

"I'm not training Shade." Diaz pointed at the young man, who flinched behind his shield. "Garreth is. I'm merely assisting."

"Train me," Nora repeated. "You and I both know you want to. At least until spring comes."

She saw him clench his jaw tight. He wagged a finger at her, then shoved her aside wordlessly. He held out a hand to Garreth, who tossed him the wooden sword the old warrior had been leaning on. Diaz caught it in midair and twirled it with a flourish. It was just for show. Still looked awesome. Her heart beat faster. She watched as he drew a wide circle into the scuff of snow on the cobblestones. The scrape of wood on stone was the only noise to be heard, until Bashan smacked his lips.

"You shouldn't indulge her, Telen," he said, waving his small knife at Diaz.

Diaz stood upright and looked at Nora. Calm had settled onto his features once more, and she wanted to rake it off with her fingernails.

"You want to become a warrior?"

"I do."

He tapped the tip of the sword twice against the stones.

"Then step into the circle."

Nora uncrossed her arms and stepped over the thin line, stopping an arm's length away from him. He threw the wooden sword back to Garreth.

"No weapons." Diaz spoke in his quiet, deep rasp. "No breaking bones, scratching, biting, spitting, or anything else that would mar this lesson. That includes vulgar language. Understood?"

Nora nodded.

"If you are pushed out of the circle, the fight is over. If you're injured, the fight is over. If you wish to end the fight for whatever reason, you must leave the circle. Understood?"

"In the circle, fight. Out of the circle, end of fight," Nora repeated.

He cocked his head to the side and stood perfectly straight with his hands folded neatly against the small of his back.

"Then come at me."

Nora licked her lips and grinned. Bashan tutted behind her. Nora gritted her teeth and bent at the knees, fists raised before her face, like every beer-induced brawler she had seen in the inn back at the Ridge. Before they mopped up the blood. It felt stupid. It probably *was* stupid. She stepped to the side. Diaz did not move, though she felt his gaze resting on her. His hands, though, were still folded on his back. She inched closer to his reach. He took her movement in without a flicker of emotion on his face.

As she circled him, he moved with her, making sure she couldn't reach his back. Nora stopped. She stared into his face. They had changed places now. She stood where he had. He half closed his eyes and took a deep breath. She let her hands drop to her sides. She wasn't a drunken brawler.

He was within reach. She was in his reach.

She swung her left hand up in a sharp, swift curve. He blocked it with a downward thrust. And her right hand, too. She aimed to chop at his throat with the edge of her left hand, but he leaned back and her fingers slashed the air. His ankle collided with her leg and swept it from under her. She lay sprawled on the cold cobblestones for a moment and watched his boots step away.

"Again," he said.

Master Diaz stood waiting for her a few paces away. His hands hung by his sides this time. At least they weren't folded on his back. Nora pushed herself up and stood, measuring the distance between them.

Then she lunged forward. But he was ready for it and blocked again. When his ankle came once more, she stepped out of its path and her own foot slid out to topple him. He jumped over and they jogged away from each other, backing off.

She didn't wait for him to call her out but attacked as soon as she caught her breath. They exchanged a few blows; he blocked hers with ease, as if he knew what she was planning to do even before she knew herself. Her heart pounded in her chest. It was exhilarating, like a jump from the overreaching branches into the pool in the brook near her home—that moment when you hung in the air, bracing yourself for the cold water below, stomach churning.

They moved in tune. It felt like they were back on their trek across the Plains, their bodies recognizing each other and falling into step next to the other. She had missed this. It felt like dancing to a slow beat, interspersed with short frantic explosions in between. One move following the other, a step to the side, a beat dictating a counter-beat, resulting in a rhythm similar to her throbbing heart. She could have laughed out loud. Could have, if she didn't know for sure that he was faster, stronger, and had longer arms. And if he hit, it would hurt like hell.

Nora ducked away from one of his snakelike grabs. But after a few near misses, he caught her forearm and held it fast, pulling her against him. She struggled to free it, flailing with her other hand, which he caught also, effortlessly. Hands pinned down, she attempted to knee him in the groin. His foot came up and stamped hers, squashing it painfully with the heel of his boot. She gasped. He pushed her away. And she was free from his steel grip but fell to the ground, jarring her hip painfully.

She rose with a groan, hearing the chuckles, and flushed.

They both stood on opposite sides of the circle and looked at each other. Her legs felt weak. The muscles in her thighs were quivering as if from the steep climb up the stairs. Maybe minutes had passed since the fight began, but Nora was panting and sweating, nauseous from exhaustion. All she wanted to do was sit down and rest up a bit. Wash and eat. And drink. Definitely drink. But here she was, in this circle, knees bent, hands raised once more, and Diaz wasn't even breaking a sweat.

Anger surged through her. Nora summoned the rest of her energy from it and dashed at the half-wight. Her movements were ever faster; she tried to hit him, hands and feet, anything to make him feel how mad she was. He either blocked or moved out of her reach. One blow hit the space where his face had just been and, for the first time, he looked surprised.

So he retaliated, and she dodged or blocked his blows as well as she could. The slap and grunt of the two bodies locked in a struggle with each other echoed across the courtyard. He upped the pace. It was all she could do to retreat, turning her body away from the blows of his hands. But a sudden sweep of his backhand hit her hard across the face.

Nora blacked out. As she came to, the cobblestones reeled under her hands. Two small drops of blood splashed next to her thumb. Her lower lip had split near the corner, and she felt a sharp sting as her tongue probed the pulsing wound. Blood mixed with the bitter taste of defeat in her mouth. She swallowed it. She looked up and saw the edge of the circle was only a hand-width away. She had held herself quite well up to now. Maybe it was time to end the show and crawl out of the circle with what dignity she had left. Laughter rang in her ears, and she looked beyond the thin line to see Prince Bashan, gloating. She blinked away the sweat from her eyes and got to her feet.

Master Diaz stood waiting for her. Calm and set. His hands were folded on his back again. Nora wiped her mouth. Blood shone on the back of her hand. The weakness returned to her legs.

"Step out of the circle," he said.

"No."

"You are bleeding."

She nodded but did not move.

"I have drawn the first blood and this fight is over. Step out of the circle."

"No." She paused. "Master."

He frowned.

This time he moved to strike first. Nora deflected his blows as best as she could, but she was edging around the snow circle, trying not to step over the line. He gave her no time to pause. There was no relenting. She held her forearms over her face, glancing through the splayed fingers, trying to guess where he'd strike next. Suddenly, his hand grabbed her right arm and twisted it painfully behind her. Then he boxed the scar they both knew was hidden underneath her clothes. She shrieked in pain and fell to her knees, all power draining from her in an instant.

"Telen!" Nora heard Master Cumi's sharp voice.

Great. More onlookers. Best thing for humiliations, she thought.

Master Diaz did not let go of her arm. He dragged her along with him by sheer force, with her scrabbling on her knees to keep up. He finally let go after they had crossed the thin trace of the line in the flaky snow.

"This fight is over," he repeated and let her fall to the ground.

Nora propped herself up on her elbows and glared at him from below. He blinked down at her, his face unreadable, then held out his hand. She grasped it and he pulled her up to her feet.

"I look forward to our next lesson tomorrow," he said, not even out of breath.

Nora nodded, not trusting herself to speak, and felt a warmth creep over her skin. Then he scuffed a patch of snow over the line and left the circle for the far sidewall.

Under the dark shadow of the statue of Scyld, Nora nodded again. She was shaking with exertion, bleeding from her lip, and her shoulder felt like an arrow had pierced it all over again. But the wind was in her hair and brought the sharp, cold taste of snow to her tongue next to the bitter taste of blood. And she'd never felt so alive.

CHAPTER 19

After another busy day, Nora dragged her feet back up the stairs with a slight headache coming on after arguing with the miller over kegs of beer he had been secretly hoarding in the half-built mill. She'd have to talk to Cumi about the order's stance on illegal breweries. As she came upon Scyld's courtyard, Master Diaz was waiting for her, circle drawn, leaning on a wooden sword. Nora groaned inwardly. It was one thing to want to train to become the world's greatest female warrior since Scyld herself, but now? Really? She was dead tired and still had dinner to orchestrate with Calla. Even though they still weren't speaking to each other.

She laid her tallying writ on the edge of the fountain and secured it there against the wind with a stone.

"No audience today? Where are the others?" Nora asked the half-wight.

"They are inside, training Shade Padarn to fight in a shield wall."

"Why aren't we inside? It's cold out here."

Diaz cocked his head.

"You think you will only ever fight when you're rested and when the weather's just fine and you have nothing else to do that day? Think again. And bow before you come into the circle."

Nora clenched her jaw and bowed her head.

"Lower."

"You're enjoying this a bit too much, aren't you, Master Diaz?" She bowed with a flourish of her arms.

Diaz allowed his lips a shadow of a smile.

"Always remember, you asked me for this."

Nora reached out for the practice sword, but he shook his head.

"No, today we will start with the basics. Today I will teach you how to roll."

"To roll?"

To roll. As Diaz explained, she would never have the strength of a man, never the reach of a man's arm, never have even odds in a fight. So he would teach her to be fast, to employ a mix of various traditional fighting styles, and for that she'd need to be able to duck, jump, vault, leap, and roll without hurting herself and hopefully come up on her feet at all times. Like a cat. Because this, he said, meant life or death.

"To be like a cat means life or death?"

He nodded gravely.

So she rolled, shoulder over hip and onto her feet, and again, and again, feeling very foolish.

Now jump and roll. Now jump from the fountain and roll. Now from the wall and roll. When training was finally over, she was bruised on both shoulders and hips from the cobblestones and strongly doubting her decision to do this. He beckoned her. She rolled one last time and rose on her feet before him, spreading her hands for show.

"Now come at me," he said. "Try to knock me over. And I will throw you, and you will roll and stand. Understood?"

"You don't think I can topple you?" Nora bounced on the balls of her feet.

"If you could, you would be training to fight in the shield wall with Padarn, wouldn't you? Instead, we are here."

She charged at him and landed on her back with a thud. Winded, she stared at the rolling clouds above Scyld's sword tip, waiting to get her breath back. She heard boots approaching, and Diaz's dark eyes shoved themselves into her view.

"You didn't roll." He loomed over her and looked down his nose with disappointment.

"I didn't roll." Nora waved a hand.

He reached down to lift her. She grasped his wrist and tugged instead, kicking his legs away from under him. It was a mean trick. But she was tired of his complacency. And anyway, weren't you allowed mean tricks in a fight? Unbalanced, Diaz let himself fall. Nora tensed, curling up into a ball, thinking he'd crash onto her, but he gracefully rolled away at the last moment and was on his feet beside her again in one effortless motion. It was depressing. He held out his hand again, one eyebrow raised high. This time she let herself be pulled up.

The next days she rolled some more. Then he drilled her in the most intriguing, most important fighting techniques, like how to breathe, how to stand, how to keep her elbows by her side, how to move from the hips and watch her opponent's hips. All the while Nora doubted he was taking this very seriously. Or maybe it was a test of how far she was willing to go before she cracked. On top of her own thoughts, she was very conscious of all the onlookers they had. Suddenly, so many people had things to do in the lower courtyards and had to pass by—it was amazing. Often during training, she saw faces at the windows onto the courtyard. She began to suspect that they practiced in the courtyard for exactly that reason. They were of the opposite sex, after all, and the nature of this training was very physical. Tongues would wag. Staring at a man's loins could ruin a girl's reputation all too easily, and didn't she know?

So they trained outside, even in sheets of rain and howling winds. Two days before Solstice it hailed, and they cowered beneath the temple's portcullis by the entrance. The cold sun shone down on the courtyard, which was filling with icy grains. Diaz wiped his face and flicked the water from his hand.

"This is why winter is normally peacetime," he lectured and turned to Nora, who was wiping the drip from her nose with her drenched sleeve. "Weather can be a powerful ally in war."

"Is that why you and Bashan will leave the temple in spring when the weather gets better?"

"To find the Blade. Not to go to war."

"Oh, I guess Bashan is going to tickle Empress Vashti off the throne with the Blade, then."

Diaz gave her a long look.

"The way of the warrior sometimes demands the death of one or a few so that many can live."

"And Bashan knows that, right?"

"*You* should." Diaz unsheathed his short sword and handed it to her hilt-first. "Show me what you know."

After a moment's hesitation, Nora took the sword from his hand and gave it a swing. Diaz watched her. Having been raised by a smith, Nora had been around swords from infancy and knew their make. Each was made according to the customer's wishes. A sword could tell you more about its owner than if that man opened his mouth, her father had always said. Like the clothes you chose to wear or the way in which you wore them. Other people might say you could tell what a man was by the scuff of his boots, but in Nora's home, it was by his weapon of choice.

This one was simple and elegant, without curves and flourishes, without gilded guards or flashy designs. There were no magic runes scratched into the naked blade, yet when she breathed on it, she saw the curling patterns that revealed how several metal rods had skillfully been pounded into one. Its point was tapered, and long grooves ran down the middle of each side.

"The hilt's heavier than it should be," she said out loud. The boss of the hilt was made of iron, as was the crosspiece, both undecorated and straight.

Diaz shrugged.

"Heavy is good. It's unexpected. She doesn't have much weight at the tip, but she's still well balanced. Makes her agile. Besides, you can always bash someone's face in with the hilt."

"She?" Nora smiled and held the sword up, mimicking the statue of Scyld. The sword's tip nearly touched the stone ceiling of the portcullis. "I doubt bashing someone's face in with the hilt is a gentlemanly thing to do."

"I've seen young soldiers get themselves killed by thinking the way to win fights is by knocking on each other's sword and shield as if there were points awarded. However, the only point is to survive. And to do so, you must kill the other man. The only gentlemanly thing is to do it quickly. Now you."

Nora nodded and gripped the sword's leather-wrapped handle. She made sure she was standing correctly and swung the blade, moving through a few basic poses. Diaz stood at a distance, arms crossed, watching his sword flash. She could see the dark tattoos on his wrists and forearms through his wet white shirt, and the burn mark on his right hand. She tried figuring out which tattoo Owen had read to know Diaz was a chieftain's son, but couldn't guess. Funny how his sword was so plain and his body so decorated. A wave of heat flushed her face, and Nora concentrated on the tip of the blade again.

She mimed hacking into his sides under the rib cage, cutting open his stomach with one swift move, thrusting downward, slashing both of his thighs. If Diaz was nervous about her handling steel between his legs, he didn't show it. The sharp tip wavered a little in Nora's hand. The sword was getting heavy. She swung it back up to pretend to slit his throat by drawing the length of the sword under his chin. Nora swallowed hard. She had killed men that way before and shuddered at the noise locked in her memory of men drowning in their own blood. The last was the heart. She pressed the tip of the blade into the leather jerkin he wore over his chest and grinned.

Their eyes met. She could feel the regular rise and fall of his chest through the sword. The blade between them made them stand apart. They had been closer before, much closer than this. She blushed, remembering the feel of his body next to hers every night on the Plains. The icy wind swept through the courtyard and her skin crawled with goose bumps, though she could swear she saw his heat make the cold air around him steam. Her hand rested on the sword's iron boss, ready to shove the blade with force through the leather and into his heart.

"Don't," Diaz said.

"Don't what?"

Nora's heart beat so hard she thought it would spring from her chest. She was breathless, but not from exertion.

"Don't think of fighting me for real."

Nora cocked her head. "That would be very stupid. Why would I think that?"

"I don't know. But I know when I'm being sized up."

Nora laughed through her nose. "I wasn't sizing you up."

"Then what?"

Diaz was taller than her. If he held out an arm straight from his body, she could probably walk under it without the top of her head brushing against him. So every time they talked, she had to look up to his face. Those pure black eyes. So unlike a human's. People said the eyes were a door to the soul. What that meant for Diaz and his kind, Nora didn't know. She gazed back, trying to find an answer to his question. The silence rang with all kinds of things she could say, but in truth, she was simply content to share this moment with him. Hearing their breathing among the steady rush of hail was enough. It filled her with calm, and that was...unsettling. The Nora reflected in his black eyes didn't have an answer, either. Hair wild and unkempt by the wind and rain, eyes wide and fierce, she used him as a mirror and didn't know whether she liked what she saw, whether he liked what he saw. She let the sword sink down and opened her mouth to say something when they heard a cry for help.

CHAPTER 20

DIAZ WAS SPRINTING ACROSS THE courtyard toward the stairs before Nora even realized he had swept his sword out of her hands. Another cry rang out through the din of the clicking hail, and Nora followed Diaz to the brink of the stairs. Looking down, she saw the boys she had met on the road to the temple. What were their names again? The youngest was the smartest. Larris! That was his name. But the other two? Larris and his friend were struggling to keep their larger friend in the middle upright. It was the sullen boy with the crap sword. His head hung limp and he was clutching his belly. Nora saw a lot of dark blood washed down his front.

Diaz reached them first and placed one of the wounded boy's arms around his neck. Larris blanched when he saw the wight's face. Diaz looked up and saw Nora at the edge of the stairs.

"Go and get Talitha!"

She ran into the temple, calling for Master Cumi at the top of her lungs. Where would she be at this time? Nora took a deep breath and headed toward the kitchens, but Master Cumi had obviously heard her yelling and came toward her at a measured pace, gathering her billowing robes high.

"Finally stabbed Telen?" The older woman flashed a grin at Nora.

"No!"

"Pity." Cumi smiled.

"Someone else is hurt." Nora panted breathlessly. "Wound to the stomach. Looks pretty bad."

Master Cumi nodded. Her lips were pressed together tightly. As they entered the foyer, they saw Diaz come in the front door with the boys, and Master Cumi ushered them all into the dining hall. It was empty. Dinner wasn't for another three hours.

"Here!" Master Cumi pointed at the floor before the large fireplace, and Diaz laid the boy carefully down in front of the glowing embers.

It was strangely silent in the large room. Nora stood back with the other two youths as the masters bent over the large boy in their middle, Talitha checking for a pulse while Diaz cut the wet shirt open to reveal a white belly covered in dark red blood.

The silent youth put his arm around Larris's shoulder as if holding the thin boy up. Nora glanced between him and the large boy bleeding on the floor. Were they related? Brothers? She had forgotten to ask back when they had met on the road. They didn't look all that similar, but the way Larris was wringing his hands and biting his lower lip seemed to indicate some greater attachment. Then it hit. Nora's perception shifted and she could see it so clearly, as if the sun had shone down in an illuminating ray through the high, slanted windows.

Larris wasn't the boy's brother. In fact, Larris wasn't even a boy. The shoulder line, the baggy shirt about the chest, the hips and legs, the small feet. Then the face: it was gaunt and filled with worry, but as free of the wisp of a beard as Nora's was. For a moment, Nora felt envy. Of course! How could she have been so stupid? Passing as a boy would have made everything so much easier. Cutting off her long hair hadn't even occurred to her—but it was just hair. It could grow back. Larris—or whatever her real name was—had been smart, and that made Nora feel dumb.

"I know you!" Larris said suddenly.

"Yeah." Nora nodded.

"Did you find your brother?"

"He's safe. Here."

Larris nodded.

The youths stood and watched Master Cumi bend over the pale-lipped boy. She wiped away the blood from the wound, felt for a pulse at his wrist, watched his ragged breathing. Then the two masters shared a look.

"What is it?" Larris's voice was the pitch of a girl's, too. Though maybe it was just the hysteria. "He'll be all right, won't he?"

"There's a lot of damage," Master Cumi said. She laid a hand over the wound. "He's lost too much blood. Inside."

"But you can help him?" Larris's voice broke. She looked as though she were going to cry.

Master Cumi took a deep breath and nodded at Diaz. "Lay him on the table. Nora, get me a deep bowl and put it under the table."

"Do you need it filled with water?" Nora asked, sweeping the cloth from the table as Diaz heaved the body up again.

"No, I just don't want all of the blood on the floor." Master Cumi pressed her hand down onto the wound, and the boy groaned weakly.

Nora emptied a large earthenware bowl of apples onto the heap of tablecloth. She placed the bowl on the floor at the masters' feet. Diaz vaulted over the table and stood on the other side. He held the boy's shoulders down.

"Ready." His rasp sounded harsh.

Master Cumi nodded. Her brow crunched together. The hand she had pressed onto the wound was covered in blood. She lifted it and rolled her wrist in an elegant motion. Blood poured out of the wound toward the tabletop and floor, but it also rose toward the outstretched hand in a dark red stream, like a fountain. The older woman made another motion, as if tugging wool with a spindle. The blood gathered into a scarlet swirl by Cumi's side, and a few drops spattered into the large bowl at Master Cumi's feet. Nora gasped and stepped back from the table.

There was a loud shriek behind her.

"It's sorcery. Blood magic. She's a witch!" Larris yelled. "A blood witch from beyond the Divide! Get off him! Get off him, I say!"

Nora turned. Larris was fighting against the silent boy's arm, screaming abuse, and spit was frothing on her lips.

"Did you know?" Larris screamed at Nora. "You knew. You liar, you said it was safe here. You said it was safe, and there's a wight and a witch!"

Nora held up her hands and tried to calmly reason with Larris.

"They're trying to help. You don't have to be afraid."

The girl heard nothing of it under the torrent of accusations. Nora threw a look at the silent boy who struggled with Larris. He shook his head and helplessly shrugged. With a glance back to the table, Nora caught Diaz's stare. He raised his eyebrows at her, then at Larris. Nora looked back at the girl. The yelling was attracting attention already; some of the Hunted Company clustered at the doors to the dining hall. The last thing Larris needed was Prince Bashan's sharp tongue.

Nora slapped Larris across the cheek. Silence rang in her ears.

"Shut up! Your screaming is not helping!" Nora pointed at the table. "Yes, he's a wight, or well, half a one. And she might be a blood witch. But even if she was suckled by the Queen of the Grave Herself, she's trying to help your friend stay alive. You said you look out for one another? Then shut up. And let them help him if they can."

There was a red mark on Larris's cheek. Tears ran down her face and her lower lip trembled, but she remained silent. Nora turned to the spectators at the door. She pointed at random into the small crowd.

"You and you, find Calla and bring her here. We'll need bandages, too. You, get clean water from the kitchens and don't you dare spill it! What are you waiting for? Go! Now!"

Nora took a deep breath and stepped closer to the table.

"Anything else?" she asked in an undertone.

A faint smile lay on Master Cumi's lips. She waved a hand in a complicated swirl. The blood orb next to her spun gently. It looked ghastly. Nora shuddered.

"More information would be nice. What happened?" Cumi cocked her head at Nora for a moment. "Think you can find that out?"

"I think she's scared and confused right now. But I'll try."

"She?"

"She."

Larris's face dug into the shoulder of her companion, and the girl's own shoulders heaved with sobs. Nora guided them down the hall to a bench. She wished she had sent someone to get tea or something else warm. The three of them were still dripping wet from the hailstorm outside.

"I know you're a girl," Nora said to Larris.

"So?"

"So I think you're clever. Can you tell me what happened to your friend?"

Larris cuffed the tears from her eyes with her dripping sleeve. She and her silent friend exchanged a look that made Larris seem more miserable.

"I don't know," she said, shrugging. A flicker of anger passed over her face as she squinted up at Nora. "And I don't know if I want to tell you. You slapped me. And you have some strange company here."

"I'm sorry I slapped you." Nora waited. Larris held up for a moment. Then her shoulders sagged.

"Fine. We were outside of the courtyards, in the woods."

She stared at Nora, daring her to interrupt.

"And?"

"We've been out poaching. Other men do it, too."

Nora smirked. *Men, ha!*

"Yeah, I know. Carry on."

"We found him in a bear trap, or something like it."

"A bear trap?" Nora repeated.

"We wanted a roast for Solstice, you know? I went with Bow. Brenn went alone. He had his sword." A dry sob escaped her lips. "We should've gone together. All three of us, I mean. Bow's got a condition. Been that way since birth. He can't talk. Got no voice. So one of us always goes with him. He can't shout out, see."

Bow opened his mouth, and Nora peered in despite herself. Two teeth were missing, as was half of his tongue. There was only a withered, fleshy flap curled at the back. Nora winced. Not being able to speak was one thing. How did he eat? The boy closed his mouth and grinned at her. Larris stared over to where Master Cumi was healing Brenn.

"And you found your…other friend in a bear trap?" Nora prompted her.

"Yeah, something like a bear trap." Larris looked up. "Hung on a spike right through his belly. We tried to lift him up, but then there was all this blood everywhere."

"On a spike?" The hairs on Nora's arms rose, but not from the chill of her wet clothing.

"And Brenn wasn't the only one in it. There were others. Women, too." Larris winced.

"You couldn't help them out, could you?"

"No point. They were dead. They were all dead."

"Think they fell in?" Nora asked, but she already knew the answer.

Larris turned her eyes to Nora.

"No. Last thing Brenn said was the man shoved him."

CHAPTER 21

THE BOY BRENN DIDN'T SURVIVE the night. He was buried the next morning in the burial grounds for pilgrims below the temple. Nora watched as Master Cumi spoke the ritual words tight-faced, while Larris sobbed in the background. Diaz took her and Bow out with a number of men, and they scoured the surrounding forests the entire day. They found the death pit Larris had described, but never any signs of the man Brenn had mentioned nor of the people who had built it. Cumi worked in the lower courtyards all day. The festive decorations for Solstice were overhung by the shadow of death, and a smell of fear mixed with the scent of spices in the air. The large outer gates of the walls had been closed for the night. The news had spread like gangrene. Only the children ran wild as ever, unheeding of their mothers' calls, eyes bright with excitement at the celebration.

In every household, the whole country over, it was tradition that the women of the house prepare for Solstice. Seeing as Cumi was in the lower courtyards and most of the girls they had recruited desired to return down the everlong stairs to their own families, only Nora and Calla were left to decorate the temple. They decked the halls with pine branches and red winter berries and then swept the fireplaces clean and heaped baskets full of logs next to them, making them ready for the celebration. A large bonfire had already been set up in Scyld's courtyard and another, larger bonfire sat ready in the square at the foot of the stairs, just in front of the red gates. The old ash was swept together and stored in large wooden buckets to be distributed to every privy throughout the temple, though some was also kept for tilling under the soil when spring came. No fire was lit during daylight on Solstice. It was the shortest day of the year, the longest night, and all would remain dark until midnight. Then every fire would be re-kindled and would blaze through the dark hours of morning to welcome the new light. For now, the fires were cold, but the ovens roared, the candles spilled golden light from the windows of the houses, and strings of paper lanterns danced in the chill breeze.

Nora and Calla were scrubbing the wooden tables and floor in the dining hall when Calla made an attempt at conversation. It was dull work, women's work, leaving the mind free to wander and the mouth free to chat.

"I shall be singing the sun hymn with Shade Padarn," she said into the silence. "He has quite a beautiful singing voice."

"Who'd have thought?"

"He plays the lyre, too."

Nora hmm'd. She was scrubbing Brenn's blood from the table, the dark brown mark still showing, though she'd rubbed it vigorously. Maybe they'd have to sand over the spot.

"Don't you think it strange that he can sing and play the lyre so well?" Calla continued. "It doesn't really fit with his...flirtatious nature."

"Well, seeing he grew up as a male prostitute, I'm not surprised he can sing, dance, and blow the flute."

"Play the lyre!"

"Whatever."

"He was a male prostitute? I didn't know that."

"Owen told me Shade grew up in a brothel. I'm making a guess as to how." Nora put her scrubber aside and turned to look at Calla. "Shade Padarn? Really? Why are you talking to me about him?"

Calla blushed.

"He asked me to go down to the festivities in the lower courtyards with him, after the ceremony here."

"And?"

"I thought you'd come along?"

"And I thought you'd ask Owen," Nora said.

"I have."

"Really?"

"He said he'll be too busy checking facts on the Temple of Shinar," Calla replied.

"Well, see? That's Owen." Nora smiled despite herself. "You won't want me as a chaperone, will you?"

"I was thinking more along the lines of a buffer. Shade...has a darkness in him that I'm not sure what to make of."

"Shade?" Nora considered the blond young man for a moment. Boisterous, loud, good fighter, fast. "Darkness?"

"It's the wrong word. I don't mean it as negative. It's a feeling of...of a shadow cast over something. A blank wall. Impenetrable. Like the watery deeps. I know there's something beyond the surface, but I don't know what or how far it goes."

"Mystery man." Nora smirked.

"Master Diaz has it, too. I thought it was a wight thing at first," Calla added hastily when she saw Nora's face. "Spiritual defenses. Owen told me the Lords and Ladies have always been rumored to be able to do that. But then I felt it in Shade, too. I didn't know humans could do it. I wanted to ask him how he does it, but I don't know how to. He's always so…and it's not an easy subject to talk about, anyway. I'm scared he won't be serious." She paused. "Will you come? Please."

Nora looked at her. Calla knelt on the floor, her knees soaked with soapy water. She had removed her silver bangles and chains and had arranged her hair in a messy bun at the back of her head, so that a few strands of blonde fell about her face. Her scrubber was in her hands, held in her lap like a flower. She was waiting for an answer. Nora looked away.

"Are those twins still all right?"

"They are growing and their mother is well. We should be able to deliver them without too many complications."

Calla's face was bright and open, with no sign of deceit. Nora chewed her lip.

"I'll be there," she decided.

✧ ✧ ✧

NORA TUCKED THE THIN PACKAGE under her arm and jogged up the stairs to the library, sometimes taking two steps at a time. The door wasn't closed. In the wet weather, the wood had warped ever so slightly. The door only closed if you first grasped the handle and then lifted it into the lock. She reached out to the handle as the door opened. It was Shade Padarn. His suddenness startled her.

He grinned when he saw her face.

"Were you eavesdropping?"

"You know I love to hear you talking, Shade. But I hear you can sing, too."

"Calla's been talking, then. Jealous? Want me to sing for you, Briar?"

"It's still Noraya. And only serenades, please."

"Of course."

She laughed then.

"What?" He winked. "Don't believe I would?"

"Oh, I believe you would. But I don't even like serenades."

"Tell me what you do like," he said, stepping closer and reaching for her fingers. His touch was light, his hands as callused as hers. She snatched her hand away; it was holding a parcel. He looked at her, curious, but she stepped around him to the door, scanning his face closely. She saw no darkness, only good looks and an eagerness to please.

"I like...folk songs," she said, a little breathless. Her fingers prickled.

"Is that so?" He laid his palm against the door, barring her way. Their eyes locked.

" *'Twas on a branch a cuckoo, fa la la la, oh, on a branch a cuckoo sang,*" he sang softly. "*She was heard by a young hunter, fa la la la, oh, heard by a young huntersman.*"

"Do you think you're a huntsman, Shade Padarn?"

"Depends."

"On what?" His lips were close to hers. She raised her chin high to see what he would do.

"On whom I'm listening to." He came even closer.

"I don't sing very well."

"Let me be the judge of that."

They broke apart when they heard footsteps on the other side of the door.

Shade cleared his throat and thumped the door.

"This is very good, er..." He spoke louder than usual.

"Oak," Nora whispered.

"Very good oak," he said loudly. "The carvings are...intricate and the details—Oh, hello, Owen."

"We were just admiring the door's woodwork." Nora smiled at her brother, who poked his head through the door.

"It's oak," Shade said gravely.

"It is," Owen said, his eyes narrowing at Nora. "I thought I heard your voice, Nora."

"You have very good hearing, brother dear."

"So, you didn't happen to bring me any cheese?" Owen asked.

"I'll see you later, then, Noraya?" Shade arched his brows.

"I'm eagerly waiting to hear your song," she said sweetly, and he grinned.

"You look...happy," Owen said as Nora stepped into the library. "Did you do something inappropriate?"

"I'm not that happy," Nora answered.

He sighed and walked her to the table in the middle of the library. After a moment, he snatched the thin parcel out of her hands. She had been holding it all this time.

"This is nice. Good cloth wrapping. Darker shade of red. Echoes the color of his cloak. Maybe an unconscious choice. Maybe on purpose. Nice touch with the black ribbon. Shows you care."

She caught the parcel as he tossed it back to her.

"Who do you think this is for?" Nora asked, smiling.

"Please don't say Master Diaz." Owen ran a hand over his face.

"It's for you, idiot." Nora tossed the parcel back.

He opened the wrapping and smiled, reading the gold embossed letters on the dark red leather. *"Tales of the Tabard Inn."*

"Bet you feel awkward now." Nora was smug.

"A little."

She watched him bury his nose into the pages of the book and take a deep breath.

"Remember sitting under the kitchen table when we were small?" She leaned against Owen's table while he flicked through the pages. "Every Solstice, we'd drag our pillows downstairs and pretend we were in a pilgrim temple. Mother Sara would read us the stories of the ancient pilgrims. I thought you might like a copy of your own."

"It must have cost you a fortune."

"It did. I slaved at the forge for over two months to order a copy from Dernberia. You have no idea how many horseshoes those pages cost. Also, I bled a bit on it on the way across the Plains. You could say it's personalized."

Owen's fingers caressed the gold letters. He looked up at her.

"It's beautiful. Thank you."

"You're very welcome." Nora bent over and kissed her brother's cheek. "It's Solstice. I have a crazy idea. Why don't you leave the library for one evening and come celebrate with us?"

"Us? You mean there'll be other people around? Shade, maybe?"

"Maybe Calla, too," Nora said lightly. "Come on. It'll be fun. We'll sing and dance and get very drunk. Throw up over Prince Bashan's boots. Then you can come back here and read for a few days all on your own to purge the dumb-people talk."

Owen smiled and rubbed his neck.

"It's funny you mention Bashan and Shade," he said. "I think this might be the first Solstice they've ever had together."

"Bashan and Shade...?" A mental picture formed in Nora's mind. She shook her head to get rid of it, but it stuck. "You mean they...he didn't make that impression…I mean, I know that some people…I mean, those two are…?"

"Father and son."

"Oh. What?"

Owen started to laugh.

"You should see your face."

CHAPTER 22

NORA FROWNED.

"Shade is Bashan's son?" Out loud it sounded weird. "How long have you known? Why didn't you tell me before?"

"I knew about five minutes after we met them. And I didn't say anything because it was so obvious I thought even you couldn't miss it. Their eyes, the jawline, the nose. The way they both stand, cock their heads, the way they both speak, their sense of self-importance. Though Shade has a sense of humor, and with Bashan, it's all earnest."

"I need you to tell me these things, Owen. I love to wallow in my willful ignorance. Not so much in the unskillful kind."

Owen snorted again and Nora smiled at him. She returned to her train of thoughts, examining her picture of Bashan with the mental image of Shade. Prince Bashan was a tall, imposing, dark-haired man, with strong features some might find handsome. His air was standoffish, though, nor did he like to let those around him forget their inferior birth. He was the legitimate heir to the Empire of Arrun, but not fit to rule as far as Nora was concerned; his temper was too similar to that of a pampered child, his art of leading was too near tyranny, and his way of seeing the world and everyone's place in it was too disagreeable. But what did she know? Emperor Fasul had supposedly appointed his warhorse as chief councilor. Empress Keren had had Queen Noraya—Nora's namesake—watch as she threw Noraya's children from the highest spire in Moorfleet onto its cobbled streets. Bashan's old man had fathered Empress Vashti through Bashan's fourteen-year-old cousin and then believed in a prophecy that led him to disinherit his only son, bringing the empire to the brink of civil strife. A streak of madness, a touch of remorseless brutality—Shade seemed different. "*There's a darkness in him,*" Calla had said. Huh. He was good-looking and knew it was all.

"I wonder how old Bashan was when Shade was born," Nora mused. "He can't have been older than we are now. Probably younger."

"Same age as us. About seventeen. I think it's safe to say that Shade is his firstborn son. There might be others we don't know about. But judging by Shade's and Bashan's ages, they must be younger." Owen paused. "The firstborn son of a ruler has great power, of course."

"You mean Shade might become a duke?"

Owen gave her a look.

"I meant power in a spiritual sense."

"What? Like magic?"

Owen sighed.

"Do I really have to spell it out for you? Is it really so hard to understand? Gods, I sometimes wonder what's going on in your funny little mind."

"Enlighten me, brother. I know you want to."

He wanted to. He launched into a long monologue, and there was little to be done about it but listen to him talk. Which he did without any intermission, quoting authorities Nora had never even heard of with a relish, sidetracking on details that went over her head, and addressing a variety of theories he had been pondering. Living Blade, blood sacrifice, power, blah, blah, blah. Nora thought about the way Shade had leaned in earlier, his lips full where his father's were thin, the spark in his gray eyes burning with fire while Bashan's gleamed cold and flat. She imagined what it would feel like to rake her fingers through Shade's golden hair, but her mind replaced the blond with dark brown hair, the pale skin with bronze, and Shade turned into Diaz, black eyes burning like volcanic stone, hardened lava. *Damn. Where did that come from?*

"Are you even listening?" Owen asked.

"Hmm?"

"Noraya!"

"I'm sorry, you lost me there a bit."

Owen muttered under his breath and searched through the mess of papers spread over his table until he found a book with illustrations. He ruffled through the pages in a huff and then held the book under her nose. His finger tapped on the picture heading the chapter titled "Of the Living Blade." She dutifully studied the picture and saw a bulky witch of a woman, face scarred, nose hooked, and hands like claws holding a baby aloft. At the top of the picture, leaning down into it, was the huge face of Dalem the Forger, god of smiths. He was easily recognizable by his broad, kindly face and pure black eyes. Also, he wore a crown around his brow with a hammer crafted on it, his sign. The same sign that had hung over Nora's father's smithy and that she had seen so often she had become blind to it being there.

"Is that Scyld offering up her child?" she asked. "Doesn't look much like her statue outside."

Owen tutted.

"And how would you know that the statue looks like her? Anyway, this is a book from the Henan Period in which Scyld's unnatural deeds often led to her being depicted as uncouth and inhuman. And yes, it's Scyld offering up her firstborn to Dalem to trade it for power to free mankind from its yoke of slavery. And Dalem—"

"Forged the Living Blade."

"He crafted the Blade from his blood and that of the child's, uniting all three kinds into one substance: the gods, the wights, and humans. You remember her child was half-wight? The first mixed child to ever be born of a human-wight relationship. It was a very special firstborn."

"I know the story, Owen. Just get to the point."

Nora looked at the baby in the picture. Its eyes were drawn closed as it cried a silent scream. Did it have the black eyes of its wight father? She thought of Diaz. Did all half-wights look like him, or were there some who were simply very tall but with human eyes?

"The power is in the blood. In the sacrifice," Owen continued. "All three kinds know the value of death, the power when one turns over the most valuable possession. All three kinds understand the need for sacrifice. I heard of the death pit you and Diaz found, and the one near here. In times of yore, the old gods demanded much blood, and usually it was human. We know so little. So much knowledge has been lost, become legends, stories we tell children as moral guidance. Because they all have the same principle in common: if you want something dearly, you must pay for it dearly. How many times did Mother Sara take you up to the Shrine of Hin?"

"The shrine?"

"Didn't she pray there for a child of her own?"

"She did. She bought the prayer ribbons at the shrine and tied them to the branches of the trees." Nora remembered the branches around the shrine being so full of red ribbons from all the blessing seekers that they drooped their fake autumn crowns like weeping willows.

"Why were the ribbons red, Nora? Reminiscent of blood, of course."

They weren't. The ribbons were white cotton stained dark red by the blood of the desperate women who would cut themselves to get divine attention. Sacrifice. But she had never told Owen this. Not all secret knowledge was to be found in books.

"Only through the death of this firstborn half-wight and the blood of the gods did the Blade pass through death and come alive," Owen said. "No longer an inanimate object, it retains the consciousness of the living sacrifice and can meld with its wielder to unleash a power so great it can change the course of the world. What would you give to change the world? The Blade has never again been as strong as that first making and the slaying of the gods, of course, but it has always been strongest when there is a direct bloodline between wielder and sacrifice. Mother and child." Owen tapped the picture again. "Brother and brother. Father and son."

"You mean like Kandar, who offered up his third son by the Prophetess Hin, right?" she asked, the hairs on her arm rising.

"I meant," Owen said, "like Bashan and Shade."

CHAPTER 23

NO FIRES WERE LIT. IT was the shortest day of the year, and from this day forward the light would slowly return to its zenith. Evening fell and all was dark. The dining hall was now full, with people pressing against each other, murmured conversation filling the air. It was so crowded that it was already warm in the hall, although the moment had not yet come when a flame would be lit and the extinguished fires rekindled. Nora stood at the back with some of the hired serving girls, closest to the exit so as to be the first to file out. Once the feast started and was humming along, Nora could delegate her duty of oversight to one of the older serving girls and join Calla and Shade. Owen was nowhere to be seen.

It was time. Master Cumi rose from her place on the dais and held her hands up high. The hall fell quiet. Nora craned her neck to see over the heads and shoulders of the people around her. But since everyone else was doing the same, it was still hard to see. Master Cumi held a short sermon, thank the gods. Nora didn't think she could endure a long sermon on change and hope and a bright dawn.

"The Darkness has ended." Master Cumi said the ritual ending words in a loud voice that rang across the hall. "And we welcome back the light."

A cheer arose, drowning the hush. As she spoke the word *light*, Diaz struck a flint stone and ignited a dry twig wrapped in cotton that he then gave to Master Cumi. She in turn ignited another twig wrapped in cotton and gave one each to two young girls, who stepped off the dais and over to the fireplaces to ignite the logs piled there.

With the fires lit, the song began. The sun hymn. It was a beautiful but haunting melody for two voices, one female, for the darkness, and one male, for the light. An invocation. Nora had heard it sung every year on the Ridge. It told of the battle between light and dark, of their yearning for each other and how they had loved and brought forth their children into the world, the ancient gods, only to lose them and then each other by the power of the Living Blade. So light and dark abided forever apart from all things, yet forever looked on, always following each other, their constancy and watchfulness a sign that the end of all time had not yet come and that one day their children would rise again. Strange how the light returning to the earth had so sad a connotation and was turned into such a mournful melody.

Calla sang with a clear, ringing voice. Shade Padarn had taken the male part—the God of Fire, Shinar—and his and Calla's voices intertwined and wove between each other like the passing of the seasons. But Nora's focus was on his face, not his voice. She saw the traces of his father in his features, in the shape of his body, in the way he carried himself. Why had Shade agreed to be killed for Bashan's glory?

"What kind of a question is that?" Owen had scoffed when she asked him earlier.

The logical one? Did he even know? If he did, who would do such a thing? Willingly, at that? What kind of a person would you have to be? Bashan stood at the foot of the dais, watching his son sing with his nose turned up at the proximity of the humble folk. He should count himself lucky there was a crowd between him and Nora. She hadn't thought it possible, but he had sunk even farther in her opinion.

The song ended and was followed by long applause. Nora watched Calla and Shade push their way through the crowd, stopped now and then by words of praise and congratulations for a task well done. When the three of them met at the temple's entrance, the bonfire beneath the statue of Scyld was already catching fire. They ran down the stairs in the cold, clear night while high above them, the bell in the temple tower rang out twelve times. As they reached the square in the lower courtyards, the throng of people around the bonfire shuffled out of the way for the torch-bearer. He paused at the pile of wood that was higher than his head and held the torch aloft for everyone to see. A murmur went through the crowd. Then a hush fell.

"The Darkness has ended." The torch-bearer echoed Master Cumi's words, and his voice rang clear over the courtyard. "And we welcome back the light."

He thrust the torch into the pile. It must have been prepared with pitch, for the flame immediately roared tall and everyone stepped back as it burst into its own crackling firesong. What followed was what a celebration of the return of light should be like, Nora thought, a celebration of life. A band began to play, drums were beaten, and young people started whooping as they danced around the fire. There was cheering and laughter and lots of alcohol. Fathers with their children balanced on their shoulders stepped forward to the fire with brands of their own to light their fireplaces. The impromptu marketplace was filled with the smell of caramel and spiced wine and beeswax candles. A hand passed Nora a cup of hot wine. She smiled at Shade as he bent over to her and yelled over the din.

"Do you dance?" He had a steaming cup of his own and was grinning from ear to ear.

"Only when I'm drunk and don't know any better," Nora yelled back and raised her cup to drink a sip. The strong wine rushed through her body, warming her.

"A challenge I like! Come on!" Shade pushed her closer to the music.

Nora pulled back, shaking her head.

"And you?" Shade asked Calla.

After a moment's hesitation, Calla nodded. With a whoop, Shade pulled her into the dancing ring. Nora watched them dance together for a while. They seemed to be talking over the music. Though Nora couldn't hear a word, she doubted they were having a serious conversation about Shade's darkness within. He was laughing as he twirled Calla. He was a good dancer, Nora thought. He kept the beat, led on, and danced at ease, making his partner comfortable. At least, Calla didn't seem to want to let him go, blushing dark red.

Around the roaring fire a wide space was filling with some dancing couples but mostly young girls holding each other's hands as they leaped to and fro, their cheeks flushed with excitement. The boys stood at the brink of the circle, watching them, working up the nerve to break their cool and dance along. Nora saw a few young couples steal away into the shadows of the stone houses on the quiet side streets. She smiled. It was as it should be.

Another circle of people enclosed the dancers, families with yawning children on the shoulders of their fathers or curled up sleeping already in their mother's arms, as well as the older crowd who stared into the fire with wistful smiles, seeing entirely different people in the flames, entirely different times. Some of the faces Nora knew from her rounds with Master Cumi. She moved through the crowd, greeting the mothers of the serving girls to praise their daughters' abilities to the skies and beyond until the mothers smiled and lifted their chins in pride. Two smiths were having a wrestling match off in a corner. Some men were placing bets on the outcome, but Nora joined in the mockery going on around the wrestlers. They were both already too drunk to actually topple their opponent, so they just stood there, hands clapped on the other's shoulders, grunting like stags locked in battle. Everywhere she went she was offered mulled wine or hot mead or cool ale, moon-shaped cakes, star-shaped biscuits, and sugar-coated roasted almonds until she was reeling with it all.

She pushed through the crowd, into a side street full of vendors, and drifted with the pull of the people around her into a small space of a former house, now crumbled and roofless, filled with rows of benches. It was quieter here, and she sat down in one of the last rows, surprised to find yet another cup of warm mead in her hand. She'd lost count of how many she'd had. The noise of the feast was a dull throb throughout her body. The smell of woodsmoke on the chill air was peaceful and cleared her head a little. She took deep breaths, the cold burning in her lungs. Away from the fires, all was held tight in winter's grasp.

Families sat here, parents with young children, the elderly, all staring at a small group of people kneeling before Master Cumi, who had come down to the lower courtyards to give a blessing. Nora took a sip of the mead. The first sips were sickly sweet, but the more you drank, the more powerfully it hit. Her legs felt heavy and a small fire kindled in her stomach. She shook her head to clear the fumes, but it didn't help. She splashed hot mead over her dress as the families on the benches around her broke out into applause and whoops of joy. A stir of movement from in front revealed the kneeling couples rising, their backlit faces turned to each other to exchange kisses, some with a hunger, some with chasteness in front of such a crowd. Four couples stood before beaming Master Cumi now, and they all looked a bit sheepishly into the rows of rejoicing and weeping people.

A cold hand gripped Nora's heart. Of course. That was Solstice, too. A good day for making a match, for marriage. Her hand reached for the silver wolf's head chain her betrothed had gifted her at their handfasting. But it was no longer there. She had given it up. Along with the life it had promised.

"Ah, such a lovely night for a wedding, and just think of all those autumn babies made tonight!"

Nora turned, looking for the voice dripping with sweetness. Two young women blurred into her vision behind her. The one who had spoken reminded her of the baker's wife, tugging at her shawl with a pinched expression around her mouth.

Nora looked away and saw Garreth's huge frame leaning against a remaining wall. He lifted a tankard the size of her forearm to his mouth, and his grin made his scarred face look like a demon of the ancient days. She raised her own half-empty cup. He was watching Master Cumi weave her way through the gathering families.

"I think some of those babies will be born earlier than autumn, my dear." The two women laughed shrilly, and Nora's focus switched back to them.

She frowned, but they didn't seem to notice; they were too busy slandering the couples in front of them. Village gossip.

One raised her hand to speak behind it into the ear of the other. "What a shame that poor Willem's bride is a whore."

Nora stiffened. Her head felt hot. With that word, so much hurt was caused, and didn't she know that already? She gripped her cup tightly, listening to the giggles behind her.

"She has a pretty face, to be sure," the other woman said. "So she's particularly attached to all her admirers and knows them to be so much attached to her."

No. Nora couldn't take their giggling.

"What a disgrace that her family doesn't have the propriety to attend to and properly guard their daughter," one woman was saying.

Nora whipped around, splashing the remnants of her drink in the faces of the two women. They shrieked in horror, and a shocked hush fell over the marriage ceremony participants.

"What the fuck is wrong with you!" she yelled at them, hurling the cup at their feet. Her shaking hands curled into fists as the women raised their hands to their wet and spoiled faces and then raised their voices, too.

"Noraya!"

Master Cumi stood in front of the crowd of people, all watching her.

"Explain yourself."

Master Cumi approached, but Nora pushed herself free. She stormed past the two young women, knocking one of them to the side.

"Bushes are over there," Garreth called as she stumbled past him.

She let herself be carried by a wave of faceless shadow people, circling the fire. Calla and Shade were on the other side, finally resting. Sweat streamed off their bodies as they drank their fill. Calla's ash-blonde braid had come undone and strands of white hung around her face, softening it. She had a sleeping newborn baby in her arms, and she was talking to the baby's mother. Shade's eyes met Nora's over the rim of his mug. He cocked his head and gestured for her to meet him under the red gates. She shook her head and pushed her way around the people to reach the gates, noticing him do the same on the other side. She groaned. Please, not now! The drummer started to play a sharp staccato and a fiddler joined him.

"Hey!" Shade leaned in close to her ear.

"Hey!"

"You're leaving already?"

"I can't...can't find Owen."

He took her hand to make her stay. His warmth sent a jolt up her spine, and he pulled her close. So close his lips brushed against her earlobe when he spoke. It prickled. She glanced down at their clasped hands.

"We haven't danced yet." His hand held hers tightly, and his breath smelled of spices.

"I don't dance. I told you."

"Come on, it's just like fighting, only to a beat. You'll be great."

Nora was about to decline, tell him her rhythm was off and he'd get bruised, when someone jostled against Shade, throwing both of them off-balance. She let herself fall and rolled to the side, coming up on her feet. Drunk, with a dress on and all. Ha! Shame Diaz hadn't seen it. But at least all that so-called training hadn't been for nothing, then. Her head hadn't quite caught up with her body, but she was standing.

Shade wasn't. He was rowing with his arms and grabbed her by the waist, dipping her low. And then they both fell over, sprawled onto the stairs. His forehead kissed her nose violently. White pain stung in her eyes and she clasped her hands over her face. He braced himself up on an elbow, one hand holding his forehead, and cursed in a language she didn't understand.

"You all right?" Shade grinned. A red blotch formed on his forehead.

"Am I bleeding?" Nora lifted her hands, wiping under her nose. The back of her hand was clear of blood.

"Don't worry. You're still pretty. It's me I'm worried about."

He helped her up. They stood close to each other, brushing off the dirt. Shade scratched the back of his head and then squared his shoulders.

"Well, wasn't that a bit embarrassing? Go on, find Owen if you must. But come back down after and I'll...sing you a song."

He squeezed her hand briefly and let her go. Nora made no promise and walked on. When she reached the first platform of the stairs, she looked down on the festivities and courtyards below, her heart swelling with indignation at the injustice dealt out so casually and cruelly. Shade was doomed to die. Of course, from a certain standpoint, they were all doomed to die, given a long enough time span. So much life. Dancing corpses. But then again, even the gods had died.

CHAPTER 24

THERE WAS NOTHING QUITE LIKE dancing and revelry, Master Diaz thought, as a charming amusement for young people and those who considered themselves as such. On numerous occasions throughout the year, people found reasons to dance, but never so much as on Solstice, when the long winter night changed even the most rational of beings into insipid celebrators of nothingness and self-import. Overeating, overdrinking, and generally overindulging. It would be insupportable to pass many such evenings in a year. Especially since the noise shook the temple walls, the drums beating a steady rhythm that made peace unthinkable even in the dead of night, even in a haven of quiet as he had found on one of the topmost levels of the temple. In a few hours, thank the gods, it would be over and everyone would be worse for wear.

However, his solitude was disturbed even here. He heard the clack of heels on the stone steps. It seemed someone was intent on enticing him to dance, he thought. It was probably Talitha Cumi come to remind him of how he was shirking his responsibilities by not stoically standing on the sidelines throughout the festivities. He shrank back into the shadows close to the door. The staccato continued in a brisk walk past him, toward the balcony the alcove opened to, then skipped down two dark steps underneath a stone-carved gazebo that cast its silver patterns, speckling the marbled floor with starlight.

It was Noraya. She had run up the stairs, and the exercise had flushed her cheeks red as much as the mead made her eyes shine. Someone enticing to dance with, indeed. He smiled to himself and made to go before she saw him. She slowed down to stand under the gazebo and looked up into the night sky through the white carvings, enthralled. Her fingers played with the thin beams of light and shadow and then trailed the delicate stonework as she strode to the edge of the balcony. A sharp night wind blew the long dark hair out of her face, flapping the folds of her dress against her legs. It was always windier up here. She should have brought a thicker cloak. He stood on the threshold to leave as she leaned over the hip-high balustrade and took a deep gulp of the wild air. Below her was only a pitch-black drop of several hundred feet.

He moved instinctively toward her. But he needn't have worried. Reeling back, she laughed drunkenly.

"The night sky amuses you?" he asked.

Nora yelped. Hand held over her beating heart, she whipped around, her face twisted in fear, and peered into the gloom. Diaz stepped out of the shadows and into the cold starlight.

"I nearly toppled over." Nora frowned. Then she smiled when she recognized him. "I didn't see you."

He cocked his head.

"I was right here. You ran past me without looking. Forgive me scaring you. It was not my intent."

"You didn't scare me." She grinned. "All right, you did scare me a little, jumping out at me like that. But if you were here first, I don't want to disturb you. I can go now. It's late anyway. Or early."

She let go of the balustrade and turned to leave, only he was in her path. He should let her go. A man and a woman alone…tongues would wag. If they found out.

"You enjoyed the Solstice festivities?" he asked, stepping into the gazebo.

"Yes, it was great. Is great, I mean, of course." Nora halted.

"And yet you're here alone," he prompted.

Nora nodded and turned to the western sky, tapping the stonework with her knuckles. Diaz stepped toward the balustrade and rested his elbows on it, hands suspended over the long drop below. He peered into the night. For a while, they stood together, over the pitch-black vastness before them, wind tearing at their garments. Side by side, it felt like they were back on the Plains together and he could just reach out and take her hand again. It had seemed so natural then. But of course, he couldn't. Not now. Not here in the temple. Nora shivered.

"Cold?" Diaz asked.

"Do you smell the snow?" Nora asked. "It smells like there'll be more snow."

He inhaled deeply. There was a scent of honey and summer rising around her.

"You liked the mead?" he asked.

Nora chuckled.

"I think it liked me more. It's quite powerful. Wait…how do you know?"

"The scent lingers on your lips," he said and looked away as she touched her fingers to her mouth. "How is your shoulder?"

"Much better. Thank you." Nora felt her scar, then brushed her fingers through her hair. Her hands settled on the balustrade once more and she stole a glance at Diaz's hands next to them.

The sleeves of his shirt were bunched up around his elbows. He caught her staring at his runes, tattooed onto his skin. The back of his right hand was covered in a deep crater of white scar. Puckers of dark color could still be seen, the rune on that hand burned away. He covered his right hand with his left, caressing the scar, reminding himself of how it had been burned. A fleeting echo of a touch flickered over his skin. The sound of a woman laughing. The memory of a time when he *had* danced. He cleared his throat. Nora saw that he had followed her gaze, and quickly looked away.

"Aren't you ever cold?" She raised her chin high.

He shrugged.

"Wights can endure extreme temperatures better than humans. Cold and heat do not affect me as they do your kind."

"That explains why you're always so hot."

He waited, allowing her the time to check the last sentence in the awkward moment that followed it and saw her redden.

"I meant—when we slept together on the Plains…wow, thank you, mouth. Always when I need you. This is just getting worse and worse. I meant to say—"

Diaz smiled. "I know what you meant."

"What do the marks mean? Owen said they're wightish runes."

"Quite right."

Diaz lifted a hand and turned his arm to let her see the marks more clearly. He pointed to groups of runes as he spoke.

"They are marks of identity. They tell those who can read them who I am, who I was born to, which tribe I belong to, my rank and status, that I am a master pilgrim, a warrior adept with blade and spear and bow."

She continued staring at his arms for a moment.

"Interesting concept. To flaunt that information on your skin," Nora said.

Diaz laughed.

"You have the same concept," he said.

Nora frowned and leaned closer. "The only people I know with tattoos are sailors."

"You dress, yes? Clothes make a man or woman, don't they? You can tell what rank a man has in life by judging what clothes he wears, what state they are in, how well he scrubs his boots."

"Well, yes. But—"

Diaz took a deep breath and closed his eyes.

"Noraya Smith. Always wearing the same leather leggings you used to wear while at the forge. Leather is hardier than cotton or wool, more practical as work wear. You wear your hair loose, uncovered, unless it's not washed. Then you fasten it out of your face. So you're not a married woman, and neither do you care for elaborate styling. Your cloak is made with the thick rich wool of the Northland breed, I suspect from the sheep that graze near Owen's Ridge. Your boots are good quality. They're buffed to a shine, but well worn."

He watched the blush rise in her cheeks.

"Your brother isn't the only one who observes his surroundings. Everyone does it all the time. We judge what we see. Just by looking at you, I know you're from a small village in the north, not married, a hard worker, and a woman who cares about what she wears but doesn't give fashion a second thought." He tapped his forearm where a dark spiral crawled over his skin. "Marks of identity, yes?"

Nora looked down. She was wearing a new dress, a rich dark blue, spun of wool with silver thread embroidery. It suited her well. Very well. Around her torso, a high-collared fur tunic kept her warm. She had made some effort on her hair, knotting the top part together at the back of her head with a leather band. The rest spilled over her shoulders in soft waves. His fingertips tingled with yearning to run a hand through it.

"I'm wearing something different now," she pointed out, winking at him. "I could pass for a merchant's spoiled daughter or a handmaiden of a noble lady. Clothes can lie. Deceive. Skin can't."

"Wights believe honesty is a virtue."

"So you burned away the mark on your hand?"

His right hand clenched into a fist and he hid it at his side. A taste of bile rose in his mouth as bitter words bubbled up. He swallowed them down. What did she know? Nothing. It was a random stab in the dark. Nothing more. He saw her freeze, one hand half raised to her unruly mouth. He willfully opened his hand, flexing his fingers against the strain. From the corner of his eye, he saw her look away, far across the Plains toward where her home had been. She tapped the balustrade with her fingers, frowning.

"I fell in love with a boy once," she said. "Coaler. I thought we'd marry one day, live out in the woods together. I don't think I really had an idea of what married life would actually be like, but I liked the idea of having my own true love. Here, look!"

She rolled up her sleeve and showed him her forearm. On it was a small circular burn, just below her elbow.

"I thought it was terribly romantic at the time. A true charcoaler's mark burned into the flesh. He told me he loved me when we decided to mark ourselves. I burned him; he burned me. We belonged together forever. That's what we thought, anyway." She rolled her sleeve back down and brushed a stray strand of hair from the corner of her lips. "Turned out his parents thought otherwise. Such is life. It was a stupid idea. Really hurt, too. But marks of identity, you said? I know what you mean."

She stood stiffly at the balustrade and gave him a sidelong glance.

"Owen told me it's probably the rune for the pilgrim's order under your burn. But he's wrong this time, I think."

Diaz leaned against the balustrade once more, making it seem casual, though his heart was pumping fast and hard, like the distant drumbeat.

"And what makes you think that?"

"Well, you're still here, still a pilgrim master. If it were the rune for the order, you wouldn't have to burn it off, would you?"

He sucked in air through his teeth.

"And because it's a burn," she carried on, not looking at him, "and burns fucking hurt. Anyone who'd do that to themselves is looking to burn away something that hurts more."

She leaned over.

"Don't worry. I won't tell Owen."

That honey scent was still on her lips as she laughed quietly into her fist. Their heads were very close. He breathed in her perfume of smoke and sage, honey and chill air. It felt soothing. No, intoxicating.

As if she felt the air between them change, Nora shifted slightly. Her posture was different now, open to him, chin raised toward his face. He caught her staring hungrily at his parted lips as he opened his mouth to say something, and his heart leaped to his throat, choking him. For a moment—a very, very short moment, he told himself afterward, a fraction of a second, really—he thought of leaning in and kissing her.

She lowered her head in the same second and stepped back, rubbing her lips with her knuckle before grasping the balustrade once more. He took a moment to gather himself, running a hand over his face, mentally shaking his head at his near foolishness. As though he were as young and inexperienced as she was! The stone was cold under his fingers, cooling his temper.

Then she gasped.

"There!" She turned to Diaz and pointed into the distance. "The fire. Is that Woodston's Solstice fire?"

Diaz stepped closer and peered into the dark. Far away to the south, an orange star bloomed in the black night.

"Yes."

"You can see as far as the Suthron Pass from here? That's incredible!"

"Not really." Diaz shrugged. "The temple and Woodston were the last of a long line of beacons from the Wightingerode to the Suthron Pass to signal when the northern part of the empire needed aid."

"It's still incredible," Nora said, eyes bright and alive with fierce joy. "I've never seen so many Solstice fires at once."

Diaz opened his mouth to comment that two or three Solstice fires weren't that many when he saw where she was pointing.

"So many fires?" he repeated, a chill wandering up his spine as he spoke. He looked down. Dozens of smaller fires littered the blackness beneath them.

"Look! In the woods between the temple and Woodston." Nora's finger shook as she froze. "Oh crap!"

"They're not Solstice fires." Diaz gripped the balustrade tightly before pushing himself away. "We're under attack."

CHAPTER 25

NORA RAN DOWN THE WINDING steps behind Diaz, cursing at her long dress, panic crawling up her throat. She had to get to Owen. Had to make sure he was safe. She hadn't looked for him earlier, but she knew where he'd be. The library, of course, poring over some ancient scroll or other, so oblivious to the festivities he probably didn't even realize it was nighttime other than the fact that his candle was burning next to him. She tripped on the hem of her dress and missed a step, and her heart upped its already frantic beat. There was the door! She threw herself against it, mildly aware that Diaz had skidded to a halt, noticing she wasn't behind him any longer. He backtracked.

"Noraya! What are you doing?"

"Finding Owen!" She threw the door open and ran into the library. "Owen!"

The table was overflowing with papers and books. His chair was empty, the wax at the top of his candle still soft. It had just recently been blown out. She punched her fist against the tabletop and, sucking her grazed knuckle, looked around. Where could he have gone? She didn't know. She didn't know and couldn't know, and he could be anywhere. Her heart was beating for them both. She took a deep breath and hid her face in her hands. She had told him to go down to the festivities. He had gone down. And she hadn't been there. And now he could be in trouble. And it was her fault. "*Why don't you leave the library, Owen? Come down and play, Owen.*" It was her fault! She had to get out of the library and find him. She stopped.

First she had to get out of this dress. She slid out of the tunic, undid the belt around her hips, and then yanked the dress over her head. It slumped in a pile on the floor like a wilted flower. Nora was on her way out the door in her woolen trousers she had worn underneath the dress (for practical reasons—standing around at night tended to get cold) and a long-sleeved shirt, pulling the fur tunic back on as she shivered from the sudden chill. Better, though—much better. She could run without fearing she'd trip over the hem of the dress and break her neck on the stairs.

Diaz was gone. She stopped shortly at the entrance to the dining hall and scanned the faces there for Owen's. He wasn't there, either. She slowed to look around once more, making sure she hadn't overlooked him, and then ran down another flight of stairs, beelining for her room and grabbing her knife. If he wasn't in the temple, he was either in Scyld's courtyard, which would be great because she could then herd him up to the highest tower of the temple and lock the door behind them both, or he was in the lower courtyards. And that would be hell, simply because he could be anywhere down there.

A sudden silence filled her ears. She frowned. The drums! The distant rhythm of the drums had stopped. It had reverberated through the stones like a second heartbeat, and now it wasn't there anymore. She ran back up to the entrance and shoved and elbowed her way against the stream of the crowds heading for the safety of the inner temple.

She ran out into the cold, ever downward, her breath a mist before her. Far below, she saw the turmoil in the lower courtyards, illuminated by the raging Solstice fire. A loose line of men ran up the broad causeway, accelerating as they saw the confused panicking human hive bottlenecked into the tight space before and behind the red gates. Sharp thwacking noises pierced the night. Arrows were thunking into the wood of the red gates and into the people below them. Men and women fell screaming, pulling others down with them. Children were wailing and being trampled. She took a shuddering deep breath, braced herself for the onslaught, and plunged into the crowd, throwing herself against them. People were pressing in on her from all sides. She was inundated with blind, raging faces and grasping hands. Suddenly there was space. She broke through the flood of people and nearly stumbled into the Solstice fire. Embers fell onto the tips of her boots. Arm shielding her face, she edged around the bonfire; there was a little space just beyond the reach of the flames and the crowd. Resin spat at her, and sparks fell like tiny orange starbursts.

Beyond the glare of the fire was a churning dark mass of men. The attack had drained the drink out of the heads of fathers and young men, instant sobriety holding them tight in its grasp. They fought back with knives and axes, roasting forks, thick logs of wood, whatever they found. Mostly desperation. Yet the attackers, seen up close, weren't much better. Most wore leather chest pieces and had crude spears and shields. Some had swords with battered edges. Knives ripped and slashed into bodies. Women shrieked. Nora made out Garreth's huge frame where the attack was heaviest, a rock in the waves, and pushed toward him. He was bellowing orders at the men around him, his one white eye gleaming, the other half of his face covered in blood that was not his own. He flashed her a tense grin and stabbed a broken wine bottle into the face of an attacker.

"Owen?" she screamed into his ear.

"Shade?" he yelled back.

Nora dodged a stabbing sword and swore, tightening the grip on her knife. Garreth turned and thrust with his blade, piercing the attacker's chest. Another arrow whisked past. Nora flinched. She turned back and scanned the mass of people pressing in on each other to get through the red gates. Across the Solstice fire—that was where she had seen Shade and Calla last. But they weren't there anymore. They could be anywhere. Owen could be anywhere. In any side street. Taking cover in any of the houses. She closed her eyes, then opened them. Just in time to see Garreth kick another attacker's knee out with a dull crunch, slicing through the downed man's neck. She briefly loosened her grasp on the knife's hilt, only to clutch it tighter.

Find Owen. Don't just stand here! Find him!

She pushed past Garreth, ignoring his shout.

Chapter 26

THE ROAR OF THE FIGHTING was behind her. Nora swallowed. Her footsteps echoed against the stone houses. Her mouth was dry. People were still fighting, dispersed in tiny pockets. Some men were making a brave stand against the attackers, and a woman was wielding a cast-iron skillet with fearsome efficiency, while others simply cowered behind the crumbling walls, trying to hide themselves and their families. Their scared faces floated like pale ghosts in the unlit streets and windows of abandoned houses as she ran by, yelling for Owen. One side street after another. The same scenes repeating themselves in variations. Two men with swords were hacking at a man on his knees with no weapon, one hand raised above his head to ward off their blows, the other shoving his wife away as she held their baby. Nora clenched her teeth. She darted in to stab the attacker's neck while his sword was still swinging high. Her knife plunged into his throat from the side, and he grabbed at the blood, his eyes widening like an owl's. The other man she slashed, opening up his belly. The stench of guts filled the street. She raked the knife up across his ogling face and kicked him down. The woman was screaming in terror as she gripped her baby and fled.

Nora wiped her brow free of her hair, which was coming undone, and found her hand to be sticky with blood. She jogged on. *Over there!* She heard the sound of metal ringing on metal. Someone was putting up a fight. She took the next corner and saw it was Shade. He had found a sword, or taken one from the attacker lying at his feet, and was circling a second man warily. They crossed swords in an explosion of movement, staring at each other intently. Nora ran up and deftly stabbed the man in his turned back. He gasped and clutched his chest, half turning to her. Shade cut him down ruthlessly, opening his rib cage. And then they stood facing each other on the dark street. She found herself smothered in a tight embrace.

"Owen?" Nora's voice was muffled by Shade's arm.

He let her go and pointed.

"He's here. Took a blow to the head."

Nora's heart leaped. Her brother lay on the ground next to a pile of rubble, his face covered in blood from a nasty cut to his forehead. She peeled his hand away from the wound and he groaned, curling up on his side.

"Gods, Nora. What's going on?" Owen said, his head lolling a bit. He looked terribly pale. She'd get him back to the temple. Master Cumi would heal him with a flick of her finger. Everything would be all right.

She grinned.

"I thought you were the guy with the answers, Owen. Come on, Shade, help me with him." Nora hoisted her brother's arm over her shoulders into a better position. "Seen Calla?"

"No," Shade said. "She was back at the fire, talking to grannies and women with babies all night. I saw Owen and thought I'd hold on to him for you."

"It was so loud," Owen groaned.

"Your brother doesn't like parties." Shade pulled a face. "So we came down here for a walk, when we heard the commotion and then suddenly these two guys jumped on us. Owen smashed the one over the head with a brick. I grabbed his sword. The other slashed Owen. You showed up. That's all I know."

Nora nodded. They kept walking with Owen between them, and then Nora yelled for Calla. A second later Shade did the same. They walked a few more paces and then repeated it. Families ran past them, heading to the relative safety of their houses, no time for the small group heading back toward the fight. Ahead, against the backlight of the fire, Nora saw men with swords herding a group of women into a house. The world went hazy for a moment. The sky fell, and the street became blacker. She heard the women whimpering and crying. Fear washed over Nora. Fear and panic filled the air. Then it was gone. She stared at Shade over Owen's head. They pressed themselves against a wall.

"I think Calla's with them." Nora gestured ahead, trying not to heave.

"Not every blonde girl has to be Calla."

"Only one way to find out," Nora said.

"Are you kidding?"

They looked at each other.

"All right, I was just asking." Shade held up his palms. "After you."

They propped Owen up against a wall close by, and Nora looked him in the face, stomach churning.

"Hey, you all right?"

"Really bad headache," Owen whispered, then grinned weakly.

"Stay here. We'll be right back."

"Don't go, please." He held her fingers tight. "Please?"

"I'll be right back."

CHAPTER 27

NORA SQUEEZED OWEN'S FINGERS, THEN let go and nodded to Shade, who followed her, weapon held at the ready. She ducked through the shadows and pressed herself against the stone wall. Shade slunk down beside her. Panic tickled at the back of her throat as if to say, "I'm still here." There was no window on this side of the house, so she circled her finger in the air, motioning to Shade that they had to go around. He nodded and, with one shoulder pressed to the house wall, moved on down. He stuck his head around the far corner and then nodded once more.

His mouth moved to form the word "window." But Nora felt Calla's fear again. It hit like a punch. A series of muffled gasps and sobs drifted out on the night wind, making her palms sweat. Shade ducked low and turned the corner. He was back at her side after a moment, wiping his brow. She wondered whether he felt it, too. Calla's projected emotions. He motioned her closer.

He bent down and whispered in her ear.

"Have you ever had sex?"

She rolled her eyes at him.

"You want to discuss this now? Really?" Her whisper came through clenched teeth.

He rolled his eyes back at her.

"No. I'm just trying to gauge if you're gonna freak out when you see what's going on in there."

He gestured with his thumb to the window. She crept around him, around the corner and under the stone windowsill. Slowly she inched her head over the windowsill. At first, Nora couldn't see much—it was dark inside. Then the bits she saw didn't fit together in her mind. She saw the white buttocks of a man jerking to and fro and thought he was having a heart attack or something. He was bracing himself against a broken table swaddled in a white tablecloth that groaned whenever he moved. Then she saw a woman's red face in the "tablecloth" of her ripped dress, tear streaked, head grinding against the hard wood, arm twisted behind her back. A second man stood behind them, by a door. Then it clicked in Nora's head and it all became one picture.

Shade gripped her sleeve and started pulling. Nora ducked low. What the fuck was wrong with these people? Down the street, by the light of the Solstice fire, the fighting was still going strong. But here, some men were already enjoying themselves. She tried to shake Shade off, but he kept tugging at her. She motioned for him to go farther around the house. They stopped beneath another windowsill next to the door.

"What's your plan, Master Nora?" He spoke into her ear, his lips brushing against her skin in a tingle.

"We go in, kill the men, save the women."

"That's not a plan. That's suicide."

"I'm not leaving Calla in there. Besides, how many men could there be?"

Shade nodded, pulling a face as he moved in front of the door.

"Think it's locked?" He smiled and then rammed his shoulder against the wood.

It wasn't locked. The door opened and Nora ran past Shade into the dark room beyond. A few women were huddled into a corner, their scared faces turned toward the door. On the other side of the room, in front of a second door, two men were grappling with Calla. The whites of her eyes were showing and she was hyperventilating. One man held her arm. He was as white as a sheet.

A flurry of sensations flooded Nora: a baby wailing for its mother; the fear, panic, and despair of the women in the room, blending into a nightmare of darkness that pumped through her veins along with blood-red helpless rage. It wasn't all Calla. She was simply the amplifier. Nora stumbled forward and tried to focus on the man holding a fistful of blonde hair. She slashed down with her knife and heard him shriek. An echo of his pain slid under her skin like splinters. She slammed into the second man, knocking him away from Calla, falling with him to the floor.

"The baby," he groaned, still locked in Calla's empathy. "Lara, Mother of Death! Mercy!"

"Did she beg you for mercy? Did you stop?"

Nora cut down blindly, opening the man's cheek. He bucked under her, his heels drumming against the floor. The tip of a sword pushed past Nora's shoulder and into the man's chest. Nora looked up and saw Shade.

"Don't touch Calla," Nora warned him and crawled off the dead man to reach her friend, who was curled up into a ball.

The second door opened and another man burst out, sword at the ready. He charged at Shade. Nora rose and held her knife tight. As Shade warded off the blow, Nora stepped around the man and plunged her knife into his back, twice. She walked through the second door and saw the rapist, blood on his groin, trousers pooling around his feet. He was fumbling for his sword.

He never reached it.

The woman on the table was dead.

"Nora!" Shade called from the other room. "I don't know what's up with Calla."

Nora went back into the first room, wiping the blood from her hand on her trouser leg. The women were still huddled into the corner. As she scanned their faces, she recognized a few of them from her rounds with Master Cumi. Shade crouched by Calla, careful not to touch her. She was rocking to and fro. A different movement caught Nora's attention. She stepped over to the squealing man without a hand, who was trying to crawl toward his sword. Shade saw her gaze and with the tip of his foot, kicked the sword away. The man blubbered, clutching the stump of his arm. Nora's eyes narrowed on him. The darkness focused, pinpointing the next step.

"Bend over," she said, raising her knife and rolling up her sleeve.

"Nora, remember we're here for Calla?" Shade said.

"Bend over!" she screamed, spit flying from her lips.

A hand gripped her wrist and she whirled around to see...Owen? He was still clutching his forehead.

"Don't," he said simply. "Don't be like them."

CHAPTER 28

OUTSIDE, THE STREET WAS NO longer empty. An angry arm of the main fight had broken loose and branched out into the side street. People with raised swords were running across the cobblestones, kicking in doors of houses, their forced entry drawing out screams from within. For the most part, when Nora thought about death and what came after, she imagined Lara, the Dark Twin, waiting to pick up each individual and then walk down a gray and silent road into oblivion with them. It was what she had been taught happened, vague though it was. But some people believed that Lara also punished the wicked with hellfire and eternal suffering. And what Nora saw now came very close to that, making it much easier to believe.

She and Shade formed a small, pitiable vanguard while Owen held Calla upright. Behind them, the captured women were streaming into the night, making for the safety of dark houses and hiding places. Nora gritted her teeth.

"We've got to make it to the gates at least," she said.

Shade nodded. Nora saw his knuckles whiten as he grasped the hilt of the sword tighter.

"Ready," he said.

"Wait." It was Calla's trembling voice. They both turned to her. "There's another way to the red gates. Through the backyards."

"Can you lead us?"

Calla and Owen shared a look. Then Calla nodded.

"Into the alley opposite, first."

"Let's go," Nora said.

And they moved, staying close together, following Calla's hesitant voice leading them through the shadows. They crouched low through a desolate no-man's-land of weeds bordered by knee-high boundary walls, then passed through the ruin of a house and found an empty washing line spanning the main room. Through an overgrown gateway, under the ivy, and suddenly they stood on a rooftop one street down from the square, overlooking the writhing mass. Garreth and Master Diaz were defending the open red gates. They had rallied the few sober men who were putting up a fight into a hasty line and met the attackers head-on. Steel clashed, men died. The ground before them was strewn with dead and dying. Other men started to run past the locked shields, looking for easier spoils in the side streets, while women and children fled through the gates and up the everlong stairs.

"Now what?" Shade asked as they carefully lowered themselves down from the roof. "We're on the wrong side."

Nora grinned.

"Now? We run with the crowd. Come on!"

She hooked an arm under Owen's elbow, raised her knife, and charged into the broad causeway, dragging the others along.

"What are you doing?" Owen called.

"We blend in," she shouted back, accelerating into a brisk jog up the causeway, following a group of attackers to the shield wall in front of the gates. "We'll be pushed against the shields and Garreth or Diaz will let us through."

"If they don't kill us first," Owen shouted, voice breaking.

"If they even recognize us," Shade butted in.

"We'll be breaking their shield wall," Owen continued.

Shade swore.

"This is a very bad idea," Owen screamed as they plunged head-on into the push-and-shove before the shield wall.

"That's why it'll work."

Nora elbowed her way through the grunting, heaving mass of men that closed in around them, sucking them into the currents that moved them ever forward. She kept her eyes on Diaz. He wasn't hard to miss, his black eyes narrowed in concentration. Nora pushed in his direction, following an invisible umbilical cord, never letting go of Owen's arm. The next wave pulled her aside a little, and she saw Garreth's white eye as someone shoved her onto his shield. Garreth turned his head after spearing a man in the gut.

"Garreth!"

He growled and lifted the spear above the rim of the shield. She flinched. He hesitated.

"Got Owen. And Shade. Calla, too," she yelled into his ear, winded by another shove in her back. "Open up."

Garreth's good eye flickered behind her.

"Fuck. Kids are back," he yelled to Diaz, who lunged forward, plunging his sword deep into another man's chest with a frown.

"Who?" His black eyes scanned their faces. For a brief second he looked confused.

"It's bloody Nora!" Garreth cried.

He cut down into the man next to Nora so hard that the head banged off her shoulder, ripped neck spraying her with blood before the body collapsed. The man behind him stepped up to fill the hole, screaming, "To me, to me!" Their tide of dumb luck was turning. The attackers around them were realizing that something was wrong. They weren't dying where they should be, hacked into pieces by Garreth and Diaz. And just as a predator sensed the weakness in its prey, they converged. Calla shrieked as the bodies pressed in around her.

Nora locked eyes with Diaz over the shield wall. She was breathless from the crush around her, squashed so tightly against Garreth's shield her own knife was cutting into her rib cage, arm trapped between shield and body. If they opened the wall, more than just Nora, Owen, Shade, and Calla would come pouring through. If they didn't open the wall…

She felt a tremor of fear pass through the crowd—fear and bloodlust, rage and greed, all amplified by Calla. Nora's knees buckled under the force. She'd go under. Go under and get trampled.

"Diaz!" She mouthed his name, too winded to speak, vision narrowing on the darkness of his eyes.

He was weighing the odds, the fucking half-wight! A pilgrim master did what must be done. Nothing more and nothing less. And right now, the lives of the many outweighed her own and the lives of those with her. She saw the conflict behind his eyes.

"Diaz!" She was drowning in the mass, Owen's forearm in her hand her only lifeline, slick with sweat. *Come on!*

"If Shade dies, Bashan will go fucking ballistic," Garreth shouted.

Come on!

"Master Diaz!" Owen yelled, his mouth painfully close to her ear. "If you and Garreth push through the wall and meet us, the line behind you will hold long enough for them to close the red gates!"

Diaz blinked.

He nodded and slammed his shield into the man next to Nora, and she heard the grinding noise as his nose broke.

"Do it!" he ordered Garreth.

Garreth muttered something under his breath. Diaz pretended not to hear, giving orders to the men around them.

The squeeze behind Nora was reaching a breaking point, meaning something had to give or she'd break. Garreth hunkered down behind his shield and glowered at her with his one good eye.

"Turn your pretty face, girl," he said and pushed forward, squeezing her between his shield and the men behind her.

CHAPTER 29

AS THE LINE WAS CLOSING the gap left by Diaz and Garreth, they managed to shove Calla through to the safety of the circle beyond. Nora saw the young woman turn back and look over the shield wall, her blonde hair falling about her face like a halo. Tearstains marked her pretty cheeks as she held out a trembling hand. But Owen's outstretched fingers were out of reach. And then Nora was swallowed by the press of men around them.

Diaz pushed through the howling crowd, stronger than Garreth, taking the lead. Nora, Owen, and Shade were sandwiched between the two men. Nora wrangled her knife free and started slashing at anyone who came at her and her brother from the side. Behind Diaz, Shade did the same. They inched forward in single file, fighting against the current until they broke through to the other side and suddenly no obstruction lay before them. They ran down a side street to regroup.

"Shade, take my shield and lock with Garreth," Diaz ordered. "Owen, take Garreth's spear and ram it hard at anyone who comes too close. But don't ever let it go! Noraya—" He sighed. "You're with me."

They arranged themselves into a tight circle. Diaz and Garreth were its front curve, Nora and Shade flanked them, and Owen was directly behind her. Next to her, Diaz, having passed up his shield, unsheathed a second short sword with a curved blade. He looked down at her. Sweat lined his brow and he was bleeding from a cut across his left upper arm. Not even an hour ago, they had stood on the balcony together.

"Now what?" Garreth was hacking down a man who had followed them.

"I think I know how to stop the men at the red gates," Owen said. Nora looked over her shoulder at him. Owen scratched the drying blood on his face, staring at the closed main gates down below. "Won't be easy, though."

"Go on." Diaz nodded at Owen in encouragement.

Owen told them.

Shade whistled through his teeth. "That's insane."

"Fits right in with everything else tonight, then," Garreth said.

Nora blushed. She and Diaz shared a look.

"There's a mill being built on the outer walls," Nora explained. "Shade and Garreth could get the things we need there while we hold the attackers at bay. The miller was using the stones from the wall and the buildings around it, so the wall must be weakened there. It must be where the attackers are coming through. The gap won't be too large. We three could easily hold it. They'd have to squeeze through the bottleneck and right onto our swords."

Diaz nodded. "We could buy Bashan a little more time to form a counterattack."

"How do we get down to the outer walls?" Shade asked. "I hate to ruin anyone's day, but we're kind of a minority here."

Garreth spat. "Hack and slash, boy, hack and slash. That's what we've been training for."

"What? Down the broad causeway? Five of us against dozens of them? I don't recall that lesson."

"There are ways around here, passageways we could use to get from here down to the outer walls without being seen," Owen said, gesturing at a crumbled wall next to them.

"Or we could go over the rooftops," Nora said. "Straight line down. We'd be faster that way."

"Yeah, faster at breaking our necks," Shade said.

"He's right," Owen said. "It's too dangerous. Some of the houses could collapse with us on them."

"Besides," Shade added. "I'm not doing anything else you say, Nora. You're fucking crazy."

"We're still alive, aren't we?" she snapped.

"Passageways would take too long." Diaz came to a conclusion, having heard all the options. "We fight down the causeway. We can do it if we focus. These men aren't trained fighters. They're rabble used to attacking sleeping villagers. Most won't dare attack us unless they highly outnumber us."

"They *do* highly outnumber us," Nora pointed out.

"Then remember your training," Diaz said.

"You want me to roll at them?"

He scowled.

"Not funny. Or appropriate."

She fought down a giggle and kept her face straight.

"I'll improvise."

"Please don't," he said.

It was decided. Nora braced herself. She took a deep breath and tightened her grip on the hilt of her knife. Owen was breathing heavily down her neck. Diaz nodded and they stepped out of the cover of the side street.

Over the next few minutes they advanced quickly onto the causeway; then they were spotted and advanced only by the inch. Diaz and Garreth shredded through the incoming attackers, Nora matching Diaz step by step, picking up whatever the tide of the fight brought to her. She ducked a swing and buried her knife into the man's ribs. He fell, and Owen's spear jabbed him viciously in the back to make sure he wouldn't get up. She blocked another sword aiming for Diaz's throat and grabbed the man's wrist, pulling him forward onto Diaz's waiting second blade. A man knocked into Shade's shield next to her, screeching something at Shade in a high pitch. She kicked the man's knee out from under him, and Shade stabbed down as Nora blocked a downward cut that would have sliced through Shade's extended arm. It rattled off her knife and slammed into the shield instead. Shade swept his blade back up, tearing the attacker open.

Next to her, Diaz's twin blades were moving as if he were two men, blocking, chopping, thrusting, and slashing independent of each other. Whenever they bore down on a single target, that man fell in seconds. Blood was spattered over his face and forearms, but he didn't seem to notice, black eyes fixed on the men coming at him.

Nora's arm grew heavy. She looked down quickly to make sure not to stumble over one of the dead. Behind her, she heard and felt Owen's ragged breathing. A cold sweat trickled into her eyes, stinging, and she had to blink it away, as her hands were busy with carnage. Owen's spear buried itself into the face of another man. His opponent fell, collapsing with a wet scream of agony. The man's sword hand was flailing, and Nora hacked at the arm's elbow joint. Blood fountained from the stump in a hot red shower. A sword flashed toward her throat, and she knocked it back with an awkward swipe of her free arm, pushing the attacker onto Diaz's blade while punching a hole into the man's side. Another few minutes of this and she wouldn't be able to lift her arms anymore. A badly parried sword thrust cut deeply into Shade's arm and he grunted, shield faltering for a moment. Nora slashed across the attacker's face. Shade's shield came back up.

They wouldn't make it down the causeway like this, let alone anywhere close to the wall where the mill was.

"We won't make it," she panted next to Diaz.

"We will make it," he said through clenched teeth.

"I won't make it," she said.

The closer they got to the outer wall, the heavier the onslaught became. They were little more than halfway down the causeway, and already signs of fatigue were creeping in. It would only be a matter of minutes before someone made a fatal mistake.

"All right," Diaz said. "We move into the next side street. Catch our breath."

CHAPTER 30

THEY FOUND TEMPORARY SHELTER IN a crumbled ruin of a house, recuperating from the broiling madness they had just faced on the causeway. Nora let her hands drop. She was bleeding from a dozen small wounds. Owen collapsed and leaned his head against a wall, gulping air like a fish on land. Shade followed suit.

"That was fucking insane!" Owen panted.

Diaz turned to look at Nora, eyebrows arched high. He had a cut across his thigh that bled freely but was too shallow to slow him down. Sweat washed down his blood-striped face, and he smudged it with his blood-soaked arm. Nora held up a weary hand.

"I did not swear this time," she explained, trying to find her breath.

"It was insane," Owen repeated. "How are we even alive right now? It's a fucking miracle!"

"Swearing is a sign of stupidity and blah, blah, blah," Nora said.

Owen grinned.

The sound of running feet thudded by the house. They all froze. Down the street, a woman shrieked shrilly. Owen and Shade got up without a word. Nora eyed the pile of stones and tiles from the caved-in roof. She stepped back, took a run at it, and scrambled up to the edge of the broken beam.

"Noraya!" She didn't turn to look at Diaz's disapproving face.

"It's only three tiers down. I can see the mill from here."

Men spilled forth from a gap just under the skeleton of the windmill on the top of the wall. A lot of men. But the gap was so tight, only two men at a time could pass through the funnel.

"Come down!"

"We can cut across here." She pointed. "It'll be easy to hold the gap."

"It's too dangerous," Owen started. "One false step—"

But she was already balancing across the beam onto another rooftop. A few steps and she was down another tier of the lower courtyards. She accelerated her pace, arms spread wide for balance, muttering, "Don't look down," under her breath. Eyes fixed on the mill, she started running, jumping over a gap between houses and rolling off her momentum in one fluid movement. The night breeze whipped her hair behind her. This was easy. They should have done this earlier.

A shingle slid under her foot. She lost her balance and skidded on the slope of the rooftop, more shingles loosening like an avalanche. Despite leaping to the side to gain a foothold on the stable part of the roof, it felt like she was running on the spot. Slate shattered loudly in the street below her. There was a shout. She had been spotted. New plan. She stopped trying to reach steady ground—or, well, roof—and let herself slide on the stream of shingles, leaping off the rooftop as they washed over the edge like a stone waterfall. She made it over the street and onto the lower roof of the house on the opposite side.

And then through it.

The roof gave way under her with a protest of old age. The falling sensation stopped abruptly as her feet slammed into solid ground once more. And though she instinctively curled together and rolled over her shoulder, the roll carried her down a set of rotten stairs, splintering under her weight. She banged against the stone wall head-first and lay dazed, staring at the patch of night sky visible through the hole she had made. Debris still rained down.

Everything hurt. Her fingers came away red when she touched her temple, and on the inside of her cheek hung a flap of flesh where her teeth had clicked shut as she impacted the floor. Blood filled her mouth, grainy with dust. She was alive, though not yet breathing normally. It seemed her lungs had forgotten how. At least her legs weren't broken. Nor her arms. And look! She was still clutching her knife. And now, breath! At last. Relief flushed her body.

Shouting erupted below her. Someone kicked in a door. Nora rolled, aching, and struggled to her feet. No rest for the ungodly. She stumbled down the next flight of stairs to the ground floor, one hand trailing against the crumbling stone wall, the other grasping the knife. A man came running around the corner, wide-eyed. He had a sword in his hand, but its point was lowered. She slashed her knife in a desperate lunge at his throat. His hand raised to the pulsing wound, and he staggered against the wall, chopping at her with the sword. She dodged it clumsily, slamming into the remains of the wooden banister. Other men came in behind him. She pushed herself upright and stuck her knife into the man's chest. At least one. At least one she would take with her to Lara's silent road. But there were so many.

Through the open door behind the attackers, she realized she had fallen through the last street of houses. The mill was just outside, the gap in the wall only a few meters away. Another man came at her with an ax. It thudded into the frame of another doorway she ducked through as she retreated through the broken house. She grabbed the edge of an ancient, moth-eaten tablecloth and threw it over the man's head. The overturned table became another obstacle. As the man roared, yanking the cloth from his face, Nora heard the tinkle of broken glass behind her and turned in horror.

A dark, sleek arrow of a man darted through the window, arms protecting his face from the glass, two blades in his hands. He came up on his feet and flung himself forward in blurring speed. She braced herself for the incoming pain. But he was past her in a flash and pierced the axman through.

"I expressly told you *not* to improvise!" Diaz said over his shoulder.

Nora closed her eyes, knees trembling. She laughed breathlessly.

Garreth, Shade, and Owen carefully crawled through the broken window.

"Stay with me!" Diaz shouted, stemming the waves of attackers, a lone rock making for the open door and beyond to the gap in the wall. "Garreth and Shade, get the flour bags from the mill. Owen, you keep our back. Noraya, at my side, where I can see you."

They rallied around him and were advancing out into the street already, men dying at their feet.

Nora pressed against Diaz, moving with him in a deadly dance of blades while Owen stood his ground behind them in a low crouch, spear at the ready. A man was charging at them—a number of men. From the corner of her eye, Nora saw Owen's spear thrust forward, jabbing a man in the side. Another man probed a spear in Nora's direction. She knocked it away from her face with her fist, grabbed the shaft, and pulled the man onto her knife. Spear still in hand, she slammed it into the belly of a man who was sidling around Diaz. She slashed at another man's side, and diverted the blade of another with her free hand, head-butting him violently. His hand came up to his nose and she drove her knife into his exposed chest, then kicked him back. And so it went on for what felt like hours but could only have been a few minutes. She fought beside Diaz, holding the gap, weaving in among his thrusts, stabbing at whatever she could whenever she could, using her empty hand to disarm and sweep man after man onto the ground or Diaz's busy blades. They melded into a four-armed beast with sharp claws.

Owen pushed his back against her.

"Master Diaz, there's something you should see back here," he shouted over his shoulder. "Someone."

"Not now," Diaz said, brow furrowed in concentration.

"Yes, now," Owen said.

But it was too late.

A cold sensation flooded Nora's veins, and her arm snapped short in the middle of a motion. A dull expanding sensation throbbed through her. She was unable to move even her little finger as a sheet of electric blue swept up between Diaz and the attackers. A yank below her navel pulled her backward violently, and the three of them were raised off the ground and thrown against the wall of the house behind them.

A lone figure stepped out of the shadows, robes billowing around her, both hands full of dancing silvery water reflecting the moonlight.

"Talitha." Diaz groaned, already back on his feet before Nora even noticed the chill of Cumi's water magic was gone.

"Quite right," Master Cumi said. "Now tell me: what do you think you are doing?"

CHAPTER 31

NORA LET OUT A STRANGLED cry. A dome of ice-cold blue closed in around Diaz, Owen, Master Cumi and her, shutting off the attackers who streamed around it. She got to her feet and stared at Master Cumi in disbelief.

"The Solstice fire," Owen breathed. "It was your signal to attack. You knew there was a force waiting in the forests. You let the miller pillage the walls to create a breach. You'd give over the Temple of the Wind? Why?"

The water swirled in Master Cumi's hands. She watched it spin serenely before her face and smiled.

"Is this the moment where I tell you my evil, evil plan? I don't think so."

"But you—" Nora shook her head, trying to make sense of what was being said. "You blessed those married couples earlier. You blessed them, knowing they were about to die because of you?"

"Till death do us part—that's how the words go, Noraya." Master Cumi's hand dropped to her side. The orb of water went with it, hovering at her fingertips. "Because that's how all life goes."

Nora saw that Master Cumi's long sweeping skirts were spattered with blood at the hem. She met her dark blue eyes.

"I don't understand," Nora said.

"Don't you? You know what they give you when you dig the deepest holes, Noraya? Only a larger shovel."

"This is not you, Talitha," Diaz said.

"And what do you know of me, Telen? You've always had a picture of me in your mind. A picture of my redemption. From blood witch to noble guardian of tradition. And there has been nothing I could ever do or say to change that opinion. Gods know I tried. Well, maybe there is this."

She gestured to the sparkling blue around them and laughed.

"Fine. I see you still don't understand. The fall of the north is just the beginning. You will find the Living Blade. The gods will return. Their treasures will be assembled. They will be woken from their slumber. The prophetess has seen it. All of it. And I convinced her of my worth in her service. And theirs."

"You killed Calla's master last summer," Owen said.

"Fast, aren't you? I know you spoke with Calla. Unfortunately, Master Rallis wouldn't see reason." Cumi smiled at Owen. "So unlike Calla, who is such a devoted girl. Devoted to the order and its silly traditions."

"And for your service, what do you get?" Owen spat.

"Freedom. To be free of the bonds that shackle me to denying who I really am: a mighty blood witch, descended from Neeze, element of water."

Diaz paled.

"Talitha, you would never be free," he said. "You would become nothing more than an instrument in her hand. This temple belongs to the order. The order you chose and vowed to serve."

Cumi raised her brows and laughed. But it wasn't her usual laugh. It sounded hollow and bitter instead of ringing out clear and true.

"What choice did I have? I was about Noraya's age. I can hardly remember the words. The years don't go by as gracefully for all of us as they do for you, Telen. I have little time left on this earth, and I don't wish to spend that time living out some fantasy version of myself that you have made up for me. For years I have let myself be bested by lesser men. Done the job and received nothing for it. Darren. Akela. You. You think I would just hand over my position to you? Why should I? Because you're a man? Because you're older? Silly traditions of silly old men, and I will no longer yield."

Cumi shaped the water into a vicious spike and hurled it at Diaz. He dodged and ran toward her, blades at the ready. She reached out to the water and pulled it back toward her in midair. It spun into a whip and slashed at Diaz, opening a wound on his arm. He winced and kept on running. The water spun into an orb above Cumi's head and then parted into tiny needles, winging toward Diaz. He held up both blades before his face and cut through the water. It fell like rain, only to be lifted up once more. Diaz was nearly on Cumi now. She concentrated and moved her hands in a complicated gesture. A silvery bolt rose from the ground and crystallized behind Diaz, speeding toward his turned back.

Nora jumped up, knife in her hand, and started to run without thinking.

"Look out!" she cried.

Diaz turned and knocked a blade through the water, sending it to the ground as harmless drops once more. He had lost his footing, though, and stumbled. He dived to the side and rolled over his shoulder and was up before Nora reached Owen, who grabbed her by the arm, holding her back.

"We've got to do something," she said.

Owen shook his head.

"This isn't your fight."

He was wrong, but Nora hadn't the heart to tell him.

Together they watched the two masters from a distance, ducking when a whiplash of water sloshed over their heads. Diaz and Talitha were dancing a complicated step, and the flash of swords and spatter of water were whirling like a churning river around them. They lashed out at each other with wide sweeps, silver streak after silver streak flicking through the night. Talitha shaped a ball of hard ice and flung it at Diaz's face. He cut through the sphere, drew his sword back, and struck a killing blow at her heart. Cumi brought her hands up, and his blade jerked to a halt just before it touched her skin. It hung there suspended, as did he. Surprise swept over his features. Then he frowned.

"You won't kill me?" He spoke softly, but his voice carried.

"It's not my place." She shook her head, sweat glistening on her brow. "For a long time, I wanted to change the world, heal it, make it better. But I can't, Telen. None of us can. All we do is make things worse. That's why we need the gods."

"To be their slaves?"

Cumi licked her lips. A drop of blood pearled in the corner of her mouth as she smiled.

"I put a curse on you, Telen Diaz. A final curse, spoken with my last breath. You will remember it and despair, and I will have that solace at least. So, listen, wight, messenger of the gods: the only freedom you shall ever have is the freedom to choose whose slave you want to be."

She let her arms hang loose and as she did, Diaz's thrust pierced her through. They both gasped. Then Talitha crumpled to the floor, dark blood oozing from a deep cut in her chest. She moaned and shuddered, curling up. The blue dome disappeared, leaving an orange glow imprinted on the back of Nora's eyelids along with white starbursts. She blinked. The light had been taken away. Darkness fell once more.

Footsteps approached from behind. It was time to move.

CHAPTER 32

OWEN CROUCHED LOW ON A rooftop on the highest level of the courtyards, closest to the temple. He shivered in the cold wind. Tiny flakes of snow were whisking through the dark around them, pure white against the black, like fallen stars. He saw the same afterimage whenever he closed his eyes. Next to him, Nora's teeth chattered. She wasn't wearing warm clothing.

He was staring intently at the mass of men pounding the wooden beam against the red gates. From the rooftop, they saw that Bashan and a number of armed men had taken up position on the first platform of the stairs, waiting for them to break through.

"I wonder how many men are down by the Solstice fire?" Nora said out loud.

"About five hundred," Owen answered, chewing the inside of his cheek.

"You counted?"

"No. Yes. Look, there are five, six men in the first row by the gates and about ten lines of men down the length of the square. Five hundred. Give or take."

"Worst-case scenario?"

Owen shrugged.

"The flour might be too damp. The explosion might be too high. Lots of very angry men will still be alive when it's done. I don't really want to think about it."

Shade signaled from the other rooftop. He was in position, overlooking the square.

"Guess that's my cue, then," Garreth said, swinging a bag of flour over his broad shoulder, then a second one on the other side. He grunted and shifted them awkwardly.

"Throw them as high as you can, Garreth. And then run, understand? Run for your life," Owen admonished him.

"Shade'll be safe where he is?" Garreth asked one last time, knees bending under the weight of the bags.

"He should be far away enough."

Garreth nodded and started to jog over the rooftop.

"We'll be safe, won't we?" Nora asked Owen.

He nodded, watching as Diaz pulled back the bowstring and readied an arrow. Across from them, Shade did the same.

"The arrows pierce the thrown bags in midair, distributing the flour." Owen spoke more to himself than to Nora. "The Solstice fire lights the whole thing up, and then...whoosh."

Diaz, Nora, and Owen watched Garreth's huge figure as he made his laborious way across the rooftops.

Nora turned to Owen.

"And the people on the other side of the red gates will be safe?"

"What people?" Owen frowned.

She pointed. In the shadows a few families stood in clusters, trapped between the gates and the lines of grim men waiting on the first platform with Bashan. Owen felt the blood drain from his face and Nora grabbed hold of his arm.

"The gates will hold under the explosion?"

His mouth opened and closed.

"Oh gods." He swallowed hard. "I, I hadn't seen them."

"Owen!"

Nora let go of Owen's arm and started to run. Diaz called her name and made to follow.

Owen pushed him back. "No! I can't shoot the arrow. You have to!"

Diaz clenched his jaw and stared after the girl chasing across the rooftops at breakneck speed, dark hair streaming behind her like a long black veil. He closed his eyes. Then planted his feet firmly and readied the arrow once more.

"If she dies—" he said, arching his eyebrows at Owen.

"I know. It'll be my fault." Owen felt like vomiting. "But she won't. You know Nora."

He watched his sister run past a surprised Garreth, and his fists curled together.

"She's lucky," Owen whispered.

✧ ✧ ✧

NORA JUMPED OVER THE GAP between the rooftops, losing her footing on a loose shingle. Not again! She steadied herself, her legs still moving, heart pounding in her ears. She whizzed past a puffing Garreth.

"Hey!" he shouted.

"Two more minutes!" she called, jumping onto the next roof—the last one before the square—her legs shuddering under the impact.

She halted and stared down at the men below. There was no way she could fight her way through them. So she had to go over the gates. That meant exposing herself to them. She judged the distance between the rooftop and the top of the gates. If she jumped—

Garreth landed on the rooftop behind her, shoulders dusty with flour.

There was no time. She just had to jump and hope she'd make it. Trust Shade to fire at anyone who'd fire at her while climbing. She ran back a few paces and took a deep breath. She fixed the handhold she was aiming for in sight and then summoned, commanded, begged, and cajoled the rest of her strength to her quivering legs.

It was seven steps to the edge. She gained speed and flung herself off the roof, tile cracking under her feet. It broke and half of the slate tile fell into the mass of men beneath her. She dropped in midair.

Then she slammed against the wood of the red gates and held fast, winded, sure her ribs had cracked, feet scrabbling for hold. She managed to hoist a leg up to the top, and an arrow thumped into the wood where it had just been. She lay on the top of the gate, catching her burning breath, when a second arrow thumped into the wood next to her head from the other direction. She sat up and stared up the steps where Bashan stood his ground and smirked. He had recognized her and allowed his men to shoot anyway. *Asshole!* Nora's vision flooded red. She rolled off the wooden ledge and let her legs dangle over the other side. It was still a long way to the ground. She let go, banged against the stone ground, and rolled off the jarring momentum that otherwise would have seriously injured her legs. Her shoulder bloomed in red heat. She rose, aching.

There were shouts around her, children crying. Desperate fathers thrust an assortment of pointy things at her face. Nora raised both palms to show she was weaponless and not an enemy.

"Get away from the gates!" she yelled. "Get away!"

Calla rushed forward and held her tightly in an embrace. No one else moved. She scanned the faces of the small crowd over Calla's shoulder to see if she recognized any. A skinny girl with short-cropped hair and a long skirt stepped forward.

"I know you," the girl known as Larris said. "You're Nora."

"I am. Now get the fuck up those stairs before the gates come down!"

"We can't," Calla said, pointing up. "They won't let us through."

Nora pushed through the people, staring at Bashan with murder in her heart. Unfortunately, he didn't drop down dead from her wishful thinking, so she had to come up with something else fast. She rammed an accusatory finger in his direction.

"That man is the exiled Prince Bashan. Your future emperor!" she shouted at the top of her lungs. "He will let you through because he knows no emperor rules without subjects. Now come on! Away from the gates!"

Ha! Deal with that, asshole! At least he wasn't smirking anymore. There was general movement toward the stairs, but not enough. Nora herded the people onto the first few steps, hoisting a crying parentless child onto her hip. The area just before the gates had cleared. But they were still dangerously close. She wondered how much more time she—

The world exploded around her.

Owen had been wrong. It didn't go whoosh. It *felt* like whoosh. She was lifted from her feet in a dazzle of white-hot pain and the shriek of the world rending. And then a quiet fell and it was warm. As though she were wrapped under the warmth of the mountain bear fur once more. With Diaz. On the Plains. Only there was no stink of bear, but one of burned toast. Her head on the cobblestones, fist-sized pieces of debris raining down around her, she sighed and finally closed her eyes.

CHAPTER 33

NORA RAISED HER HEAD FROM the pillow as the door opened with a faint click. Light hurt her eyes. Sunlight glared from the white stone walls. She had fallen asleep again. The headache was finally gone, but whenever she moved too fast, her head throbbed painfully. With nothing to do but heal, she had taken to reading and napping. Mostly napping, though, as even the words she had just read were gone in an instant, and she reread the same short passage of the *Tales of the Tabard Inn* over and over again.

She rubbed her eyes, which were gummed shut from the fine flour dust that still seemed to be everywhere, and saw Owen creep into the quiet room.

"Hey," he said. "How are you feeling?"

"Bones heal, flesh seals. Face still looks like shit."

Nora pushed herself upright. Calla had let her look into the mirror once after she had woken, her reflection spinning in the dark room, a piercing stab whipping through her head. Hair black like ebony, skin as white as snow, damage on one side of her face red with blood and burns. Her heart had sunk. None of her visitors had the courage to tell her—not Shade, not Calla, not even Owen—but she knew she looked like Lara. The Dark Twin. Half beautiful woman, half mangled corpse. It would be poetic, if it hadn't been her face. With Master Cumi gone, Nora would bear the scars for the rest of her life.

"I'm bored mostly."

Owen grinned as he saw the open book on Nora's lap. It was still showing the same page it had the last time he had come by to visit. Nora snapped the book shut and put it on the small table next to the bed, re-arranging a jug of water, a cup, and a half-finished bowl of cold soup to make everything fit.

"Maybe I can find something more entertaining for you to read than stories of pilgrims," Owen said. "There's a thin treatise from Niccolo of Aerenfurt called *Daggers in Combat* in the library. If you're interested…"

"I'm not." She sighed. Daggers in combat actually sounded interesting. "I don't want to *read*, Owen."

"Then what do you want?"

Owen sat down on the edge of the bed. Nora shrugged.

"I want to get up and do something. I want to help in the kitchens, help with rebuilding. Even Calla is helping tend to the wounded."

"Anyone wounded worse than you is already dead."

"I'm just sick of staying in this room. In this bed." She punched the blanket with her bandaged fist. "Everyone else is up and doing something. Even Bashan."

When the red gates had exploded into nothingness, Bashan had charged down the stairs with his men and plowed through the remnants of the attackers with ruthless efficiency. The prince was the hero of the day and had taken over the rulership of the temple temporarily at the behest of the people he'd saved. He filled the position extremely well, too. It made Nora feel sick to the bone. You had to give it to the prince; he knew that it was never who you were, but who you seemed to be to others that mattered. Still.

Dust specks danced on the sunbeam across the wall. The dust was everywhere. She could taste it as a film on every cup of water she drank, gritty and slightly bitter, saturating the temple with a scent of bread and woodsmoke and blood. While he stared at the wall, Owen was fidgeting with the leather bands that bound his loose shirtsleeves together at the wrists. He was thinking.

"You took the vows, didn't you," Nora said.

"Hmm?" He turned toward her, seemingly oblivious to what she had just said.

"You took the pilgrim vows. You're one of them now. Punish the wicked. Protect the innocent. Guide the lost. The road becomes my bride. No ties to family and kin. Blah, blah, blah."

"I know you disapprove—" he started.

"I don't, Owen. I know it's what you wanted. What you're suited to do. I'm just—" She shook her head, remembering Master Cumi's words. Not her last ones, but all the ones in between. "I wish I was so sure, is all."

"If you took the vows, too, I'm sure Master Diaz would take you on as a student."

"Yeah...Diaz."

She studied Owen for a trace of innuendo, but her brother's face was empty of smirking winks. His mind was probably too pure now for those kinds of thoughts. He *was* nervous, though. His fingers intertwined with her own. They were sweaty. Why would Owen be nervous?

Realization hit her hard then. Of course he had taken the vows. Taken them and was going on his pilgrimage with Diaz and Bashan. Going alone. That was why he had come here. To leave her here. Alone. After all she had gone through to find him, to be with him again, for them to have each other. Bandits on the Ridge, mountain bears and death pits on the Plains, the long journey spent dependent on Diaz, the time here, the people here. All of it meant nothing because he would be fucking leaving her.

"Over my dead body," she said through gritted teeth.

"What?"

"Did you come here to say goodbye, Owen Smith?"

"Er…I don't know what you mean." He pulled a face. Yeah, he knew exactly what she meant.

"Stop lying, because you suck at it."

Owen took a deep breath to compose himself and glanced at her.

"I have spoken to Prince Bashan. We will move southward when spring comes to consult the prophetess at the Temple of Shinar."

Another look at Nora. She didn't say anything.

"So. I know you want to come along. But I also know you want to help. And you would be of great help to Calla when we're gone. Bashan will be leaving most of the Hunted Company here for protection. But his men know and accept you more than they would Calla, for example. If you gave them an order, Bashan thinks they'd probably do it. You're like a lucky charm, they think. You have Garreth and Shade to thank for that, by the way. Gossipers."

He grinned weakly. He was trying to deflect the damage. She kept her mouth shut. It wore him down. It always did. Even though he knew this tactic, he stepped right into it every time, trying to fill the silence. He cleared his throat.

"The people in the courtyards have seen you with Master Cumi and Calla, too. Some of them remember you from before the gates. Some remember they would be dead, that their children would be dead, if it weren't for you. You would be a great help. If you stayed here."

Nora waited for more, but Owen just licked his lips and fiddled with his leather band.

"Are you finished?" she asked.

"Think of all the good you could do here, Nora."

"I am thinking—" she started.

"And besides, we shall pass through here on our way farther north when we have divined the exact location of the Living Blade. We will see each other again." Owen spoke fast to jam in one more *reasonable* reason.

"I am thinking," Nora repeated slowly, reaching for the book on her nightstand, "of the fact that you fucking don't know me that well if you think you can just leave me here and skip away."

She threw the book at Owen, who caught it awkwardly and gaped at her.

"With fucking Bashan."

The cup she hurled at him made Owen jump off the bed and run to the door, the book still clutched to his chest.

"I know you're a bit angry right now—"

"And fucking Diaz."

The water jug exploded into shards next to Owen's head. He grabbed the door handle and stepped into safety.

"I'll come back later with a different book," he shouted.

The door closed.

"You do not want to see me get out of this bed, Owen," she screamed as she heard his footsteps leave hurriedly. "Don't make me follow you."

When she heard nothing on the other side, she allowed herself to laugh.

Laugh until her ribs hurt. As if he really didn't know nothing would stop her from following him.

✧ ✧ ✧

THE COLD WIND TUGGED AT Owen's collar, but it also brought a scent of new green from the woodlands. Though snow still drifted in the corners of the courtyards and slumped against houses, and icicles hung like diamond teeth from the rooftops, spring was showing her blue banner of promise in the skies. She kissed the earth from its winter slumber, though it was but a brush of the lips.

"Have you said goodbye to Nora?" Calla asked.

Owen turned to look up at the window to Nora's room. It was high above, and though he fancied he saw the outline of a person looking down, in reality he knew that was just wishful thinking. He knew that from this distance, he wouldn't see anyone's face.

"I tried," he said. "She won't see reason. She—"

He knew Nora wanted to come along. And deep down he wanted her to come with him, too. But that was a selfish reason, Owen told himself. A selfish desire to be with his twin, to have her roughness complement his smooth edges, her stubborn head compensate for his yielding spirit, and her loud mouth saying things as how they were to contrast his speaking logically and reasonably. But—

But that was simply selfish. Nora was still weak. Too weak for such a long journey. Besides, the Temple of Shinar was a temple of the pilgrim order, yes, but it was also the largest brothel on this side of the world. It was not a place he wanted to take his sister. She'd probably enjoy herself too much.

And having Nora here with Calla would help his beautiful companion. He glanced over. Calla's hair was braided loosely and the wind lashed strands over her face. Some stuck in the corners of her mouth. Shadows lay under her eyes, but at least the silver chains were gone.

He looked down the causeway and could see Bashan, Shade, and Garreth under the arch of the outer gates. A small crowd of men gathered around the prince, seeking his good favor. Yes, it really was the best solution all around if Nora stayed here. But—

But the niggling of doubt crept up on him. He had been wrong before. To send her away from him. Maybe—

"She's being very obstinate." He finished his own train of thought.

"And vocal, I heard."

"I think everyone in the vicinity heard." Owen grimaced. "And besides, we shall pass through here on our way farther north when we have divined the exact location of the Living Blade. We will see each other again."

"I look forward to it."

"I meant Nora and I—"

"I know." Calla simply smiled, her blue eyes fixed on him for a moment, making his heart miss a beat. She then greeted the family walking past the two of them but said nothing more to Owen until they reached the gates.

This was it, then. Bashan, Shade, and Garreth were waiting already. They made small talk and shouldered their gear, making ready to leave. Master Diaz was lurking in the shadows, hood pulled deep over his eyes. Even after so much time, even after the battle at Solstice, the residents of the lower courtyards flinched when they saw him pass by.

He nodded in greeting.

"Master Calla." Bashan turned. "I bid you farewell. Look after my temple while I'm gone."

Calla bowed her pretty head.

"The temple belongs to the order of pilgrims, my lord. We shall look after your men for you, though."

Bashan grunted and made ready to go.

"May your journey be swift." Calla said the ritual words. "May the miles fly by on wings like an eagle. May you not travel down the silent road. May the way become your bride.

"And may your return be just as swift," she added.

Owen turned to Calla one last time.

"You'll talk with her, won't you?"

"I'll try." Calla smiled. "When she's not so mad. I'll tell her it wasn't an easy decision for you to make. That you left doubting whether you had made the right choice."

"That'll placate her, for sure. She loves to be smug."

"It's also the truth."

Owen was unsettled for a moment. He looked down at Calla's gloved hands. After Solstice, she had turned to wearing leather gloves that reached up her entire forearm. He thought it was to help her not sense her surroundings, not feel the emotions of the person she was talking to.

"Only if the person is someone I'm not close to," she said, and a faint tinge of red crept into her cheeks. Owen watched, fascinated by the change in her complexion.

She stepped closer and spread her arms wide for an embrace.

"Come back soon, Owen."

"I will."

As he felt her arms rest on his shoulders, he made himself think of good things, of beautiful things: a rainbow, the sound of summer rain, the silver melody of the springs in the temple, the scent of woodsmoke and sage, Nora laughing out loud, tossing her hair back as she did so.

"You don't have to do that for me," Calla whispered into his ear as she hugged him tight.

"I know."

They stepped apart and Owen turned around, concentrating on the road before him, trying not to see Shade winking and hooting.

Every step now would take him farther from a desire he didn't even know he had. He focused on what lay before him, the road to Woodston and the Suthron Pass, to the Temple of Shinar. Knowledge was his ultimate desire, he told himself as his heart beat faster at the idea of finding the Living Blade, of finding more than just the Blade. What lay ahead excited him far more than an embrace could.

They walked down the road to Woodston for the rest of the day, only stopping shortly for a midday lunch on a grassy mound to the side of the ancient imperial road. At dusk, Diaz signaled them to move under the trees, and they found a small glade, perfect for shelter. After the long stay in the library all winter, Owen was exhausted by the journey. He made his bed and fell asleep quickly without even reading a page or two in the books he had brought along.

Diaz shook him awake a few hours later.

"What?"

Diaz held a finger to his lips. Only then did Owen see the sword in Diaz's hand. He nodded, bleary-eyed, understanding when he heard the crunch of breaking twigs come from the direction of where he supposed the road was, invisible now in the pitch-black night.

It was probably just another weary traveler who had seen their small fire and was looking for shelter under the trees. Despite his rational thoughts, Owen's hair rose. Too many bad things had happened. Whoever their nighttime visitor was, he moved as quietly through the woods as he possibly could. Why? Owen held his breath as Diaz melted into the shadows.

The rustling stopped. Owen jumped in fright as he felt cold fingers slide over his eyes.

"And? Did you miss me?"

Nora laughed at his surprise, tipping back her hood.

The Living Blade: Book Three

Black Hole

CHAPTER 1

SNOW COULD CHANGE EVERYTHING. NORA looked up at the blue spring skies. The winter snows were beginning to melt, and heaps of it grayed into slush along the roadside. The earth was visible after the long winter, dark brown, wet, and receptive, ready for plowing. They traveled a week on the road and passed Woodston, still shut to travelers, with ease. At the front of their small company, Owen harangued Prince Bashan for days about the ongoing possibility of snow until they reached the Suthron Pass, leaving the road that led to the heart of the Kandarin Empire and taking to the woodlands with their gradual climb. If they made it past the Suthron Pass without snows, then their journey would be smooth, Owen said. They'd reach the Temple of Shinar in about two and a half, maybe three months. But only if the snows—

"I heard you the first time," Bashan said icily, patience finally breaking.

Owen blushed and instinctively fell back to where Nora and Shade were dragging their feet, then he flinched, probably remembering he was still mad at Nora for coming along. He stayed by Garreth's side instead, silent.

Bashan had pressed his lips together tightly in an uncharacteristic display of self-restraint at Nora's arrival, and he hadn't sent her back. Yet. Garreth had shrugged at her presence in that nonchalant way that said if she wanted to die horribly, what was it to him exactly? On their first morning on the road together, Diaz had handed her a wooden baton the length of her forearm. She'd given it a puzzled look.

"For training," he said and winked.

At dusk they made camp, talking low around the fire. Bashan looked up at the sheet of clouds that had rolled in during the evening, barring out the faint starlight.

"Sun sets early still," he announced to no one in particular. "I want us to get a start before dawn tomorrow. Make it over the pass and camp in the fields of Rheged."

"Mercy, lord." Shade grimaced. "A growing boy needs rest."

"It's not yet eight." Bashan scratched his jaw. "That gives you plenty of time to rest. Provided you go to sleep now."

"Now? Owen's going to read his books until midnight," Shade said.

Owen looked up from his book, startled by the sound of his name.

"I'm figuring out the most direct route to take south so as not to lead us too close to the military camps of the imperial guard," he said, shadows dark under his eyes.

"Least Owen's not whining," Garreth said, wiggling down close to the fire and pulling his cloak over his face, knowing he would relieve Diaz of guard duty in just a few hours. "So shut up and good night."

"We haven't even eaten anything," Shade pointed out.

"Whining, boy," Garreth rumbled. "Next time you open your mouth I'll punch it shut for you. Then you won't be able to eat anyhow."

Bashan sniggered. Over the fire he gave Shade a look. Though he mumbled something rude, Shade deferred to his father's wishes.

Three months of this ahead of her, every single night. Nora rubbed her hand over her face and winced. The wet cold made the freshly healed cuts and burns feel taut, the skin stretched uncomfortably tight across the damaged side of her face. Warmth helped. But if she moved too close to the fire, the heat made the cuts feel dry and itchy while the burns flared up. She pulled out the small leather pouch Calla had given her and dabbed some ointment here and there, then carefully massaged it over most of her left lower jaw up to the cheekbone and a bit of her forehead, too. A piece of burning debris had fallen on her head after the explosion at the red gates. It had singed away a large part of her hair just above her ear, burning the scalp, but if she left her hair down, it didn't show. Much.

She caught Owen watching her from across the fire and finished up, running a fingertip doused with ointment along a deep cut across her cheekbone. He quickly lowered his gaze, pulling up his shoulders, hunching over his book. This fight had gotten tired two weeks ago. It was time he let it go.

Nora got up to go behind the bushes, taking a light from the fire with her. Nature was having its way with her body again. It was that time of the month. As she threw the soft moss into the dark, the blade of a sword slid silently between her bare legs, grazing her thigh. The sting made her think something had bitten her at first, and she hastened to pull her trousers up but couldn't. She stared dumbly at the silver tip shining between her knees, then realized what it was. Her trousers pooled around her feet, and she rose slowly and raised her hands.

"No one should walk alone in the dark," Bashan's voice drawled behind her. "You least of all. There could be all sorts of dangers—wild animals, poisonous snakes, evil men."

Not to mention the poisonous snakes impersonating men, Nora thought, pulling a face at the dark trees around them.

"My lord," she said.

"We should be over the Suthron Pass tomorrow," Bashan said, twisting the sword to see the reflection of her intimate parts in his blade. "It's still a bit of a climb. So stick close or you'll get lost. But the end of the journey, the Temple of Shinar, warms every man's heart and quickens even the heaviest feet—such a place of beauty, filled with beautiful women. Did you know, in ancient times, when it was still a temple devoted to the god Shinar, all the unmarried girls living in its vicinity had to travel to the temple to be initiated into the sacred knowledge of being a wife? It's true. Ask your brother. They even came from as far as the outskirts of the City of Arrun itself. Each girl had to wait in the courtyards until a man, any man, came to choose her as his vessel for divine instruction. The uglier they were, the longer they had to wait. Pity about your face, isn't it? All that scarred mess on the one side. But you know, if you shaved between your legs, maybe you'd find someone willing to teach you what you really need to know instead of how to wave a knife around."

She remained silent.

"However, I understand that it's hard to scrape a blade across something you can't see properly. Perhaps you'd like assistance?"

"No, thank you, my lord."

"It's really no problem. You just ask away when you're ready." Bashan laughed at his own joke.

The tip of the sword quivered and cut her once more. She sucked in air between her teeth.

"Oh, look. I've made you a woman. You're bleeding a bit." Bashan chuckled. "I'd say I relish these little chats of ours, but really, I don't. It would be far simpler if I had the guarantee you'd keep your mouth shut and behave decently for a change. But we both know you're not very good with obedience."

He sighed dramatically, removed the blade, and tapped Nora on the shoulder.

She turned to face him dutifully, gathering saliva in her mouth to hawk into his eye at a convenient time. He looked her up and down like a butcher assessing a cow for slaughter. She didn't swallow the spit but just stared into his dead fish eyes, scanning his face for a good target. Directly into the right eye, she decided.

"Just so we're clear..." Bashan leaned in closer. "I don't mind you coming along if your only purpose is to warm Shade's bed. The boy is going to die for me, so whatever makes the rest of his short life pleasant is fine. What I do mind is that you're a tragic accident waiting to happen. Unless Diaz is always there to save you, of course."

He moved in closer, pressing her against the tree behind her. She could feel the tenseness in his muscles, ready to uncoil and strike fast with the sword still in his hand. He bent down to whisper in her ear.

"I like when things go smoothly. So let me tell you now in good faith that your pull on him is nothing in comparison to the power of Shinar."

She did swallow the spit then, reaching slowly for her knife instead.

"Are you a man of faith, then, lord?"

"Faith is the evident demonstration of realities not yet beheld. My life's motto, one could say. Bear with me just a moment longer, as I will bear with you." Bashan tossed his head back and frowned at the celestial bodies twinkling into appearance. "I'm trying to prove a point."

"And what point would that be?" Diaz stepped out of the shadows, his deep voice broken and raspy like the bark of the thorn trees.

Bashan smiled down at Nora.

"Aren't you lucky?" He turned to Diaz. "Oh, it's nothing. Nora tried to seduce me with her peasant wiles. It seemed like fun. But I refused."

He walked away, and Nora wished she still had the spit. From where she was standing she'd get a good shot at the back of his head. She pulled up her trousers, face hot. Tears swelled in her eyes, but she would not cry now. She fumbled with her belt and stalked past Diaz, head held high. A trickle of blood ran down her leg and itched in the hollow of her knee.

"Are you hurt?" Diaz asked in a low voice and caught her arm. "You're limping."

"I'm just fine." Nora ripped her arm away and walked to her bedroll next to Shade, who was already sleeping. Owen looked up briefly from his book.

"You all right?" Owen whispered.

"Just peachy," she said, rolling up in her cloak with her back to the fire.

She stared out into the deep dark blue. Three months of this ahead of her, every single night, she thought. *Yeah. Nothing to it.*

CHAPTER 2

THE SUTHRON PASS WAS A narrow stretch of rugged terrain that separated the north from the south, a land bridge left over from ancient days. They crossed the high pass on a forgotten wagon road. It was so narrow that the rocks, though weathered by age and howling winds, still bore the wheel marks that had rolled over them in exactly the same spot. Smuggling wagons, for sure. Anyone else would use the imperial road below and not risk the narrow path, not risk the landslides tumbling to the ocean far, far below. The peak opened suddenly before them, and Nora took a deep breath from the rushing wind that tried to claw it from her lips. She looked out upon the world at her feet.

To her right, mists hung over the western sea below, roughing up the cliffs on the far shore. The vast body of water stretching beyond the horizon shimmered a dark blue as though reflecting a summer night sky. To her left, another sea lay long and silent, its waters cobalt blue, and in some places, emerald green. Many days', maybe even weeks' travel into the sunrise by boat, somewhere in that enchanted ocean, lay the Blessed Isle of Nessa, Master Cumi's point of origin, a kingdom of blood witches and mermaids. The otherworldly color of the water made it easy to believe the stories she'd heard.

The country before her broadened after the pass, rolling gently into a plain with small fields and whitewashed settlements touching the land with human hands, though in two days' travel on the main road, they'd passed not a single soul. The way descended through woodlands of pine into forests lined with oak and juniper. Spring had reached the south. Green invaded everywhere Nora looked. Blackbirds and robins twittered. Crows croaked when they walked along the endless plowed fields where sprouts of wheat greeted the warmer sunshine. The lands of Rheged were often called the breadbasket of the empire. If they followed the main road farther inland to the east, where mountain ranges paled in distant blue, eventually they would come upon the imperial City of Arrun, heart of the world. Whether Bashan was tempted to see his home, his city, was hard for Nora to tell. But she saw his gaze fix on that direction for days while they walked ever toward the south.

She often woke before dawn, listening to the chatter of the birds in the semi-darkness, watching the last embers of the fire die slowly before she rose. In the quiet time before the others awoke, she trained with Diaz out of earshot.

Today, a deep crease wrinkled his forehead as though he were plagued with headache. He had borrowed Garreth's shield for his protection, so she knew this lesson would be intense. At least she didn't have to roll anymore, and though they weren't practicing with swords, it was much closer to the training she had imagined when she had first asked Diaz to train her. She swung her wooden baton for feel as he took up his position opposite her.

"Hit me when you can," he said.

Nora nodded.

The drill was the same routine they had gone through the last few days. They'd start gently, circling each other. Sometimes there would be an opening, but she was a pace or so out of reach. Other times he'd tease her by turning his open side to her thrust, only to close it fast as she darted in. Whenever she managed to touch him, he nodded or gave commendation. When she made a wrong move, she got smacked on her upper arm. The resulting bruise was dark purple, surrounded by yellow and greenish spots. She didn't mind. It would fade sooner or later. Every day he tapped her on the arm less and less.

After a few minutes of warming up, Diaz increased the difficulty, striking back at Nora to make her watch her footing, throwing unexpected blows where she was ill-guarded. He swung his baton in a wicked curve that would have opened her stomach if it were a real sword, spilling her guts. But she sidestepped and skipped back to have more room, more time to rethink her approach. He watched her over the rim of the low shield, waiting at ease. She gave the baton a twirl. It was longer than her knife, but lighter, if only a little.

"How did you know?" she asked, stalking around him to find an opening.

"Know what?"

"That I'd come and follow you," she said. "You had these batons made when I was still in my sickbed. So how did you know?"

He lifted one shoulder a fraction.

"You dragged yourself half-dead across the Plains in winter to get to your brother." Diaz cocked his head to the side. "What could stop you?"

Nora tossed her head back, grinning.

"How do you know I followed Owen and not you?"

Exactly as she had hoped, his face froze over while he was thinking of a reply. She charged in then, but his baton came up ready and they connected in a flurry of blows and counterblows. After a minute or so, he signaled for a pause.

"You don't cover yourself. That makes you vulnerable," he pointed out.

"I thought I was supposed to be on the offensive, acrobatic, like a cat."

"Yes." He nodded. "But your over-commitment is too much of a risk in a real fight. We'll have to work on that balance more."

"All right," Nora said and took up a fighting stance once more.

Diaz removed the shield from his arm.

"Not today," he said, shaking his head. "It's past dawn."

"And you've had a rough night."

His frown deepened. "I did not."

Nora shrugged. "You look like it."

"Two days south from here is a settlement," Diaz said, ignoring her observation as they walked back to the camp where the others were stretching and waking. "I want you to go and scout ahead, maybe pick up some supplies while you're there."

"On my own?"

He looked down at her.

"Women don't travel on their own. You may take Owen and Shade."

"What does this have to do with my training?"

"The way we act in times of calm determines how we act in times of crisis. Keep your eyes open and your mind sharp. And, Noraya…" He paused. "You're here because of Owen. So talk to him."

"He's the one not talking to me," she huffed. "I don't know why he's so mad. It's not like he doesn't want me to come along, because I know he does. I can feel it in my bones."

"He does," Diaz agreed. "But every time he sees your face, he feels guilt. And it weighs heavy on his mind."

"But it's not his fault." Nora touched the scar under her eye.

"I never said it was." He raised his eyebrows high. "So talk to him."

CHAPTER 3

FROM A RISE IN THE land a few miles out, the three of them looked down upon the settlement that lay along the crook of a river. It looked much like every other settlement they had seen from afar, sprouting alongside the imperial roads every day's worth of miles. Smelled like them, too—of cooking and human waste.

"Hmmm." Owen scratched his nose. "Looks like a military encampment with the fence around the compound, but there shouldn't be one this far south. According to the map, we're already in the no-man's-land between Shinar and the southernmost borders of Kandar."

"It's not military," Shade said.

"How can you tell?" Owen peered at the settlement.

"See the central structure? The large house with the domed roof? It'll belong to the matriarch, the woman in charge here. We have to enter the settlement from the side. It's customary for travelers to not enter through the main gates. That's reserved for family. And we'll have to ask the matriarch for permission to stay the night."

"You seem to know a lot about this settlement," Nora said, tugging her hood up around her face. It was traditional for married women to cover their hair, and that was their guise. Also, it kept the sun from burning on her head, irritating the scarred skin.

Shade grinned. "Not this one in particular, but if you've seen one, you've seen them all. And I grew up here. And have seen them all."

"You grew up here? In the south?" Owen looked over Shade's light hair and his blue eyes. Shade could have been a street urchin from Dernberia in the north. Owen and Nora, with their dark hair and tan skin, looked more like they came from these parts. "You don't sound like it. No accent."

"I had good training. But, yeah, I can do the talking."

The settlement was shored up on the red alluvial plain and had been built among the ruined pillars of a town or a temple, slumping back into the mud of the meandering riverbank. The three of them crossed a wooden bridge leading over the brown sluggish waters to the white square houses. The poorest-looking houses on the bank were roofed with tight-set planks if they weren't sporting the typical flat roofs of the better homes, with their second living room under the open skies. Toward the center where the domed building stood on its own, the houses were set with mortared stones, some with intricate carvings, probably pillaged from whatever ruins these were around them.

The fattest woman Nora had ever seen came out of the domed house and approached them, her skin a rich brown like the river, black tattoos on her forehead and cheeks matching her black dress. A widow. Or, well, she could be a charcoaler, but Nora didn't think that likely.

The woman's balding head was covered with ornaments that dangled and jingled as she moved, as though she were wearing a wig of gold. When she smiled in greeting, they saw she had only one tooth left in her mouth, a striking white among the red gums.

"Peace unto you," she said in flawless Kandarin.

"And to you, Mother," Shade replied. "We are weary travelers and wish to—"

"Is she sick?" The fat woman pointed a thickly ringed finger at Nora, who tugged the rim of her hood farther down over her eyes. "What's wrong with her face?"

Shade sucked air and looked at Nora.

"Um," he said. While working out a simple story, they had overlooked a reason for Nora's facial scars.

"She is not sick, Mother," Owen jumped in and pulled Nora's hood down. "My sister was assaulted and we, my brother-in-law and I, are hunting the dogs who did this to her."

The sun glared down and Nora shut her eyes at the sudden exposure. She tried to keep her gaze cast down, but she heard the gasps of the men and women who stood nearby and she could have throttled Owen. This was not the story they had settled on.

On account of their likeness, there would be no denying Owen and Nora were brother and sister, though they could drop the twins' curse, maybe. Shade, though rough-looking, wasn't old enough to be hired for protection, so Owen had suggested Shade and Nora pose as a newly married couple. Shade and Nora had traded a look, trying not to grin. Yeah, they could make that work. But now Owen was improvising the rest about righteous retribution and avenging a damsel in distress. Nora gritted her teeth as the gathering townspeople stared at her disfigured face.

"Who did this?" the fat woman wanted to know.

"Our village was attacked in the night. My sister was trapped in her burning home. Many died. My parents are dead. Only we three managed to escape with our lives." Owen hung his head sadly.

It seemed to be working. The bits and pieces of the truth mixed and matched together. The question was whether the fat matron would swallow it.

"Who attacked you?" The woman repeated her question. "It was none of mine, I can assure you."

"No, I'm sure they weren't, Mother." Owen shook his head and reached into his garment. "But they were carrying this."

He held out one of the gold daggers they had found among the attackers on Solstice. It was the same make Nora had seen on the Ridge. The same one Owen nearly had been killed with on his way to the Temple of the Wind when they had been separated. She watched the fat woman's face as the matriarch bent over and inspected the weapon. She recognized it but hid that fact well.

"It's a ritual dagger, that's all I can tell you." She shrugged and pulled herself upright. "I'm very sorry. It could be from anywhere. We have one in our shrine to Shinar at the back of my house. Every settlement you pass from here on out will have one in their own shrine."

Shade said something in a language Nora didn't understand. It sounded demanding, imperative, but maybe that was just the language's melody. She looked to Owen, who was following the rapid-fire conversation between the fat woman and Shade with a scrunched-up face. The woman raised her voice in pitch, making broad sweeps of her hands while she spoke. Then just as abruptly as it had started, the conversation ended.

"Come, come," the woman said, flashing her single tooth once more. "Stay at my house for the night before you continue on your search."

✧ ✧ ✧

DARKNESS AND COOL MET THEM as they were ushered into the domed house. Over the chattering and bustle of various young women coming in to greet the strangers with friendly smiles and plates laden with food, Nora grabbed Owen by the arm.

"What was that all about?"

"I'm not sure." He frowned, glancing over at Shade, who was immediately surrounded by a cluster of dark-haired beauties. "Shade seems pretty fluent in the ancient language of Shinar. I've only read it in scriptural texts. He asked the Mother whether she had retired from—"

"I didn't mean Shade," Nora hissed. "What's up with parading my face around in public? I thought you were on a guilt trip about it."

"What?" Owen seemed taken aback. "No. You're failing to see the larger issues at hand."

"Like what?"

One of the girls around Shade giggled, and Nora shot her a pointed glare.

"Nora, think! The north is in turmoil. There's no clear leadership there anymore. There's a gaping black hole that is looking to be filled. But by whom? And how? Everywhere you look, there are marauding bands, each spearheaded by a man with a golden dagger. Even the attack on the Temple of the Wind was clearly an organized and planned event."

"Planned by Master Cumi."

"*After* she had been visited by female pilgrims from Shinar. Think of what she said before she died. It wasn't just her behind the attack. All the signs are pointing toward an instigator in the south, maybe even the prophetess we're about to see. Who would be better in that position than the one who gave Bashan's father the self-fulfilling prophecy that cast the heir to the throne out on the quest to find the Living Blade? Bashan said she was a manipulative bitch. His words. Not mine."

"Bashan?"

"He sent me and Shade to scout ahead. See what we could find out."

Looked like prophetesses weren't the only manipulative bitches around, Nora thought. She scowled at another girl who had rested her hand on Shade's. The hand whipped away.

"Look, I am sorry about your face," Owen said.

"It's not your fault, Owen."

"I know."

She turned her attention back to her brother and squeezed his arm tighter. "It's really not."

"It was my idea to blow up the gates." He didn't look her in the eyes. "Over three hundred people died because of me."

"Most of them were attacking us."

"And you nearly died, too."

"But I didn't."

He nodded.

"I wish you had stayed with Calla," he said softly after a moment.

"Forget it. I'm with you. Always."

Owen smiled and leaned back.

"Well, you might want to reconsider. Your 'husband' is about to be taken from you."

"They can try." Nora smiled back. "He knows whose bed he'll be sharing later."

"I'll pretend I didn't hear that."

Nora laughed.

CHAPTER 4

REUNITED WITH THE OTHER THREE, the small company followed the unspooling river, bowing east for a while, then back south. As they traveled ever farther, the landscape gradually changed, became more barren and wasted, empty. The only settlements they saw now were small gatherings of sunbaked mud-brick houses, herdsmen with stables for their domesticated animals, mostly goats. They passed through mazes of cliffs and sun-kissed rocks, natural ravines that shaped the land around them into a wild and rugged place. At night they heard jackals and the roar of lions. At least Shade said they were jackals and lions. He could just as well have told her they were fire spirits howling out in the desert plains and Nora would have believed him. With every week that passed, they came closer to their destination.

Nora rubbed her hand over her eyes. The red dust made them dry, and irritated the healing skin on her face. She had picked at the scab under her eye after Calla's ointment had run out, and now that side of her face was divided into an upper and lower half by a thin, jagged scar.

She had retreated under Diaz's fierce blows during training and moved away for some space. Now she lifted the baton to signal she was ready again. This time he attacked first with a strong horizontal blow. He had reach and used it, but she had flexibility and stepped aside, making to beat his baton down. Dawn came early now as the days grew longer, and Nora had been listening to the lions roar with Shade last night. She missed a beat, and Diaz's baton landed on her arm once more.

"Concentrate," he said.

"I *am* concentrating." Nora massaged feeling back into her arm.

"You're everywhere but in the moment. That's why you make mistakes."

She raised her baton and charged at him, dealing out blow after blow, forcing him to parry her strikes. They had dropped training with the shield a few weeks ago, leaving him unprotected. But now their training was more like a well-choreographed dance. Nora turned, ducking under a high blow, and managed to graze her baton over Diaz's shoulder before he spun.

"Good," he said, but unrelenting, he kept coming at her.

She skipped a few steps back to make room before launching into another busy round. Something was off, though. The energy between them felt disturbed by a presence. She glanced to the side to see if one of the others had come to watch. Sometimes Garreth rose early and gave her some extra advice or told funny stories of female mercenaries he had known. No one was there, though. Still, it felt as if someone had thrown a large stone into a small brook and now the water had to flow in a different direction. While her arm was cutting through the air in a forceful blow from above, Diaz stood there, unmoving.

She called out in warning, suddenly scared she'd hit him square in his face. The baton was blunt and only made of wood, but a blow was painful and could do serious damage. She pulled her arm back as best she could. He blinked then and moved sideways at the last second, so instead of hitting him in the face, she whacked his ear. The lobe split under the blow and started to bleed.

Diaz sucked in air between his teeth and pinched the injured cartilage with a flicker of anger passing across his otherwise calm features. He held up his other hand to signal for a pause and turned away.

"Gods, Diaz," Nora said, shaken by the sight of blood pearling between his long fingers. "I'm so sorry."

He grunted and looked at the blood on his hand with a frown.

"It's fine."

She stepped closer, a hand on his upper arm to make him turn back and look at her, needing to see how he felt, but he pulled away.

"It's fine," he repeated. "Leave me be."

"But I—"

"Training is over, Noraya. Go, get some breakfast." He marched off with long strides, out onto the sandy ridge surrounding their camp. Alone.

"I said I was sorry," she called, angry he was walking away, but if he heard, he didn't answer.

✧ ✧ ✧

THE FINAL LEG OF THEIR journey was a climb up into the Red Canyons, and it was brutal. It was early summer, yet the sun was oppressive. The red earth beneath their feet burned fiercely with flickering heat, under them and next to them and above them. The wandering crags and canyons offered only sparse shadow, but when they did, it felt easier to breathe and easier to walk. The thirst was terrible. The more Nora drank, the more she sweated and the thirstier she became. Her waterskin had been full when they started the climb this morning, but now it was nearly empty and the lukewarm water tasted brackish. She felt dizzy and kept stumbling, catching herself on the jutting stones that scorched her hands when she touched them.

The last stretch was the hardest. The climb was steep, and though the way itself was not long, they had to go around and around on winding paths to reach the hidden city of Shinar. By the wayside stood little figurines with huge heads and closed eyes, smiling serenely on their dainty feet. Some stood under little roofs made of stone slabs; some wore shirts of faded, tattered red cloth. Some had little bowls before their feet, the rims marked with white lines showing how high the water level had been before it evaporated.

"What are they?" Nora asked Owen quietly as they passed another group of smiling bigheads in a crevice. She felt the hairs on her forearms rise despite the heat.

Her brother shrugged.

"No idea. Shrines to Shinar, filled with protective spirits for the pilgrims on their way?"

"Each figure carries the soul and ashes of the miscarriages of the women in Shinar." Nora jumped as she heard Diaz's voice, harsh on the ears. He looked grimmer than usual. "Those unborn, the unliving. They rest here."

"So many?" Owen asked.

Diaz blinked solemnly. He opened his mouth, then shut it again.

"There are many women in Shinar," he said simply.

"Is it still far?" Nora asked.

"No." Diaz's lips were chapped and dry. Nora licked her own in sympathy. "We will reach the temple tomorrow."

"Do you think I'll be allowed in?"

He gave her a long look.

"I hope not," he said finally and pushed to the fore, taking the lead.

"What did you do?" Owen asked Nora after a few paces.

"Me?"

"You must have done something. Else he wouldn't be so…" Owen made a face.

"Yes?"

He must have heard the warning in her voice. "I'm still looking for the right word. It's too hot to think."

"Yeah, right." Nora grinned lopsidedly. They walked on. "Shade's been strange, too."

"How so?" Owen's brow knit together and he pointed to a crevice. "Scorpion."

"Just some things he's said." *In his sleep*, Nora added in her mind. She gave the scorpion a wide berth and wiped the sweat from her face. "Didn't sound like he had many good childhood memories."

"He's probably anxious," Owen said after a while.

"Shade? That's what I just meant, Owen."

"No, I meant Diaz. Being here again."

"He's been here before?" Nora took another sip from her waterskin. The water still tasted brackish.

"On his pilgrimage to all the temples and shrines." Owen shrugged. All pilgrims were wanderers. Since Owen had taken the vows, this journey counted as the first leg of his own pilgrimage. They carried on a few steps before Owen added as an afterthought, "Maybe he had a lover here."

Suddenly Nora was spluttering, choking, with Owen thumping furiously on her back. She coughed the accidental sip back up, tears running down her cheeks. Owen motioned with his hand that the others could continue.

"A what?" she croaked.

Owen grinned sheepishly. "Well, I've yet to see any mention of celibacy in the code. So why not?"

Why not? Nora thought darkly, staring at the back of the half-wight who led the company through the red ravines. That was indeed the question.

CHAPTER 5

SHADOWING HER EYES AFTER THE twilight of deep ravines, Nora stepped out into the glaring sunlit white space. Beyond the dull red stone tunnels, the sky was tall above a large plaza, a perfect square lined with potted palm trees, but it took her eyes a few seconds to adjust to the brightness.

"My gods," she said, fighting the sudden urge to shield her face from the glory and fall to her knees.

The Temple of Fire was built of pure white marble into the red rock mass of the natural ravines. The clean lines of the central block tower speared the blue sky and reflected the sun with a blinding brilliance. Two wings flanked the central tower, their stonework etched with curving, twisting spiral patterns that moved in the glimmering heat, pure white-hot tongues of fire licking the stone. Its sheer size was mind-boggling. She lifted her gaze to take it all in but then bowed her head, eyes watering in pain from the glare. Standing before the immense white walls dwarfed everything else—the purity erased everything else, the vast weight of the towering stone looming over her head like the fist of a wrathful god sticking his middle finger up at the mortality of the world.

"I think I need to sit down," she said, mouth dry.

"Two hundred thirty-four," Owen said, head tilted far back. "Two hundred thirty-four steps high. The shrine's spire in Dernberia. This must be...this is at least...a lot higher."

He rested his chin on his chest, rubbing his neck before raising his eyes up to the apex of the central tower once more, hand still at the back of his head.

"I wonder how they built it," Owen said, shaking his head, lips pressed together. "So much knowledge we've lost. We can't build like this anymore."

"Where did they get the stone?" Nora asked. "And how did they get it here? There's no way they brought it through the ravines."

"It was built by Shinar Himself." Shade knocked Owen's shoulder. He was grinning at the slack-jawed country bumpkins Owen and Nora currently resembled, but the grin didn't reach his eyes. "Take off your shoes. You stand in the presence of the divine."

"Come on." Bashan rolled his eyes and hoisted his backpack on his shoulder. "Looks like we're expected."

He pointed at three figures coming toward them under the great gates, the points of their spears reflecting the sunlight in flashes of silver. They wore black leather jerkins and had curved swords at their hips. A symbol of three flames was worked onto their breastplates and the tips of their helmets. The cheek pieces of their helmets reached so far into their faces all Nora could see were dark pools instead of eyes. The effect made them appear disconcertingly like Diaz's eyes. Nora shot the half-wight a glance. His lips were pressed thin, as though he was about to vomit on the plaza's trodden red earth.

"Prince Bashan, Master Telen Diaz." The guard had a deep voice. He took his helmet off as a courtesy, brown hair plastered to his skull by a band of sweat, and bowed low. "My queen has seen you from far off and welcomes you. She is awaiting your presence in the throne room."

Bashan turned to Diaz and raised his eyebrows. Diaz's shoulders sagged a fraction, but he nodded.

"Very well. We shall follow you," Bashan told the guard.

The guard bowed once more and then gave a cry to the other two. They bowed and then pushed open the gates, which were as high as six men and as thick as Nora's thigh, as easily as though they were pushing aside a linen curtain.

"There must be some kind of mechanism behind the gates," Owen whispered to Nora as they passed through them. "The hinges must be as thick as my arm. I wonder, how do they open them so easily?"

I wonder whether Diaz is going to puke, Nora thought, walking behind the half-wight. *And I wonder whether the gates open from the inside just as easily.*

Behind the threshold was another smaller plaza lined with a ring of white-bark trees that cast their dappled shade over the dusty red ground. In the middle was a fountain, and the sound of water in this dry place was refreshment to the wanderer's soul. As they left the small grove, they could see the city. A city built within the red rock, several stories high and upheld by many mighty pillars of stone etched with carvings and statues. Everything was a balance of red and white.

The group followed their guard of honor toward three great arches that led deep into the rock. The middle arch was the largest, towering over their heads with a dizzying height. In the stone dome above, lit up by flickering torchlights, Nora could see the same abstract spiral patterns that were on the walls outside, until she recognized a round shape and her view suddenly adjusted. The figures carved into the red stone were men and women in various positions together, some positions…interesting, others incredible, repeating themselves over and over, filling the ceiling and reaching down to the floor. They were so lifelike that Nora, stretching out a hand to touch a couple, was surprised at the feeling of cold stone under her fingertips, half expecting the marble-veined woman to sigh and move.

They came into a cavernous hall that held a long flight of stairs leading farther down, deep under the earth. It was cooler already, and Nora shivered pleasantly at the chill on her skin. Grand pillars of white stone touched the high ceiling, each one shaped in the likeness of a beautiful woman, a serene smile twinkling in the whites of their carved marble eyes. Between the pillars, shafts of golden light fell from above. Where the light shone, clusters of potted plants grew well tended, bringing green and life to the reign of red and white. If the temple was a body, the hall with its high red naves and white columns was the backbone, and from it streets of houses jutted like ribs. Hewn from the solid rock, every house was fashioned like the settlements they had seen on their journey.

A bustle erupted on the long stairs as they walked down among the calls and waves of the women welcoming the newcomers. Tight skirts, men's shirts slipping off their pale shoulders, easy smiles on guarded faces, all those pretty girls. Nora tossed her scarred head high and stared back. A city of women. No, a brothel. The air was thick with want and desire, heavy with a rich scent of perfume and secrets. On every flight of stairs pungent smoke wafted from copper braziers, dulling the senses like a hammer blow and making Nora retch. It wasn't a woodsmoke scent she recognized, more like an herbal concoction than resin.

When they finally reached the bottom of the long stairs, they halted before twin doors of normal height, interlaced with gold. The carvings around them had changed. Stylized flames blazed in the darkest hues of red stone, uncovered by the white flagstones. When she touched the jagged points, they were sharp and pricked her finger. The tips of flame gleamed, polished until translucent like candle fire while their bases were the color of freshly spilled blood. The two guards with the spears took each of the doors' handles. Before they pulled them open, though, the chief guard without a helmet turned toward Bashan's company once more and bowed.

"No weapons allowed," he said. "You may leave your swords and daggers and spears in our keeping, and they will be returned to you in the guest houses to which you will later go."

The prince nodded. It only took a few minutes. They all stripped off their weapons, leaning them against the polished walls of flame. Nora placed her knife on top of her backpack, next to Owen's spear and bag. Diaz took his time. He unbuckled his sword last and handed it over to the chief guard, catching Nora's gaze. He cleared his throat and squared his shoulders.

"Come," the guard said. "Enter before the throne of Suranna, the Queen of Shinar."

Chapter 6

THE DOORS SWUNG OPEN SOUNDLESSLY, and beyond them lay blackness. The group filed into the room, their eyes slowly adjusting to the darkness within.

The throne room felt vast, yet everything was black and that made it seem close at the same time. It was a strange, ambiguous sensation Nora couldn't quite handle, as though she were standing in a ball of shadows, a dark womb. The walls were hung with heavy black tapestries, embroidered with the three-tongued stylized flame, making her feel small, wishing she could hide behind them like they were her mother's skirts. The floor mirrored the midnight surroundings, the flagstones smooth on their surface but puckered underneath like lava. *Obsidian*, Nora thought. She had once seen a dagger made of obsidian, and even her foster father had been speechless at the sharpness of the stone blade. And at its price. She felt like kneeling down and running her hands over the floor, but she straightened, taking in the rest of the throne room. Three shafts of light divided the space, each ray hitting the surface of an oblong pool of still, black water. And beyond the pool, between two high copper braziers, stood the throne itself.

It was placed on a dais in the middle of the room, all of black stone, nothing more than a straight, clean seat built out of one huge block, obscured by transparent silk veils. A figure sat upright on the throne, arms resting on her knees. Next to her, Nora heard Shade take a deep, rattling breath. The veiled queen held up a hand and the guards bowed low and left, closing the doors behind them. The shadowed woman rose from the throne and stepped through the veils.

Nora gasped. The queen was a goddess, tall and proud, black hair cascading down her naked back, her skin a tone of gold and without blemish, young and firm and perfect. She came down the stairs of the dais slowly, deliberately, one bare slender foot after the other, moving with natural poise and grace, a faint chime of her golden bangles heralding her presence in the pregnant silence. There had never been a woman as beautiful as the Queen of Shinar. Or as desirable, or as strong. She was the essence of everything Nora had ever wanted to be, could ever aspire to be. The eyes of the queen were all she could see, and she wanted to lose herself in them forever. Forget she'd never be as beautiful, that she could never be anything other than a monster. The Dark Twin. Cursed and twisted, fire-burnt and ugly, her right place was on the floor and groveling.

"My Lord Bashan." The queen's voice rang deep and clear, golden honey dripping from her lips. With her appearance and just three words, she held the entire room enthralled.

Around her throat, Suranna wore a coiled snake of gold and black and crimson. She wore the neckpiece and her flame-shaped golden crown and nothing else. Nora's breath caught. Like with the glory of the temple above, Nora's eyes hurt with the onslaught, scanning the flawlessness for details, any detail, that would reveal the artifice of the creature standing before her. But her eyes registered nothing—no hair, no spot, no wrinkle, no scar, no powder to hide any imperfection.

"My lady." Bashan struggled to stand tall. The tip of her crown let Suranna stand taller than him. "It is my pleasure to kneel before one who is so fair."

She laughed at that and gave him her hand to kiss as he fell to one knee. As his lips brushed her knuckles, his hand trembled and he lingered over her fingers a bit too long, the creep. Suranna didn't seem to mind. She withdrew her hand slowly, her eyes wandering over his body as though it were her possession. Suranna smiled and shifted her attention to Shade. She held out her arms wide.

"Brisin, welcome home."

Shade paled, then stepped into her embrace.

"Myvar," he started. *Mother*. Nora recognized the word from their short stay with the matriarch. The rest of the short, intense conversation she didn't understand. Owen sucked in air next to her.

"Brisin," he repeated in a whisper and leaned closer to Nora. "It means sapphire. I knew Shade wasn't his real name."

"Really?"

Still, sapphire was a nice name…for a girl. Nora's lips twitched with a smile as Shade sheepishly stepped away from the queen. He rubbed the back of his neck and shrugged at Nora as she silently studied his face for a likeness to Suranna's. *Mother*. Was she really? Would the queen have serviced the empire's fledgling herself? Hard to imagine, though the brief image of those lips pursed in a soft moan sent a jolt of warmth deep down inside Nora. She clasped a hand to the base of her own throat. It was probably more an honorific title, Nora decided.

Suranna caressed Garreth's cheek in passing and then came to a halt before Diaz. She lifted her eyes, batting long lashes at him, lips slightly parted. The air felt charged, dense with unreleased energy, like a summer thunderstorm, clouds amassing in the humid heat before the first lightning struck and the rain finally fell. Nora gritted her teeth and fought down a flurry of emotions, watching who of the two would make the first move toward the other.

Diaz turned his head away.

The rain fell.

But the burning of summer's heat lingered in Nora's chest.

Suranna's golden eyes ran over Diaz's body with approval, and she stepped closer.

"Telen." Her voice was soft and she raised her hand to touch his face. "It has been far too long."

He leaned back, away from her fingertips.

"So cold?" She reached out with a hint of a smile playing around her full lips and ran her fingers down his throat and let them rest over his heart. Nora saw his hands curl into fists behind his back.

"Don't stand so close." Diaz's voice shook.

He glanced at Suranna as she laughed, pressing herself against him. One hand rose and ran through his hair.

"But I want to," she whispered, her lips brushing against the corner of his mouth.

Nora watched with a pounding heart as Suranna ran the tip of her tongue up Diaz's throat before sinking her teeth into the soft flesh of his earlobe. The tip of her nose touched the tiny blood-red rip Nora had caused. He sucked in air audibly and shifted his weight as Suranna squeezed him in a tight embrace, his hands still folded against his back.

"We came for information." Diaz sounded breathless. "Information on the whereabouts of the Living Blade."

"I know exactly what you came for, my love." Suranna chuckled. "I wouldn't be much of a seeress if I didn't."

Her golden eyes met Nora's, and Nora recoiled as though Suranna had landed a physical blow. A sense of heat washed over Nora's body as Suranna focused on her. Intense heat. When a charcoal clamp broke and Owen and Nora were frantically shoveling earth to close the leak again, the hot air wavered underneath them, making them want to shield their faces from it.

Such was the power of Suranna's gaze. Nora wanted to raise her arm before her eyes to hide from the queen's piercing stare. Her mouth was dry, and her throat clicked when she swallowed.

"Twins." Suranna nestled her chin on Diaz's shoulder, as though it had always belonged there, still staring at Nora with her falcon eyes. "Dedicated to Tuil and Lara, the Divine Twins of life and death. I have seen you in vision. Give me your name, girl."

Nora's feet shuffled, but she squared her shoulders.

"I'm Noraya Smith. My brother, Owen."

"Owen." The queen tasted his name, then bedazzled Owen with a smile. "I can see my girls will like you."

"Er…thank you, milady." Owen bowed low and Nora saw his ears burn red.

"You, Noraya, come." Lady Suranna motioned with a flick of her wrist.

Nora stepped up despite herself. So close to Suranna, she could smell the sweet perfume that lingered on the woman's silky black hair, on her honey skin. The queen reached over Diaz's shoulder and touched Nora, holding her chin to make her look up into those black-rimmed eyes. A tingle remained where her fingertips rested.

"Tell me, Noraya Smith, why should I let you stay and see the secrets of Shinar?"

"Your secrets do not interest me."

The queen's smile broadened. Not letting go of Diaz, she grasped Nora tighter by the chin, pulling her toward her perfect face.

"Then maybe we shall have to find something else that interests you."

She was close. Her lips so close. The goddess. Nora opened her mouth to say something in response, but nothing came. Instead, a rosemary scent overlaid with sweetness filled her nostrils. Nora closed her eyes for a moment against the reeling sensation, but then the queen's lips brushed lightly over her own, and without thinking Nora stepped closer, squashing against Diaz's back to let the queen in, a jolt like a tongue of flame running deep down as their lips met. It was a very thorough kiss, leaving Nora's knees buckling. The only things holding her upright were the scorching hands on her skin and the mouth that dripped with the sweetness of pears. The queen pulled away first, licking her lips as though savoring Nora. Dazed and confused, Nora stepped away.

"You will be my guest. All of you will be my guests," the queen said, her warm breath tickling Nora's skin. "You may leave. Rooms are waiting for you. Rest. Your journey was long, and yet you still have far to go to find the

Living Blade. And you will find it, my lord prince, for I will help you."

Queen Suranna turned to speak to Bashan, and Nora withered from the heat, heart beating like the wings of a caged bird. Owen touched her elbow and she stood straight, shoving a strand of hair back behind her ear. Nora looked to the golden woman again, her lips still prickling from their kiss. She had felt the energy, the power Suranna had held back but could release like a wildfire, devastating the barricades of the soul and laying waste to any thought other than being one with her. Her knees were still trembling.

Suranna clapped her hands twice, and from beyond the blackness a few shining beauties stepped forward with eager faces to escort the gentlemen to their rooms. A young blonde woman as naked as her queen stepped up to Nora and took her elbow with a wink.

"Er..." Nora raised her hand and strained to pull her arm away without touching the girl's nipples.

"Come on," said the blonde girl, cradling Nora's arm against her soft breasts. "I'm fun, I promise."

"Not her." A sharp command from Suranna stopped the girl, and she let go of Nora's arm immediately. "I want her for myself."

The girl bowed her head and clasped Owen's arm instead with a question in her eyes. Suranna nodded and Owen, sporting two girls, beamed at Nora, then looked a bit overwhelmed.

Suranna's eyes flashed. She reached out to caress Nora's cheek, but like a serpent striking, Diaz caught her hand and held her wrist hard. Nora saw a triumphant smile flicker over Suranna's beautiful face as she gazed defiantly into Diaz's eyes.

"Touch her one more time..." Diaz spoke quietly with a threat in his raspy voice.

Suranna laughed and stroked a finger across his cheek.

"Jealous?"

"Suspicious."

"I see she is special."

"Special?" Nora echoed.

"Special?" Bashan spoke the same word in an incredulous tone.

"Yes." Suranna smiled, pulling her arm out of Diaz's slackening hand. "Every year many young girls come to this place, Noraya. Hundreds. Some years, even thousands. Some come as supplicants to Shinar Himself; they pray at the Deep Shrine and beg him for visions. Some come seeking refuge from the harshness of a man's world and wish to stay here, taking up work as cooks, as cleaners, as laundry women. And we take them gladly, because this city always needs helping hands. Others, a handful only, come and pay for services they can't find elsewhere in the world. Others come looking for…a different line of work. But in the end all are led here by their desires, whatever those may be."

Suranna stood before Nora once more and smiled, reaching for her hand. Nora gasped at the dry heat.

"You, though," Suranna said, "you have not come to worship. You have not come to seek refuge or seek satisfaction. You're here, but you don't know why you're here. Yet. That blank slate makes you special. Unique. Stay with me a little while longer and I can show you your purpose."

"My purpose?"

"No." Diaz crossed his arms. His face was unreadable.

"It's all right," Nora told him, but her eyes never left Suranna's face. "I'll be fine."

"No," he repeated, shaking his head.

"In Shinar," Suranna said, her honey-tongued mouth filling out Nora's vision, "it is always the woman who decides whether she wants to go with the man. Do you want to go with him, Noraya?"

And to her surprise, Nora found she didn't.

CHAPTER 7

DIAZ MARCHED OUT OF THE throne room without looking back. Owen shrugged at Nora and followed him. As Bashan passed by, he grabbed Nora's arm and pulled her close.

"I need the Blade, so I need Suranna happy," he whispered into her ear with a smile on his face. "If you fuck this up, I will make you watch your brother die."

He pushed Nora away from him and raised his eyebrows at her to make sure she understood. He left with his hand on the bare bottom of a redheaded girl. The doors closed behind them, and Nora was alone with Suranna in the vast black room. Nora shuddered.

Suranna was watching her silently. Then she gave Nora a broad smile.

"What do you think of him?" she asked with a purr.

"Of whom?"

"Your master."

"Diaz is not my master," Nora said.

"Quite right," the queen said smoothly and ran a fingertip across her smiling lips.

She inclined her head and beckoned Nora to follow her back to the dais. She clapped her hands once, and another set of girls stepped out from the shadows, each carrying a golden tray. They stepped close to Suranna, who spread out her arms to let them dress her in a luxurious white linen garment.

"Battle dress," Suranna said over the servants' bustle. "Make your vulnerability your armor; then, nothing can hurt you anymore."

Another servant girl came out with a tray, a golden cup and pitcher balanced on it. Suranna took it and the girl left.

"So, Noraya." Suranna reclined on the black stone steps of the dais. "Tell me about yourself. You wish to find the Living Blade?"

"No."

"Yet you are on the path that leads to finding it."

"Who wouldn't want to be part of prophecy fulfilling itself?" Nora lifted a shoulder in a shrug.

When Suranna's eyebrows rose in a perfect arch, she added, "My brother said that."

"He desires greatness?"

"No." Nora shook her head. "Not Owen."

"Ah, but he does and you know it." Suranna poured from the pitcher and held the cup out to Nora. "Thirsty?"

"Yes, thank you."

Nora's mouth felt parched. She took the golden cup and looked inside. The fluid was clear like water, but the scent was fruity and sweet.

"Drink," Suranna said with a smile.

Nora hesitated.

The queen rose. She took the cup from Nora's hand, brushing her fingers against Nora's with a shock of heat. She took a sip, then licked her lips.

"It's not poison," she said, smiling.

Nora took a sip. It was a kind of wine. The first taste was a tooth-paining sweetness, but after she swallowed, a hint of fig lingered in her mouth. Another sip and she grimaced. It was very much like mead, she thought. First sweet, then you tasted the sharp alcohol.

"Do you believe in fate, Noraya?"

Nora's tongue felt heavy already. This stuff was potent. She wished for water instead.

"No."

"Do you believe you will become a mighty woman warrior like Scyld or Master Siha, wielders of the Blade? Shapers of destiny?"

"Er...no, not really." Nora laughed breathlessly.

Gods, what was this? There was a faint tingling in Nora's fingers and her tongue felt numb. Suranna showed no sign of intoxication. She was walking up the stone steps of the dais with no problem. Nora followed tentatively and wiped the sweat from her forehead while the queen wasn't looking. She swallowed another sip of fig wine, but her thirst seemed to grow.

"Why not?" Suranna sat on her throne, the veils drawn to the side now. Nora stopped at the foot of the dais.

"I'm just...Nora." She shrugged.

"What if I told you, you were to play a very important role in this history?"

"Have you seen a vision?" Nora asked, half mocking, half in earnest.

She felt a hand on her shoulder and turned her head, half expecting to see another servant girl, requesting the cup back. But no one stood there. She frowned. And looked down. Her feet glided with the black floor an elbow's length away from where she should be standing. She gasped and ripped her head back up quickly. Suranna sat on the throne, still smiling.

"I could cast bones into the fire so you may see a vision yourself," she said.

But at the same time Nora felt Suranna's naked arm stretch around her from behind, pressing her into a tight embrace. She heard the queen whisper into her ear.

"I know exactly how you feel. You despise not being in control of your own life."

"What?" Nora shook her head.

She looked down into the cup, but it was empty. And it wasn't even in her hand anymore but had fallen to the floor. Suranna sat on the throne, a divine queen. But she also stepped gracefully around Nora in one fluid movement and cupped her face gently in her hands. Nora's mouth was dry. She closed her eyes. The sweet scent was overpowering so close.

"You feel it, don't you? The helplessness?"

Nora swallowed hard and tried not to look at Suranna's soft lips open just a little, drawing in her breath as though sucking it from her lungs.

"You want to be free."

The blackness spun before her eyes, a single ray of golden light blurring softly into a tear on the inside of her mind. Nora raised her hand to steady herself against the queen's shoulder, but her arm went through Suranna's form like a wisp of smoke. Still, she could feel the queen at her throat. Nora's knees went weak and bent of their own accord under her weight. The cool black stone was under her hand now, perfectly smooth. And when Nora opened her eyes, she saw her own pale reflection in the black, her own dark twin. Lara, Death Herself, was staring right back at her with her skull grin. Nora gasped in horror, and panic squeezed her heart, making it miss a beat.

There must have been something in that drink… something…

She saw her black mirror image standing tall and upright beneath her, gazing up at her in dawning horror. The world flipped and Nora stood looking down, watching herself scream silently, veins bulging in her forehead. She saw herself pounding her fists against the black surface as though trapped under a thick sheet of ice. The ice at the bottom of the world.

"Let go."

I can't.

"Show me what you're afraid of."

Something broke. Her world came crashing down, and Nora fell backward, into the swirling black that shattered like glass under her falling frame. But she couldn't hear anything, couldn't see anything. Frozen to her core, she fell…

CHAPTER 8

NORA LANDED ON HER FEET, pulling herself upright after an almighty jolt. Gods, she'd tripped over that fucking cobblestone. The door was just a few more steps away. She staggered toward it and fumbled for the key at her belt in the dark. *Stupid lock. Stupid key. Come on!* A scratching sound behind her made her look back, but the town square had emptied. A few last stragglers from the slaughter feast were standing around the gleaming coals of the fire pits, talking in low voices, their faces lit from below. No one was close by. No one looked up. Funny, it felt like someone had brushed against her. She shook her head. She shouldn't have had the last cup of wine, she thought, and opened the door. Back home.

The kitchen was silent and dark. A sole candle gave off its golden light on the table where her father sat. He looked up at her from his cup.

Oh gods, no. Anything but this.

Nora stood in the memory of that dark kitchen of her mind and watched herself square her shoulders. It looked just as pitiable from the outside as it had felt on the inside.

"Nora," her father said, half rising from the kitchen bench. "I didn't think you'd be back before morning."

"I'm back." She hung her cloak on the knob behind the door.

"I'm back." Real Nora spoke the words along with her counterpart. She wished Memory Nora would just keep walking to the stairs. *Go upstairs.* She concentrated on the words. *Go upstairs.* But to no avail. Memory Nora wouldn't listen. She wouldn't go up the stairs, and it would all happen all over again.

"You can't change what happened," Suranna said, suddenly standing at Nora's side, her long linen garment fluttering in a breeze that didn't exist. The sight calmed Nora a little. This was a memory. Of course you could change what happened. If she didn't want to see this, she could just pretend she *had* gone upstairs, gone to bed. People lied to themselves all the time, telling themselves how things had happened over and over again until it became the truth.

A heavy weight pressed down on her, distorting everything. For a moment, she watched Memory Nora smile at her father and then make toward the stairs, one step heavier than the next, her boots sinking into the wooden floor as though it were a tar pit.

"Don't." Suranna held out a hand and the memory halted. "To be free, you must face what you fear."

"Close your eyes and make a wish, Nora."

It was Mother Sara's voice. Nora turned. Over the fuzzy outline of her halted memory, another layer was added. Mother Sara scratched the tip of her small, sharp knife across Nora's upper arm and pressed a piece of white cotton onto the bleeding wound. This Nora was nine years old. She squeezed her eyes shut at the welling blood, trying not to cry.

"One day I'll marry Father," she said.

Mother Sara smiled as she hitched up her long skirts and ran the knife across her thigh. On her white skin, paler knife-etched scars showed the signs of the many wishes Mother Sara had made at the Shrine of Hin.

"Maybe you will," she said as the blood gushed forth.

I had forgotten this, Real Nora thought, wincing at the memory. *Gods, Sara must have known she was ill already.*

Sara pressed a cotton strip against her flesh and watched with grim satisfaction as it slowly turned deep red.

"If you give the gods your most valuable possession, they may grant your wish."

"Like Owen?"

"Is he your most valuable possession, sweetie?" Mother Sara's voice echoed into the memory kitchen, and the picture before them unfroze.

Real Nora shuddered. *Here it comes*, she thought again. Unstoppable. The twins' curse at work.

Her father's lips crushed against hers. She opened up to him, letting him in, and for a short glorious moment, the two of them were alive in each other's arms, her tongue exploring his mouth with zealous passion. She heard him moan and it made her knees weak. He pulled her closer, his strong hand gliding below her waistline. She ran a hand through his hair, grinding her hips against him. Feeling his readiness there made her blood quicken.

Real Nora braced herself. *Here it comes.*

Her father stepped back as though stung and made the warding sign over his heart. Just like the villagers did when they saw her passing. It was the sign against evil. Against *her* evil. The evil seductress. The dark twin. The force of the simple sign was crippling. Worse than if he had raised his hand against her in violence. Because that would only hurt for a while and then fade. This was going to stay with her for the rest of her life.

"Oh, gods, you believe it too?" Nora pointed at the sign, wiping her wet mouth with her sleeve.

"Nora," he started to say and quickly dropped his hand to his side.

"You think I'm evil? You raised me!"

"This shouldn't have happened."

"It's what you wanted!"

"Go to your room, Nora."

"Or what? You'll spank me?" The grin on Nora's face was twisted in spite. As though he could still be her father after this. She stood, trembling hands clutching her sides.

He wagged a finger at her.

"Now you listen," he started. "I never—"

"*You* kissed me!"

"It doesn't matter, does it?" Suranna interrupted. The scene before them froze once more. The queen had seen enough. "Everyone will believe it was you."

"It was a mistake. I, I was surprised."

"You wanted him."

"I wanted my life to stay the way it was." Nora pulled herself up straight. "Is that so bad? I wanted us to live together. As a family. We already were one, for crying out loud! I'm not a monster."

"You're afraid everyone is right." Suranna was watching her closely now. "Afraid it was your fault."

"No."

Nora stormed past her kneeling father, running up into the dark, two steps at a time. She'd grab the door handle of Owen's room, and this was where the story would start. She wiped her face with her sleeve and pushed the door open…

CHAPTER 9

...AND STEPPED OUT ONTO THE balcony of the Temple of the Wind. Her momentum carried her steps a bit farther to the white stonework. She looked back, recognizing the scene, searching for Diaz, who surely sat meditating in the shadows by the door. Only he wasn't. He was already at the balustrade with Nora.

"And because it's a burn," Memory Nora was saying. "And burns fucking hurt. Anyone who'd do that to themselves is looking to burn away something that hurts more."

Real Nora watched herself blink, then lean in to Diaz.

"Don't worry. I won't tell Owen."

She laughed quietly, a knuckle pressed against her lips. Then she looked up once more at Diaz, who had bent down to her, their faces close. He seemed about to say something but didn't. She lifted her chin as his hand caressed her cheek. Their lips met in a gentle kiss. A touch, an invitation. As though they were back in the training circle, testing each other's strength. So, a challenge, then. She pressed her body against his and took his mouth violently. They kissed like they fought, hard and unrelenting, his burning touch always a promise of more hidden underneath, holding back. Maddening. She grabbed his belt and hooked her leg around his loins. His hand slid under her thigh, hoisting her up and against the wall in one smooth move.

"Aren't you passionate?" Suranna said beside Nora, amused.

Nora jumped, startled.

"Er...this never really happened," Nora stuttered, blushing. In the background she was still in Diaz's embrace, moaning loudly as they moved together.

"I know," the queen said. "It's what you imagine when you touch yourself. The mind doesn't distinguish."

They both watched in silence.

"I see a pattern," Suranna spoke. "Forbidden father figure?"

"No," Nora sniffed.

Suranna smiled.

"Knowing what you want is the first step forward to freedom. So many people are stuck in denial, stuck with the shoulds: who they should be, how they should live." Suranna tapped a finger against the corner of her mouth. "Telen is like that. He isn't a casual lover. He can't find joy in satisfaction and then walk away. When he loves, he must give himself over completely, and if he can't, he won't allow himself to, even if he were burning for you. Do you want him to burn?"

"No."

"You should. Connection bestows great power."

Suranna snapped her fingers and the floor beneath them changed to black water. For a moment Nora felt the cold under the soles of her feet. Then her body plunged down, rushing into the chill. The water pressed in around her and she was flailing, unsure which direction was up. She took a deep breath and her lungs filled with water. She broke through the surface, coughing and choking. A burning sensation spread in her chest as she took a rattling breath. A stabbing pain in her gut made her bend double, face splashing into the water again. A hand cupped her face and pulled her upright as she sputtered. She clutched at the arms, holding on for dear life. The pain, though! Like a dagger twisting in her stomach, the white-hot blinding pain of steel penetrating. She gasped.

"Noraya!"

Two voices called out as one. The panic and pain subsided as she was pulled out of the water, first onto the red stone of the floor, her naked body pale as death. But then she was pulled higher, out of her racked body until she was floating just under the domed ceiling of a room that was unknown to her. Suranna was next to her. Below, she saw Diaz next to her writhing body, soaking wet himself but clothed, hoisting himself out of a small round pool. He bent over her as she bucked underneath him in some kind of seizure.

"What's this?" Nora asked Suranna. "I have no recollection of this."

"It's happening right now." Suranna turned toward her. "You're suffering the aftereffects of the potion I gave you. Intimacy isn't always romantic. First thing I tell all my girls when they come here: illusions are for poets."

Nora looked down at her own face screaming silently as her body arched against the pain. She could feel its echo inside her, squirming like a live thing trapped within.

"Will I die?"

Suranna shrugged. "Of course. Everyone dies. Even the gods."

"I meant now?"

Suranna's full lips were slightly parted. Her mouth opened and Nora saw fangs too large to be in any human mouth. Under Suranna's cracking skin, a red gleam like hot coals burned ferociously. Nora tried to back away but couldn't.

"I'm not finished with you." Suranna struck out, and her nightmare mouth closed over Nora's.

CHAPTER 10

NORA WOKE UP AND INSTANTLY wished she hadn't.

Even the dim reddish light gouged at her eyeballs. She shut her eyes tightly once more. Her heavy head was filled with a piercing, shrieking glare that left an afterglow of throbbing pain sludging through her veins. It felt like someone had poured acid into her ear while she slept and her brain was liquid slosh. She groaned. The rustle of clothes betrayed a stirring beside her. She opened one eye again and squinted into the blurred face of Diaz. He looked just as poised as ever, his black eyes taking her in with what might pass for relief.

"You're awake."

Her hand instinctively reached for her face to protect it from the onslaught of sound and vision. The hand fell on top of her face, her arm too weak and numb to guide it properly.

"You're loud." She winced.

He pushed her forearm away from her eyes and laid the palm of his hand on her forehead.

"The fever's down. How are you feeling?"

"Not…good," she managed after a lot of thought.

She groaned once more. Her skin felt raw, the memory of wrestling with a fiery serpent still etched into it. She peered down at the pale limb lying next to her, recognizing it dimly for her own arm, part of her, though not yet under her command. There was nothing to be seen, no flayed skin, red burn, or mark whatsoever. It felt like there should be, though.

She moved her head a bit more to check whether…oh, good. She wasn't naked. A sleeve covered the arm by her side. That was good, right? Soft linen had slipped over her shoulder and pooled around her elbow. It wasn't one of her shirts.

She frowned.

It must be one of Diaz's shirts. Over her arm…covering her…*oh my gods*!

She'd puked all over herself, and he had cleaned it up and seen her naked…and then cleaned *her* up—she vaguely remembered something with water—and then dressed her in one of his own shirts. And she had been naked. She'd been naked in his arms and couldn't even remember.

She hid her face in her palms. Diaz touched her elbow and she reluctantly looked up, hands still over her mouth, wishing she'd just die now, please. He held a cup before her and his hand pushed under her hair, a tingling sensation spreading where he gently touched her aching head to lift it. She drank a few sips, washing down the sour taste in her mouth, then turned her head away.

"Stop being so gods damn nice to me, Diaz." She grimaced, rolling her weight on one elbow to push herself up. She flopped back down, then tried again, aware of his raised eyebrows.

"Why is it," he said, "that you never want my help?"

She snorted. Her tongue was thick and heavy, a fat flab of useless flesh in her numb mouth.

"I want your help. But not…when I'm helpless."

She managed to prop herself up on one elbow and waved a hand at him as though to shoo him away.

"That doesn't make sense." He rose and vanished from her sight. "Rephrase that thought when you're sober."

"Why don't you just say it?" She spoke through clenched teeth. Sitting made her lightheaded, and something was stabbing into her skull, etching fancy carvings on the inside.

"Say what?" His voice came from far away through the blinding white pain.

"I told you so."

He hunched down beside her and shrugged. He offered her the cup, which she took and emptied.

"Why would I say that?"

"You wouldn't. Because you're so perfect, so controlled, so considerate."

She wiped the bitterness from her lips with the back of her hand and looked away.

He laughed quietly and she turned to glare at him. He saw her face and, before she could speak, shook his head. "I wish someone had told me so all those years ago."

She groaned and grasped her head. "I can't understand. Not a word."

"I woke here. In this room. In a state much worse than yours. The first time I had ever been beaten." He opened his mouth as though wanting to say more, but stopped himself and shook his head again.

"So I'm not that special, huh?" Nora frowned. "Why did she pretend I have a purpose?"

"Well…" He leaned in. "You can ask her that yourself. You have another audience with her. In about two hours."

He pointed to the wooden door. Nora saw a small wooden trunk next to it.

"She even sent you something clean to wear."

CHAPTER 11

THE BLACK OF THE THRONE room was a consolation to Nora's eyes. It muted the pain a little. Harsh daylight colors danced before her eyes when she closed them. Her legs were still shaking from the descent to the throne room. Better not throw up on the new dress Suranna had sent her. It was made of raw, stiff silk and embroidered with gold thread. You'd never get the stains out.

In the darkness, a pool of gold shone upon the dais where the throne stood. Suranna's symmetrical beauty was shrouded by sweet-smelling smoke from a copper brazier before her. Her eyes flashed a smile at Nora's costume.

"I'd ask how you feel, but, well…" she said.

Her slender hand passed through the smoke, forming it into a rough ring. If the potion she'd shared with Nora had affected her, Nora couldn't tell. Suranna pointed to a low bench at her side and gestured for Nora to take a seat. Nora bristled at the thought of complying, but she still felt exhausted enough to be grateful to sit down.

"Poison has no effect on a snake," Nora said slowly as she carefully arranged the gown underneath her legs.

"Is that what you think of me?"

"You tell me."

"Upset?" Suranna seemed amused.

"Upset that you drugged me, crept into my head, and snuck around in my most intimate thoughts and memories while I was puking my guts out?" Nora raised her eyebrows high and layered the sarcasm thick. "No. I had such a great night."

Suranna smiled and twirled the smoke with her fingers, shaping it as Master Cumi had shaped water. Orange sparks lit up the white smoke and, for a moment, Nora thought she saw a flickering image in the twisting curls. She blinked and Diaz's face was gone.

"I merely did what I had to do," Suranna said. "The potion I gave you lowers mental barriers, allowing me entry from a distance. Alcohol works to a certain extent, blurring the lines between the mask self and the raw self. I need to know who I'm dealing with in order to find out your purpose. I need information that you might not even have known about yourself. Much simpler to go directly to the source and extract what I need from your subconscious mind."

"Yeah, 'Why ask for consent?' said every rapist ever."

Suranna actually laughed. "My dear girl, would you have told me what I wanted to know if I had asked politely?"

Nora lifted her chin, fingers curling around the edge of the bench.

"Maybe."

"Did you ever tell Owen what happened between you and your foster father?"

Nora remained silent.

"See?" Suranna said. "Our time is short as it is. Bashan must find the Blade. And he must do so soon. Time is of the essence, or else all will have been in vain."

"Do you know where the Blade is?"

"It is hard to pinpoint where exactly it is, for the Blade—as its name suggests—is very much alive and doesn't want to be found if not by the right person."

"And that's Bashan? The Living Blade must be very stupid, then."

"It becomes all the person sacrificed to reforge it was. That is why that person must do so willingly. The last person was Emperor Kandar's own son by his liaison with the Prophetess Hin two thousand years ago. Who now can tell what kind of a person he was? Even the eldest of wights has not lived that long. Much less I, a humble human."

A human who has lived unnaturally long enough to sleep with Diaz. *She should look older*, Nora thought with a pang of jealousy. Talk about aging with grace, but Suranna's youthful vigor was freakish. There was nothing humble about her.

"And by when would Bashan need to have it?" Nora asked, rolling the tension out of her shoulders.

It was uncomfortable sitting on the low bench in the asymmetrical dress. The material stretched tightly over one shoulder, hemming in her natural movements, forcing her to sit straight, chest out. She hid her legs beneath the bench as best as she could since a slit in the dress reached nearly to her upper thigh, and with Suranna sitting opposite, Nora was suddenly very conscious of all her blemishes and unshaven extremities.

Suranna bowed her head a little, tugging a smoke trail into place like a spinner tugging a strand of wool into shape on the spindle. This time Nora was sure she saw a figure like Diaz pacing through his training routine. Her eyes flickered back to Suranna, who was smiling.

"Do you believe in destiny, Nora?"

"No."

"So sure?"

"The gods are dead." Nora tossed her head back. "How can there be a predestined fate when there's no one left to predetermine it?"

"But what if the gods didn't predetermine it? What if they understood themselves to be slaves of destiny, forced to play out their part in the time given them?"

"Then it's good they're dead, the fuckwits."

Suranna gave Nora a look through the smoke.

"Do you know why the people in the north leave twins out in the wilds after birth? It is because in times now long gone even the common folk understood that some people are marked by the gods, chosen by them to stand out. Twins like Lara and Tuil, like Owen and you, but also people who speak in tongues, have the gift of second sight, or far-sight, of vision, who survived shipwrecks, fires, or other dismal fates miraculously."

"You forgot insane people," Nora interrupted.

"Touched by the gods, you mean." Suranna smiled. "When I look at you, I see a strong female twin, an outcast from a bigoted society who by all rights should be dead, but who has survived again and again, who is outstandingly lucky when tempting fate. And whose face is becoming a reflection of Lara, Queen of Death Herself." Suranna reached out and touched Nora's cheek. Her fingers were hot and Nora was sure the queen had singed her skin. She gasped and flinched away.

"To be holy means to be separate from all else. I see you and call you holy, Noraya. Dedicated to the gods to do their will, though beyond their direct reach. Do you know what revolution means?" Suranna asked.

Nora opened and closed her mouth a few times. "It's a word for disgruntled, unentitled people to say they want a turn at fucking over others for a change."

"It means a return to a former state."

"Nah." Nora shook her head. "Are you sure?"

"It's what we need now," Suranna continued, ignoring Nora's question. "A return to order and stability, to a strong hand led by divine fortune. You have seen it. There is something inherently wrong with the world of mankind, Nora. But what it is you cannot name; you can only feel it. And its cure is simple: we need the Living Blade. And now, look: a constellation of heroes aligning despite differences to find the Blade at the right time. A powerful seeress, an exiled prince, his shadow, a warrior of the elder blood, twins. The appointed time is coming. Look into the smoke and tell me what you see."

With that, the queen reached into the brazier and took out two glowing coals with her bare hand. Nora held her breath, expecting screaming and the stink of burning flesh. Instead Suranna formed the rising smoke in the cup of her hand, and Nora saw Diaz's face outlined to such a resemblance it was as if Suranna was holding up a mirror. Nora leaned in closer. A slender finger reached into the smoke and caressed Diaz's cheek. Nora saw his eyes open in surprise and his hand reach to where he had just been touched. The smoke writhed and twisted to reveal him from his head down to his hips. Suranna scratched her nails down his back, and Nora swallowed hard as his lips parted in a silent moan while he shivered. She licked her own lips and caught Suranna staring at her, golden eyes like slits.

"Tell me what you see."

"Is it—" Nora shook her head. "I mean, could he...feel that?"

"Oh, yes." Suranna laughed quietly, making Nora uneasy.

"How?"

"'This is at last flesh of my flesh, bone of my bone.' You know the words?"

"Diaz is your *husband*?"

Yeah, he'd failed to mention that along the way. Inclusion of celibacy in the code or not, one thing pilgrim masters were not allowed to do was marry. Even Nora knew as much. She stared at Suranna, heart racing, stomach churning bile.

"Twenty years ago he bound himself to me," the queen continued, as though unaware of the effect of her words on Nora. "Our bond goes much deeper than matrimony. Much deeper than he likes. Still, I would give him to you. Teach you how to touch him as I can. Do you want to learn from me?"

Her own personal love slave, unable to refuse her. Nora shuddered, but not with pleasure. She should not have to make decisions like this. Was not in the position to make them. No one was.

"In exchange for what?" she asked, surprised at how level her voice sounded.

Suranna leaned forward.

"In exchange for a true revolution."

CHAPTER 12

TWO GUARDS ACCOMPANIED NORA BACK to the guesthouse she had woken up in. She leaned against the closed door, waiting for her eyes to adjust to the twilight inside. A table with two chairs, a still life of fruit arranged on top of it, an alcove for washing, another decked out with cushions and costly sheets. The bed. Only one bed. But large enough for two.

Diaz was training. But she knew that already. She had seen him. He turned once, acknowledging with a quick glance that he had noticed her entering.

"You're not covered in vomit, nor are the whites of your eyes showing," he said, going through his movements with routine and precision. "It must have gone well today."

Nora nodded, not trusting herself to speak freely to him. Still under the impression of Suranna's smoke and illusions, the silent vision of Diaz moaning, she swallowed hard.

The wood of the door was smooth under Nora's fingertips. It was cool inside the room, but she felt warmth steal into her innards as she watched him move. He had stripped and wore only his trousers, rolled up around his knees, his tattoos curling on his skin, glistening sweat.

His face was calm, a mask of concentration as he fought the ghosts of at least three warriors around him. His sword flashed, catching the dusty rays of sunlight that fell in through the blinds of the windows. It took a master to make it seem as effortless as he did. His muscles hardened and tensed, and her knees were still weak from the poisoning. Or maybe just weak from a sudden, mad desire to kneel before him and lick his bronze skin, taste him, possess him. Her heart fluttered and maybe a sound had escaped her lips, because he came to a finish, sword point stretched at an arm's length without quivering.

"You didn't wear shoes?" He nodded at her bare feet, toweling off.

She looked down at the slit in the gown that exposed a long stretch of leg. So much nudity. Why had he noticed her feet?

"The shoes she sent me didn't fit," she said.

"Hmm." He rubbed the back of his neck just under the hairline. "Is something wrong? Or why are you still standing at the door?"

Nora licked her lips and registered with slight disappointment that they weren't salty from his sweat.

"Why am I here?" she asked slowly.

He pulled a shirt over his head and took his time answering, tucking the fabric neatly into his trousers.

"Are you sure you want my 'philosophical bullshit' answer?"

She smiled. "You won't forgive me saying that, will you?"

"We're here because we need information on the exact location of the Living Blade. As the queen is the strongest seeress—"

"I mean why am I *here*?" Nora interrupted. "With you. Why are we sharing sleeping quarters? Suranna must have…I don't know how many people and guesthouses. It can't be that hard for her to find a place for me to stay. Yet here I am. With you. Why?"

He remained silent.

"Why, Diaz?" She stepped away from the door, drawing nearer to him.

"It's like training, Noraya. It's all a test."

"A test of what? Or should I say whom? Me or you?"

He drew a deep breath. "The queen—"

"Why don't you say her name, dammit?"

A dark gleam entered his eyes as he looked down at her, and not a trace of pleasure could be found in his gaze.

"Names have power, Noraya. They seal and bind."

"Bullshit cliché. Answer my question."

"I just did."

"You know which one I mean."

He fell silent once more.

"Of course it's you. I'm just the means to an end." Nora shook her head. "If it's a test of your self-control, well…we both know how disciplined you are. We could be staying here for a long time. A very long time. I could be old and shriveled before you—"

"Noraya," he warned.

"Is it a test of…manhood? If she's simply curious whether you are still capable of wooing another—"

"Noraya!"

"—then I say, let's just get it over with. See what she comes up with next."

He snorted. "Why do you have to talk like that?"

"Like what?"

"Vulgar. Like you aren't…a virgin."

His voice dropped to a hoarse whisper when he said the last two words. As though they were sacred. Holy Nora. The worst was, she thought, he believed it. He'd always believe it.

"I trust you with my life," she said, shrugging. "I think I could trust you with my virginity."

She saw his jawline tense, but the rest of his face remained frozen in a carefully arranged non-expression. She smiled but made sure not to laugh. "Are you blushing yet?"

That broke the spell, and annoyance flashed over his face. He cleared his throat.

"Always trying to provoke me."

"No, I *am* being serious."

He flung the towel into a corner and raised a finger to admonish her to be silent. She closed her mouth.

"You don't know what you're asking," he finally said.

"I have a rough idea."

She groaned inwardly. *Shouldn't have said that. Thank you, mouth.*

"No. You do not." He made as though he wanted to say more but then snapped his mouth shut.

"Diaz—"

"This conversation is over."

"I—"

"Not one more word! I will *not* speak to you on this matter. Go, find your brother if you feel well enough. Go or I will go."

"I'll stay right here."

"Then I shall leave."

He made for the door. She caught him by the sleeve as he passed.

"We need to talk about this," she said.

"You forget. I am the master. I decide when we talk, and what we talk about."

He knocked her hand away and left.

Nora stared at the closed door for a moment, waiting for him to return. When he didn't, she started swearing and didn't stop for a long time.

CHAPTER 13

DIAZ DIDN'T RETURN THAT NIGHT. Nor did he show up in the morning. Five more days passed that way. Occasionally, when she came in from wandering the many streets of the temple-brothel, it seemed he had been in to collect some things, change his clothes. Sometimes Nora had the impression that she heard the door close quietly behind him when she woke, as though he had been there during the night, watching over her sleep. But most of the time he wasn't there.

Having little else to do, she went exploring. The temple was enormous and couldn't be seen all in one day. It took her three days to roam from one end to the other, and the temple's black heart was the throne room. She paced down the main streets, the girls there calling to her, beckoning her to come in. Some danced to the strange notes of a foreign wailing music on an instrument Nora had never seen before. Their lithe bodies writhed and shook, making the bells around their ankles ring. They wore nothing else. Off the main streets, there were food stalls and auditoriums where some girls sang and played music and entertained in many different ways. She sat around for a few afternoons, listening to the sad love songs and watching the older men weep silently in the dark seats before the stage.

A few days later, Nora also found a library, similar to the throne room in scope but in a quieter part of the temple. When she walked through the many rows of books, she saw a couple making out in the shadows between the rows, living out some weird fantasy. She would have turned and left when she saw them, but curiosity got the better of her and, well, this was a library after all, so maybe…nope. The man wasn't Owen.

Her brother sat at a long table, books piled high before his face, staring in concentration at the paper before him. A particularly loud couple was doing their thing on the other end of the table, but Owen didn't seem to notice. His frown only deepened as the table shook. Nora sat down beside Owen for a while, but he was so immersed in what looked like accounting ledgers that he didn't notice her, didn't notice anything. Not even when the couple was finished and the girl walked over to Nora, wearing nothing but a bead chain. Talk about uncomfortable clothing. Nora's eyes flickered upward to the girl's face. Her cheeks were red and she was wiping between her legs and down them as she nodded at Nora and said something.

"Sorry?" Nora said. "I don't speak...er..."

"I said that guy there, don't bother with him." The girl reached over and took a large gulp from a pitcher filled with water. "I've never seen anyone with such a lack of interest. Watch."

The girl ran a hand over Owen's nape and the tip of her tongue traveled along his throat to his ear. She raised her head and winked at Nora. After a moment, Owen's hand came up to wipe the wet away. His eyes never left the numbers before him, though two breasts dangled in front of his face.

"When you sit on his lap, he merely grunts and asks you to leave," the girl said. "Polite. But...no money there."

"I'm his sister," Nora told her. The girl simply shrugged and walked away.

"Please be in there somewhere, Owen." Nora waved a hand in front of her brother's face. "This place scares the shit out of me."

"Hmm?" Owen turned his head, but his eyes were still stuck on the page. "Nora? How long have you been here?"

"Long enough." Nora shuddered. "Owen, do you sleep here in the library?"

"I'm trying not to."

"What, sleep?"

"Mmhmm."

She waited, but he didn't say more.

"Owen?" She sat closer, a hand on his forearm, voice low. "I've never seen so many vacant expressions. This is no place to be. Owen? I'm scared. And lonely. Please talk to me."

"Uh-huh."

Nora rolled her eyes. She leaned back and tapped the wooden table with her fingernails.

"I'm with child, Owen. I'm carrying Diaz's love child. It'll be reborn as Shinar's chosen one, and together with Suranna we will rule this world as a holy fucking threesome."

"Not now, Nora. I'm reading. Hey!"

She snatched the book out from underneath his hands and snapped it shut. He groaned and ran a hand through his unkempt hair.

"What do you want?"

"I want to talk to you, brother dear."

"Why? I mean, why don't you go train with Diaz?" He made a grab for the book, but Nora held it higher.

"I can't. It's complicated."

"What did you do?"

"You're always quick to assume *I* did something."

"Did you?"

"I might have said something inappropriate." When Owen groaned, she quickly added, "But it was true. Not like Diaz keeping quiet about his marriage to the whore queen. Gods, I hate her. Always yapping on and on about Shinar this and Shinar that."

"Diaz was married?"

"Is! He *is* married. Aren't you listening?"

"But it's against the code." Owen's frown deepened. "Master Diaz would never go against the code. He doesn't—"

"That's the whole point! She's making him. She's an attention-demanding lunatic who has no respect for other people's boundaries."

"So unlike someone else I know," Owen muttered.

"Want your book back? Then start talking fast," Nora snapped.

Owen threw up his hands. "Imagine you don't belong anywhere. The wights don't socialize with you, and humans flinch whenever you approach. You meet someone. Someone beautiful, someone interesting, someone powerful. And that person reaches out to you. For the first time in your very long and lonesome life, you are touched, desired, wanted."

"As though she really felt that way," Nora scoffed.

"What matters is that he believed it. Is it really so hard to see what he saw in her? You've felt her influence yourself. I saw you two kiss and it was...stimulating, and I'm saying this as your brother." He made a face. "And another thing. You're not here to talk with me, Nora. You're here because you're bored. You're bored and I can't fix that for you. Only you can. Go and find something to do. You're in the middle of the biggest distraction palace of the world. You don't need me to entertain you."

"Did you even touch those two girls you left the throne room with?"

"Why would I? I've read books and seen illustrations on genital diseases. One word: chlamydia."

"Ew. Why do you even read that kind of stuff?"

"Go and find something to do, please," Owen said more softly. "There, we talked. The book, please..."

She stared at his outstretched hand, taking in his determined expression, holding up a moment longer.

"Fine. Have it your way, then." She rolled her eyes once more as he snatched the book from her hand. She watched as he flicked through the pages until he found the right spot. He always found the right spot. She got up and left.

✧ ✧ ✧

LITTLE HOUSES ADORNED THE STREETS in most areas, houses hewn of the red stone, but some were whitewashed with intricate patterns stenciled into the white. These whitewashed houses were larger, airier, sometimes two-storied, and when Nora peeked inside of an open door, she saw with surprise that it was a tavern of a sort. At least, in the background was a bar and a girl as a barkeep. Instead of the usual wooden tables and benches, each tavern had comfortable-looking alcoves separated off from the main bar room and filled with lush cushions. Where the curtains were drawn closed, she heard high-pitched laughter, and sometimes clouds of sweet-smelling smoke cascaded into the lower floor of the tavern like rolling fog banks.

In one of the taverns Nora spotted a familiar face at the bar, so she walked into the nearly empty place and took a seat.

"Hullo, Garreth," she said.

"Blech." He gave her a look with his good eye and took another sip.

"Rough night?" the seemingly ageless woman behind the counter asked, looking Nora up and down. Her mouth was painted the same shade of dark red her hair was colored, and she had a voice like gravel.

"You speak my language?" Nora asked, surprised.

"Hon, alcohol speaks everyone's language," the woman said and set down a glass holding a pale golden liquid.

"Ain't that the truth," Garreth said, and half of his face moved into a grin. The scar down the entire length of his face, splitting the eyelid of his blind white eye, transformed his smile into a demonic leer.

Nora took a sip and grimaced as she swallowed. She needed to stop drinking whatever they put in front of her here.

The barkeeper woman set a small silver box between her two silent guests busy with their drinks. When she opened it, Nora saw a little heap of finely ground salt, only it was a pale gold salt with flakes of red sprinkled throughout. The woman winked and stuck a tiny, delicate silver spoon into the substance, then told them it was on the house before stepping behind a curtained-off area.

"Great, you scared her off with your ugly mush," Garreth rumbled.

"What's this?" Nora poked the silver box.

"Sun Dust."

"What do we do with it?"

"You could lick your finger and take some. Works better if you rub it into your gums. Other people sniff it. Others smoke it. But what do we do with it? You and me? We don't take it, girl. That's what." He downed his glass in one go.

"It's a drug, huh? Is it good?"

He scowled and turned in his seat.

"Do I look like a wight to you? Black eyes, miserable face? Then stop teasing."

Nora laughed. "What are you doing here, Garreth? Money run out?"

"Nope, everything's on the house for us select few. Haven't been billed for anything." He burped. "And it's a rotten shame."

"It is?"

He rolled his shoulders.

"I'm not a complicated man. I don't pretend to have complicated pleasures. Expect nothing and you can enjoy everything, Nora. Expect everything and you won't enjoy anything."

"That's...pretty deep," Nora said, stunned.

"It's better when you pay for things you value. Things have worth then."

"Stop it, you're creeping me out. Let me check your eyes aren't black."

When he laughed, it sounded like he was choking up phlegm. She nearly slapped him on his broad shoulders.

"Know what's better than paying money, though?" he asked, scratching his nose thoughtfully.

"Tell me, oh wise one."

"Taking it from some poor sod with a bad hand at betting." He cocked his head and gave her a critical look-over. "How's your training with Diaz going? You two ever sparred down in the training hall?"

"There's a training hall?"

"There's something even better."

His grin was contagious. Maybe there was something to do here after all.

✧ ✧ ✧

NORA HUNCHED HER SHOULDERS UP against the loud revelry she had stumbled into on Garreth's account. The old warrior had led her deep down into the temple, a part she had not yet visited. They had passed under an open wooden gate and now stood in a round space, like the bottom of a deep well, where the light from the open sky high above them filtered through an orange sun sail that was ripped and tattered in places. Shafts of light spilled into the red stone pit where groups of men brawled while others stood on bleachers to the side or wooden stands scaffolded up high on poles, cheering and calling out. The wooden boards and poles were black with the dried blood of who knows how many gamecocks that had died there, or fighting dogs. But the center of the pit was reserved for fighting humans, and in its middle was a large table, the quiet eye in the storm. This was where the bets were made. This was where the referees of the fights were sent forth from. This was where Garreth stood patiently, arguing with a man who looked more like a scribe than a game runner. After a while the old mercenary ambled over to where Nora stood and dropped something into her hands: a wooden cuff with a number.

"Now, remember, this isn't about killing people," Garreth said gruffly. "Don't fight like you mean it. You're an unknown entity, and a woman fighter at that. So don't expect great opponents. In fact, choose people you know you can easily take down. See that girl over there?"

She looked to where he pointed. A young, beautiful girl with almond-shaped eyes was twirling two sleek curved blades like she knew how to use them. Her moves were jittery, though; a buzz ran through her body. Nora nodded and pulled the cuff over her forearm.

"See the red in her eyes?" Garreth went on. "That's why we don't do Sun Dust. Easy target. And see that woman?"

He pointed at an enormous woman warrior who was pounding a wiry young man into the red sand with her bare fists, each of her breasts the size of Nora's head.

"It'll be just like training," Garreth said, watching Nora's doubt play over her face. "Only I'll be making a bit of money for the both of us, because I know how good you really are."

He slapped her shoulder and made his way to one of the bleachers, nestling in with a large group of drunks.

The almond-eyed girl came closer along with one of the referees, who was dressed in white to stand out more.

"Are you ready?" the referee asked Nora in a bored tone, suggesting he didn't care if she was. She nodded, clutching her wooden training baton, feeling very stupid. The referee asked the pretty girl the same question, then held up a black flag to signal the fight had started.

The pretty girl twirled her blades in complex figures before and around her slim body. She threw one in the air and caught it by the handle as Nora bent her knees low, on guard for an attack. But instead the girl dodged blows that Nora hadn't even thrown. She jumped and pirouetted around, waving her dual swords in a fancy-looking way. Nora had to duck and sidestep a few wild hits, but the girl wasn't actually doing anything except showing off her mad sword-wielding and acrobatic skills. She actually posed before jumping high to stab Nora from above.

Nora was getting tired of the antics. Maybe the girl was high as fuck, but this was no way to fight.

As the girl let out a high-pitched shriek, sighting in on her supposedly easy opponent, Nora leaned back and head-butted her. One of the two blades clattered to the floor as the girl clutched her smashed nose. Oh gods, was she crying? Nora rolled her eyes, stepped closer to the sobbing girl, and cupped her head gently in her hands. The girl looked up, her beautiful eyes red with burst veins. Nora nearly felt sorry for her.

Nearly.

She broke that pretty face on her knee and called for the next fight.

Chapter 14

A small but heavy purse hung from Nora's belt as she made her way back to her rooms, elated because her muscles felt sore and used for once. And because she'd had a few drinks to celebrate with Garreth. Oh yeah, and because she had won against all odds, of course. That too. She walked on and on through the dusk-lit temple, staring at the bright torchlights above her and the loud, ugly people around her. Music beat heavily on her eardrums from a tavern close by. There was some kind of commotion going on.

She stopped in the cavernous hall, gaping wide-mouthed at the marble pillars of the women. So beautiful. Why was something so pretty when it was so messed up? People pushed past her, jostling her. She moved to the side, but there were still so many people walking by—lots of men, very few women. Nora was bracing against the stream when she heard the baby cry.

First she looked up, then around. This was not a place she had expected to hear a noise like that. She looked down at her hands, checking whether they were covered in blood. The baby in Calla's blood-soaked memories had cried like that. A newborn baby cry. But Calla wasn't here. Nora let her empty hands drop to her sides. There *was* a baby crying. And a woman, too, farther down in the cavern's deeps, leading toward the black throne room, where everyone else was going. She joined the crowd and let herself be carried down with it. The gates to the throne room were open, and people were pushing through to get inside. Nora was still at the back of the throng when a hush fell.

The baby had stopped crying.

Nora elbowed her way closer to the front and caught a glimpse of Suranna standing before the gates with a baby swaddled in cloth in her arms. A young woman had thrown herself before Suranna's feet. Rough hands had torn her black dress, and she kept trying to pull it over her full breasts as the milk dripped out of them in answer to the baby's cries.

"Daughter." Suranna touched the young woman's blonde head, her voice smooth and soothing as honey. "What is this you bring before me?"

"My queen, I didn't mean wrong. I, I simply loved my baby so much that I hid him from you."

"Don't cry, Keren." Suranna stooped low with the baby in her arms as the woman called Keren started to sob once more. "If the wind changes, your face will stay like that."

"Please, I just want to keep him. Please."

Suranna sighed deeply, as though arguing with a rebellious child. "The rules are the rules. This is the Temple of Fire. We never water truth down."

"Please. I beg you, Great Mother."

"Yes, I am the Great Mother. All life born in this temple belongs to Shinar. This little one is ours."

The young mother screamed violently as the women standing among the crowd took up the chant, echoing Suranna's words in an eerie singsong of various tongues. It made Nora's skin crawl.

"All life born in this temple belongs to Shinar. The little one is ours. The little one...belongs to Shinar. All life is...Shinar."

"Don't!" the young mother screamed. "Please. Don't throw him into the fire! He's mine. He's my baby. Don't make him pass before Shinar." *Shinar. Shinar.*

Nora shuddered. The crowd pressed in on the young mother as Suranna turned her back to them and strode into her throne room, the baby still in her arms. The gates shut soundlessly behind the queen's regal figure. The other women were still chanting, closing in on the young mother. Men grabbed the sobbing woman, and two of the other women closest to her pulled her dress over her head. She was naked, her breasts gleaming wet and her belly still soft and stretched from the recent birth. She didn't fight, just let herself be laid down, gently, as though going to sleep, as though exhausted from crying. She didn't even gasp when the first man entered her.

Instant sobriety hit Nora and she shoved automatically toward the sinister circle. The crowd rippled and flowed into a new shape around her, like a shoal of fish swarming around an obstacle. Men jostled each other to form a line while the chanting women pooled together around the young mother. Communal judgment. Nora was squashed between two men. One looked down at her with a sneer. He was loosening his belt already. She grabbed him by the shoulder to punch his face when she felt an arm hook under hers and drag her backward, nearly toppling her. She spun around to see who dared stop her.

It was Shade. Only he didn't look much like Shade. His face looked gaunt and solemn, as though years had passed since they had seen each other last, not days. Shadows lay under his eyes as he dragged her away from the circle.

"Do you have a death wish? Let me go." Nora struggled to get out of his firm grip.

"Keep walking. You can't help her, Nora," he said grimly, tugging her farther. "This isn't the Temple of the Wind."

"I can't just stand by and do nothing." Nora ripped her arm away from him and shoved him. He grabbed her wrist as she moved toward the circle pressed in the tight space before the gates and hauled her back. Nora stumbled into his arms, and in a short scuffle, managed to stamp on his foot and slap his face.

"Hey." A guard came ambling by, a spear in his hand. "Need help?"

Shade forced himself to echo the guard's laughter.

"This is just foreplay. She likes it rough," he said, shuffling Nora through the final ring of men as the guard joined the crowd.

"What are you doing?" she whispered through clenched teeth.

"Saving your ungrateful ass. Just keep walking. Please."

He shoved her against the stone wall as more men came by, pressing his body against hers so tightly a carving ground into the small of Nora's back. As she opened her mouth to protest, his lips smashed against hers in a fierce, wet kiss. She pushed back as his hands groped her breasts.

"Play along, stupid," Shade hissed into her ear as he necked her. "They won't go for the chanters, but right now every other woman is just meat. We need to get you out of here fast."

"But they'll rape that poor woman to her death."

"And there's nothing you can do, Nora. Nothing. Come on. We'll get you home."

Shade was playing that they were both overcome by lust, putting up a show for the passersby that this girl was already taken. As they made out in small nooks along their way, though, the pretense confused Nora's drink-addled body, so she gave up and fell into it, her mouth smudged with salty tears, hands shaking.

"Touch me," she moaned and pulled him closer. "Gods, Shade, hold me tight."

She bit deep into his lower lip, hearing him moan as he ground her against a wooden door.

"We're here," he said hoarsely.

"Oh, yes, we are." She ran a hand through his blond hair, grabbing a fistful.

The door opened behind them suddenly and Nora fell back, Shade landing on top of her, squashing the air from her lungs with a badly placed elbow. As she struggled for breath, she looked up to see what idiot had opened the door.

Dark eyes shone down at her. For the first time in a long time, Diaz was home.

Chapter 15

If Diaz had yelled at her, it would have made things easier, Nora thought as she followed the guards silently through the deserted throne room, passing through the veils into a small chamber. His grave silence and vague sense of disappointment had irritated her more. Both he and Shade had agreed that Nora should not spend the night alone with a mob outside. So Shade had left, and Diaz had taken a seat at the small table in their rooms as though he hadn't been gone. It made her so mad she felt like stomping over and slapping him, but instead she lay down on the bed and pretended to sleep, stomach churning. She knew he wasn't staying to protect her, but to check she didn't run out and kill those men. *Don't do something stupid, Nora. Wait until the morning, Nora.* She clenched her teeth tight and kept her eyes closed.

It was morning now, and she had called for an audience with Suranna. Guards had come to pick her up. The room she was in was lit by golden lampstands. It looked like a prop room, an anteroom to the throne room. The only thing that seemed misplaced was the huge four-poster bed and, above it, attached to the ceiling, an equally enormous copper mirror that reflected the light and, on occasion, whatever happened in the bed.

Beyond the bed was a door. A common wooden door. In the black heart of Shinar, with its veils and curtains and open spaces in the most private of settings, finding a door with a lock felt like something special. Beyond the door was a long corridor stretching out to the left and right. Servants scurried about, carrying golden pitchers or tablets of food. Whenever they passed them, the servants curtsied quickly or bowed but never stopped whatever it was they were doing.

Of course, Nora mused, the best magic was worked unseen. To encompass so many desires, much must happen off-scene, hidden from the theatrical spectacle. Here in long corridors, the wheels and cogs turned day by day to make everything else seem to run effortlessly. Food and drink, comfort, laundry, light, basic sanitation, heating—if you dazzled them enough, they'd believe you to be a sorceress, a seeress, a goddess even. Suranna, the goddess of efficiency.

They went down another corridor to the right, then down a flight of stairs. Nora looked over her shoulder as the guards led her ever deeper into the secrets of Shinar. She told herself she could still find her way back on her own, if she had to. It wouldn't be easy, but she'd manage after a while. They finally stopped and opened a black door, indistinguishable from the myriad of other doors they had passed along the way.

Beyond was another black room. It was nearly empty except for a large rectangular shape on a pedestal in the middle of the room. The guards shut the door behind Nora and she was alone with what looked like a silver pea pod, a long round coffin. Nora had asked to see Suranna, had demanded an audience. She had been led here, to a complete anticlimax. Lacking an immediate target, her fury defused somewhat. After looking around, Nora stepped closer to inspect the coffin.

If the thing was made of metal, she thought, it was a metal she didn't recognize. It seemed to be formed from one block, as though poured, perfectly smooth to the touch. No welts, no carvings, just one pure slab of metal.

"You wanted to speak?"

Nora jumped in surprise.

Suranna had entered, standing wrapped in nothing but a loose linen towel. It seemed she had appeared out of nowhere. But having walked through miles of corridors to get here, Nora didn't believe the queen had conjured herself from thin air. Rather, there was probably a passageway behind where she stood, shrouded with black veils. Divert the attention from your hands and any old card trick seemed like magic. It was all deception. Smoke and mirrors. Nora nearly laughed, but then she remembered why she had come.

"Well, then speak," the queen said, letting the towel slip from her shoulders.

"The woman." Nora came straight to the point. "Why did you sentence her to death?"

"I did not." Suranna shrugged and stepped closer. Nora held her ground, lifting her chin. "The god Shinar demanded her death. I am nothing but his servant girl. May I?"

She reached past Nora without waiting for an answer and pressed her hand against the metal slab. It cracked open soundlessly where before there had been no seam. The top part drifted to the side and hovered there, a foot above the ground. Nora stepped back instinctively. An orange light pulsed forth from the insides of the…thing. Suranna smiled like a cat before a dish of cream and dipped her hand into a milky liquid. She raised it high for Nora to see, and the white ran sluggishly from her fingers down her forearm.

"Come closer and take a look."

"What is it?"

"My bath. Care to join me?" Suranna laughed at Nora's face. She carefully lowered herself into the milk—if it was milk—and started to sponge herself off.

"The woman." Nora cleared her throat, becoming aware that she had been staring at Suranna's breasts for a while. They were full and firm and gravity had no hold on them. It was hypnotizing to watch the milk run between them, pearling off the smooth skin. The Great Mother, indeed. "Why did she have to die? What did she do to deserve such a death? What about her baby?"

"Do you think I'm a monster?"

Nora swallowed down her reply and chose a more tactful approach. "I don't know what you are." *But it's not human,* she added in her mind.

Suranna laughed quietly. She raised her finger, signaling Nora to wait. Then she lay back and submerged herself under the milk, or whatever it actually was. The texture seemed to be viscous, like cake batter, but not as sticky, oozing off her body as she rose again. She wiped her face.

"Did you come through the corridors on your way here?" she asked Nora as she stepped out of the bathtub, reaching for the towel.

"Er…yes."

"Every level of the temple is connected through these back corridors. They are the most direct route to any room for quick maintenance or help, should any be required. There are small intimate rooms for two, maybe three, but also large halls, depending on the need, and all are interconnected. Thus the structure of the temple resembles the structure of our society. We are all interconnected and interdependent. We all stand by each other, and though each of us may have a different role or import, all are equal before the face of Shinar."

"You stole her baby to sacrifice it to your god and then did nothing as she was raped to death. Doesn't seem equal from where I'm standing."

"Every society has its rules. Rules that one must live by. You know this, Nora. If you do not live according to the society's rules, if you do not fit, then you are quickly cast out, and when you are cast out, the rules that bind everyone else do not apply to you anymore." Nora remained silent, thinking of her home village, thinking of the many refugees at the Temple of the Wind and the rounds she had gone on with Master Cumi. Rules, yeah, she knew those too well.

Suranna continued, wrapping herself in her towel once more. "Here we have but one set of rules. The safety of my girls must always come first, not only their immediate safety when together with a customer, but also their long-term safety. Here they are not cast out when they become old or too sick to work. We take care of each other. We work together, not as competitors. But thinking long term also means that population control must be a priority. A necessity. We live in an oasis in the middle of a harsh desert. If every girl were to become pregnant as often as she wanted, very soon none of us would be able to stay here, live our lives to the standard we have become accustomed to. Thus weighs the greater good of all. And so our laws are quite simple in this regard. If a girl becomes pregnant here, she has many choices. She can choose to abort the child or give birth to it. If she desires to give birth, then she must decide whether she wants to keep her child. If she does, she is free to collect her wages and leave Shinar at any time before the baby is born. But she must leave. Many cattle farms and settlements owe their prosperity to the choice of a girl to raise her family outside the gates of Shinar."

Nora thought of the matriarch with the gold wig. She thought of the little bighead statues lining the way through the ravines. "And if she chooses to stay?"

"Then the child becomes our child. Every life born here is a gift of Shinar. It is born of the mother but then brought to me as high priestess of the god. And I then commune with the god over the fate of the child, whether it should pass through the fire and reside with the god, or if it may stay here with us and become part of our society."

"Like Shade?"

"Brisin is a beautiful son of Shinar, and our god graciously chose to bring him back to us once more as a most beloved son."

Nora snorted. "Yeah, like it wasn't cold calculation on your part to keep Bashan's bastard alive. To influence the heir of the Kandarin Empire, your powerful next-door neighbor."

"I see you still lack faith." Suranna's eyes were slits, but she spoke calmly, slowly, as though reasoning with a child.

"You sacrifice newborn babies by throwing them into the fire. The new mother is raped to death with everyone's consent just because she chose to keep her child here. So, yeah, I lack your kind of faith."

"Every society must sacrifice. By choosing to keep her child, she was working in direct defiance of our laws for peaceful living together. She stole from all of us, stole our child, stole the god's child. A life for a life."

"But it's wrong."

"Your mother lived by the same rules." Suranna shrugged.

Nora opened her mouth to retort; Mother Sara would never hurt a child. She had saved the twins from certain death and raised them as her own despite the stigma they carried. But then she realized Suranna wasn't talking about Mother Sara and shut her mouth dumbly.

Suranna smiled and stepped closer. "No. Really? You never wondered where your real mother came from?"

She touched Nora's face. The scarred side began to tingle as though it had been numb and was now waking. Nora touched her cheek and scratched at the healed cuts.

"I've seen you when you were still being woven in your mother's belly," Suranna whispered, her golden eyes soft. "This is your home, Noraya. This is your destiny, Child of Shinar. Stay with me. Stay by my side and together we will rise as free daughters, casting off the tyranny of men and placing them under our heels. The likes of Bashan will never do us harm. They will serve us, or they will die by the hand of our living god."

Nora shook her head, confused. When Suranna was so close it was hard not to want to kiss her. She backed away. You couldn't cast off tyranny simply by becoming a different kind of tyrant. A world in which women treated men the way they had treated women was just as shit. Not worth making.

The smiling queen drew a circle before her with her fingers, smoke trailing from them, pulling a handheld copper mirror out of thin air.

"Look into the mirror."

She did, expecting to see Diaz in a vision once more. She gasped, hand reaching for her cheek.

Her face was mending. The scars left from the explosion at the Temple of the Wind were knitting themselves together, the skin was smoothing, the damage was being undone. The tingling increased until it was like an itch.

"Shinar is a place of desire, Nora," Suranna spoke, but Nora was transfixed by her own reflection. "Anything you desire can be fulfilled, child. Anything."

CHAPTER 16

DIAZ WAS WORKING THROUGH HIS sword-fighting routine on his own. Nora stood by the door of their house on the lookout for Shade and watched Diaz go through his drill, while touching the taut skin of her still scarred face. He spent most days in their rooms now, and when Nora wasn't out making money in the fighting pit, she trained with him again. Now, though, dusk had fallen over the temple, and she enjoyed when the lights softened the gathering darkness into a golden glow.

"Try not to come home drunk," Diaz called over his shoulder.

She rolled her eyes at him.

"Yes, Mother. I heard you the first time." She spotted Shade jogging around the corner and hurried toward him.

"Hey!" he said, a little flushed from jogging.

"Let's go." She gave him a peck on the cheek and hooked her arm under his.

"Everything all right?" he asked.

"I just want to leave before Diaz gives me a curfew," she said. Shade laughed, and for a moment the shadows under his eyes were gone. Nora smiled. "So what's the plan tonight?"

"Are you hungry?"

"No."

"Do you want to sit around in the library with Owen?"

"Tempting, very tempting. You sure know how to take a girl out."

"I think I might know a few bars we haven't yet been to..."

"Great, let's go."

"...but if this really were a date, I thought you might want to spend it in a way you could actually remember tomorrow." He grinned at her sheepishly.

Nora laughed. "I'm game. Where are we going?"

"Somewhere we're not supposed to."

"Now you're talking."

He led her through the main streets first, then through the industrial parts of Shinar, past the cauldrons of the laundry and the steaming kitchens, down alleyways that became tunnels so tight they had to walk through them sideways. Beyond she saw the light of dusk, an orange sun balancing precariously in a red stone bowl. They stepped into the last of the sunlight and stood in a natural ravine filled with long rows of fragrant herbs, tended beds of vegetables, and date trees as far as Nora could see. The setting sun had already cast a deep shadow in the ravine. The night wind brought refreshment from the heat, the scent of fennel, and the chirping of insects. Streams gurgled their melodious songs. A verdant, vibrant scent hung over the gardens, a soothing balm after the barren red stone. The gardens were empty. No one else was around. Nora took a deep breath.

"Like it?" Shade stepped closer to her and took her hand in his.

"It's incredible." So peaceful. So beautiful. She squeezed his hand. "Thank you for this."

"Well, I'd be lying if I said I hadn't hoped it would inspire a certain...mood." He grinned. "Come on, let's walk. There are fields of flowers here, too, for the perfumes. Some only bloom at night."

And so they walked through the rows of lush green life, content to just be near each other, brushing against each other to feel the other's presence, sometimes accidentally, sometimes not so accidental. Every now and then Nora would stoop low and inhale the scent of the flowers around her or touch the springy leaves of the plants. Shade led her into the middle of the gardens where an oasis of date trees rustled their branches in the breeze.

"I used to come here a lot," Shade said, touching a low-hanging branch of a lemon tree. "Hung around an elderly couple who worked here. She had retired from her...work here, and he had stayed with her. Really sweet together. They let me help them sometimes, though now that I think back on it, I might not have helped that much but just ate my way through the vegetables."

"Didn't you get enough in the temple, you poor starved boy?" Nora smiled. Shade was wiry, but not from hunger.

"Oh, we did. More than enough." He hesitated and gave her a sidelong glance. "The children who are born here and aren't given over to Shinar in sacrifice get everything and more. We were spoiled rotten with treats and sweet things, rich clothes, attention of the Great Mother, and her protection, of course. No one could touch us."

Nora thought about what Suranna had told her about her own origin. She would have grown up like Shade, a servant of the temple.

"You make it sound like it was a life to be envious of," she said.

He shrugged and looked up into the velvet sky of many colors. "I didn't know life to be otherwise. But…I liked life here more."

They held hands, and turned toward each other.

"Shade," Nora started, leaning in closer.

"Yes?"

"I'm glad you brought me here."

"How glad are you?"

She laughed, her lips brushing against his. "Very glad."

"Undress, then."

She snorted with amusement and felt him smile under her lips. They shared a look. Then his lips pressed against hers, his tongue hot and greedy. He pulled away suddenly, and they broke apart, breathless.

"Come with me."

Shade grabbed Nora's hand and pulled her away from the pathway, toward the date trees. She followed, giggling, pushing branches out of her way as they ran faster, always faster, until they reached a small artificial clearing among the tall trees. In the middle of the clearing was a pool filled with water, its surface black with depth, a cistern to keep the gardens fresh and alive. They halted abruptly, and Nora rowed with her arms to avoid falling headlong into the round pool reflecting the stars, a piece of sky cast on the ground. Shade, grinning, gave her a push and she shrieked, splashing into the cool wet.

Underneath the surface a quiet pressed against her eardrums, the only sound her beating heart. She opened her eyes and looked down as she felt her sandals slip off her feet. She saw no floor beneath her. Only the surface was lit; below yawned the pitch dark. There was no way she could tell how deep the cistern was. She resurfaced and took a singing breath. Treading water, she wiped her hair from her eyes. Shade had bent down low over the cistern and was grinning.

"Are you wet now?" he asked, eyebrows waggling.

She moved an arm over the water and sent a wave splashing at his face, making him laugh.

"You didn't know I could swim. What would you have done if I had drowned?"

"I'd have saved you." He threw out his chest and flexed his biceps.

"You'll pay for this."

He laughed again, pulling off his shoes as she swam a few strokes to the rim of the cistern. She hoisted herself up and hooked her fingers under his belt, pulling him down with her. As he broke the surface, she flung more water at him, and for a few minutes they splashed around, dipping under, relishing the respite from the heat of the day. Then he grabbed her hand and pulled her close once more.

Nora hooked both of her legs around his waist, nearly weightless in the water. They were still panting heavily from the play fight. Shade pulled his head back as she leaned in to kiss him, a teasing smile on his face widening as he swam both of them to the rim of the cistern. Pressing her into the stone that was still warm from the blaze of day, he made his next kiss slow, burning against the chill of their wet clothes in the night breeze.

"Tell me to touch you again," he whispered between kisses.

"Touch me." Nora bit into the flesh of his earlobe. "Oh gods, if you don't touch me I'll scream."

He chuckled and took her nipple between his fingers, playing with it until she moaned and arched against him. She pulled up his wet shirt while his hands moved over her body. He groaned loudly as she squeezed her thighs tighter around him, excited by his touch and his readiness.

"Gods, I want you," he murmured, his breath hot against her clammy skin. "I really want you."

He let go of the rim to hold her with both hands, and they went under. She kicked up and broke through the surface the same time he did. He made a face as she giggled.

"I'm sorry," Shade said. "I can't. Not here."

"It's hard without a foothold."

"That's not what I meant. I meant this place…maybe wasn't such a good idea."

He let her go and climbed out of the water, reaching down to give her a hand up. The water dripping from them spattered darkly on the red ground.

"We'll go someplace else, then." Nora rose, taking his hand. "Come on, show me."

He laughed without humor.

"It's not this place, Nora. I thought if there was any place I could…you know…it would be here. At least better than in one of the houses. Better than in your rooms with Diaz watching."

"What is the matter with you? Why are you bringing him into this?" Nora pulled her wet shirt back down, aware that the chill made her nipples stand out anyway. She crossed her arms over her chest.

"Oh, please." Shade gave her a look. "As though I'm not simply a substitute. As though you weren't imagining him whenever you closed your eyes just now."

"I was not—" Nora gritted her teeth. "Fuck you, Shade."

"Not here in my childhood memories. Not with the feeling that you'll get what you need, get up, and walk out on me." He sighed. "Look. I'm trying not to be an asshole."

"Well, you're failing, then."

"But I don't want to feel like you're just another customer."

He knelt before her among the palm branches, eyes earnest, shoulders sagging, still dripping wet. His blond hair was plastered to his skull, making his features stand out more, making him look more like his father. *Damn it all.* That wasn't helping.

"What am I to you, then?" she asked softly.

Shade shrugged.

"I'm not sure. But maybe we'll find out someday." He rose and tried to brush off the red clumps of dust on the knees of his trousers.

"Someday?" The hairs on her arms rose, but not because of the wind. "You mean when we're back on the road, like a quickie up against a tree?"

He half grinned.

"Well, no. That's not what I had in mind. Though I like your dirty way of thinking." He cleared his throat. "I meant when all this is over."

He doesn't know, she thought. *And I am not the one to tell him. I can't tell him. Can I?*

"I wonder sometimes," Shade continued, oblivious. "Prince Bashan has the Living Blade and goes off to be emperor. Master Diaz goes off to become guardian of the order in the north or whatever. Owen becomes a pilgrim master somewhere. What are we going to do then? Ever thought about that? Become sellswords like Garreth? Maybe make up our own crew? We'll have loads of time then. Together."

Her stomach felt like it was going to heave.

"Oh gods, Shade." She shook her head as he reached for her hand.

And the hits just keep on coming. She opened her mouth to tell him he was going to die, then closed it again. What had he ever done to her that she should be so cruel? To tell him people would just use him all his life, right up to the manner of his death—that was no service.

"I, I need to tell you..." she stammered.

"Yes?"

She couldn't tell him. Suranna had told her that the sacrifice had to be willing. If he didn't know he was going to be sacrificed, how could that count as willing? Bashan would never get the Blade. And, oh my gods, she really couldn't tell him, because what if by telling him, he would then choose to become the sacrifice? His blood would be on her hands, whether he went willingly or not. Fucking hell. She needed to talk to Owen. She needed to take Shade in her arms and give him what he wanted. She needed to get out of this temple. And she needed…she really needed…

"I really need a drink now."

CHAPTER 17

OWEN TOOK A DEEP BREATH, turning the last page in his book. Then he put the book down before him, palms of his hands flat on the cover, and stared off into space, as though savoring the fleeting moment of accomplishment. Nora watched him. It was quiet in the library today. It seemed she and her brother were the only ones there.

"And? Better now?" she asked.

"Nora?" Owen looked surprised to see her. His red eyes focused on her face. He had been going strong for some time now, keeping himself awake with a concoction that smelled divine but tasted bitter as hell. Nora had tried some herself, but it made her heart race and her fingers shake. Owen stretched.

"Ah. You know that melancholic feeling when you're nearly finished with a book and know that afterward there will be nothing left to read? And it makes you happy and sad at the same time?"

"No," Nora said, licking the tip of her finger to turn a page. "Is it like: '*post coitum omne animalum triste est*'?"

"How do *you* know that?"

She grinned at him over the cover of her book. "Read it."

"But who translated it for y—never mind. I don't even want to know."

She laughed and poured him a glass of water as he rubbed his eyes.

"What *are* you reading?" He squinted at the title of the leather-bound book in her hands.

"Words." Nora flicked back a few pages. "Lots of words. Here, listen to this: 'She moaned lustfully as he thrust his quivering love lance—'"

"Ew. Why do you even read that stuff?" Owen clasped his hands over his ears. "And no, I don't want to hear your answer."

Nora chuckled and placed a bookmark between the pages. The table in front of Owen looked as though he had been trying to build himself a book fortress but had failed because someone kept opening the bricks. She drew herself up and put on a serious air.

"Shade doesn't know," she announced.

Owen stared at her with wide eyes. His hair was ruffled like the feathers of an owl.

"You didn't tell him, did you?"

"No." She frowned. "Should I have?"

"No." Owen looked shocked. "That's not your business."

"Amazing how often people tell me that."

Nora leaned back in her chair and stared up at the domed ceiling. Ages ago, someone had stained the red stone a rich dark blue to depict the night sky. It was flaking in spots, leaving blood-red gashes in the painting. You could see constellations of stars imprinted within the outline of an enormous man who stretched from one horizon to the other, his back arching to hold the heavens up, stars scrawled onto his blue skin. Specks of light in night's dark cloak. Light and dark conjoined, though forever apart. A paradox. A divine mystery. The fixed star was the man's navel, but the most prominent constellation was just below: the Axis, a row of four large stars with a heart-shaped trace of smaller stars below. Typical. Even the heavens revolved around some guy's testicles.

"Does Master Diaz know?" Owen asked.

"Why does everyone believe we're together?" Nora's voice rose a pitch higher in exasperation.

"Aren't you?" Owen peered at her down his long nose.

"No, for fuck's sake."

"Fine. Why are you so mad, then?"

"Because..." She stopped and held her head in her hands. Because she wanted what Suranna had had. Because she wanted Diaz unreservedly. Because it wasn't fair to use Shade as a substitute. Because she knew that Diaz would never be with her the way he had been with Suranna. He couldn't. Because he was the master and he didn't see her as his equal. And because being with him would change everything between them, and she didn't want that either.

She took a deep breath before continuing in a more calm and dignified manner: "Tell me why you've crawled behind all these books the last few weeks, Owen. Tell me about the Blade. Suranna told me the sacrifice for it had to go willingly. That the Blade somehow...remains the person who was turned into it. Why hasn't Bashan told Shade yet?"

"Maybe he is waiting for the right time."

"Bashan?"

Owen shrugged and offered another theory. "Maybe he is so sure that

Shade will want to volunteer that he hasn't told him yet."

"How so?"

"I'm not sure, Nora. Do I look like I know what Bashan thinks? Or Shade?" Owen ran a hand through his greasy hair, ruffling it even more. He was paler than usual, making the curved scar on his cheek stand out. There were shadows under his eyes and was that…? Was that the ghost of a beard around her brother's mouth? Did he have to shave already and hadn't? She used to be indistinguishable from him, snotty-nosed, charcoal-smeared face and all. Nora folded her arms. She'd never tell him they had narrowly escaped a life of whoredom by grace of a mother they didn't know.

"Even if you don't know, I'm sure you have a theory. So share," she said instead.

He swallowed a gulp of water and wiped his mouth with his sleeve. "Where should I start?"

"Tell me of the treasures of the gods. Tell me of the prophecy and the quest you're on to find the Living Blade."

"So you can mock me and them?"

"Owen." Nora fixed her eyes on her brother's face. "There are thousands of people, maybe even tens of thousands, who would mock you. They say the gods are dead, that magic is gone or dormant. They say we should put our faith in men. We should follow the pilgrim's order. We should bow our heads to the Kandarin Empire. Should, should, should. These people would say your search for cauldrons and blades and cloaks and horns is so much nonsense it betrays a deluded mind. Belief is frowned upon; faith is for the gullible. They would mock you, Owen. But I won't. I am here. By your side. And if they dare mock you to your face, I'll kick their ass. So you owe me."

Owen stiffened while she spoke, but he smiled at the last and then nodded, hunched forward between his books.

"Owe you? Interesting line of reasoning, that. So. The treasures," he said, never able to resist imparting his knowledge, "are what remains to us of the gods. For a long time, the wights kept those treasures from us, which is why we saw them as messengers from the gods, their mouthpieces. And the wights taught us that in the beginning, before the dawn of men, there was only one land, the ancient Blessed Isle, Nessa. No other lands existed, just Nessa and the wide sea, covered with swirling mists.

"There were seven tribes of wights then, seven kings, seven great feasting halls, and seven gods. And the gods walked among the wights as they do, in physical form on the land. And one of the gods, Arrun, fell in love with a wight maiden. To keep her at his side forever, knowing she was mortal,

Arrun gave his woman the first treasure. The Cauldron of Arrun. Whenever she began to grow old and feel time's sting, she only had to fill the Cauldron with water, immerse herself, and be young again. Thus, in all her beauty, she could walk beside him always. They were married, and the First Empire was forged from that marriage."

"And thus love conquers all. The end," Nora interrupted. Owen gave her a dark look. She knew it wasn't how the stories went and so gestured for him to continue.

"The other tribes were jealous, resentful of a forced unification of what seemed so diverse. So each tribe prayed for their god to give them a treasure matching the power of the Cauldron. But the Cauldron had been forged not only by Arrun, but by Dalem the Forger, who had brought humans to the Holy Isle. And he hid himself in his mantle of sky while his brothers and sisters searched for him to help them with their treasures, so that they were left to make their own treasures.

"Soon each tribe but Dalem's had their own treasure, and each tribe could use its holy gift to summon their god. Only once a year could they summon their god, but when they came, the summons gave the tribes great power in the terrible wars that followed. The lands were sundered. The world was broken. The seas were swept up in tempest and forever subjected to the push and pull of the moon. Many died. Many more were enslaved. Every time a god's spear fell from heaven, thousands perished, until Dalem could no longer watch in the shadows and came out of hiding. The son of the king of Dalem's tribe had fallen in love with a human woman, and he bade his god to give him the means to protect what he loved from extermination."

"Wait." Nora sat up. "That's not how the story goes. I know the 'Lament of Deeyan.' His lover is the woman warrior Scyld, and *she* asked Dalem to protect humans. In return for her firstborn child, he forged the Living Blade for her. You can't make it about a guy when it's about a girl hero."

"There are as many versions as storytellers, Nora." Owen raised an eyebrow. "Now the prophecy?"

"What about the Blade itself? What do you know?"

"I just told you what I know. The Blade was made so long ago, even the wights don't remember it clearly, only in creation myths and legends. The last time it was reforged was two thousand years ago. What we know is mere guesswork, an approximation of the truth."

"Approximate away. I trust your educated guess."

Owen sighed. "The Blade and the Cauldron are the two greatest of the treasures. The one gives the wielder the power to stand against the gods, and the other bestows everlasting youth. The Blade itself, when dormant, is some kind of fluid. There's a transcript of an ancient Nessan scroll somewhere here in which the dormant form is described as the Tears of Indis, also known as quicksilver." He started looking through his book heap but only managed to topple a few to the ground. "Anyway, the fluid encompasses the sacrifice whole and incorporates the living body to remake itself."

"How?"

"Magic?" Owen scrunched up his forehead. "There's the transference of matter that puzzles me, to be honest. I mean, a sword is never as long as a body or as thick. Where does all the…leftover stuff go?"

Nora pulled a face.

"Anyhow," Owen continued, "the Blade, now no longer dormant, can somehow communicate with the wielder. They become one. A perfect union. More than the sum of their parts. But it also destroys the wielder from within. Maybe it's the guilt of the sacrifice, maybe just the strain of holding all that godlike power inside you, maybe the secret knowledge of the makeup of the entire universe fries your brain—whatever the case, every wielder has gone insane and taken his or her life after a span of a few years. So, the sword of destiny is a two-edged one."

"Is this something you really want to be finding for Bashan? Because the more you tell me about it, the more it sounds insane to be doing this. If we ever do find it, we should destroy it before it falls into his hands."

"How would you destroy it, Nora?" Owen scoffed. "It's an artifact of awesome power and ancient knowledge and—"

"It's called the Living Blade. Anything that's living can die, Owen." Nora slumped in her chair. She took a moment to think about what Owen had told her. "Suranna told the prophecy to Bashan's father, didn't she? That his son, his only son, would destroy the empire by finding the Living Blade. Bit too much of a coincidence."

"Well, that brings us back to the Cauldron. It was lost in ancient Nessa, but I think someone must have found it. It has survived through all the centuries." Owen sat up straight. "I had this thought when we first reached the Temple of the Wind. Why try to find the Blade, with its many downsides, when you could find the Cauldron instead? Imagine having the lifespan of a wight, or even longer, and everlasting youth and health—think of what good you could achieve if you steered the fortunes of a kingdom or empire over centuries. One man. One vision. One direction to greatness. Or one woman, in this case."

Owen paused for dramatic effect, but Nora took the wind out of his sails.

"I know Suranna has it," she said.

"You—what do you mean, you know? I had to sit here reading three-hundred-year-old tax reports to find the evidence that she has been ruling here for at least that long."

Nora lifted a shoulder.

"She bathed in it while talking to me. She's also been Diaz's wife for the last twenty years, and since she doesn't look a day older than twenty-five and he doesn't seem the type to marry little girls, I figured she must have access to some pretty powerful magic. Ta-da." She threw up her hands dramatically, seeing Owen's disconcerted look.

He scratched his chin.

"Don't be clever, you," he said after a while. "I'm the smart one."

Chapter 18

Sun Dust. Nora gazed at Suranna's moving lips from a faraway place in her mind. It was tempting to numb herself with drugs. They should be an escape from the queen's ongoing effort to win Nora for her god. But they simply lowered her mental barriers and allowed Suranna to trespass on her most intimate thoughts. No retreat. The same with alcohol. It didn't seem fair. Nora felt cheated, having to sit through the audiences with the queen entirely sober and well rested. Falling asleep was not advisable when the one sitting opposite you could walk into your mind and wreak havoc.

She slouched while tuning out the lecture. How could you block someone when you couldn't use your physical body? How could you stop the breaking and entering when every time your thoughts wandered you not only left a door unlocked but opened it wide? Nora had been practicing over the last few days. She found that if she focused on the speaking without actually hearing the words, Suranna didn't bother her. Drunk on her own power for too long, she didn't even consider that anyone listening might not be paying rapt attention. That was a lesson learned on leadership, right there before Nora's eyes. One that Bashan would do well to ponder, too. Power was just as addictive as any other drug. And Suranna was high as high could go. Had been for the last few centuries, according to Owen. Three hundred years of life and power, everlasting youth and beauty. There was no other way she could live now. Maybe she had once been a young, innocent girl. Or maybe Suranna had been like Nora. Regardless, she could never go back.

"Fish cannot fly. Birds cannot swim. And humans are not fit to rule over each other. Thus we need the gods back with us. To help us and guide us. Do you agree?" Suranna asked her.

"I do." Nora nodded.

She did, in fact. It was all true what Suranna said about the incapacity of mankind to rule one another. The blind leading the blind. Need for change. Blah, blah, blah.

However, the way Nora saw it, the problem with theocracy was that you needed a god to rule. And all the old gods were dead. So in reality that only left their human mouthpieces and their interpretations of divine will. That was the crux. If there ever was a living god, Nora hoped there would finally be some smiting and laying to waste of the unjust, because that would set some people straight or conveniently get rid of them altogether.

She hurried to sit straight as a servant approached the queen and whispered into Suranna's ear. Suranna nodded regally.

"Let him in," she said with her honey voice.

The servant bowed low and disappeared behind the black veils. Nora gave Suranna a puzzled look. The queen smiled as she adjusted her seat on the throne.

"We will have an audience," she said.

"Aren't we already having one?" Nora frowned.

"Observe and learn," Suranna said, concentrating on the opening doors.

Nora turned on her stool to see who entered. For a moment, Nora hoped it would be Diaz, and her heart fluttered at the thought. Then she really hoped it wasn't.

Prince Bashan entered, chin high. His noble face was clean-shaven. He held himself with utter poise and confidence that the room was a better place since he had graced it with his presence. He was one who could do with some smiting, Nora thought. She nearly smiled when a flash of anger spoiled Bashan's collected appearance as he realized Suranna was not alone. He caught himself quickly, though, and bowed low before the throne.

"My lord prince, what honor," Suranna said, sweetness dripping from her lips. The atmosphere in the throne room changed as she let loose a current of power. The effect was instant. Nora felt like kneeling and worshiping the golden goddess before her.

"My lady." Bashan moved up a few steps to kiss Suranna's outstretched hand. "I see you are inconvenienced." He waved a hand in Nora's direction with a throwaway gesture.

"She is my guest, as you are." Suranna's smile widened.

Bashan made a noncommittal noise at the back of his throat. He glanced at Nora.

"Are you enjoying yourself?" he asked her.

Nora shrugged and cast her eyes down.

"I do my best, my lord."

"Shaved your legs at least," Bashan commented. Nora swept them under the hem of her long garment. "Not much improvement in your face, though."

"You wished to speak to me, Lord Prince?" Suranna said. "Then speak."

Bashan gave Nora another long look before he turned to Suranna, hands folded neatly against his back.

"My lady," he started, articulating the words so that they resounded with thankfulness and warmth. "We have been your guests now for four weeks. The hospitality of Shinar is renowned and has been spectacular as always. Yet, I cannot help but wonder how much progress you have made determining the location of the Living Blade, our common endeavor."

"My lord prince." Suranna spoke down to him. "You are justified in asking, and I wish I had good news to share with you. Alas, divining the exact location is proving to be difficult."

Bashan's eyes narrowed.

"Why?"

"The trail of this legendary item you seek has been cold for over two millennia. Its magic has been asleep for so long that it is hard to tap into the correct lode of power to find it. Give it time, Bashan. Give me time."

"Could I be of more assistance? Just say the word and I will put heaven and earth into motion for you, my queen."

"I feel your impatience as acutely as you do. However, there is no way you can help with the divination unless you have the sight yourself."

Bashan shook his head. "Unfortunately, I do not own such powers. Which is why I must rely on you, my beautiful lady. I can only hope your time isn't frivolously wasted with people who do not appreciate you as much as I do."

"I never waste my time, Lord Prince. I enjoy it too much."

Nora saw Bashan stiffen and laughed quietly through her nose. *Yeah, he just got burned.* She suppressed her smile as he turned to stare at her, eyebrows high, the corners of his lips pulled downward. He turned back to face Suranna.

"How much longer do you think it will take you to find the location, my lady? You must know that our return journey will be a long one. I fear if we tarry longer, we might not make it past the Wightingerode before the next winter comes."

Suranna arched one perfect eyebrow.

"Patience is a virtue. Virtue is a grace, my lord prince. Wait, and I promise you will not wait in vain. The Blade will be yours. Soon. And with it, you will destroy your father's empire, just as I have seen it."

"To rebuild it larger and more magnificent than even my forefathers could?" Bashan asked sharply.

Suranna nodded, a silky black lock of hair falling into her face.

"Of course."

Bashan pressed his lips together tightly, then smiled, flashing his white teeth.

"Then I shall await your divination with patience and grace. Though I cannot promise virtue."

He strolled out of the throne room, chin still high, hands clasped at the small of his back.

When the doors had closed behind him, Nora turned her attention back to the queen, who was watching her attentively.

"What do you think of him?"

"Well." Nora folded her hands neatly in her lap, trying to think of something else to say other than, *he's a slick asshole*. "He can be charming when he wants to be."

"Agreed."

"What about Empress Vashti? Will Bashan really rebuild the Kandarin Empire?"

Suranna shrugged. "With the Living Blade, all things are possible."

Nora stared at Suranna for a long time while the smile on the queen's full lips broadened.

"Go on," the queen said, laughing finally. "You may ask me."

"Do you already know where the Living Blade is?"

"Of course. I wouldn't be much of a seeress if I couldn't find one of the greatest magical items in the world. That would be comparable to not seeing the only candle in an otherwise darkened room."

"Well, if you're standing in the proximity of another candle..."

"The Cauldron of Arrun amplifies my power of divination. As does the Horn of Tuil, the Mirror of Neeze, and all the other divine treasures."

Nora frowned. "Then why pretend—"

"There is an appointed time. It is not now."

Nora stared at the beautiful creature before her and realized something: Suranna wasn't a woman. She wasn't Diaz's wife. She wasn't even a goddess. She was a spider sitting on a web she had built herself. And Nora prayed that if anyone could summon the gods back to rule over mankind, they'd be so pissed off they'd take it out on Suranna first.

CHAPTER 19

THE DOOR OPENED AND THE draft blew out the candles. Nora stood on the threshold, swaying slightly, peering into the darkness within to see...nothing.

"Diaz?" she whispered hoarsely.

"Here." His disembodied voice was accompanied by the sound of splashing water. He must have been in the bath at the back of the room.

Light flickered, casting long shadows as the candles were relit. Nora entered, closing the door behind her. When she turned, he had wrapped a towel around his hips, water pearling off his body.

"Drunk again?" He looked down at her disapprovingly.

"Best way to meet the end of civilization and bring on the revolution," she declared solemnly and then spoiled the effect by giggling.

Nora managed to take a seat at the small table, lifting her leg high over the bench with a drunkard's care, and listened to the soft rustle of clothes behind her back. She stared at the swirling wood under her hands, ears hot, wondering whether his whole body was tattooed, working up the courage to quickly peek—

"Have you eaten something?" He stood beside her and pulled the breadbasket toward her.

She shook her head.

He sat down opposite her and they shared a small meal of fresh, soft bread, olives, and nuts. Nora reached for the wine, but Diaz poured her water instead.

"The kitchens here must be huge," Nora mused between bites. "So many people to cook for."

"I'm sure you would be allowed to see them if you desired to."

She shook her head.

"I was just wondering out loud. It's not a burning desire to be back in the kitchen."

He shrugged. "In Shinar all desires are equal, and all can be fulfilled."

She gave him a look over her piece of bread. He sounded like Suranna.

"You ever thought all the food here is loaded with Sun Dust?" she asked.

He nodded. "And the drinks, too. It's addictive and makes everything taste good. Makes people want to come back for more. The craving draws you in. Desire holds tight reins."

Nora broke her last piece of bread and picked at it. Maybe she *had* had a bit too much drink. His words…they sounded like a cue. She felt dizzy; a slight spin held her fast in its grip.

"This place…" she started. Maybe she shouldn't continue? It was the drink doing the talking, making her braver, more daring. Reckless. She could stop that, though. She looked up and met his eyes across the table. Her mouth felt dry. Yeah. She could stop her mouth any time. "This place doesn't fulfill all desires."

"Keep hold of that thought."

He was miming his usual oblivious self. She tapped a finger against the beaker. The water was condensing on the side.

"I desire to taste your lips."

The silence rang loud in her ears. For a long time, she didn't dare look up. Scared of seeing his face and then having to laugh. Make him think she was joking. Another minute or two of silence grated her patience to shreds, so she lifted her gaze.

He was staring at her, his forgotten cup still half raised to the lips in question.

"Well?" Nora tossed her hair out of her eyes, lifting her chin. "Say something."

Diaz blinked as though coming out of meditation. He carefully put the cup down and folded his hands neatly before him. He cleared his throat, too.

"Excuse me. What did you just say?"

Nora snorted. "You heard very well what I said. Don't make me say it again."

He stared at a spot just beyond his fingertips for some time.

"You understand," he said slowly, "that what you think you feel and desire…could simply be an illusion here. It might not be something that arose in your own heart. Someone might have put the desire into your head. A thought like a marble, going round and round. A touch of…lust. You know of whose influence I speak."

"I know." Nora nodded and took another sip of water, grimacing at the sobriety it brought. He still wasn't using Suranna's name.

"I know," she repeated. "But the feeling is not something that arose here."

She ran a hand through her hair, fingers rubbing over the stubble slowly growing back after the burn.

"I felt it first on the Plains, only I didn't know what it was then. At the Temple of the Wind...at Solstice." She kept her eyes fixed on the rim of her cup. "There was a moment when I thought you would kiss me. And in that moment I knew that if you did, I would kiss you back. And since then I've known that I really wanted you to."

Now she looked up to see his reaction. He kept his face as expressionless as he could, but the tension in his shoulders betrayed that her words had rattled him.

"Noraya." He spoke her name as though she was talking of something impossible, like walking across the sky.

"It never happened, but it would have been...good. I think."

"You think?"

Her gaze fixed on his lips.

"Then let me cure you of your curiosity."

Diaz rose from the opposite bench suddenly, nearly knocking over his cup. He stepped around the table in two quick strides, tugging his shirt over his head.

Her heart skipped a beat and though her knees were just as suddenly like melted butter, she stood, shaken but excited, and pulled at her own sleeves. Diaz threw his shirt into the corner and for a moment, she saw the tattoos on his back move over his rippling muscles. Then he turned toward her and she hurried to pull her tunic over her head.

"What are you doing?" His jawline was clenched tight.

Nora let her tunic drop onto the bench. This was supposed to be the part where she'd walk up to him, hips swaying from side to side and filled with yearning. Diaz would sweep her up into a long, deep kiss. Only, he didn't seem very inclined.

"Er..."

"Why did you take off your top?"

"You took off your shirt first." Anger rose in her cheeks. "Cure my curiosity, you said. And you were headed toward the bed! I thought..."

"What did you think?"

"Well, the obvious."

He snorted and then stretched out his hand.

"Give me your hand."

"Yeah, that doesn't sound dirty at all." She rolled her eyes. "You know, you're making it very hard for me to believe you're not headed in a certain direction."

"This is not—" His mouth snapped shut. His teeth were going to crack under the pressure one of these days, Nora was sure of it. "Give me your hand."

She slapped her hand into his with a clap. He caught her wrist and pulled the rest of her toward him. His skin was hot to her touch. Her own bare skin prickled as a shot of warmth plunged downward, deep into her. If he looked away from her face, he'd see her hard nipples through her chafing cotton breast band. He kept his eyes up, though. A true gentleman.

"There is something you should know about me," he said. "Let me show you."

"All right," she laughed, a little out of breath.

He clasped her hand to his chest, over his heart, holding it there with his hands. She felt his heart beating slowly. She felt his skin against the sweating palm of her hand. She felt his chest rise and fall with his every breath. She felt...nothing else.

"And? Is it good for you?" she asked.

He frowned. "I was sure this would work."

"Well, your heart's just fine if you wanted to know."

He shook his head as one hand dropped to his side. He gave her a look she knew from sword practice. It was a calculating look—the one he would give her before dealing out a blow to test if she could meet it. In this context, though...it wasn't a sword he was holding. She bit her lower lip.

His thumb caressed her fingertips.

Her breath faltered. Eyes locked onto his, they stepped even closer, her free hand brushing against one of his scars, just above his hip. Her fingertips ran along the visible part of the jagged semicircle that stood out from his skin like a line of white sugar among brown. The curved scar started below his ribs and must end somewhere below his hip. She looked down briefly.

"Where did you get this? Sawmill blade?"

"I got it here, in the arena." He followed her fingertips with his gaze. His breath was warm and ticklish on her cheek. "A fighter with a curved Nessan blade nearly got the better of me. But he wouldn't even have come close if I hadn't been distracted by—"

He drew in breath audibly.

Nora winced as his hand curled into a fist around hers, squashing the bones together.

"I'm sorry," she said quickly, trying to keep the smile from her mouth.

"Distracted by?"

"No." He pushed her away, staggering back a step.

His heels knocked against the mountain of pillows and cushions that made up the bed. Diaz, the fearsome warrior master Diaz, stumbled and, after rowing with his arms for a moment, fell back.

Nora crossed her arms before her breasts, trying to ignore the wet dribble that began to run down her thigh as he moaned, bedded before her, biting his lower lip. She closed her eyes, struggling to ban the image she knew would appear uninvited over and over again. When she opened her eyes once more, his hands were clutching the pillows as though bracing himself for great pain…or great pleasure.

Then she saw what he had meant to show her and gasped. "What the hell is that?"

Black imprints of hands moved under his skin as he squirmed. As though made of charcoal dust, they ran in pairs all over his body, smooth across his scarred chest, caressing his cheek, smoky fingers touching him inside and out. He pushed himself up to his elbows.

"You see it now?"

"It's Suranna?"

He nodded, his face turned away, letting her see a dark hand stroking down his neck. Gods, she hated that bitch.

"It's powerful ancient magic." He swallowed hard, voice breaking. "I thought it was terribly romantic at the time, letting myself be bound to her. We belonged together forever. That's what I thought, anyway. Turns out she thought otherwise. Such is life. That's how it goes, isn't it?"

Shock ripped through Nora. He had repeated what she had told him on Solstice. His black eyes were watching her face intently. She carefully kept her expression as neutral as she could and, oh crap—so that's what he felt like all the time!

"Is it two-way?" Nora asked. "Can you—"

"No."

"Idiot."

He laughed through his nose, but nodded.

"Well, can you break the spell?" Nora wondered.

"It was woven with the power of one of the ancient treasures of the gods."

"Means no, then."

One shadow hand was inching slowly down to the rim of his trousers. He laid his own hand over it as it crawled on downward. So she wouldn't see. He couldn't stop the smoking trail under his skin. He licked his lips.

"Only magic stronger than the one used to make it can undo the spell. That's why I need Bashan to find the Blade. It's my hope that he'll grant me freedom from the curse for my help in finding the Blade."

"But he'll never release you from service to him afterward."

"It's like Talitha said." Diaz pressed his arm to his abdomen as he rose—as though wounded. "I don't know how she knew. I can choose slavery to Suranna or servitude to Bashan."

"Gods, Diaz." Nora shook her head.

"Bashan won't live as long as I will. And he is malleable to a certain extent. And every wielder of the Blade has died by their own hand after only a few years. So my term will be short."

The shadow hands took his body into their possession and, with a sudden sweep, disappeared into his pants. He made a strangled sound and squeezed Nora's shoulder tightly.

"You should go now." His hoarse voice sounded like gravel. "Go."

He pushed her toward the door.

"It's not fair," Nora said, grabbing hold of his wrist. "I want to stay. With you. I could help. Maybe. I want to."

She made to touch him, but he pulled away, shoving her roughly against the wooden door at arm's length. Nora was breathless. The sight of the hands all over him made the blood pound hard in her temples.

"I, I want you," she corrected after a moment's hesitation.

He swore in his own language, then bowed his head. His shoulders shook. Was he laughing? At her? Her cheeks were hot. His hand snaked around her waist as he looked into her eyes. Then he shivered as one of the shadow hands reappeared and traced the outline of his lips before sinking back below his waistline. He suppressed a moan and tightened his grip.

"Where were the two of you when I was seventeen?"

His eyes were on her mouth as he lowered his head. She leaned into his embrace, her knees weak. Her lips were but a hairbreadth away from his, but he then stopped. He tossed his head far back, inhaling deeply through his nose.

"I cannot."

"Please. Diaz. Just one kiss."

He looked down into her eyes, lips opening.

"Please," she repeated.

"All heartbreak starts with just one kiss," he breathed. "Forgive me. I do not want to hurt you."

"Don't worry, you wo—whoa."

The door opened behind her and a falling sensation took hold of her instead. When she sat back up, hip aching from the improvised roll, she saw the door close before her.

Then she heard the sound of the lock.

Then she realized Diaz had shut her out.

She jumped to her feet as the window shutters were closed from within, barring entry.

"You!" she screamed at the door. "You fucking half-wight. Open this door right now and I'll kill you!"

"Don't you mean 'or'?" a voice said behind her.

Nora turned and scowled at a woman and her lover passing by. "Fuck off!"

She kicked the door and nearly broke her toes doing so. The pain flooded her with red rage, and she found herself pummeling the door with her fists.

"Open the door this instant, Diaz. I won't let you just meditate this off, asshole. Open the fucking door."

"Is there a problem, my lady?"

The voice from behind sounded amused. Nora whipped around and saw a small group, gathered to see what the commotion was about. At the head of the crowd were two guards, leaning casually against their spears.

"Is there a problem?" one of them repeated.

"No, of course not. Everything is just fine. Thank you very much for asking."

"I'm afraid you're disturbing the queen's peace. I must ask you to quiet down."

"Oh, the queen's peace, eh? I'm sorry, but right now, do you know what I say to the queen's fucking peace?"

"If you don't calm down, my lady, I'm afraid you'll have to come with us."

Nora opened her mouth to say something wickedly rude but then stopped herself.

"Actually," she said loudly, "I think that's an excellent idea. Yes. I'd like an audience with the queen, please."

The guards chuckled.

"The queen's busy right now," one of them said.

And I know with whom, Nora thought darkly.

"I'll wait," she said.

And then I'll tear out her fucking spine and dance around with her entrails, she thought. And smiled.

CHAPTER 20

MASTER TELEN DIAZ SAT CROSS-LEGGED in the middle of the red-walled room and meditated. Or at least he tried to. Palms open, eyes closed, he went deep within and far without, concentrating on a ball of white healing light, his own energy condensed in his mind to a pulsing sphere. It wasn't much. But he had found that full meditation in the proximity of the queen was the soul equivalent of lowering the drawbridge and destroying the outer walls. What was meant to guard him, to protect him, was instead ripped wide open, allowing her entry into his deepest being.

So he concentrated on the white sphere, imagining ice-cold mountain-tops and wading through hip-high snow. She couldn't reach him here. No one could. He found a quantum of solace in that.

He heard the knock on the door and ignored it, deeply breathing in the scent of snow. Focus on the light. The white, clean, blank slate. Nothing to be seen. No one here.

"Do you smell the snow?" Nora asked. Her red lips parted. "I want you."

There was the knock again. He gritted his teeth as the white ball faded, grayed into the dim light of the room.

Concentrate on the light. Choose a different setting. He took a deep breath. He was walking the high north, the endless wastes of the Wightingerode, the cold sunlight reflecting silver on the water that came up to his knees. No one was here. He was alone.

"Master Diaz? Are you there?" A man's voice came from the other side of the door.

With a sigh, Diaz gave up and got up.

Two guards stood before the door and snapped to attention when he opened it. The front guard bowed his head.

"I'm sorry for the disturbance, master. But there has been...an incident with your...apprentice." The guard smacked his lips at the practiced words. "You should come immediately."

Diaz closed his eyes. It wasn't Nora's fault. He should have done something to hinder her acting on her impulses. Should have done something *else,* rather, but what? Doing something with her was what was out of the question.

"Where is she?"

"In the throne room."

Ah. It would be faster and less painful if he just impaled himself on his sword now. Instead he gritted his teeth and inclined his head.

"I shall come," he told the guard.

He followed the two guards to the throne room entrance and waited as they opened the golden doors. Beyond it was pitch black. He heard a moan and instinctively stepped inside the darkness.

He shuddered slightly, a sense of dizziness holding him fast as his eyes adapted to the dense gloom, pupils widening in a second. The doors closed behind him, shutting out the last of the natural light. The black lightened fast, became washed-out shades of midnight, like a charcoaler's clothing. A red flame flickered in a brazier in the middle of the room, before the throne, but he could make out no other light source. Odd.

Diaz saw Nora, illuminated by nothing but the brazier, struggling between two men, guards. He groaned inwardly. She hung by her arms, which one of the guards was tying together behind her, still wearing nothing but her breast band and a pair of loose trousers. He saw her muscles flex as she kicked out at the other guard, mad with helpless fury. The three had not yet noticed his entry. One of the guards slapped the girl around the face.

Diaz's hand automatically moved to his belt, to the hilt of his sword...that wasn't there. Of course it wasn't. It was still back in the room. Why should he have thought to take it? He felt the anger rise in him and didn't try to push it back down. He wouldn't need a sword for this.

"Do that again," Nora said quietly, calmly, and full of hatred, "and I will fucking kill you."

Her black hair hung in locks before her face, and her cheek sported a red welt. Her eyes shone fiercely.

"Vixen," the guard laughed. "Make sure to tie her up tightly."

"Legs, too?"

"No," the first guard said slowly with a smile. "Maybe we can have some fun while we wait."

He reached out fast. Nora turned her head away, bracing for more punishment, as his hand grabbed her breast band and pulled it down. Nora curled together, trying to hide the flash of pink nipples.

Diaz charged.

He tackled Nora to the ground, and his hands closed around her neck. She bucked beneath him in fear and her eyes grew wide.

"Master Diaz! What…?"

"Change," he growled.

The guards disappeared, vanished into smoking wraiths.

"I, I don't understand—"

"Change the face, Suranna."

Nora smiled then and her eyes flashed golden. A ripple went through her, changing the skin, softening her borrowed features, padding her curves until it was Suranna underneath him and no longer Nora.

"How did you know?" Her fingers caressed his forearms while his hands still itched to choke her.

"I know you. You know me. Please don't insult me by thinking I wouldn't recognize a trap when I walked into one."

As he let her sit up, she made no effort to cover herself. He turned his head and looked away demonstratively. She laughed again.

"You haven't changed, Telen."

He looked at her, keeping his eyes high, looked at the long black hair framing her beautiful face, long black lashes framing the warmth in her hungry eyes. He looked away again and tried to picture snow. Cold, cold snow.

"Neither have you, it seems. Where is Noraya?"

"Perfectly safe and sound."

"Where?"

She shrugged and her breasts moved with her shoulders. Catching his gaze, she leaned back on her elbows, displaying her attributes.

"Drowning her frustration with Brisin? Shall I look into the fire and divine her location for you? Is that what you desire?"

"No." Diaz stood up to leave. "Call us when you've divined the location of the Blade."

"You want to leave me so soon?" She grabbed hold of his sleeve.

"Yes." The sooner, the better. He should shake her off. But he didn't do so immediately.

"Tell me what you want, Telen."

He stiffened. *I want you to leave me alone*, he thought. *I want the past to never have happened. I want to stop—*

"Don't you know?" he said out loud. "You are an all-powerful seeress, are you not?"

"Don't pretend to be coy with me. Of course I know what you want. I just want you to tell me. I want to hear your voice break, my name on your lips."

He pressed his lips tight together.

"Don't talk like that."

"Like what?"

"Like you care." He tried to calm the emotion in his voice, ran a hand through his hair, and took a deep breath. "So after I ravished you in Nora's form, may I ask: what was your plan?"

Her foot ran up his leg. He folded his arms in front of his chest, not sure what to make of her silent smile.

"You left me to die," he said.

Her foot ran higher.

He stepped back and turned to the door. "I'm not your plaything."

"But you are mine," she purred after he had gone a few steps. "And now that I see someone else reaching out to play with my toy, I want it back. Badly."

He snorted and shook his head. But he had stopped instead of leaving.

"Don't think of it as love," she continued. "Think of it as possession. You swore you'd be mine till death do us part. You're still alive."

He gnashed his teeth. She laughed and rose with a sweeping gesture. Anger had always excited her. Nora's black clothes vanished as though burned from Suranna's golden body, and in their place, red flames enclosed the naked flesh in a transparent linen garment that clung to her every regal, sensual move.

"Forgive me," she said, coming closer. "I know you want to."

"No." His voice shook. Gods, she was still so beautiful. Beauty was a thing of terror, far worse than any onslaught he had ever faced. She nestled into his arms, those traitorous arms that took her in without him wanting them to. Her sweet scent of myrrh overpowering him, her hair tickled under his chin as he rested his head on top of hers.

"I missed you, too." Her lips brushed against his skin. "Kiss me."

He looked down into her eyes and they were warm. Like they used to be. He bent down and kissed her lips; her hot, soft, and yielding mouth. Just like it used to be. Another illusion. It wasn't real. A mild pain in his chest was warning him to stop. But her fingertips made his skin tingle as she touched him on the outside and underneath at the same time. He moaned and shuddered with pleasure.

"Take your clothes off," she commanded between kisses.

"No."

Her index finger ran over his shirt, so scorching hot it burned through the fabric and left an angry red welt on his chest. He sucked in air between his teeth. She pulled the ruined shirt from his arms and threw it into the gloom.

He stood very still as she walked around him, her hand traveling over the scars on his body, every touch leaving a burning trail. Her hands came to rest over his heart, her gaze sultry under her long lashes. She kissed him again, thrusting herself into him until he grew weak in the knees. She smiled triumphantly when she heard him gasp for air. Her hands crawled over and under his skin, pulling him down to the floor with her.

Her skin was soft under his touch. He brushed his lips against her naked shoulder and followed the curve of her flesh down to her breasts. She moaned in his ear as he drew a circle around her nipple with his tongue, grabbing a fistful of her glorious silky hair as she reached down between his legs and touched him.

He was half raised above her, frozen by her touch. Her golden eyes were slits of longing as she caressed him, massaging him. Yes, she knew what he wanted—he felt cold suddenly. And drained. One shaky hand reached up to her face and covered those golden eyes, but it didn't help. He closed his own eyes and tried to conjure up Nora's face as he bent down to kiss Suranna's full lips, but that just made the gnawing feeling in his gut bubble over and he felt himself slipping away from her grasp.

"What is it?"

He sat up, kneeling between her legs as she propped herself up on one elbow. He ran a hand over his face.

"I just…this does not work for me."

She reached out for him with a smile.

"Let me make it work."

He stopped her hand, but she wouldn't let go.

"I cannot. Let you. Do this to me. Again."

"But you want it. Go on. Beg me."

Her touch sparked a fire. He gasped as the heat spread through him from his root to his pumping heart, energizing him once more, making him hard and ready, greedily devouring all thoughts of cold and snow and loneliness. A strangled cry came from him as her hand started moving again.

"I, I won't beg," he said, breathless.

"You will. The only question is how long it'll take."

Two hours later, she fell asleep with her head on his shoulder, leg over his loins. But he didn't, couldn't sleep, exhausted and lightheaded though he was. He waited a long time before slipping out from under her to search for his clothes in the dark. She arched her back as he pulled his shirt over his body, feeling her golden eyes rest on him once more.

"I used to be the one who crept away from you," she said. "Some things do change."

He couldn't find his belt and cursed silently.

"Where are you going?"

He remained silent, scanning the blackness with his adjusting eyes.

"Back to her?"

There it was. He walked over to the belt and picked it up. He could feel the toothmarks still.

"Aren't you worried she'll smell me on you? Or wonder where the scratches came from? Or maybe she'll just realize how calm and collected you seem now and draw her own conclusions."

He sighed. "Did you always talk so much?"

"Will you lie to her, Telen?"

He surrendered to her conversation. "Silence is a virtue."

"And virtue is a grace." Suranna smiled. "You're her hero. And you'd just be ordinary. Just like any other man. Isn't that what you always wanted?"

He pulled the belt tighter, clenching his jaw as his stomach churned.

"I can see it behind your brow, the guilt rising, the anger at yourself for losing control."

He turned around and met the queen's eye.

"What do you want from me?" he asked, annoyed.

"A child, of course. Oh, your face is so divine when you're shocked."

She shrugged, fingering a long strand of silky hair.

"The small alcove on the left. You remember the one? No, not the one with the bed in it. The other one, where you would watch me?" She saw him glance over to the piece of the wall where the alcove was hidden behind a heavy, black curtain. She rose, stepping closer to him, and whispered into his ear: "Guess who's there right now, watching you?"

Diaz closed his eyes against the sinking feeling. It was going to be another show. Another trap. He walked over to the alcove anyway, knowing what he'd see, who would be there, preparing for the hammer fall. One hard whisk of the curtain to the side and—

An intense look of hatred met his gaze, making him recoil. Then Nora looked away.

The girl's hands and feet were tied together, the thin cord cutting into her flesh. Because she'd fought. She'd always fight. She had been gagged, and he saw lines streaking down her bruised face where the tears had washed a clean path. His heart felt like an icy fist was squeezing it tight. It was another illusion, he told himself, not even believing his own words. He'd forever be at Suranna's mercy until she let him leave. His knees were still trembling and now he felt sick. Two guards stood over Nora with their swords to her throat.

"She's been very well behaved, hasn't she?" Suranna sidled up behind him, leaning against him. "So quiet. She came in here ranting and raving a few hours ago about the injustice of life and love. I see why you like her. Remember when you last felt such passion?"

"This isn't happening," he murmured.

"I assure you, it is." Suranna gestured at the guards and they hauled Nora up to her feet. She groaned into the piece of cloth between her teeth. "Take her to the Pit."

"Yes, queen," the guards said in unison.

Nora swore through the gag as they hauled her out of the alcove.

Diaz swept around. At least, he tried to. He was rooted to the spot.

"I wondered when you'd feel it." Suranna stepped up from behind.

Diaz wrestled against unseen chains. In vain. He was as a stone marker set in the ground. Even when he strained his entire will, he remained paralyzed. Trapped. Like the fool he was proving to be.

"What are you doing?" He spoke in a low menace. "The Pit?"

"How well have you trained this girl? Do you think she'll last as long as you did?" Suranna paused for a breath before adding, "In the Pit?"

"You're going to test her?"

"No. I'm going to watch her die, Telen. And you are, too."

He struggled more then, jaw clenching until it hurt. She laughed and slapped him on the cheek. His body mistook the sensation as rough foreplay.

"I should kill you now and rid the world of your presence once and for all," he growled at her from deep inside and stopped fighting.

She lifted one hand up to his arm and with a finger made the mark of a cross on it. The fabric of his shirt burst into flame, searing the flesh underneath it. He pressed his lips tightly together, but a groan escaped them anyway as the fire ate into him.

"Try. But know you are not the one to give me death."

"You have seen your own end in vision?"

"You brought it here with you."

Diaz winced, but not at the flames licking his skin.

"Noraya?"

She shrugged. He laughed a bitter laugh.

"Attempting to change fate, then?" he asked. "Don't tell me you're scared."

She swept her hand up, and the fire on his arm died with a flicker, leaving behind a raw and open wound.

"I am not. For I have seen the future. But you haven't. Guards!"

Four men in heavy armor appeared from the corridor and leveled their spears at him. Diaz licked his lips. He had no weapon, yet. But it would be easy to take down these four despite the pain in his arm, if only she'd let him go.

"No. You will enjoy doing as I say." Suranna smiled then and moved her hand in a complicated gesture.

He knelt before her then, his legs moving of their own accord as he fell rigidly to his knees. He shuddered and tried to get back up. He couldn't. His knees scraped across the stone floor as he approached her on them like a penitent sinner and kissed her outstretched hand.

Her smile broadened as she caressed the scar on the back of his right hand.

"Burning the mark only made the bond stronger."

She waved her hand again, and he had to rise and follow her to the Pit.

CHAPTER 21

IT WAS THE NOISE THAT told Nora where they had brought her. The noise she could feel like a numbing punch, along with the stench. Both made her head reel. The heavy iron gates before her, rusted in part, were hauled open and she was shoved forward into the white light beyond.

A step and she nearly fell to her death. The hand had roughly shoved her onto a thin wooden plank that shuddered and bounced under her feet. To each side of the plank, she saw below her a death pit. The stench was worse here. People hung spitted on stakes, some dead, the others slowly dying, broken and whimpering. Throwing out her arms for balance, she staggered three steps farther to cross the plank and stand in the gleaming white sun on hard-baked sand.

The ropes binding her hands together had been cut, and whoever had done so had also put tight leather bracers on her forearms. She hadn't even noticed. The gag still remained. Realizing her hands were now free, she reached behind and tried to untie the knot, giving her watering eyes a moment to adjust to the glare.

The heat was unbearable. She pulled the gag down and tried to lick her dry lips with a parched and heavy tongue, but the sun drank all the moisture that was left.

She was in an arena. Opposite she could see another gate just like the one she was standing before. On the left and right were two more gates. And all around the arena ran the circular death pit.

The walls of the arena reached high, but the spectator rows went even farther up, deep into the shadow of the rock. The arena itself was a natural shaft in the red stone, wider at the bottom than at the top. Above she could just see the penetrating blue sky and the merciless eye of the sun beaming down the shaft, burning the sand that spilled over into the death pit.

It was loud and hot and stank of men and urine. The scent of blood was strong in the air, and she could taste it on the back of her tongue. Death lurked here in this pit, though the white sand suggested innocence. Excitement vibrated through the walls. She covered her ears against the throb, but it didn't help.

A flash of silver landed just before her feet in the sand. Ahead, a number of men were fighting and bleeding, to the roar of the spectators. But the fighters had not yet noticed the newcomer. Nora looked up.

A balcony or a booth sat just above the gate she had entered through, partially sealed off by curtains blowing in a faint breeze. She squinted against the brightness.

A gong sounded and a deafening roar from the crowd went up. The veils from the booth were swept aside, and the queen stood in all her golden glory in a sleek black dress and a golden band. She raised her golden-cuffed wrists and silence settled over the entire arena. Nora's heart skipped a beat as she saw the lady, but more so when she saw who stood behind her. In the veiled shadows she could just make out the dark eyes and bronze skin of…that half-wight, and her heartbeat doubled as her jaw clenched.

The queen pointed to the sword at Nora's feet with a sweeping gesture.

Nora looked down. Yeah. She understood what she was supposed to do. She was supposed to die.

Everything in her screamed to grab the sword. Grab it and protect herself against whatever was coming. It was a chance at survival. It was defiance in the eye of death. But she hesitated. She recognized the sword. The unfurnished, plain blade. A sleek killing weapon with a hilt heavier than it needed to be. His sword. The half-wight's. So she stayed on her feet and didn't move.

Nora watched as one of the fighters pounded another man's face to pulp before lifting him up onto his shoulders to the cheers of the crowd. Thus weighed down, the victor staggered across the sand to the moat of death and looked up at the crowd, who began to chant.

"Shinar! Shinar! Shinar!"

The name of the god reverberated off the walls, making the very stones tremble. A sacrifice to the gods. The people wanted to see blood. They shouted, screamed, yelled for it. Someone must have tipped the fighter off that the queen was present, because the man turned around to look up to the booth. His gaze flickered over Nora dispassionately, maybe assessing her challenge and finding it risible. He sneered, then looked up to the queen, and she nodded ever so slightly. The man shrugged his opponent off his shoulders and into the pit. Nora heard the screams of the man impaled on the spikes, turned her head, and vomited, making a pattern in the sand next to her shoe.

She wanted to just pick up the sword. She really should. The man ahead flicked the blood of his opponent from his hands and came steadily toward her. But what was the point? She was going to die here. There was no way Suranna would let Nora out of this alive. The sword was just another way of humiliating her. Fight for your life with his sword, your mentor's sword. Shade's voice rang through Nora's mind: *"The sword is a symbol for a man's best part."* She swallowed hard and her throat clicked dryly. Yeah. No way she was going to pick that thing up. They wanted to see defiance? She pulled her cracking lips apart and grinned at the approaching fighter.

✧ ✧ ✧

SURANNA LEANED FORWARD, BREATH BECOMING more rapid as she watched the brawler walk toward Nora. The queen turned to see Diaz's face. Her full lips were parted slightly, aroused, drunk on her own power.

"What will she do?" she asked him.

He strained against her hold but still couldn't move.

"She'll kill him."

"How?" Suranna licked her lips. "Tell me."

He shook his head—he couldn't even do that. A bead of sweat trickled down his forehead and into his eye.

"I don't know."

Suranna turned back to watch.

Gods, he really didn't know. If Nora didn't pick up the sword now, she would die. And there was nothing he could do about it. She should pick up the sword now. The man would be on her any moment, and she still wasn't moving. He knew her to be fast, but she wasn't going to be fast enough if she didn't pick up the godsdamn sword now. He blinked as the sweat stung in the corner of his eye. Any moment now. One more step, and the window of opportunity would be gone. One more step. He took a deep breath.

✧ ✧ ✧

"TAKE THE SWORD!"

Nora heard Diaz's shout over the din of the crowd as the man came closer.

"Noraya! The sword! It's your only chance."

Pfft. What did he know? She gritted her teeth harder as his voice broke with strain. It was too late now, anyway.

The man's foot landed hard on the flat blade, grinding it into the sand. He chuckled triumphantly and swung his blood-speckled fist at her. Nora watched it coming. It was like vertigo, she thought. Owen had explained the word to her. It described when you stared down from a height and suddenly felt the urge to jump. She stared at the fist knuckling toward her and nearly wanted to feel it smashing into her face. Nearly. She pivoted away just before impact, slamming her hand into the man's elbow and, using his own momentum, propelled him forward into the sand, joint dislocated.

For a moment, he lay there winded, his face puzzled as the pain crawled up his nerves and into his slow brain. The noise in the arena dropped in intensity, though a murmur still ran in the background. Any bets would not have been in her favor. But right now, Nora knew, they would be changing fast.

She eyed the big man warily. He lay close to the edge of the death pit, but there was no way she could push him over. She could maybe stamp on his throat and hope to suffocate him that way, but the chances were slim. Besides, this wasn't about beating him.

She was lucky, though. A second man was coming at her with a sword.

✧ ✧ ✧

"SHE HAS A KNACK FOR putting on a good show." Suranna smiled at Diaz and stroked his cheek. "You know what will happen to her once she's bested."

"She'll be raped." His stomach churned with bile.

Suranna's smile widened as she drank in his disgust.

"There are fifteen men left in the arena, my love." She licked his upper lip before biting into the lower one. "Fifteen."

He groaned and closed his eyes. At least she allowed him that while she kissed him. The crowd cheered, and Suranna's attention snapped away from reveling in his suffering, back to the arena.

Nora had impaled a second attacker on his own sword. As he slid off it into the sand, she gave it a twirl. Diaz strained to see, heart racing wildly. Fourteen men now. Maybe she could make it. If Suranna didn't order in more fighters, at least Nora had a chance now that she had a sword.

The crowd groaned collectively as Nora threw the sword away, into the sand. She stood waiting as the first brawler got back up to his feet and lumbered toward her, angry at the girl who had made him look a fool. Still. She still had a chance.

Diaz glanced at Suranna, who was watching him carefully. She shook her head.

"You're right," she said. "Hope leads to the worst kind of desperation. Let's even the odds a little."

✧ ✧ ✧

NORA JUMPED AT THE LOUD squeal of a rusty gate behind her. She shuffled closer to the edge of the arena, closer to the pit, wary of what was going to come at her through the gate. The big man was shouting abuse at her, picking up speed, his fat lips sprayed with spittle and his bald head reddening not just with the heat. Nora danced nervously between him and the opening gate. Whatever was going to come through, it wouldn't make a difference, she told herself. She was going to die here. Her best bet was to make the fighters angry enough that they'd kill her by mistake so that she'd be dead when they took it out on her body. That was the only plan she had. It wasn't a good one.

The gate shuddered to a halt, and two young men were pushed through it. They stumbled along the wooden plank with their hands bound before them. More sacrifices, then. She turned back to watch the big guy approach and thought about throwing a handful of sand in his face. Would that make him angrier? Probably. But would it make him kill her faster? Probably not, if he couldn't see properly. Dammit.

"Nora?"

She turned back to the two new victims who had just entered the arena. She saw Shade first, then Owen behind him. Owen, who was running up to her with his hands still bound, his face worried.

"What are you doing?" Her twin brother clutched her arm awkwardly. "Why don't you have a weapon?"

She closed her eyes briefly and swore.

New plan. Right now.

CHAPTER 22

NORA FELL TO HER KNEES and cast about in the sand for the sword she had just thrown away. There. She snatched it and slit through the ropes that bound Shade and Owen before pressing the hilt into Shade's hand.

"Keep him alive." Nora's lips met Shade's in a hasty and hard kiss. She heard the crowd roar as they should.

"Er...," Shade said.

Nora looked at her brother.

"Oh." Shade nodded, gripping the hilt of the sword tighter. "With my life."

She swept down and gathered a handful of sand. The big guy was still coming at her, arm dangling at an unnatural angle. She started to run, to sprint toward him, head level with his stomach as though she was going to ram herself into his squishy parts. He was in pain and angry, but he realized through the haze of both that what she was planning to do would bring her into immediate contact with him, and he laughed.

His good arm swung around to beat her, punch her head right off her shoulders. She let herself fall backward and skidded neatly between his moving legs, rolled elegantly, and was up and running before he spotted that she had publicly humiliated him again. He yelled as the crowd laughed. But he turned to pursue her, leaving Shade and Owen alone for the moment.

The sand was treacherous under Nora's feet, making it hard to run fast. But she needn't. Let the big guy come close. Nora looked up at the booth and her eyes met Suranna's, a hot flash of hate tearing through her body.

I'll give you your fucking show if you give me my brother's life, she thought and concentrated on the patch of ground just below the queen's balcony. She spotted the flash of silver that betrayed the only good weapon in this arena, the only one of quality that wouldn't break spectacularly when she needed it most. Damn that it was Diaz's, and damn the symbolism, but right now she needed metal to get Owen out of here alive. The pounding feet behind her told her that the big guy had caught up. She skidded the last meters on her knees, picking up the sword, turned on one knee to face her pursuer, and threw the sand in her fist into his eyes. His good hand went up, and she slashed the sword across his uncovered belly, opening it to let the innards spill out. The crowd went wild.

Nora rose and stood over the felled man, who was clawing his insides together, blood pumping into the sand. She finished him, then raised her blood-tipped sword aloft and pointed it directly at Suranna's smiling face. That was defiance, bitch. Deal with it.

Shade and Owen had shuffled closer.

"Any strategies?" Owen asked.

"I was going to ask you," Nora said.

"Just stay alive? Last ones standing win?" Shade offered.

"Is that the only objective?" Owen licked his lips, eyeing the cluster of men before them. "Because then I want a weapon, too."

"We won't make it out alive," Nora answered. "That's not the point."

"What did you do?" Shade asked.

"Me? Nothing," Nora huffed and pointed the sword at the booth. Owen and Shade looked up.

"Is that Diaz?" Shade asked. "I thought they weren't together anymore."

Great, so everybody had known about Suranna and Diaz, except for Nora.

"Well, they are now," she scowled.

Owen was watching her face. "He might not be at her side voluntarily," he said carefully.

"Looked pretty fucking voluntary to me. So give me a plan, mastermind," Nora said, aware that her cheeks were flushed and not with exertion.

"You want to take on the queen?"

"Hell yes."

Owen nodded shortly.

"There'll be bets on the outcome of the fights. They'll be turning in our favor. In your favor." He stepped closer to Nora. "If too much money is at stake, you'll force the hand of the queen to let us live."

The noise in the arena changed in pitch, making Owen look up. They all turned and watched as the slaughter at the other end gave way to a small group of survivors forming a tentative coalition force against the three newcomers who had won the fickle crowd's favor. The men spoke with each other, one man leading with gestures, working out a strategy and not even bothering to conceal it. There were nine men left. Nine experienced pit fighters against the three of them. The men before them spread out more, coming steadily closer, raising their various weapons. All at once, then. That was their plan. Kill the newcomers and then battle it out among themselves.

"I need to get into that booth," Nora told Owen.

She and Shade made a stand before Owen, brandishing their swords.

"You'll die," he said.

"I'll die," Nora said bluntly as she frowned at Shade. A thought had just entered her mind. Now it was lodged there like a tick. She looked back at Owen, who had followed her gaze. His mind was already working at high speed. His eyes had that distracted look they always got when he was puzzling over something. "You stay alive."

"Killing the queen won't necessarily ensure we stay alive."

"The booth, Owen. How?"

"Er…guys?" Shade nudged Nora.

The men were coming closer in tight formation.

Nora heard Owen sigh as she sighted on a target: a burly man with an iron mask pulled over his face, a longsword in both his hands and his chest uncovered but for a guard of leather over his heart. Idiot. Brain must be cooked already in this heat, and on top of that he wore an iron mask.

"I need time," Owen said.

Shade remained standing at Owen's side as Nora ran forward, hearing the cry of the crowd thunder around her. Her man had a companion just behind him, a man with more armor and a long spear that he stabbed at her.

Nora rolled and rose behind the man with the spear. The man in the iron mask held his sword high above his head. It came down slow. Too slow. She slashed her blade over his naked stomach and stepped around the dying man to push him forward onto his companion with the spear, like a living shield. Or a dying shield, anyway. The spearman recoiled in surprise at his mate's sudden death, and the weight of the body pulled the spear downward. She hacked down into the spearman's throat. Blood wet on her hand, she gripped her hilt tighter.

The fighter behind him was a lithe man with a halberd that he stabbed at her deftly. She let him, sidestepped the blow that would have run her through, and grabbed the wooden shaft, yanking it around as she spun toward the next man. The halberd man didn't let go, though. He pulled his weapon back to take it from her grasp and stab at her again. She let it go suddenly, and he punched the iron tip deep into another man. Nora ran over the strong wooden beam of the halberd and killed its wielder with one fell stroke.

His warm blood spattered against her face and onto her lips. His head was gone from his shoulders and his body toppled over, still gripping the wooden shaft, tugging the impaled man to his death.

Over the roar of the crowd, she blinked the sweat out of her eyes and took a breather.

A thud of wood on wood caught her attention, and she turned again to see Shade and Owen. They were in trouble. Two of the fighters had large circular shields and, after a moment deliberating, seeing the slaughter, they had changed their plan and were now forming a makeshift shield wall. A whoop arose from the crowd. Enough veterans of the wars had been in shield walls to recognize what was happening down in the arena.

The two shield men rallied, and behind them crouched two spear fighters. Four against Shade, who stood tall, one man dead at his feet.

"Nora," he called, licking the sweat from his upper lip. He shielded Owen with his free arm and they both withdrew a few steps to the edge of the death pit.

She looked around in the sand while keeping an eye on the man advancing toward her. There! She rammed Diaz's sword hard into the blood-red sand and ran over to one of the death-pit victims. A net thrower, he hung on a stake through his back, his mouth a perfect O. She grabbed his net and a small circular shield that lay close by.

The crowd laughed at her mistake as she straightened, holding the small shield by the wooden pommel inside instead of putting her forearm through the leather hoops. In her other hand she held the net and let it drag behind her. Give them a show. Well, this was the show of the dumb girl who had just made a terrible mistake. She watched the fighter come closer and she retreated. The gap between her and Owen was getting ever wider. Her breast band clung to her skin with sweat and blood. It itched. She rolled her shoulders, but that didn't help.

The body of a man lay behind her. She banged her heels against his dead arm and slipped, losing balance, nearly dropping the shield. The fighter roared and jumped at her. He was fast, faster than she had expected. She distributed her weight and threw the shield at his face. It smacked into his nose with ice-cold precision, cartilage breaking under the impact. Howling and blinded by the gush of blood, he clutched his face and staggered, leaving a free line of sight for her to throw the unused net away. She reached for the hilt of a sword still embedded in the body behind her and swished the blade in a graceful arc.

Owen yelped behind her. Nora swiveled around. Shade was moving away from her, keeping ahead of the shield wall, knocking the spear tips away with the sword. He kept Owen behind him always, but her brother had taken a thrust and now bled onto the sand from a cut just above his knee. The crowd boomed.

Nora turned around to see the broken-nosed man hurtling toward her, a spear in his hands.

Good, he was angry. Really angry.

She dodged his first thrust, then feigned retreat, showing him her back and legging it over the sand as fast as she could. He howled and ran after her, blood streaming down his face. The shield wall moved as the spear warriors tried to catch a glimpse of what was going on behind them. They should see a young, blood-spattered girl running at them in a last desperate attempt to reach her friends; behind her, a battle-hardened pit fighter looking for vengeance. Maybe a few seconds ago they would have turned around to face her. But now, having drawn blood and sensing weakness, they felt confident enough not to bother. One of them jabbed his spear at Shade's head, laughing. They could smell terror, they could smell defeat, and they could nearly taste their own victory.

But Nora didn't stop. She didn't break her stride to slow down or to curve around the shield wall in front of her. She just ran on and the broken-nosed man closed in behind her, leveling his spear. One of the spear warriors turned his head as he heard them approaching, but he was too late. Nora jumped up, her foot firm against his hip. She stepped onto his shoulders next and then used his helmeted head as her springboard.

An eerie silence hung in the air with her. The crowd inhaled.

Her head was upside down as she turned in the air to land on her feet. She watched the dawning realization on the broken-nosed man's face as he tried to stop but couldn't. He slammed his spear straight through the unprotected back of one of his teammates. Her own spear warrior banged his helmeted head against the shield man in front of him, and for a moment, a precious moment before she landed, she saw the shield wall open as that man lost his balance. Shade saw it, too, and stabbed down hard into the opening.

Then Nora landed in front of the shield wall and rammed her sword into the face of the broken-nosed man, pulled the blade out of his shuddering body, back-swung, and hacked down at her human catapult. He died as Shade killed the last shield man. And then it was over.

She stood beside Owen and Shade once more, sweating, tired, and thirsty. But alive. Yes, very much alive while there was death all around them.

The arena filled with the sound of silence. For a moment, all she could hear were the singing breaths the three of them were gulping. Then she raised her sword high above her head, toward the booth of the queen. As though the crowd had been waiting for her signal, a cacophony of sound washed over them from the rows of the spectators.

"So?" Nora asked Owen.

He nodded and picked up a spear from the fallen men around them. He ran a few steps despite his leg wound and hurled the spear at the wall underneath the booth. The long shaft shivered but held in the wall. The queen flinched with surprise. The crowd went wild. Guards stepped out of the shadows to protect their queen. Shade and Nora jogged to where Owen was standing, Shade carrying another spear in his free hand.

"Spears," Owen panted. "Use them."

"Crazy," Shade said breathlessly, pulling his arm back to hurl his spear at the wall. It thudded into the stone a notch higher than Owen's.

"Yes," Owen agreed, wiping his face free of sweat.

That was why it would work. Maybe. Nora nodded. The wall was still pretty high. She visualized herself climbing it, visualized falling down and breaking a leg, then falling onto the spikes in the death pit below in several versions. She shuddered. Enough visualizing. She stared at Diaz's sword planted halfway between herself and the wall to the queen's booth. One goal. One direction.

The noise from the crowd grew even louder, so that the three of them had to cover their ears. Nora looked up and saw commotion in the rows. Guards were herding the spectators out of the arena. The show was over.

Or rather, it was beginning. Suranna was clapping her hands.

CHAPTER 23

SILENCE FELL IN THE ARENA once more so that all Nora could hear was the queen's steady clapping.

"Well done," she called, and her voice rang out loud and clear. "Very well done. You killed a group of imbeciles, to the excitement of the masses who wagered on their deaths. Yes, your master must be proud of you. However," Suranna carried on, after flashing a smile at Diaz behind her, "maybe he isn't. Maybe you should fight a real opponent to prove yourself."

"Here it comes," Nora said quietly to Owen.

"What?"

"Remember I said you mustn't die?"

"I remember."

"I mean it. I can't win against Diaz. I'm not getting out of here alive, Owen."

"Stop saying that," he said.

Suranna clapped her hands together twice. When she spoke next, her voice was deeper, more guttural. She sang a sentence in the language of Shinar. Nora didn't get much except the word "Brisin." She glanced sideways at Owen, his lips working the words around to translate. He looked up, astonished.

"She just said…"

"I got the gist."

They both turned to look at Shade, who blushed then paled.

"What?" He grinned, flashing his teeth.

His eyes darted to and fro and he stumbled backward as though drunk, swaying his arms, brandishing his sword wildly. Suranna repeated the sentence, raising her arms, and Shade touched his head and fell to a knee, groaning. Owen moved toward him instinctively, but Nora held him back. She clutched the fighter's sword tighter and looked over her shoulder back to where Diaz's sword still stood upright in the sand. She should have seen this coming the moment she recognized Shade walking into the arena. Clairfucking-voyant. She would have wished for Diaz to come down so she could at least hurt him before he took her out. But Shade? Fuck. It seemed she'd never have a normal relationship, ever. Shade shook his head like a dog shaking himself free of water. He rose and his eyes seemed broken. He nodded and answered his "Myvar" in their own tongue.

"Er…I think he's not quite himself," Owen said as Nora pushed herself in front of him, sword raised. "Nora, put the weapon down."

"Fat chance."

"It's a method of mind control. He's been conditioned to—"

Shade bowed low to the queen and turned to Nora and Owen, sword raised too.

"I don't think that matters now, Owen," Nora said, licking her lips in vain. She stepped backward, trying to get closer to Diaz's sword.

"Actually, I think it does. You see, the Living Blade can only be—Nora!" Owen tugged at her sword arm. "Put your weapon down. It's Shade. What are you going to do? Kill him?"

Oh gods, please don't make me do that. Not in front of Owen.

"Depends on what he does next," she said out loud.

Shade said something; his sword tip didn't waver.

"He says disobedience is not an option," Owen translated.

"Fine. The hard way, then. I really like you," Nora said slowly to the approaching Shade. "But if you touch Owen, I will kill you. Translate, Owen, in case he missed that."

Owen stepped up and opened his mouth. Nora struck her brother over the head with the hilt of her sword. He fell into the sand out cold, and she crouched down by his side, feeling for his pulse. It was steady. The skin behind his ear had broken open, and the wound bled freely. Shade moved awkwardly toward them.

"Don't," she told him and held up a hand.

"For the life of your brother, what would you give me?" It was Shade's voice, but not the way he talked. The melody was wrong. Nora glanced up at the booth. Shade was nothing more than a mouthpiece.

"What do you want, Suranna?"

"What was it like, seeing him that way? What did you feel?"

"I felt nothing." Nora wiped her brow.

"Liar." Shade laughed. "I felt your pain."

"Then why do you ask?" The longer Suranna talked, the longer Nora had to figure out what she was going to do next.

"Take a lunge. Go on. Kill me."

"Oh, I want to kill you. It's just Shade I don't want to kill."

"He's touched."

Shade lunged. Clangs of metal rang out as the blades crossed. They each dealt a few blows. Nora danced away, the tip of her sword held downward. She was in grasping range of Diaz's sword. Suranna was talking through Shade, but his hand was wielding the sword. This was going to be tricky. Shade was fast. But Nora could probably beat him. Already had the first time they tussled. So, what now?

Shade stepped over Owen's prostrate body. For a moment, Nora felt the ice-cold certainty that Suranna would have him stab down at her unconscious brother. A wave of panic clawed at her chest. But Suranna didn't want Owen's death, it seemed, for she let Shade pass on by. This wasn't about hurting Nora, then. Because that would have been the deathblow, right there. This was about something else. Someone else.

"To obey one's master is not a weakness, Nora," Shade said as though Suranna had been reading Nora's mind.

"To obey a dumb master who makes unreasonable demands is, though."

"You're saying your Master Diaz is dumb?"

"I'm saying *your* Master Shinar is dumb, Suranna."

Shade lunged at Nora once more. They exchanged a flurry of blows. Nora was tired. It was hard to even lift her sword. Hard to concentrate on her surroundings in order not to trip over the bodies lying around. Sweat stung her eyes. She was retreating before the blond boy with no idea of how to go on, edging ever closer to the wall with the booth, warding off Shade's blows as best she could without maiming him. He yelped. Her blade had cut across his face, and a trickle of blood ran down. He touched his cheek and winced.

"You'd mar this face? I thought you said you liked him."

"He'll heal."

"Maybe you only like men with scars?"

Nora remained silent. Diaz's sword was just behind her now. She reached for the hilt and held it fast.

"Do you think he'll regret not having touched you when he could have?"

"Who exactly are you talking about?" Nora wobbled the hilt to loosen the sword from the grip of the hard earth.

"Oh please." Shade rolled his eyes.

The sword pulled free. She kept it hidden behind her back. That might be stupid because Suranna could see her holding it from her vantage point in the booth, but Nora waited to see what would happen.

With a suddenness Suranna must have thought surprising, Shade jumped at Nora. He made to drive her across the arena with slashing blows, but instead Nora retreated to the edge of the death pit, until she was underneath Suranna's booth. She lunged with both swords then and, targeting Shade's shoulder, thrust one of them into his flesh. Master Cumi had once pointed out an important vein than ran just below the collarbone, and Nora took pains to miss it. Instead, Shade's sword fell from his numb fingers into the red sand. Nora grimaced. She let the blade stick in his shoulder, just in case pulling it out would let him die of blood loss. She knew exactly how he felt, the white-hot pain flooding the body. She swung her other hand around and gave him a clout with the hilt of Diaz's sword. Shade's gray eyes showed their whites, and with a moan he fell to the ground. Blood pulsed from his temple, but he was still stirring. Would Suranna be able to keep him under her influence when he was hurt?

A pain flickered through her stomach. She clutched her middle and groaned. There was nothing to be seen—no wound, no cut, not even a graze. Still, it felt like someone held a torch to her insides. A stream of fire crawled up to her chest, burning her up from the inside, forcing its way out. She rocked to and fro, holding it in. But it inched up her throat and hit the back of her mouth like a stream of lava gushing forth. She retched and turned her head away in case she would vomit. But nothing came when she opened her mouth except the heat and the fury of a scream that would not stop. Her whole body shook under that scream; her lungs ached as she fought for air. Screaming all the while, her head hot and her throat raw, she threw Diaz's sword and watched it spin over the rim of the parapet in a silver arc and fall inside the booth.

Blind with rage, Nora jumped. She grabbed the first spear and pulled herself up against the wall, feet scrabbling. The infernal scream had stopped now that her mind had caught up with what her body was doing. Propelling herself from the spear shaft that was losing its hold under her weight, she flung herself upward and reached for the next spear. Below her, the spear Owen had thrown clattered into the death pit. Bodies hung spiked on the sharpened stakes, and she feared she was going to join them any minute now. The rage and the fear battled with each other for control over her, but rage won out, shouting louder. She dangled for a moment, then kicked her legs to hoist herself still farther upward and grabbed the edge of the balcony in wild triumph.

She grasped the ledge with both hands and pulled up her legs to crouch against the wall, giving her enough leverage to climb the last meter or so. A heavy boot came crashing down on her one hand and she screamed in pain, only one handhold separating her from a short drop and a painful stop. She looked up and for a brief moment saw Diaz's face. His left eyelid was twitching nervously as he drew up his leg to kick back down again. A jolt of intense heat stabbed into her stomach and she grabbed the edge with her flailing hand once more. And then she was on top of the parapet, under the shade of the veils, out of the burning sun. There was a commotion going on behind the queen as more and more guards piled into the small booth to protect their lady from this raving mad thing from the arena. Nora was aware of them but didn't care. In front of her, Master fucking Diaz stood utterly still, his hands folded neatly before him, sweat dripping from his brow. His dark eyes opened in surprise. *Yeah, surprise, master.*

Like a serpent striking, his hands were around her neck and choking her, lifting her from the parapet. Again her feet dangled. She kicked out and heard from his groan that she had managed to hit him, but his steel grip wouldn't budge. Her vision was dimming, although she couldn't close her eyes. They were drying in the heat but were wide open in her fight for breath. A needle of pain stuck in her side. And suddenly freed, she gasped and landed sprawling on the floor. Her arms were cooked noodles. Flames were spreading from her side throughout her whole body, followed by a numbness where the flames had been. A foot placed itself on her head as she turned it.

She blinked at its owner. The queen knelt before her, those full lips pulled into a smile. She held a sharp pin before Nora's eyes.

"A paralytic," the queen explained. "Very effective. Only a pinprick will paralyze a person for hours. A touch more and your lungs would stop working. More and your heart would stop in an instant."

Nora's body started to twitch on the floor.

"Just...kill...me." Breathing was hard, and already Nora's tongue was numb.

"What would I kill you for? You're very entertaining. Take her away, dear."

As the last of her vision faded, Nora saw Diaz bend down to pick her up, and a cold sensation overwhelmed her that the only times she'd ever been in his arms, she was unable to do anything.

CHAPTER 24

THERE WAS A KNOCK ON the door. There hadn't been knocks on his door for a long time now. A week, two weeks maybe? It was hard to tell. Reality felt fuzzy sometimes, especially when Suranna was close by. Also, Diaz had a terrible throbbing headache. It was like someone stabbing him with a pin just behind his left eye.

If knocks could reveal what kind of person stood behind the door, this knock should have been the thoughtful, pensive yet determined knock of a tired young man, he mused. Instead it was the short, hard rap of the guard, who then let Owen enter. The young man looked as though he too had a headache, eyes slitted, with dark rings under them. He looked like he hadn't slept in a long time. He still wore the same clothes he had worn in the arena, Diaz noticed. The blood from his head wound had turned a dark rusty red on his grubby, stained shirt. As he came closer, so did his smell. He tossed his head about, taking in his surroundings, Diaz's surroundings. Taking in the costly dyed carpets and lush rugs, maybe; the unmade bed and all the airy space the new suite held. Or maybe Diaz's new clothes. Or rather the complete lack thereof. Owen's expression was guarded but disapproving.

"Owen, what can I do for you?" Diaz took a last sip from the fragile bone-china cup and placed it neatly on the saucer on the table next to him.

"Master Diaz." Owen inclined his head. He glanced at a piece of paper before he crumpled it in his fist and shoved the paper ball into his pocket. "I asked to see my sister. I was told to see you. She's not here, I reckon?"

"She is...imprisoned, unfortunately," Diaz said slowly, carefully weighing his words lest they trigger an unwanted response.

"She's alive, then?"

"Yes."

Owen's shoulders sagged in relief as his hands curled into fists. Diaz knew that stance, knew it from...*Don't think her name. Don't even think it.*

"I wasn't sure," Owen stammered. "After I woke up—no one told me..."

"I'm very sorry."

Owen caught himself quickly. "I want to see her."

"No."

Anger flickered across Owen's features. "I wasn't asking for your permission, Diaz."

Diaz closed his eyes. Gods, he had forgotten how similar they were. It was so easy to forget at times as Owen was such a scholar and, well, she…the one he shouldn't think of was not a scholar. A bead of sweat rolled down Diaz's forehead. It was getting close to midday. Again. Midday was the worst. He swallowed hard, his mouth already dry again.

"Good," he answered. "For I am not the one to give permission, Owen."

He blinked, hoping Owen would get the message.

"Please," the young man said, stepping closer. "I just want to see her for myself."

"No, you don't. Trust me."

But he rose from his chair anyway. He rose despite not wanting to. Just as he walked over toward the balcony although he didn't want to. Suranna had taken his body from him, and he had no way to stop her. He motioned Owen to follow and took a deep breath. It wasn't a sigh of resignation, but it was as close to it as she would allow him. He waited at the waist-high parapet for Owen to step up and then directed the poor boy's gaze in the proper direction.

Beyond the balcony was nothing but the Great Far Reach, the sand desert beyond the ravines of stone the temple was carved from. This was dry land. A short distance to the west, thirty, maybe forty miles, lay the ocher backcountry that reached unimaginably far, the luring emptiness of the desert. Dark pits, some empty like the desert, most filled with water and thus covered with heavy wooden shields, lay immediately below the balcony. And in one of them was Owen's twin. Diaz looked down at the red stone, drawing the clear, dry air into his lungs. It was high enough to break his legs, but not high enough to kill him. Suranna held him tight by her reins, and he stopped a foot from the edge. He watched as Owen placed his hands on the parapet, leaning over to see better; he waited for the signs that Owen had made out his sister.

Owen gasped. His hands clutched the parapet tightly. So he had seen her.

It was midday. Midday held no shelter in the cistern from the sweltering sun. She lay naked on her side, unmoving, curled into a ball, skin blistered and broken, burned raw but dry. She was nothing but a piece of skin stretched tightly over a forlorn heap of bones. The vultures would have picked them clean already were she lying in the Great Far Reach and not so close to human settlement.

"She stopped raving a few days ago," Diaz said.

For a moment, he was sure Owen would punch him. *She* would have. And Diaz would have welcomed it. But Owen had himself better under control. He merely pressed his lips together tightly and stared at his sister below with an intense, feverish look in his eyes. After a while he turned to Diaz.

"I've seen enough." His voice broke a little.

Diaz nodded and they moved inside, back into the cool shade. Owen sat in one of the wicker chairs, and Diaz silently poured him a cup of peppermint tea.

"So," Owen said.

"So," Diaz echoed.

"How complete is Suranna's hold over you?"

"It is very complete."

Owen looked Diaz up and down. "She can make you move although she isn't near?"

"She is always near," Diaz said bitterly, tapping the side of his head. "But yes, I did not want to get out of this chair. I did not want to gaze at your sister's broken body. Again."

Owen nodded sagely as though they were making conversation about the weather and Diaz had just said it wasn't likely to rain for the next few months.

"What about thoughts?" Owen wanted to know. "Can she read your mind, too?"

Diaz took a sip before answering. He winced, then looked pointedly in the direction of the bed.

"Only when she's very close," he answered.

"And how often is that?" Owen muttered, cup pressed to his lower lip.

"Whenever the queen desires," Diaz said. "It's my free will that has been impaired, Owen, not my hearing."

Owen held up a hand for peace. He set the cup and saucer back down on the table, rested his elbows on the chair's arms, and folded his hands before him like a businessman.

"I want to speak to the queen."

"No, you don't."

"I have a proposition I'd like to make her," Owen continued.

"A proposition pertaining to your sister?"

"No, not directly." Owen shook his head. "This is about Shade. Or

Brisin."

Diaz arched his eyebrows as high as he could.

"If I tell you what I want to tell her, can I count on an accurate retelling on your part?" Owen asked.

"Tell me and I will hear you."

"I'm going on the assumption that Queen Suranna has already or will soon determine the exact location of the dormant Living Blade. It seems to me, though, that Shade is not a suitable candidate as a sacrifice for the Blade."

Diaz stared at Owen across the table. The young man carried on.

"On a superficial level, he seems to be ideal. He is an illegitimate child, a direct descendant of Bashan's, blood related. That's a powerful bond. A bond powerful enough to make a powerful Blade. Plus, when Bashan is emperor, he'll need legitimate children, so sacrificing Shade beforehand seems to clear the path for a glorious future. Only there's a problem, isn't there?"

Diaz waited.

"Shade has been prepared. Unknowingly, true, but still. He's been conditioned by Suranna to do the bidding of anyone who speaks a certain formula, a sentence she has indoctrinated into his mind from infancy. A sentence she has undoubtedly made Bashan aware of by now. So, what Bashan really has is an unwilling, unknowing sacrifice. And blood or no, that's a heavy gamble on his side. What if he says the magic words, sacrifices Shade, and nothing happens? The Blade does not assemble itself?" Owen took a sip from his cup and made a point of fussing with the saucer as he set it back down. He looked up at Diaz before continuing.

"Bashan will be standing in wight territory with nothing but his dick in his hand. He will have to rely on you to get him out of there fast." Owen folded his hands neatly once more. "I wonder whether Suranna's hold over you reaches that far north?"

"It does not." Diaz smiled without mirth.

"Poor Prince Bashan." Owen flashed a smile, too, but there was no warmth in his eyes. "There is a solution to his problem, though."

"Is there?"

"I offer myself willingly as a sacrifice."

Diaz grasped the arms of his chair tightly.

"You cannot be serious."

"Do I look like I'm joking to you?" Owen took a deep, shuddering breath. He squeezed his eyes shut for a moment before he continued. "The Blade is a source of infinite power. But it is also a source of infinite knowledge. Knowledge that I seek. I'm not of Bashan's blood, true. But the

Blade remade by my blood, with my personality, might still be an advantage for him. I ask that you do whatever you can to make the queen convince Bashan I am his man. She can be very convincing, I'm sure. After all, she managed to convince Bashan's father to send his son away, which led him to go on the quest for the Blade in the first place. And...well, she's got you doing exactly what she wants you to do. The only question left is whether you can be as convincing."

"Owen, I cannot allow you to throw your life away—"

"You can't allow me to do anything anyway," Owen interrupted. "And besides, I'm not throwing my life away. I'm making an educated guess, that's all. I'm not doing this for Shade or Bashan. I'm doing this for me. Although, there is a condition for my sacrifice, of course. I offer myself willingly only if Suranna lets Nora go free. With us. You see, I am motivated purely by selfish reasons."

Diaz shook his head. Sweat pearled down his naked back, but he felt chilled to his heart.

"Your sister would never allow it. If she knew what you are planning—"

"Then Nora must never know." Owen gave Diaz a hard stare. "I trust your discretion."

Diaz was speechless.

Owen stood and made to leave.

"Think on what I said."

CHAPTER 25

THE HEAT BEAT DOWN ON her naked skin like a leaking charcoal clamp. Nora reached out to find the shovel's handle, then remembered she wasn't tending charcoal anymore. She opened one eye and searched for a flash of metal that would betray a knife or a sword. She needed one. She was in the arena and she'd be up to fight next. No, wait. That wasn't what had happened last. Suranna. And Diaz. Especially Diaz. With a groan Nora stirred, moving to get the blood flowing again. She coughed, cleared her throat, and spat out sand with a gob of gooey, sticky phlegm. She sat up, leaning her hurting head against a burning stone wall, and looked around.

She was at the bottom of a dry cistern. High above her she saw the cloudless sky and the merciless sun. When Shinar traversed the sky in his fiery chariot, shadows would creep down the wall of the empty well until all was dark and cold with nightfall. Now, though, it was just past midday and only a sliver of shade darkened a patch of bare rock. She rose on wobbly legs, running a hand over the smooth walls of her prison as she paced the circle of it. Four and a half long strides wide, thirty-two normal paces when she walked around. A rusty iron door had been built into the rock. A water valve for when the cistern was full. Nora felt no chink, no weakness in the ironwork. She looked up. At certain irregular points in height, the cistern sported small holes in its walls, holes guarded by iron gates. For the rain, Nora guessed. They would channel the precious water into the cistern, flooding it within moments, depending on the torrent, or filling it slowly, over days. Would Suranna risk poisoning the fresh water with Nora's rotting corpse? Would she drown in a suddenly full well? Or exhaust herself trying to keep above the rising water and drown that way? She would already be dead when the rains came, though. In this heat, she'd dehydrate within hours, be dead in two, maybe three days. Could she reach the lowest of the rain channels? Grab the iron gate, loosen it, and crawl through the rain channel to find a crueler kind of freedom in the barren rocks and canyons that made up Shinar's realm?

Above her head the walls of the cistern wavered in the heat. Nora raised an arm over her face. Already her head was a hammering mess of dull pain.

Prison was not meant to be comfortable.

At least she wasn't in chains.

Sometimes a slit in the iron door rattled open and half of a small bottle gourd plant was shoved through, splashing its costly wet. It tasted brackish, earthen, but she didn't mind. The few sips ran down her parched, sore throat like liquid balm. But all too soon she was thirsty again. The drinks came irregularly. Sometimes they would leave her without water until the thirst grew so strong her lips cracked and she cried out, tasting her own blood, her hoarse voice echoing against the dry walls. Sometimes Nora cried until the tears stopped coming and she simply sat at her favorite place against the wall, heaving dry sobs, allowing herself to wallow in self-pity. Sometimes she tried to scale the wall to get to the lowest rain channel for what seemed like hours. Every day, when the sun reached its zenith, she curled up, sweat dripping from her head resting on her knees, her back bearing the brunt of the worst heat, turning into a red burning sore with the skin flayed from her. She tried to sleep then, because at night it grew so cold that she couldn't, shaking and shivering as her teeth chattered. Most days she tried to come to terms with the fact that she would be kept alive, just alive enough, until Suranna got bored and finally had her killed. Other times, though, she panicked and howled and stomped her feet and gnashed her teeth and called Suranna all the filthy words Mother Sara had forbidden her to use. But after a while she would stop. Screaming was exhausting, and worse, it made her thirsty, and who knew when there would be water again?

Without the possibility of deep sleep, her mind tricked her into seeing images even when she was awake. Faces and scenes passed before her ever-more-confused, heat-addled mind. Sometimes she saw her brother with her in the cistern, other times Shade as he had been in the garden, in a cistern just like this one, only full. But most of all she saw Diaz. Always Diaz. With Suranna. Over and over again, until she wasn't sure where the dream image of the queen stopped and where her own self began. After a while she stopped trying to make a distinction. She had stopped counting the monotonous days, too. Sun up, sun down. It didn't matter anymore. The sun burned deep within her, etched into her darkened skin and spreading like a fever throughout her whole body, a fire in her lungs whenever she breathed. Maybe she should just stop. Yeah, stop breathing, stop hurting. Not long now.

She was laying in her corner when the door opened. Her eyes were half caked shut, and when she tried to raise her head she felt sick. She had to tug her head free from where it rested. At first she thought her face had melted and stuck to the stone. But she had vomited bottle gourd juice earlier and, body too weak to get up, her hair was baked into the hardening clump.

People. People in the cistern with her. People were walking. Yes, they were walking around, doing...something. Must be a new vision. She closed her eyes and when she opened them again, she felt two shoulders beneath her weak arms. Her head lolled, but she was carried into the center of the cistern where two poles stood erect, iron chains dangling from them. Her hands were clapped into the iron, forcing her upright unless she wanted to have her shoulder joints dislocated. Her legs shook, though, and she was sick again.

The people said something in a foreign tongue. Annoyance. Disgust. Or something. Nora couldn't remember the correct word. A hand pressed something against her skin-flaked lips. It was cold, liquid, and tasted of the metal ladle it had been poured into. Water? Was this...actual water?

More water was thrown over her. The impact made it feel like her cooked flesh would fall off the bone. But by some kind of miracle, it remained on her outstretched arms. They scrubbed her all over. It hurt and she screamed a bit. Then someone shaved a mat of black tangles and knots from her head. It would grow back, Nora told herself as she saw the lank strands of her dark hair falling around her feet. It could grow back. There was absolutely no reason to cry. Someone else rubbed her skin with aloe, and another someone clothed her in a simple white shift. The best, though, the best was a dark sun sail someone hung above the working people, casting out the glaring sun. Then the people left and she was alone again, slow thoughts dripping irregularly through her aching mind.

"Do you think me a monster now?" A honey voice intruded on her.

Nora opened her eyes and saw herself. She closed her eyes, then tried again.

Suranna stood before her, smiling, waiting for an answer.

Nora made a noise that was supposed to be laughter. Didn't sound right. She frowned. What did laughter sound like?

"Allow me," Suranna said and reached out to touch Nora's face.

A heat rushed from Suranna's fingertips, spreading warmth through Nora like strong liquor, revitalizing her as much as it made her head fuzzy. The nausea stopped. The throb in her burned skin dulled its sharp edge. She looked up into the queen's golden eyes.

"And? Do you take me for a monster?" Suranna repeated.

"Lady," Nora spoke, voice breaking from disuse. She glanced down at her clean self, up at the iron bands that held her hands high above her head. "I don't know if you're real right now."

"I am real." Suranna was wearing a simple black dress, and a thin band of gold rested on her silky black hair. "Your brother is alive."

Nora let herself hang by her sagging shoulders for a moment. Her lower lip trembled.

"Thank you," she said.

"I didn't say he was well."

"Bitch."

Suranna laughed.

"I see the defiance hasn't died in you. Keep it. It will serve you well."

"Really? In prison?"

"Make me an offer for your freedom, Nora. In truth, though, you have nothing you could give me."

"How so? Getting bored of torturing Diaz?"

Suranna's smile broadened.

"Never. But alas, the quest must come before my selfish needs."

Nora's head still felt like she was wading through a dense fog. Her tongue felt huge in her mouth.

"Quest?"

"Bashan's quest for the Living Blade, of course. The time is now. To achieve our revolution, Bashan needs Telen to guide him north. And so my love will leave my service soon. There is no point in keeping you here."

"So you'll set me free? Just like that?"

"Every day you'll see each other on your journey, and you'll be reminded of how you're both bound to me. It's far more effective a prison than any empty cistern could be."

Nora groaned.

"Bashan is just doing your legwork," she said bitterly. "He's supposed to get the Blade for you. Then you'll have all the gods' treasures, all their power, won't you?"

Suranna clapped her hands in mock delight.

"Aren't you a clever little girl? I do hope you don't tell anyone."

"What do you want with me? I mean nothing to you. I am nothing. No one. Just kill me already and have it done and over with." Nora closed her eyes.

"Look at me." Suranna bent down to see Nora's face. Nora obeyed. "I was once your age. I saw the world as it truly is: dark and ugly on the outside and worse within. Then I met him and everything changed."

"Diaz?"

"Shinar. He came to me in a vision. A vision of how I would summon Him back into existence. I saw you, too, your coming as a herald to a glorious free future where we all, man and wight, shall be the children of the gods once more."

Nora remained silent. She had no answer to that amount of crazy.

The conversation died and Suranna left.

Nora was alone for a while in the shade, heat gone, thirst gone. Her arms ached and her legs were still weak, but she knew it would be over soon. And so she waited.

After what felt like hours, the door opened once more.

Owen stood in the doorway, holding the key to her shackles. The start of a scruffy beard lined his jaw, and his face seemed leaner than she remembered, grim and hard. A lump tightened Nora's throat. She stood still, fighting the urge to strain against her bonds and reach out for him. Owen did not move except to look her up and down, as if he were memorizing every detail. The need to touch him grew unbearable. What if it was a trick? What if it was Suranna returning and he—

"Owen." Her voice cracked.

As though hearing his name broke his trance, he stepped up swiftly to open the shackles with trembling hands, catching her as she tumbled into his arms. She rested her head in the nook of his shoulder and felt his grip tighten around her. As she breathed in his familiar scent of ink and old books, she allowed herself to relax. It *was* Owen. Touch of iron, she thought. Touch of home.

STRANGE FIRE

Taken from the Indigo Girls: *I come to you with strange fire, an offering of love.* Sounds way better than Author's Note, Afterword or Acknowledgments, doesn't it? Yes. Yes, it does.

Well, I guess if you made it this far, you really want more, don't you? Personally, I love long Author's Notes – the longer I get to stay in my favorite books, the better, say I – but let's do this Nora's way: hard and fast.

On charcoal: First off, why make charcoal? Simply said, no other combustible substance generates the heat necessary for the forging of metals, which is why blacksmiths today still prefer using charcoal and why large parts of Central Europe were deforested during the industrial revolution. So it kind of made sense to have my main characters have this profession in a book titled "The Living Blade" with its focus on blades and knives and stuff and things, you know? I mean, not everyone can start their Hero's Journey as moisture farmers on Tatooine.

Charcoal has been made by various methods. "The traditional method in Britain used a clamp. This is basically a pile of wooden logs (e.g. seasoned oak) leaning against a kind of chimney (the logs are placed in a circle). The chimney consists of 4 wooden stakes held up by some rope. The logs are then completely covered with soil and straw, also moist clay, allowing no air to enter. The clamp is then lit by introducing some burning fuel into the chimney. The logs then burn very slowly and transform into charcoal in a period of about 3 to 5 days' burning (depending on size – *as so much does*). If the soil covering gets torn or cracked by the fire, additional soil must be placed on the cracks to control the leak. Once the burn is complete, the chimney is plugged to prevent air from entering." (And let's all go donate to Wikipedia now. Thanks Wiki – we love you!)

Charcoal burning is a delicate art which is why professional charcoal burners (or colliers) usually comprised whole families who lived together tending their piles. (Er...log piles that is.) In the Harz Mountains (in Germany, so, not far from where I live) the word for collier "Köhler" is still a prominent surname, attesting to how widespread this profession was and, for tourist-y reasons, you can still find shelter on hikes through the mountains in "Köten" or "Köhlerhütten", that is: in traditional, conical coaler's huts.

Twins are thus perfect for tending a burn. One of them would stand watch over the burn while the other slept. If they both fell asleep for more than about ten minutes, all the charcoal could be lost. A coalman's weapon of choice is the curved spade or shovel with a long handle, and this is used to maintain the layer of straw, turf and mud on the clamp throughout the burn. It's heavy. Tending a burn builds lots of muscles. It builds callouses. It develops tolerance for sleep deprivation, for standing up for long periods, for extremes of heat and cold (often at the same time). It also accounts for not learning social norms that would behoove young girls. I'm looking at you, Noraya Smith.

Fuck you!

Stop swearing!

Pfft!

On Flour: Flour and sugar mills were seldomly built within a medieval town or village, but usually in quite a distance from any settlement. Why? Well, historians who focus on architecture have postulated a number of sage reasons, of course, but my personal favorite is the one Owen utilizes to blow up the Red Gates at the Temple of the Wind: flour explodes. Yup. Think about that, next time you bake muffins.

Chemistry teachers can explain this better than I can. But what basically happens is that by scattering the fine dust of the flour over a flame, you create a much larger surface area that reacts much better with the oxygen, so you get a really good *whoosh*. (Watch this: youtube.com/watch?v=evXhs1-exMo – go ahead, have fun learning stuff.) This is why grain elevators nowadays still have such thick walls. And you thought fantasy was all about magic.

Obviously, Owen would have read about this in an ancient tome *On Alchemy,* heard of a flour mill burning down and put two and two together. There certainly was never any burning desire on his part to actually try this out. Like ever. Really.

On Shinar: Many of the dreadful things that happen here are actually taken from our own history as testified by numerous ancient sources, the Bible, and archeological evidence, unfortunately. If you read Deuteronomy 18, you can find that magic, spellbinding, spiritism, and sacrifice of their children by fire were among the Canaanites' detestable practices which condemned them to divine judgment. According to Merrill F. Unger: "Excavations in Palestine have uncovered piles of ashes and remains of infant skeletons in cemeteries around heathen altars, pointing to the widespread practice of this cruel abomination." (*Archaeology and the Old Testament,* 1964, p. 279) The Canaanite goddesses Ashtoreth, Asherah, and Anath are presented in an Egyptian text as both mother-goddesses *and* as sacred prostitutes who, paradoxically, remain ever-virgin (literally, "the great goddesses who conceive but do not bear"). Their worship apparently was invariably involved with the services of temple prostitutes (female *and* male, actually), pretty much as Bashan explains it to Nora. These goddesses symbolized the quality not only of sexual lust but also of sadistic violence and warfare. The goddess Anath, for example, is depicted in the Baal Epic from Ugarit as effecting a general slaughter of men and then decorating herself with suspended heads and attaching men's hands to her girdle while she joyfully wades in their blood naked. I can totally see Suranna doing that, can't you?

(Oh, and the Latin phrase Nora quotes? It means: *All animals are/feel sad after sexual climax*. Just so you know. I didn't. I had read it in a book and couldn't figure out what *coitus* meant and instead of turning a few pages in a Latin Dictionary (Google wasn't around back then), I asked my Latin teacher. In class…I was a very popular kid at school. Don't be like me.)

I'm going to go all Roland Barthes on you now. You know: a "text is a tissue of quotations", drawn from "innumerable centers of culture." (*Death of the Author*) So, did you find the Easter Eggs? No? Look again. In Book One, which reference is made to Philip Pullman's *His Dark Materials*? In Book Two, whose words does Master Diaz echo when he talks to Nora about his art? And in Book Three: which dogmatic, but equally charismatic mentor figure does Suranna paraphrase? Know the answers? Found more Easter Eggs? DM me over at Twitter @timwhitecastle with #easteregg and I shall applaud and love you dearly, you pop culturally savvy reader, you!

And while we're deconstructing the author, I must point out to you that, while it's my name on the cover of this book, I certainly couldn't have done this on my own. Before I say my thank yous, though, I want to take a short moment and ask you to imagine (if you can) a serious, non-reckless, non-swearing version of Nora. Okay? Okay. (See what I just did there? Another quote.) Now that was what Nora used to be. But then I got myself an editor who knows Story like Bruce Willis knows how to Die Hard.

Nora wouldn't be Nora if it weren't for Harry Dewulf. (harrydewulf.com)

Now, if you have a story you're thinking about publishing and would like some editorial advice, I would recommend Harry.

I would, that is, if he weren't a very busy man already and back off! He's mine. I saw him first!

So, what I would *really* recommend you (*she said, glowering*) is to head over to Udemy to get the next best thing: hours of Harry coaching your individual story to make it awesome. The Read Worthy Fiction Course helped me when I ran into an issue in the first third of this book. It made me rethink Diaz's character and realize he had so much more potential and impact on the story I'm trying to tell as a hero on his own journey. www.udemy.com/read-worthy-fiction You're welcome.

I'd also like to thank Kira Rubenthaler (www.bookflydesign.com/editing), copy editor extraordinaire, who basically tells me to cut, cut, cut, and insert more Oxford commas. She makes the torrent of words flow much more gracefully and I am highly indebted to her advice. Also from Bookflydesign, I'd like to thank James T. Egan for his patience, excellent typography, and making the cover stand out.

And talking about covers, words cannot express how indebted I am to the awesome, eye-wateringly beautiful artwork that graces the cover of this book (and my desktop, and my smartphone's home screen, and my ... ok, you get it. It's everywhere and I just can't get enough.) The artist's name is Tommy Arnold. You should check out his other fantastic art at: www.tommyarnoldart.com and because I know you just won't get enough, look here, too: tommyarnoldart.tumblr.com

Huge thanks go to my beta readers over at www.fiverr.com: Cate (Msalwayswrite), Sarah (Woadwarrior), HermioneB, and Anaiya who test drove this narrative for you and pointed out the unintelligible, bumpy spots along the way.

And a big thank you to my husband Tobias who – without knowing – "lent" me his RPG character name in slightly changed form for Nora's lurrrrve interest. Ahem.

But lastly, I need to thank you, dear reader, for picking up this book and reading so far. I love to entertain you. Here's how you can express your enjoyment:

Buy the book. *Done.*

Read the book. *Done.*

Review the book.

Sign up to timandrawhitecastle.com/join to be the first to know when the next book comes out.

Buy the next book.
Read the next book.
Repeat.
Thanks.

About the Author

Timandra Whitecastle lives on the original Plains of Rohan (Lower Saxony) in Germany, with her family. She is a native speaker of both English and German, but she's also fluent in Geek, Gaming, and Whale. Reading is an obsession that borders on compulsion most days.

Tim has never bothered to get a life because she feels like she's been trying to lead three different ones already – and, yes, she totally stole that line from Terry Pratchett. Also, she's partial to Mojitos and Baileys … er, just in case you meet her in a bar and want to buy her a drink, say. (She knows people don't actually read author's biographies, but feels mentioning this might be worth a shot … or two.)

CPSIA information can be obtained at www.ICGtesting.com
Printed in the USA
LVOW11s1622111016

508320LV00003B/702/P